SEIZED & SEDUCED

SHELLEY MUNRO

MUNRO PRESS

First Munro Press electronic publication April 2015
First Munro Press print publication February 2025

DEDICATION

For Paul, my husband, partner in crime, and fellow adventurer.
Every day is a good day.

INTRODUCTION

During a routine stop en route to Viros, Jannike Hondros is kidnapped and incarcerated, her destination a planet she'd hoped to never, ever visit again—Manx Two, the planet where she was accused of murder.

Prince Lynx Leandros of Viros, second-in-line to the House of the Cat, and his bodyguard, Shiloh Tetsu, are caught in the same trap as Jannike. Destined for sale as a breeding pair and a spare, escape seems impossible, and now Jannike informs the feline shifters they're showing mating signs. Impossible. Neither Lynx nor Shiloh believe her, yet they can't deny their relationship has turned strangely touchy-feely.

A lucky break sees them fleeing for their lives, but danger lurks over every sandhill in their race for safety. The two men are becoming even closer. Jealousy and yearning stalk Jannike. She can't fall for either feline and certainly not for both, then nothing matters when she comes face-to-face with her past and death stalks her with its beady eye.

Contains two headstrong alpha shifter males and their female match, enough kitty cats to make a leap and some hot lovin' in the great outdoors, the indoors and places in between.

CHAPTER ONE

A shrill cry echoed through the arid valley. Unexpected, it set a shudder rippling the length of her body. Jannike Hondros, second-in-command of the Indefatigable, came to an abrupt halt, her stomach twisting even as she grabbed her blaster from her hip holster and flicked off the safety.

"Tracker lizards." At her side, Ry Coppersmith, captain of the spaceship, confirmed her fears. He edged his petite mate behind him, but Camryn O'Sullivan wasn't putting up with his overprotectiveness.

She neatly sidestepped him, wincing at a repeat head-splitting shriek, closer this time. "What are tracker lizards, and why are they making that infernal noise?"

"Trackers are the best available means of trailing an object or person. They never fail to capture their target. *Never*. The cries mean they're on a scent," Jannike said, her voice terse as she scanned the far end of the valley. Not a single tree softened the landscape, the sparse grasses, the same beige brown as the rocks and dust. The lizards' screeches bounced off the rocky walls of the valley again, pulling a wince from Jannike. She'd experienced their tenacity and hadn't emerged on the winning side.

"Us." Ry glanced at Jannike, and with the ease of long friendship, they came to a decision without words.

Jannike gave him an imperceptible nod.

"We need to split up," he said, attention on the horizon.

In the distance, maybe four or five clicks, Jannike caught the swirl of approaching dust. "You need to shift, change your scents."

"But Mogens said shifting might be dangerous." Camryn cupped her slim belly in protest.

"We're gonna have to risk it." Ry didn't hesitate. "It's either that or capture."

"Capture? What's going on? This sort of thing doesn't happen on Earth. Usually," Camryn added, obviously thinking about her own kidnapping.

"I'll keep going away from the ship." A lump the size of a rock closing up Jannike's throat, making her words gravel-rough. She swallowed, silently cursing both the situation and this god-awful heat from the planet's sun. The dry temperatures sucked the juice from everything, animal and vegetable. "Go." It was surprisingly difficult to force out the order.

Camryn still frowned, not understanding. She squinted at her husband, shifted her attention to Jannike. "But—"

"Change. Now," Ry ordered. "Jannike, if you're captured, we'll come for you. We will not give up. That's a pledge."

"Same goes." Secs later, she started running, veering around the pile of rocks and sprinting down the rolling sandhill away from Ry and Camryn. It had to be the cargo ship they'd seen earlier, but why had they set tracker lizards on them?

A thought sprang into her mind, and she stumbled before

regaining her balance. *Grata!* No, it couldn't be her. No, that was impossible since Jannike was far from her home planet.

Behind her, the baying shrieks of the lizards intensified. Sweat trickled down her forehead, stinging her eyes. She slipped in the shifting sand, arms flailing before she toppled, hitting the ground hard enough to punch the breath from her lungs.

No time to baby ouchies. Had to move. Had to give Ry and Camryn time to get to the ship. Faster. *Faster.* Her blue tunic clung like a second skin. A skin wet from sweat. The dry rocks in her throat closed her windpipe. She panted, a painful wheeze.

Goddess, she had to keep going.

She twisted, rolling and pushing to her feet. She lurched her first steps, only her fitness and determination propelling her forward.

Concentrate on running. Forget the trackers. Don't think about the past.

The landscape stretched in front of her—one big, inhospitable sandpit. The planet's sun beat overhead, frying everything in its path. And still she kept trying to run. One foot in front of the other, leading the trackers farther from the Indy. Faster. The Indy's crew were her friends, her family. She'd do anything to keep them safe. *Faster.*

Determination gave her a burst of speed, but a glance over her shoulder told her the trackers had closed the distance margin. Their brown-blue bodies glinted in the bright light, strangely beautiful despite their ferocity. Their baying cries filled her head, lent panic to her adrenaline-fueled flight. She rounded a corner and came to an abrupt halt. A box canyon. The wall of rock stretched into the distance as far as she could see.

Trapped.

Nowhere to go.

Slowly, chest rising and falling in uneven gasps, she turned to face the four snapping trackers. Their bulging eyes blinked, their wicked teeth white against the brown blue of their skin. Their stubby tails shifted lazily from side to side, strong muscles in their haunches poised to spring should she attempt evasion. She edged along the rock wall, and they advanced with her. She'd heard their bite was nasty, and some people were allergic to their saliva.

But she refused to go without a fight. She reached for a handhold on the rock wall, dug in her fingertips, attempted to lever her body upward.

"Ho, my beauties. What have you caught me today?" The mountain of a man rode up on a cyberbeest—a combination of machine and cheetahbeest by the look of the tawny coat and spots. The cyberbeest snorted, pawing at the ground, restive under the firm restraint. The large rider wore a tight, light gray suit shaped to his body. The man was all muscle with no fat. With his left hand, he controlled the cyberbeest while his right rested on a coiled whip.

Jannike glanced left, speared a look right. A tracker bite or the nip of Mountain Man's whip. Both would hurt.

"You won't escape," Mountain Man said with almost a kind smile. But the smile didn't reach his wintry-blue eyes and she knew, deep in her gut, he wouldn't hesitate to act in order to capture her.

Grata, her past had *come back to bite her in the bum. There was no other explanation.* "Why are you chasing me?"

"Why did you run?" the man countered.

Jannike gritted her teeth, not relaxing a bit. She sidled to the left, and one of the trackers snarled, the snap of its teeth returning her to the spot she'd vacated.

The man cocked his head, gaze wandering her body in lazy insolence. "Yes, I think you'll suit our purposes. The boss will pay handsomely for you."

"What purposes?" Jannike tried to ignore the faint stirrings of fear. They'd need to drag her kicking and screaming the entire way. Besides, the more trouble she caused, the more time the *Indy* crew would have to escape.

She hoped.

The man smiled again, calm and sympathetic, but underpinning the friendliness was amusement and cunning. Determination. The perfect attitude to increase her unease. "You're female. You're strong and appear healthy. And even better, you're fetching to the eye. Yes, you're perfect for our needs."

She still had her weapons. One hand slid behind her back and her fingers closed on the hilt of her knife.

The creak of wheels and the roar of an engine fighting to gain purchase on the sand grabbed the man's attention. He glanced over his shoulder, and Jannike threw her blade with a precise flick of her wrist.

He let out a grunt, turned back to her and beamed, despite the weapon protruding from his chest. "Ah, the transport has arrived. It was fortuitous we noticed you out for a walk this morning."

The man was part machine, the same as his mount. "And I'll just be moving along," Jannike said, her hand slipping downward to grab the dagger in her right boot.

"I don't think so." His good humor never faltered. "You're going to walk into the transport so we can ship out." He clicked his fingers, and the trackers closed in, teeth snapping at her heels.

Jannike edged along the wall of rock. A second snap didn't miss, the tracker nipping her calf. She cried out and clutched her leg. Damn, he'd taken a mouthful of her black trews along with skin. Blood smeared her fingers.

"Come along," the man said in a brisk manner. He jumped off his mount to grasp her arm, the knife still jutting from his chest. "I'll take the rest of your weapons." Big hands frisked her efficiently. "I don't have all cycle. Damn hot out here. Quicker we return to the ship, the sooner the medic can inspect your leg. Use this cloth to stop the flow of lifeforce."

When she balked, he gave her a hard shove, and she stumbled onto the sandy floor, the pad of fabric he'd offered her striking the back of her head. Secs later, the doors of the transport locked, the high barred window letting in heat and minimal light. The vehicle lurched into motion, a bump-and-shudder across the hostile terrain.

Frustrated with her capture, Jannike slammed her hand against the wall. Outside, the trackers snarled and started baying. The ghostly howls made the hair at the back of her neck stand to attention. With a low curse, she rubbed the sudden chill from her arms and lurched to her feet. Her breath hissed out in a sharp exhalation.

Damn, that hurt. She probed the wound, wincing at the red blood that coated her fingers. She wrapped the cloth Mountain Man had given her around her calf, gritting her teeth at the dart of pain. The seepage was sluggish, but the wound throbbed, the jabs of sensation relentless pinpricks in her flesh. A harsh laugh rippled up her throat. She just *had* to be one of those who were allergic.

The transport hit a rut, jogging her back to commonsense. She needed to see where they were going, had to watch the 'scape and note the landmarks. Goddess, she hoped Ry and Camryn were safe. They'd be back at the ship by now. A pained groan escaped when the vehicle hit yet another rut. Her friends would come for her. All she had to do was survive whatever Mountain Man threw in her direction.

A whimper from the far corner had her whirling. "Bloody fuckin' hell." One of Camryn's colorful curses croaked free as agony in her leg almost felled her.

Someone was in here. Panic tore shreds in her before her mind jerked into gear again. They wouldn't lock her in with anything dangerous.

The whimper repeated, the creature—whatever it was—transmitting fear not danger.

"Who's there?" Jannike's voice was a rasp, not a show of confidence. She swallowed, tried again. "Come out. I won't hurt you."

Despite the light coming through the window, she couldn't see into the far corner of the transport.

A scuttling, scraping noise sounded, and a black missile sprang at her before she could react. Violent pain swept from her calf, radiated upward, shoving blurry edges to her vision. "Bloody hell."

Strong, skinny arms wrapped around her, a long tail anchoring a furry body at her chest. She braced for teeth. Instead, the creature whined, snuffling loudly as it took in her scent. The beat of her heart settled to a fast jog as she and the creature stared at each other. Big fluffy ears, a little on the pointy side, swiveled and twitched while its furry black body trembled.

She stretched out a careful hand and ran it over the black fur on its back. When the animal didn't bite, she settled into a series of strokes and low murmurs. The creature—she had no idea what it was—relaxed against her chest, the whimpers fading to low sighs of pleasure. Jannike's hand stilled, and its tongue darted out to lash her cheek.

A surprised chuckle escaped, and taking the animal with her, she limped to a position at the window. None of the 'scape appeared familiar. They hadn't seen the cargo ship after landing the *Indy*, had never considered there was a threat.

The transporter lurched around a corner, and a gasp escaped Jannike before she could bite it back. The cargo ship loomed over them, big and solid and black, even bigger than she recalled and far more menacing now that she'd become a captive. Panic slipped back in force, and the creature clinging to her cried out, picking up on her fear. Ry wouldn't get here before they departed.

Their hauler ground to a halt. Mountain Man whistled shrilly, and the trackers trotted up the ramp after him and his cyberbeest.

She couldn't let them take her onto the cargo ship. She'd lose her mind if she landed back in jail. Now that the trackers were gone, maybe she'd have a chance. Of course, they could free the trackers again, and she had no idea where she was in relation to the *Indy*.

Maybe Ry—no. There was no point endangering all of them. When Ry and the rest of the crew came for her, they'd take a clandestine route. And until then, she was on her own.

Plodding footsteps sounded outside the transporter. The rear rattled as someone unlocked the door. Jannike sprang out low, before the door was open. The animal clinging to her screamed in surprise but didn't let go, tiny claws piercing her tunic and digging into her flesh.

Someone hollered. Jannike didn't look back. She sprinted across the sand, off-balance because of the creature but not stopping to fling it off. It, too, was a victim. She ignored the wash of pain, the agony darting the length of her leg.

Behind her another shout roared through the air. Mountain Man.

"Stop running," he hollered.

Not bloody likely. Jannike dug for energy, knowing this was her last chance.

A weapon fired. Something hit the ground beside her right foot. *Zigzags. Run zigzags.* A difficult maneuver, given the weight of the clinging creature and the soft sand. Her breath sawed from her throat, her lungs cried out in harmony with her leg. She kept running. Another weapon fired. Something sharp hit her shoulder. Another struck her butt. Numbness spread across her shoulders, crept around her chest, down her legs.

Must keep going. Keep going.

Someone grabbed her and her fists flailed. She whacked a face, a nose. Heard a vicious curse, then one of her captors thumped her. Hard. Blackness surged around her vision, and she felt herself falling, falling, falling.

10

"How long do you think she'll sleep?" Lynx Leandros stared at the unconscious blonde female the guards had dumped in their cell.

The small creature clinging to her hissed when he ventured too close, the calibore's black fur fanning around its skinny body, long tail flicking a secondary warning. A rare animal that would fetch a large price in the collector market.

Lynx backed up a fraction. "Do you think she's gonna be all right?"

"No idea, but I'm sure she'll be happy to find herself incarcerated, bound for auction."

"The guards could be messing with us." Lynx glared at his business partner. Keeping a careful eye on the hissing calibore, he crouched beside the woman and touched his hand to her grubby cheek. "Shush, fella. Not gonna hurt her." He removed his hand, and the calibore closed its mouth, hiding sharp teeth. The long tail stilled. "We don't know the ship's destination for sure."

"If it squawks like a crow." Shiloh Tetsu shrugged as if he didn't care but his gaze remained watchful, his muscles tense. He looked like the fierce feline warrior he was, a man Lynx trusted to protect his back. His friend, albeit testy at present. Neither of them enjoyed feeling helpless.

"Shut the phrull up with your whining. She has a temperature. Feel her forehead." Lynx scratched his chest.

Shiloh stayed across the other side of their cell—a square room with three plain sides and a front wall of strong bars. Bars made of a substance too sturdy for them to break or bend. "Feeling a little guilty, my prince?"

The taunting tone had Lynx's hands curling to fists. Yes, he was remorseful. His urgent need to nail a curvy barmaid had landed them in this mess. His chest tightened, his breath dragging over scent receptors and filling his nose with Shiloh's musky fragrance.

Aw, phrull. He backed up until the bars of the cell halted his retreat. His feline rolled beneath his skin, a snarl of fury echoing

11

through his mind.

Wrong. Wrong. *Wrong.*

Unable to hold his breath any longer, Lynx sucked in and relaxed when the air held only a smidge of Shiloh, the stench coming from the captives in neighboring cells muting the dark temptation.

"Swarrk. Swarrk. *Swarrk!*" An unknown, unseen creature cried out, the pain and terror in the tortured sound lifting the hair at Lynx's scruff. So much pain. Confusion. So much terror. He knew how they felt. Even though they couldn't see each other, couldn't communicate, the same despondency writhed inside him.

Freedom. If they managed to escape this mess, he'd never take liberty for granted again.

"Cat got ya tongue, Prince?"

"Shut it." Lynx scanned the area beyond their cell, tension bleeding from him when he found it guard free. He turned back to Shiloh, fury a heavy drum in his veins. Before the thought formed, he sprang halfway across the cell and pushed his face into Shiloh's. "Don't call me that."

"If the robes fit..." Shiloh sneered, his top lip curling upward, sardonic through and through.

"Enough with your damn attitude." Lynx gnashed his teeth, his canines shoving into prominence when his fury escaped his tight mental grip. They were arguing when they needed to stand firm, but hellfire, guilt played with the mind.

A laugh emerged from Shiloh, throaty, mocking, and Lynx snapped his mouth shut, confining his temper to an aggravated scowl. So far, they'd hidden their feline natures, both sensing if their captors learned the truth, they'd never escape. Ignoring the demands of the feline, though, was becoming harder each day since he and Shiloh were active males in their prime, used to shifting at will. And sex...well, the less he thought about that the better.

"We have to hold it together."

"You think?" Shiloh's green eyes bled into cat, the pupils

narrowing to black slits. A low snarl escaped Lynx before he bit off the telltale sound. "Truth hurt, or are you afraid they'll cast you as chief stud at the auction since you have the royal breeding?"

Another damn secret. Their cell was thick with them, and tension arced in the confined space, tempers flaring at the slightest provocation.

Lynx shot a quick glance at his friend, his heart giving an extra hard thump. Shiloh was a big, muscular man about five inches taller than his own six foot. The beginnings of a beard had appeared on his hard jaw, the last application of stop-beard having ceased doing its job. His mouth...no! Lynx wrested his gaze away from his friend's strong features and landed on his hair. Shiloh's black hair, already long at the beginning of their capture, reached halfway down his back. Wild and untamed yet sexy...

Phrull it!

Lynx turned his back to stare at the still woman.

Only the Gods knew for sure how long they'd inhabited this cell since the cycles blended into an endless passage of time. Their attempts to mark the passing cycles and rotation portions on the wall was stymied by the guards who sanitized their cell with a foul-scented spray that made them both sneeze.

Lynx stole another look at Shiloh and caught him staring. Both averted their gazes, the tense silence like a heavy weight pressing against their cell. They both fought it, ignoring the monster in the room, but the simmering awareness between them had grown worse.

He wasn't sure what to make of his craving, the constant gnawing for physical contact with the man who'd been his best friend from childhood. He sure as hell wasn't brave enough to broach the subject.

He sucked in a breath, attempted to center his mind in the way Shiloh's father, the head of security on his birth planet Viros, had taught him as a child. The air puffed back out in a harsh sigh.

"Look, I'm sorry. How many times do I have to say it? I made a mistake. It's my fault we're in this predicament."

"Just remember you owe me for keeping your identity quiet."

"Yeah, yeah." Despite the inherent threat, Lynx wasn't concerned. Shiloh was frustrated and the aggravation ignited his temper.

Lynx glanced at the woman and when she remained unmoving, he began to pace a circuit around their cell, his feline restless and struggling with confinement. Sighing, he stalked past their sleep pallets and glanced back at the woman and the calibore guarding her person. The guards had attempted to separate the two and given up after much cursing. "The calibore hasn't left her side."

Lynx caught the scowl Shiloh flung at the woman. He saw Shiloh open his mouth and drag air across his receptors. His friend gave a tiny shudder, and Lynx understood since uneasiness stalked him too.

The musky scent filling their cell acted like a drug fogging his mind and stirring up his feline. An echoing tremor swept him, his edgy mood urging him to action. He stalked a second circuit of their cell.

"We need to keep alert in case we have an opportunity to escape," Shiloh said. "No one knows we're here, but perhaps the woman has people who will demand answers about her disappearance." He slid a hand beneath his shirt and gave his chest a vigorous scratch. "They need to fumigate for biting insects."

"I thought it was just me," Lynx said. "Both my chest and back are itchy as hell."

"It smells in here."

"Yeah." Lynx caught a whiff of Shiloh as he stomped past to grip the bars of their cell. "It's you."

Shiloh whirled around. "No it's not." He lifted an arm and sniffed the cat tattoo on his biceps. "Hell, you're right. Maybe they're putting it in our food." He stalked over to Lynx, leaned over and smelled his neck.

Lynx shuddered, both shocked and weirdly turned on by Shiloh's proximity. He gasped when Shiloh grabbed his shoulders, the touch tearing down his body to pool in his groin. Whoa! That wasn't normal. He shot a quick look at Shiloh, saw his friend's fierce frown. Lynx had the weird urge to burrow into Shiloh's embrace, to seek comfort and give in return. He wanted to place his lips...

Aghast at the idea, he lashed out with his fist. He clipped Shiloh on the jaw and bounced on the balls of his feet, battle-ready.

"What the hell was that?" Shiloh rubbed at his jaw. Then his mouth tightened, green eyes flashing irritation. He dropped his hands to his sides and prowled toward Lynx, a snarky smile twisting his lips. "Getting frustrated because you're thinking about taking a trip to the wild side?"

"You're the one who does men," Lynx spat, not even trying to pretend he didn't understand. But the urge to run his hand over Shiloh's back and lean into his best friend's hard chest dominated his mind. He bunched his hands to fists while he groped to understand the compulsion. He could guess what his father and older brother would say, but he found himself staring at Shiloh's sensual mouth, wondering if his lips were as soft as they appeared. He shook his head, attempting to rid himself of the weirdness. "I don't do men."

Voicing the denial seemed to make it real. Heat pooled in his groin. His balls throbbed. When the craving hovered a tad shy of him taking action, he swallowed and shoved Shiloh so hard his friend rattled the cell bars.

Shiloh came at him snarling, his canines pushing below his top lip.

Lynx smirked and gestured with both hands. "Bring it."

Shiloh gaped then his roar erupted, vibrating his throat even as he sprang through the air, his fists swinging. His first punch struck

Lynx's jaw. Pain ripped through him. Instinct rammed his elbow into Shiloh's belly then spun him away. Humor scrubbed at his angst. Damn if it didn't feel good sparring with Shiloh.

A low sweeping kick took his legs from under him, then Shiloh was on him, a hard muscled body pinning him in place.

Lynx cursed, swung his fists, grunting when he connected. In the distance, he heard shouts, feet running. He didn't stop ramming his fists into Shiloh's belly. His feline shrieked, demanding release. Claws bled from beneath his fingernails, sharp canines pushed into prominence.

Without warning cold water struck him. He hissed and released Shiloh as it soaked into his tunic and trews and dripped down his face. His quick glance at Shiloh showed him just as bedraggled and wet.

"Break it up," one of the guards snarled.

Lynx grunted and kept his face lowered, the strands of his black hair hiding any sign of the cat. Beside him, Shiloh did the same thing, his wet locks falling over his face to hide his eyes and mouth from their captors.

The guard's hard stare dared them to do more, and he appeared disappointed when neither of them moved. "Do again and I be chaining you like the fight-dawgs in the cell at the other end of the ship. Truth, aye?"

Shiloh grunted, and the guard seemed to take that as agreement. He ambled away, scanning the other cells before vanishing from sight.

Shiloh ripped off his wet shirt, and the damnable scent hit Lynx again, musky and so good he almost moaned aloud. Stunned he backed away to squat in the far corner of their cell, head bowed to conceal his reaction. He took shallow breaths through his mouth, limiting the drag of air across his receptors. But he could still smell Shiloh and the desires coursing through him scared the phrull out of him.

CHAPTER TWO

Shiloh dragged his aching body into the opposite corner, chest heaving from exertion. Idly, he rubbed his fingers over an itchy spot on his chest. The prince had learned to fight dirty since their childhood scuffles, but so had he. Memories slid through his mind in a fast-moving vid. Days of innocent childhood fun and learning he'd become bodyguard to the second prince of the House of the Cat, following in the footsteps of his father and his older brother, Ellard.

Shifting for the first time at twelve rotations and running in feline form with the prince. As they'd matured, they'd discovered females—in his case, males too—and indulged themselves, their friendship becoming solid and real instead of one of employer and employee.

Neither enjoyed the strictures of prince and bodyguard, and they'd both rebelled, going into business together as interplanetary traders, much to the disapproval of their parents. A good life and one they reveled in until Lynx had dragged him into the middle of a honeytrap and imprisonment.

Now their lives had changed into before capture and after capture. He was beginning to wonder if they'd ever escape. The guards remained efficient and never relaxed their security.

But that wasn't all. Shiloh bit out a curse, unable to look at Lynx because then he'd want to take the next step and join him in his corner. Touch him. Phrull, yeah. That would be a colossal mistake.

Throughout their argument, the woman had remained silent and still. Now she moaned, tossing and twisting on her pallet. Shiloh went to her and touched her brow, ignoring the anxious hiss and the bared fangs of the calibore. Her forehead was hot and sweat beaded her skin.

"Call a guard. There's something wrong with her."

Lynx hollered from the cell door. Eventually a guard appeared, and Shiloh heard Lynx request medical assistance.

Shiloh crooned to the calibore and the creature ceased hissing. "Easy, fella. Not gonna hurt her. Come over here so I can turn her over." He held out his hand. The calibore whimpered but allowed Shiloh to stroke his head.

Lynx strode over just as the calibore crept into Shiloh's arms. "Still full of charm, I see."

"Male or female, they can't resist me." Shiloh ran his hand over the calibore's back and it sighed and cuddled closer. "Can you check her out?"

Heavy footsteps approached. "What be happening? What you do to her?"

"Nothing," Lynx snapped. "She's sick. She requires medical help."

The scrape of keys in the cell door grabbed Shiloh's attention. He tensed, gaze tracking the keys before lifting to study the guard's face. The guards seldom risked opening the door because he and

Lynx had almost escaped. Ah, they weren't taking chances today. Three guards, and two of the three trained weapons on them, their expressions full of mean promise. A trace of smugness. Not good odds and the guards knew it.

A humanoid ambled into the cell, a black satchel in his hand. His slouch and careful movement indicated age, and his amber eyes were shrewd in his bronzed face. No, a scaled face. He came from a reptilian race. Shiloh shot a quick glance at Lynx, saw the tension in his muscles, the prince's watchful air. Slowly, he retreated to join Lynx.

"Stay back," one of the guards ordered.

The calibore cried for the woman, but the guards didn't react. They continued watching, weapons raised while he attempted to calm the calibore.

"They're not taking chances with us," Lynx murmured.

"Not this time." No, they'd be silly to attempt anything now. Evidently Lynx agreed because he remained in place, vigilant but apparently resigned.

The reptilian man crouched to examine the woman and hissed aloud when he saw her ripped trews and swollen leg. "Why didn't someone tell me she was injured? I was told she was healthy."

"She darted during escape attempt. Thought she wake once the drug wore low," one of the guards spoke for the rest.

"She has a bite. It's inflamed. Poison, maybe." The elderly man rose and turned to face him and Lynx. "Did you do something to her?"

"No!" Shiloh snapped. "We're not murderers."

"We haven't touched her." Lynx placed a warning hand on his shoulder.

"Doc, you help her?" one of the guards said. "Boss, he gonna be irate if we lose her. Need us a female and male to get good price, true."

Doc *tsked* under his breath and reached into his bag for supplies.

Shiloh and Lynx watched, not moving from their corner of the cell.

"Do not harm her. We have in two males, one female," the guard said, his face flat and uncaring. "Truth, aye." The gesture at his weapon left Shiloh in no doubt as to his meaning. The woman was valuable while they required one male to make a breeding pair for whichever collector purchased them. The other would go to the slavers.

"If she's so valuable, why is she in this cell?" Lynx demanded.

"Need space for a new specimen. Once loaded, we be off for home. 'Bout time. I be craving me a bottle or two of verjuice. Can get on Manx Two."

With that info, Shiloh's insides twisted into knots. Once they offloaded on Manx Two, the chance of escaping grew slimmer.

"What happens when we arrive?" Lynx asked.

Shiloh waited, silently applauding Lynx for asking the question. Information was power.

"Special collector customers invited to view specimens. Arrive a few cycles after we land on Manx Two," a hulking guard said, his expression screaming satisfaction. "Good sale. Extra wages."

"What about those not chosen by the special collectors?"

"Open to all, aye. Collectors, those wanting slaves. Even circus owner comes."

Phrull, they could end up in a circus. Gods, he could wring Lynx's neck for getting them into this mess. Of course, he might give in to his sexual inclinations before he choked his friend to death.

When he found himself staring at Lynx, he ripped his gaze away. *Focus on the woman.* Maybe she'd clean up well and offer distraction.

"Wait, what happens if the woman dies from the fever?" he asked. "You can't put that on us."

The guard spokesman frowned. "Doc will fix."

A disdainful sniff came from the doctor, but Shiloh watched the man's competent actions. His nose twitched at the sharp medical tang when the doctor soaked gauze to place on her leg. After cleaning the bite, he dressed the wound. The doctor gave her a shot before rising to speak to a guard.

"If she hasn't improved by next feeding, call me," the doctor ordered.

"Aye." The guards straightened.

The doctor hesitated then turned to Shiloh and Lynx. "The shot I gave her will make her sleep. She might act confused when she wakes. Call the guards if she requires further attention." With a final curt nod, he departed.

The guards backed from the cell, their shoulders relaxing once the key turned. He released the whimpering calibore and it scuttled over to the woman. The animal patted the woman's blonde hair repeatedly, distressed at her stillness.

"Steady, boy," Lynx said, moving closer.

Shiloh studied the pale woman. "Hope that doctor knows what he's doing."

Lynx squatted beside her, speaking calmly to the calibore while he scanned the doctor's work. He held out his hand for the creature to sniff. "I'm not going to hurt either of you. The leg looks okay. The doc might act for the enemy, but he does good work."

The calibore cocked its head, pointed ears twitching. It sniffed Lynx's hand for a second before its tongue flickered out.

Shiloh caught his breath at the grin that spread across Lynx's face and the husky chuckle of delight. He'd been trying not to admit he found his friend attractive. And failing.

Lynx's face was one of beauty. Golden skin. Even features. Green eyes. Dark stubble because the guards didn't run to stop-beard supplies. Sexy profile. Muscular body gained from hard physical work along with weapons training, and a cat tattoo on his right biceps, the same one that he bore on his own arm... Phrull!

Shiloh wandered over to the woman. "I wonder who she is.

21

Hopefully, someone is searching for her."

"With the way our luck is going?"

Shiloh grunted. The calibore sniffed then reached for him. Grinning, he held the creature against his chest and watched while Lynx brushed the woman's hair from her face.

"She looks like a warrior," Lynx said.

Shiloh silently agreed as he scanned her body. She wasn't as beautiful as some women he'd known, but she was sleek and muscular, her features bold and striking. Not his type. Probably not Lynx's either. He glanced up at Lynx and found the prince watching him. A bolt of lust struck him so hard he gasped.

"Gods," he muttered, not releasing Lynx's gaze.

Lynx gave him a nervous smile but didn't glance away either. "It's not just me who feels as if I'm about to jump out of my skin?"

"No. I know what I want to do. It's probably not wise."

Lynx swallowed, the strong chords of his throat moving noticeably. "Tell me."

"I want to rip off your clothes and touch you." Shiloh was amazed he could keep his voice steady with urgency crashing his mind. When Lynx didn't reply, Shiloh continued. "I want to put my mouth on you, rub our cocks together. And I want to fuck you." His left hand clenched against the calibore's fur. "That graphic enough for you?"

"Yes."

Shiloh barked out a hard laugh. "Sorry if I've shocked you."

"Hellfire." Lynx raked his fingers through his hair, his normal easy expression absent. "Never wanted to jump another man. Do you think they've done something to us?"

"What?" Aware he was gaping, Shiloh pressed his lips together. The partnering of two men wasn't acceptable on Viros, and hearing Lynx's confession did strange things to his insides, played with his mind. His friend was the younger prince, second-in-line to rule the House of the Cat.

"Can't fight it any longer. I don't know what is wrong with me, but I think of two things. My cat and you. If I can't touch you soon, my feline will take charge. Having trouble controlling him."

Shiloh fought the images trying to invade his mind, fought for control. "The queen wouldn't approve."

"My mother isn't here."

"The queen thinks I lead you astray."

Lynx grinned and Shiloh's stomach bucked at the glint of mischief. He found himself stepping closer to inhale Lynx's scent. The blood drained to his cock, his thoughts drifting...

"No." Shiloh forced himself to stop. "You heard what the guards said about it not mattering if one of us dies. What if they decide we're both defective?"

"We deal with this cycle and each successive one as it comes. Chances of rescue are slim, so the rules change." Lynx's forehead wrinkled then he gave an impatient huff. "We concentrate on staying alive."

"And if this weird attraction doesn't go away?"

"No idea." Lynx glanced at him then away, which gave Shiloh a big hint about how off balance his friend was at this hint of sexual attraction.

"Do I disgust you? Does the idea of me touching you—"

"We touch each other all the time."

"This is different." Shiloh wasn't sure why he was belaboring the point. "Will you let me touch you now?"

Lynx swallowed and glanced through the open cage bars. Apart from the other prisoners, they were alone. When he turned back, his eyes glowed with an inner fervor. He raked his nails across his chest, scratching vigorously. "I feel as if I'm going to burst out of my skin if I don't get closer to you, but we can't let the guards catch us. To have any chance of escape, we have to stay together. What if they have surveillance?"

"We've checked the cell from top to bottom."

"True." Lynx's gaze went to Shiloh's mouth, and it was as if invisible fingers played over his flesh.

Shiloh fought to contain his shudder of pleasure. One of them needed to remain in control. For Lynx to admit his feelings proved he wasn't doing well, which meant he had to step up. It was how their partnership worked, how their business had become successful. "We can touch each other in a casual manner. Maybe the physical contact will be enough."

Lynx reached behind to scratch his back. "Phrull it. You'd think that nasty disinfectant the guards spray everywhere would kill off the bugs."

"Come over here." Shiloh slid down against the rear wall of their cell. "I promise if we get out of this alive, I'll continue as normal and won't throw this in your face. Surviving is the important thing. It doesn't matter how we do it."

Lynx searched his expression and must've read the sincerity, the honesty Shiloh tried to project. Lynx had seen him commit acts of stupidity over the years, screw up sometimes—just as he had—but he'd never once lied.

Finally, Lynx nodded and the knot of fear inside Shiloh subsided. "If we need to remain close for longer, we can pull our pallets together after the blacklight feeding. Once they adjust the illumination."

"Yes," Lynx said, and he slid to the floor beside him. They leaned against the wall, the vibration from the ship's engines throbbing through their bodies. Time for departure if they'd switched on the engines. For a short time, they said nothing. Shiloh wanted to smile but knew this wasn't the moment to make fun of his friend. Instead he slid nearer until their arms and shoulders touched. Both still stared straight ahead, but some of the strain faded.

"I've been racking my brain, but I can't recall much about Manx Two. We passed through once, but from memory we took on fuel and left straightaway."

"It's a hostile planet. Lots of deserts," Lynx said. "The city is built under a temperature-controlled dome."

Shiloh sucked in a breath and felt the tautness fade from his muscles. The proximity seemed to be working, and Lynx appeared more relaxed.

"Remember, that was the place where they'd predicted a big sandstorm. Another reason we didn't dally."

"We haven't been home to Viros for almost an entire rotation. I kind of miss it after a while," Shiloh said, more for something to fill the silence.

"The folks will nag us. The usual stuff."

"Ellard's not so bad."

"Better than my brother," Lynx said. "I wonder if Jarlath still has a stick up his arse."

They glanced at each other, and Shiloh grinned.

"Yeah, he probably does," Lynx said.

The rest of the cycle crawled while they waited for the evening meal. The woman didn't stir, but the calibore watched them in wary interest.

A guard appeared, holding a weapon. Two guards behind him carried something—the last prisoner. They entered the empty cell opposite them, placed the large body on a pallet on the floor, locked the door and retreated. A threatening growl from the prisoner made them laugh. Still joking amongst each other, they departed without a backward glance.

The prisoner struggled to his feet, and Shiloh bit back a gasp. A tremin. He'd heard tales and thought the talk the stuff of myths. The male's skin was rough and uneven like the bark of a tree, his entire body exposed apart from his groin. He wore a brown loincloth to preserve his modesty. His hair was green and rustled when he checked the door of his cell.

"Thy is rude to stare," the man said in a deep voice that boomed between his cell and theirs.

"My apologies." Shiloh stood and strode to their cell door for a better look.

Lynx joined him, and Shiloh couldn't restrain his compulsion. He moved closer until their hips touched and Lynx's scent swirled around him. Lynx groaned, a low, tortured sound that twisted Shiloh's guts into knots.

"Steady." Shiloh kept his voice low. "Take shallow breaths. I'm not going anywhere."

"Where are they taking us?" the tremin asked.

The hum of the engines increased, the deck beneath their feet vibrating.

"Manx Two," Lynx said. "They're taking us to an auction house."

The tremin's jerk of denial set his leaf hair rustling. "I be the owner of me." He pounded his chest with one large brown fist, and another rustle sounded.

Hope surged in Shiloh. "Does anyone know where you are?"

"Thy do." Confidence radiated from him for a sec before fading to leave his features pale. "I...I forgot. They're dead. They killed my family. My wife. For a sec, I forgot."

The tremin retreated to the rear of his cell and dropped to his knees. He clasped brown boney hands and dipped his head. He was still praying when the guards arrived with their meal.

Lynx stared at the bowls of stew and fruit and vegetables, some alien to him with their glossy-colored skins. "Do you think they're putting something in the food?"

"It would make sense if they wanted to keep us calm, but I doubt they'd want to make us horny."

Lynx spluttered out a laugh, the sound carrying a hard edge of tension. "Doesn't matter either way. I'm going out of my mind."

Shiloh moved closer to Lynx and slid his arm around his friend's shoulders. Something inside him calmed at the contact, and Lynx leaned against him with a soft sigh.

The illumination lowered, signaling blacklight, the time of rest. Shiloh checked the woman and the calibore. She was still unconscious, but the calibore remained awake and watchful. Shiloh cautiously petted the creature's head and it sighed.

Lynx pressed his fingertips to her forehead. "At least her temperature has dropped."

"She should have regained consciousness."

"The doctor didn't seem worried." Shiloh scowled at the still woman and scratched an itchy spot on his chest. He glanced up to see Lynx staring at him. "What?"

Lynx's gaze skittered away before darting back to him. He swallowed. "I need..." He trailed off, his discomfort clear at admitting his requirements, years of conditioning working against him, despite him accepting Shiloh's sexual proclivities.

For once Shiloh didn't fire off an insult about stuck-up royal princes. Instead, he extended his hand and waited. This last bit was up to Lynx. Damn if he was going to force the issue and have it come back to bite him on the arse.

The little contact they'd done to date had helped settle their felines. Maybe that would be enough.

The firm clasp of Lynx's hand in his sent a jolt to his groin. He grunted and tightened his grip, closing his eyes for an instant. His next deep breath drew in musk and desire, and he tugged Lynx to the rear of their cell, eagerness a compulsion thrumming through his veins.

"Gods, Shiloh." Lynx trembled as they settled on their pallets. His face held uncertainty, instead of his usual confidence.

"You can change your mind if you want."

"No." Lynx rolled toward him, and his green eyes glowed catlike in the darkness. His fingers stroked Shiloh's cheek. A harsh breath tore up Shiloh's throat in reaction. A groan. "Damn."

"Nervous?"

Lynx gave a bark of laughter. "Hell yeah, I'm nervous, but I'm not gonna let that stop me." And with that, Lynx mashed his lips against his. It wasn't pretty, contained nothing but raw need. Hands slid beneath tunics, ran over pectoral muscles and tight bellies. They changed the angles of their heads and suddenly, they fit, their lips moving in sync, hard bodies grinding together.

It was like igniting a torch. The intense desire Shiloh had felt for the last cycles flared into desperation. On the plus side, his feline purred, making him realize how jittery he'd been.

"Clothes," he mumbled, lifting his head. "I want to feel skin."

Lynx didn't reply but ripped his shirt over his head. He kicked off his boots and underskins then tore his trews down his legs.

Shiloh stared, his hand trembling when he reached out to touch. His friend was all lean muscles and tanned flesh, his cock full and erect. His gaze drifted upward and came to a halt on the curve of Lynx's lips.

"Like what you see?"

Shiloh shed his clothes. The first touch of skin against skin sizzled through him. They moaned in unity, sliding against each other, lining up their hips. Then they were grinding together in mindless urgency. Shiloh gripped Lynx's shoulders, kissed his mouth, his neck, letting the erotic assault to his senses and body wash over him like a sonic wave. Lynx's breathing went shallow even as he rocked his pelvis forward. Shiloh strained against Lynx, biting back his roar of pleasure as the engorged length of his cock slid across firm muscles. Gods, this was good. So good, and exactly what he'd needed.

The electric feel of climax rushed from his balls, up his cock until heat and pressure rampaged through his body. He gasped and with a convulsive heave, his orgasm exploded through him. Lynx's skin felt hot against his, and his friend shuddered, jerking a fraction when Shiloh reached between them to grip his shaft. Shiloh pumped his fist. Up and down. Up and down. The entire time he watched Lynx's face. The initial panic. The uncertainty.

The groan of surrender. He heard Lynx's breathing turn shallow, gloried in the hungry sound of pleasure.

Lynx could handle more, Shiloh decided. Using his other hand, he cupped the heavy weight of Lynx's testicles.

Lynx grunted, his features full of desperate need. "Please."

Shiloh kissed Lynx, sliding his tongue inside while he moved one hand lower. His finger pressed down on the smooth skin between his balls and hole and slipped closer to his entrance.

Lynx gave one long groan and came, his come erupting from his cock in hard spurts. Shiloh continued with the slow caress of his hand until Lynx muttered a protest.

"I was—" Shiloh cut off his indignant words when Lynx smiled and wrapped his arms around his shoulders.

"I get a bit sensitive after I come."

The annoyance bled from him at Lynx's confession, the tightness releasing from his muscles. He pressed against Lynx, he who never lingered or cuddled a lover, and realized he'd never felt this satisfied. The crawling, itchy sensation beneath his skin had subsided, and his cat settled with a lazy purr. "I thought we were going to restrict ourselves to touching."

"You know me. Leaping before I look. I...it seemed right."

"What happens if we've made the longings worse?"

"I feel tranquil now. At peace," Lynx said with not a shred of hesitation.

So did he, for the first time in many cycles. Shiloh ran his hand down Lynx's sweaty back, content with his lot, despite their captivity. Lynx gave a happy sigh and curled himself around Shiloh. The weirdness of this situation struck Shiloh again. He'd just ground against the prince, spurted his seed on the prince's chest and belly and the kicker was he'd do it again in a heartbeat.

Her eyes were light gray.

"You're awake," Shiloh blurted, his hand stilling on the calibore's head.

Lynx's hand jerked from her arm, a dull red filling his cheeks. "Sorry."

"I should think so," the woman said. "The last man who attempted to do that had his stones crushed."

"Stones?" Shiloh asked, unfamiliar with the term.

She cast a quick glance at his groin, her lips twitching.

"Ah, of course." Shiloh rolled to his feet.

Lynx rose too. "We weren't intending any harm. We wanted to make sure your temperature was back to normal."

The calibore chattered insistently, wriggling and indicating its desire to return to the woman. She grimaced. "Let me get up first." She stood and took in their bare cell at a glance. "How long have I been out?"

"Almost two cycles," Shiloh said. "How long have you been awake?"

Amusement flickered across her face. "A while. It was noisy in here."

"You watched...why didn't you say something?" A wash of red appeared in Lynx's cheeks.

Shiloh wanted to curse. Great. Just phrullin great. Lynx would backtrack now that the woman was conscious. Yesterday he wouldn't have cared, but now he'd touched Lynx, tasted him, and he didn't want to take a step back. Finally, he understood the true reason he'd agreed to leave his family and everything he knew to follow Lynx all over the universe.

Her gaze darted to the feline tattoos decorating their biceps. "I didn't want to attract attention until I decided if you were friendlies. How long until we reach our destination?"

"We're not sure. All we know is the ship is bound for private auctions on Manx Two. They're gonna auction off the specimens they've collected," Lynx said. "That's all we know."

"Grata," she muttered, her shoulders hunching inward. Her head dropped, and Shiloh noted the faint tremor of her hands before she clasped her fingers in a tangle. "Will anyone try to rescue you?"

Shiloh bit down on his tongue, and when he was sure he could contain his fury, he said, "We were visiting Chatta, a new destination, to pick up goods for trade. We went to the tavern for a meal. This idiot let a sweet-honey pick him up. She drugged him in her room, and when I went looking for him, we both got doped."

"I've said I'm sorry." Lynx blew out a noisy breath. "How many times do I have to say it?"

Instead of his usual angry retort, Shiloh decided to investigate a theory. He sidled over to Lynx and wrapped his arm around Lynx's shoulders. "They would have got us anyway. We made it easier for them."

"You're from Viros?"

Shiloh's bodyguard defenses rose in suspicion. They had to take care. As much as Lynx might annoy him, he'd never disclose his identity. Their captors hadn't worried about people searching for them, which told Shiloh someone with a great deal of power and money backed this enterprise. It occurred to him it wouldn't be silly for their captors to plant a spy in order to decipher their value. They'd need to watch their chatter until they discovered more about this woman.

"Will someone miss you?" Lynx asked.

A series of differing expressions shimmered over her face, so quickly he didn't know what the hell they meant, except he got a sense of wariness. Finally, she said, "Yes, hopefully they're tracking me now."

"How?" Shiloh asked.

"All the crew has trackers embedded in our arms. The *Indy* should be able to find me as long as they don't let this ship get too far ahead. How many guards are there?"

"We've seen the men who feed us plus the doctor who treated you," Lynx said. "Six different ones."

"Do you know who is in charge?"

Lynx grimaced. "That would be the man they call Piros. Big dude. Rides a cyberbeest. At least he's the one in charge of captures."

"Same guy who captured me." She fired questions at them with the ease of someone used to taking charge. Her natural leadership skills raised Shiloh's curiosity, and he could see the same interest blooming in Lynx. Lynx shrugged off Shiloh's arm and strolled closer to the woman.

Something akin to jealousy fired to life in Shiloh, and he cursed under his breath. What the hellfire? Even though he was aware of the weirdness, his unusual behavior, he couldn't stop himself from moving closer to Lynx to exert ownership. Near enough for their shoulders to touch again and to send a message to the woman.

Lynx was his.

The woman stroked the calibore even as she narrowed her gaze. She lifted her head and sniffed the air, leaned a bit closer, and sniffed again. "Steady, boys. I'm not going to interfere in your mating. Leave me alone, and I won't bother either of you."

"What the phrull are you talking about?" An itch gathered momentum on Shiloh's chest, and he slipped his hand beneath his tunic to scratch.

"Take off your shirts," the woman ordered.

"Why, sweetheart? Are you trying to figure out which of us you'd prefer?" Lynx's smirk was predatory, the grin of a charmer, a feline who knew how to seduce a woman. Shiloh clenched his teeth so hard his jaw ached.

"Just do it, and I'll answer your questions." She stepped back, still stroking the calibore. The creature let out a drowsy purr.

Shiloh glanced at Lynx then shrugged. He lifted his tunic over his head, the wash of cool air strangely soothing. Beside him, Lynx whipped off his tunic, and Shiloh gaped at the wealth of black bruise-like splotches decorating his pectoral muscles and belly.

"What's wrong with your chest?" Lynx asked, staring in return.

Shiloh glanced down to see the weird black splotches on his chest, the same patches marking Lynx.

"Turn around." The woman had a weird tone in her voice. "Ah! You have the marks on your backs too. Well, and here I thought incarceration would bore me. Seems as if things are about to get interesting."

CHAPTER THREE

"What the hell are you talking about?" Lynx demanded.

Shiloh frowned at the amusement in her gray eyes. She knew something. "What's your name?"

"Jannike Hondros, second-in-command on the *Indefatigable*."

"Shiloh Tetsu. Lynx Leandros." Shiloh gestured at the prince, his words abrupt and decisive as blaster shots. "The rash. What's so funny?"

"You're feline shifters." Her brows lowered, and she pursed her lips—flower pink, Shiloh thought. The pale sort his mother favored and placed in vases around their apartments in the castle. "Don't you know what the marks mean?"

"No," Lynx said. "What are they?"

Shiloh shot a glance at the nearby cells, scanned for guards, and lowered his voice. "How do you know we're shifters?"

"Superior brain power."

No mistaking her words for anything but smug. Anger flashed through him, a searing heat. He stepped into her space. Instead of retreating, she met him halfway, her jaw lifting in determination. Between them, the calibore chattered uneasily. Meantime, they stared at each other, neither backing off.

"Knock it off." Lynx grasped his arm and yanked him away. "Tell us what the marks mean. Please."

Her anger dispersed, revealing incredulity. "Goddess, you don't know. I've seen the cat tattoos on your right biceps."

"Yeah, we have tattoos." Shiloh glanced at his arm, expecting to see the familiar inky-black tattoo he'd borne since he hit rotation twelve. "What the hell?" He checked Lynx's tattoo. It had faded and lost vibrancy in the same way as his.

Beside him Lynx cursed, his eyes bulging in a double take. "Tell us."

"You're in the beginning stages of mating." Her blunt words toppled Shiloh into an adrenaline rush. His stomach lurched up and down as it did whenever their ship hit turbulent space. He gaped at her, waiting for her to crack a grin. She didn't.

"What?" Astonishment coated Lynx's yelp. "You're lying."

Shiloh narrowed his gaze on her, scrutinized her closely. They'd fooled around, kissed each other. That was all. Nowhere near full penetration.

"How do you know? You're not from Viros." Shiloh kept watching her, his gut telling him she wasn't intent on mischief. She was telling the truth as she saw it. No, mates were a myth. Arranged marriages were the norm on Viros with benefits accruing to both parties.

But is she lying? his conscience prompted. *Don't you feel something for Lynx? Have the urge to keep him beside you, far, far away from her.*

"We were on our way there. My captain was born on Viros and wanted to visit."

Lynx sent an anxious glance over his shoulder. "Mates don't exist."

"Try telling that to my captain and his mate," Jannike said.

"Who is your captain?" Shiloh demanded.

"Ryman Coppersmith."

Shiloh caught Lynx's faint shrug. He'd never heard of the man either.

"We're both males," Lynx said. "We've known each other since we were kittens. Why hasn't this happened before?"

Jannike shrugged. "You're exhibiting all the symptoms. Camryn didn't want to mate with Ry either. They're expecting a child now. How long have you been locked up here?"

Shiloh frowned. "We've lost track. A while."

"Maybe your close proximity has kicked the mating heat into gear."

"No," Lynx said, emphatic in his denial.

Shiloh saw Lynx's feline shift under his skin, felt the same agitation in his own feline, but what she said about them being incarcerated together made sense. It was true that in the past they'd seen each other most cycles. Yet, they'd also spent time apart with friends, other felines, people they dealt with for business. "Careful," he warned. "We don't want to attract attention. She might know we're feline, but they don't."

He reached for Lynx, half expecting a punch in return. Instead, Lynx closed the gap between them until their arms touched again. Shiloh sucked in a breath, filling his lungs with their combined scents. Both felines settled, prompting curiosity. He'd never experienced anything like this before. Could the woman be right?

"So you're saying the splotches signal the start of mating?" Lynx asked.

"Ry and Camryn experienced the same symptoms. Are they itchy?"

"Yes," Lynx said.

Her slow smile spoke of relief. "At least that makes me safe."

Famous last words, she decided after what she thought was several cycles or days as she often thought of them after their Earth vacation. It was difficult to gauge the passage of time on board the cargo ship. The guards played with the lighting because of the different species and time blurred together into a lump of boredom. She slept a lot, and she'd wondered if they doctored the food to make them fall into deep slumber. And now this...

Why, oh why, hadn't she kept her big mouth shut? The prickling sensations that had started as a minor itch had morphed into something much bigger and insidious. Jannike prowled back and forth in front of the cell bars as she tried to ignore the tickle of sensations rioting across her back, over her chest, and streaking down her belly to simmer between her thighs. Casually, she stretched, the pull of muscles stilling the irritation for an instant before it sprang to life again. *Not good.*

None of the feline mating dance made sense. Close quarters. Bad timing on her part. Maybe. Since she only had Ry and Camryn for info, she was running in the dark. Somehow, she'd need to deal with this situation, extricate herself. She scowled at her hand and forced herself not to claw her fingernails into her tingling breast. The two feline males had known each other for rotations. She'd presumed the forced proximity had made the heat commence for them—a guess—but she had no bloody idea why fate thought she should get stuck in the middle of the mess. Ironic, for sure. She marched along the front of their cell.

The animal—a calibore, according to Lynx and Shiloh—clung to her the entire time, appearing to take comfort from her body heat. The calibore never liked to leave her for long, although he tolerated the two felines for short periods. The guards terrified him, and he usually hid in her bedding or pressed his face against her chest.

Another one of those annoying itches had her scratching vigorously.

Bloody, bloody, damn. The commencement of mating heat was the least of her problems.

Manx Two. They'd been galaxies away from Manx Two, but now it appeared she was heading back to the planet of her birth, and wasn't that a kick in the arse?

She shot a glance at the two felines lying on their pallets at the rear of the cell. Two beefy guards ambled past and peered through the bars at them during food distribution. One pushed a trolley with a creaky wheel.

"Why they ignore female?" one asked. He was a pale lilac color with white eyes that gave her the creeps. It was like staring into a pool empty of emotions.

"Maybe different species," the other guard said, disinterest threading through his guttural words.

The two guards unloaded food at their feeding station and moved on, their trolley still squeaking a protest as they wheeled to the next cell.

Jannike glanced at her cellmates. Shiloh and Lynx were touching, running hands over each other, and a tiny voice at the back of her head wished she were in the middle to create a pile of bodies and questing hands.

A harsh breath whooshed in and out, her chest rising and falling with the force of the action. No!

Not gonna happen.

She'd keep away from the two felines. At least the longing wasn't crippling as it had been for Ry. He'd been unable to function when the need hit bad, not until Camryn joined the *Indy*. Copious amounts of sex and Mogens' slumber drugs had helped him.

Maybe it would be all right. She didn't seem that bad. *Yet.* The thought wasn't reassuring. So far, her attraction to them was more of an insidious yearning plus the itchiness that plagued her. Could be her mind playing her. The panic at learning of their destination of Manx Two wasn't helping.

Forcing herself to ignore Lynx and Shiloh, she stared through the cell bars while stroking her hand over the calibore's back. He let out a vibration that came close to one of Ry's purrs while her mind raced.

None of the crew on board the *Indy* still took the potions Mogens, their seer, used to whip up while Ry was single. Once Ry mated with Camryn, he'd ceased to be a danger to any of them. Heck, she could count on the fingers of one hand the times they'd met others of Ry's species.

Goddess, she didn't understand any of this. She should have remained safe since the mating process between the two men had commenced before she'd arrived. Asking questions didn't help since she knew more about the subject than the two Virosian natives. She gave her head an irritable shake and the calibore ceased his purring to issue an irritated grunt.

"Sorry, fella," she whispered. "Perhaps I should give you a name." The creature cocked its head. Its profile was regal and proud. "How about Royal?"

"Come and sit over here with us," Shiloh said.

"No, that's not a good idea." She forced a smart-ass grin. "I don't want to catch feline cooties."

The men were both taller, and she didn't look up to many. Like Ry Coppersmith, they had green eyes and black hair. Lynx had facial hair outlining his mouth and skimming his chin. The beard wasn't heavy and bushy. Instead, it framed his mouth in a real sexy way and she found herself wanting to test the bristles with her hand. Shiloh's beard was a little heavier but not unattractive. His physique was bulkier than Lynx's.

"We won't bite," Shiloh promised.

"Speak for yourself," Lynx said in a sensual purr. "I'd enjoy biting." The direction of his gaze left her in no doubt of his starting point, and her breasts prickled under his heated attention.

Shiloh growled, low and fierce, jerking Lynx's attention back to him.

Jannike backed up until the cell doors were at her back. "Easy there. I'm not intending to let either of you bite me. You don't need to when you can nibble on each other."

"Steady." Lynx petted Shiloh's shoulder in reassurance. "The guards will hear."

Shiloh grabbed Lynx, holding him firmly against his chest. His throat worked in an audible swallow, and he sucked in hoarse gasps while he fought for control. Long secs later, he'd regained self-discipline and he bowed his head. Jannike noticed he didn't release Lynx, and when he glanced up his pupils were catlike and glaring in challenge.

"We need to pool resources, make a plan to escape should the opportunity present. We need to work as a team, not bicker with each other," Jannike said.

"Who made you the voice of reason?" Shiloh's deep voice held mockery, and it echoed in his gaze. The challenge didn't shift, and she knew if she weren't careful, he'd attack. He gave off an air of confidence, that of someone who could handle himself, and she wondered how she'd manage if he pounced.

"Why are you staring at Shiloh?"

Jannike sighed, a heavy gust of air whistling past her lips. *Oh shit. As Camryn said, this was gonna be a hell of a ride.* "We need a plan." She squared her shoulders and strode across the cell floor, stopping a few feet from their pallets. "Do the guards stick to a schedule? I haven't noticed one so far."

"They come and go at odd times. We think it's because some of the prisoners require specialty feeding," Shiloh said.

"Have you seen the other captives?" Jannike had heard noises at all hours, some of them alarming.

Lynx scratched his chest, grimacing when he met her gaze. "The opposite cell. That's all. You've heard the others calling out. Crying." He scowled. "Sometimes they scream. It's been like that since our capture."

"There's no point trying to escape while we're on board. There's nowhere to hide," Shiloh said.

"You're right." Jannike tried to keep her voice businesslike when each cycle her panic escalated. *Manx Two.* "You said they're selling us to collectors. We can't let them split us up. The best place for my friends to free us will be once we arrive. The guards might laugh and joke, but they're watchful. Overpowering them isn't an option."

"I agree," Shiloh said. "The best thing to do is wait and attempt to plan for contingencies. Neither of us has spent much time on Manx Two. Have you?"

Jannike closed her eyes, battling the trepidation stalking her mind. Oh yeah. She'd been there before.

"Jannike?" Lynx prompted.

She opened her eyes, striving for calm. "I was born on Manx Two."

"Getting locked up with you might be a good thing. You say you have people who will rescue you, but you come from Manx Two. You have contacts, right?" Shiloh asked.

"Not exactly." Their association with her might get them killed unless Ry and the crew managed to get them first.

Shiloh studied her like a specimen. "Spit it out."

Jannike forced herself to hold his gaze. "I was in jail, charged with murder."

"Who did you murder?" Lynx asked.

Jannike's lips twisted at their wary expressions. They were like springs ready to explode if she made a wrong move. Indignant but resigned, she backed up to give them the illusion of safety.

They should fear her expertise. Since leaving Manx Two, she'd made it her mission to learn how to kill and defend herself. She wasn't the same gullible kid she'd been back then.

"Tell us." Shiloh edged closer to Lynx and planted himself half a step in front, standing ready to protect his mate.

Jannike had never told anyone, not even Ry, and he was her closest friend. She sighed. Maybe it was right to tell them the truth. Someone should know because she doubted she'd remain alive, not if the widow discovered her presence on Manx Two.

"My family was poor, barely managing to exist with too many mouths to feed. My stepfather took me to the market one day and sold me." Even now, she recalled the determined expression on his face as he'd shunted her into the pens holding those offered for sale. She swallowed, forcing herself to continue. "A wealthy merchant purchased me or rather his majordomo did. I worked in the kitchens until the master noticed me. He seduced me with pretty talk. Our affair continued for some time until the mistress discovered us in their bed. Seven cycles later, the master was dead, and I was in jail, accused of his murder."

"How did you escape?"

"I used my body," Jannike said, proud of her matter-of-fact voice when she still had nightmares of the experience. "The head jailer took a liking to me."

Shiloh lost some of his fierceness. "How long were you there?"

"Half a rotation." This time it was harder to restrain her instinctive shudder. "One hundred and eighty-six days. I mean cycles."

"Maybe no one will recognize you," Lynx said.

"They'll recognize me. I bear the Verena brand on my right shoulder."

"Maybe they won't recognize the brand," Lynx said.

Not a chance, Jannike thought. She was doomed the second she set foot on Manx Two.

"Damn, tell me this itchy sensation fades." Lynx slipped one hand beneath his tunic and scratched frantically. "It's driving me crazy."

"It stops." Jannike strove to keep her dread contained. At least it should for them. She didn't know what the outcome would be for her.

"After what?" Shiloh displayed shrewd understanding, taking the leap to the unpleasant.

"After fucking each other stupid," Jannike replied as she fought the urge to rip off her tunic and let the air drift across her heated limbs. "There doesn't seem to be any way to resist the heat once it starts."

Lynx groaned. "It seemed better when Shiloh and I started messing around. Now all I think about is running my hands over him and letting him do whatever the hell he wants." He fluttered his eyelashes in Shiloh's direction and offered a sultry, fuck-me-now smile. "Anytime."

"Really?" Shiloh's brows shot upward.

"I wouldn't say it if I didn't mean it."

Jannike watched the two communicate and stomped on her flash of envy. It was easier for them. She had death at the widow's hand in her future. "Go." She gestured. "I'll drag my pallet over there to give you privacy. Maybe I can stuff something inside my ears." She sent a sideways glance at Lynx. "You're very vocal."

"I'm not."

Shiloh hooked an arm around his neck. "You are, and I like it." He guided Lynx to their pallets without another word, leaving her alone.

Jannike recommenced her prowling, back and forth, back and forth, back and forth, edgy fear doing a number on her nerves. The sounds coming from the rear of their cell didn't help. The two men had wasted no time in getting busy. They didn't need to worry about death by whatever gruesome method of disposal the widow decreed.

Royal made a chittering sound and patted her cheek. Jannike halted her frantic pacing and stroked his soft fur instead. "Are you hungry, boy?" She strode to the fruit and nuts the guards had left—food the calibore enjoyed—and selected a nut. Royal sniffed it before crunching the shell with sharp teeth.

Maybe she should attempt to sleep. No. She'd go through her exercise routine. Keeping fit while waiting for an opportunity to escape made sense. Besides, it would give her something to do during the long hours of captivity.

Around four cycles later, Jannike went through her routine, arms flowing fluidly, clutching a pretend sword. She ignored the guards while they carried out their duties, as she did every endless cycle, but overlooking the constant prickle of her skin took a more concerted effort. The crawl of invisible bugs beneath her skin tormented and teased, made her crave physical touches. She halted her routine to scratch her belly. Her tunic felt heavy, the weight unbearable against her breasts. She yanked at her bra, considered taking it off. No. She righted her clothing and centered herself, ready to restart her sequence.

It took longer than it should, the itch on her belly, on her back a barrier to concentration.

Royal sat on her pallet, a piece of fruit between his front paws. The two males remained in their corner, arms wrapped around each other. Neither wore a stitch of clothing beneath the light cover, but she tried not to recall the glimpses she'd caught when they'd ripped off their clothes, desperate for full body contact.

No, no, no! She bit off a pithy curse, drew a sharp breath, and forced herself to flow into a sequence of defensive moves.

Her skin prickled violently, and she faltered, the sensation of claws raking her from the inside throwing her off her stride. She screwed her eyes shut while she rode out the discomfort.

The pain was becoming worse.

"You are suffering from the same malady as the males," a voice boomed.

Jannike whirled to face the front of their cell and spied the brown man with the rustling green hair. From the corner of her eye, she saw Lynx and Shiloh stand and pull on their trews and tunics. "Who are you?"

"Kelvin Tremin."

"You don't know what you're talking about," Jannike ground out, anger a hot, bittersweet syrup in her mouth. Understatement. *Lie.* No matter how she tried to twist the facts, the tremin was correct.

"No point lying to yeself."

The appearance of three guards dragging a trolley bearing food and liquid sustenance had Kelvin sliding to the rear of his cell. Lynx and Shiloh joined her at the cell bars, one male stepping into place on either side of her. Immediately, the stinging that writhed across her skin ceased, and she took a steady breath—the first in a long time.

"What ya think ya doin'?" one of the guards demanded. Not one of the purple ones this time.

"Just exercising," Lynx said and retreated to the rear of the cell.

Jannike and Shiloh followed, and all three turned to face the guards. The calibore scuttled across the floor of the cell and scrambled up Jannike, twinning its arms around her neck and hiding its face in her hair.

"Six regular guards," Shiloh murmured.

"Yes," Jannike agreed. "Wish we could be sure of the numbers.

There will be more who aren't involved in the feeding and care of their captives."

"We need to know how long until we reach Manx Two," Lynx said in an undertone. "Once we hit land, we need to be ready to move."

"Seize any opportunity," Shiloh agreed.

"They'll have shuttles." Lynx puckered his brow. "If we could get out of the cells, we might manage to take control of one and escape that way."

Jannike stroked Royal. "No, they'd set the tracker lizards on us. My leg is still tender where one bit me. We need to gather facts, wait until we land. With other people around, we'd blend better. They couldn't set the tracker lizards free in the city."

"Good point," Shiloh said and Jannike found herself basking under his approval.

She shook her head to clear it. Focus. She needed to think. "Once we arrive in the city, they'd need to transport us into the dome. The ships land at the spaceport outside."

"They could still set the tracker lizards on us at that point," Lynx pointed out.

"More people around," Jannike said. "Assuming they land at the regular spaceport. They might have a private area. It's been a while since I left the planet."

"But you remember the city?" Lynx asked.

Jannike watched a guard open the feed slot of their cell and shove in three bowls of some sort of stew. One step up from space rations, but still tasteless. "As long as they haven't changed it too much. There was always rebuilding."

"How much longer do we have to put up with this crap food?" Shiloh demanded in a gruff voice.

"Not much longer." The guard's lips curved into a toothy smile. One of his teeth was broken off at an angle and it resembled a fang.

"Why?" Lynx barked out the question, an imperial order.

"Two cycles and we arrive on Manx Two," he said, and Jannike noticed the matching tooth on the other side of his mouth. They were fangs.

"Drinks. Females," one of the other guards added. "Chance to spend our wages."

"Hurry up your arses," the third guard said. "Got to finish feeding."

He tugged on the trolley and moved it to the next cell. A rustling sound came from the cell, the grate of the feeding slot. A snarl. The guards snickered and the squeak of a wheel indicated their progress to the next cell.

"Two cycles," Jannike whispered, fear sweeping through her in a violent rush. Two cycles until she arrived back at the beginning. She'd wondered about her parents, her family over the cycles. Part of her had wanted to confront them, even though she understood the need to sacrifice one to save the majority. The tiny innocent child cowering deep inside her mind kept crying out, *Why me?*

She lifted her chin and forced away that helpless self. She wasn't that person any longer. Her name was Jannike Hondros, and she was a competent second-in-command. She was a warrior.

Damn if she'd go down without a fight.

CHAPTER FOUR

U rsola Verena, widow of the wealthy merchant Neot Verena, who had died many rotations ago, strode from her office.

"Computer, lock door." She scarcely paused for the central control unit to obey her command, eagerness taking her from the austere business section of her mansion to her more luxurious private apartment. Her slippered feet made no sound on the tiled floor, only the faint rustle of the fabric of her wide-legged white trousers marking her rapid progress.

A door opened halfway along the passage. On seeing Ursola, the young slave froze. Secs later, she turned to face the wall, her slight shoulders trembling beneath her gray uniform tunic while she waited for her mistress to pass.

Ursola ignored the slave and continued her ground-eating steps, in a hurry to reach Cayle.

"Computer, where is Cayle?"

"Slave Cayle is on the shade deck." The husky male voice surrounded her, coming from all angles.

Ursola skipped the remaining steps to the door at the end of the passage. Joy bubbled up inside her, the pressure of business and maintaining her position shoved aside in the excitement of meeting the man she loved.

"Cayle! Cayle, where are you?"

Cayle, a tall, muscular blond man with skin several shades darker than her own pale complexion, stepped from the shadows of a planter box. A green plant resplendent with water-loving scarlet flowers spilled over the synmetal sides. Beyond, a stunning view of the pink sandstone city buildings and the curve of the dome drew attention. Cayle smiled at her, the expression taking him from handsome to stunning, and she forgot about the view.

Hers.

All hers.

"I missed you," Ursola said, a smile forming on her own lips, such was his magnetic pull. *Cayle.* Her heart beat a little faster, sexual desire stirring her excitement. No matter how many times they were apart or how long he warmed her bed, the heady sensations of first love didn't retreat. Instead—to her shock—they'd grown stronger.

She was in love, and that astonished her even more. Humor spurted inside her at the thought. If others of her station discovered her depth of feelings for this slave, she'd lose face. The power she'd struggled to amass since her faithless husband's death would erode under snide gossip.

Why did he have to be a slave?

Cayle went to her, kissed her once, twice. Not enough to appease this ravenous hunger, her appetite for him endless. "I thought you were busy with your empire."

"Not too busy to miss you." She claimed his mouth for the kiss she desired. Deep. Sexual. All encompassing.

When their lips parted, she fought for breath, her breasts heaving. She gasped, her entire body alight with urgent need. She stared at him, the gray of his eyes. So seductive. Magnetic. Every time he touched her, kissed her, he left her wanting more. He was addictive, this slave, and she knew she was behaving out of character, yet couldn't stop.

He made her feel feminine, wanted and desirable.

For the first time in her life, she felt loved.

The man accepted her for who she was, what she'd become in order to survive.

"Have you eaten?" Cayle grasped both her hands in his. "I had the cook prepare a light repast in case you felt hungry."

"I'm starving, but not for food. I'm ravenous for you."

One of Cayle's smoke-gray eyes closed in a wink. "Soon, lunaheart. If you want to beat your business competitors, you need to maintain your health. That means good food and rest."

"The sex keeps me going."

Cayle grinned, and her heartbeat picked up in pace. "Manx residents cannot live on sex alone. Did you have successful business negotiations?"

He led her inside, away from the heat from the solar-star—the amount the scientists allowed to pass through the dome. "It's cooler in here. I don't want you to burn that gorgeous creamy skin."

"But I've taken my star-pill. I can stay outside on the roof garden for a short time."

"I'd rather not put it to the test. Come, I've programmed the holo in your suite. I bet you'll never guess what I've designed for us."

He tugged on her hand, and with a chuckle, she allowed him to guide her to her suite.

"Close your eyes," he whispered.

She shuddered when his touch became more intimate, his

fingers pressing into her shoulders.

"May I unfasten your hair?"

"Can I open my eyes yet?"

"This isn't a business negotiation. Let me direct our private time. Please?"

Even after all these rotations, Cayle still maintained his place—that of slave. Ursola sighed. His behavior was impeccable, no matter what the situation. She wished things were different. She wished...

"Ursola?"

"Of course you can. I trust you." No less than the truth, yet other merchants, other folks of her social standing would consider him property. Not fit for anything except service. He could come to her bed—of course. She had the right to demand he service her, which was how this relationship had started. He'd pleasured her with competence and skill, yet he'd never taken liberties or tried to benefit over the other slaves.

He'd be the perfect man—if he didn't wear the mark of slave.

The gentle massage of her shoulders continued.

"I'm going to lead you to a couch, but first, let me make you more comfortable." Gentle fingers removed the pins from her hair until the intricate braids unraveled. The work of two slaves destroyed in secs. She should be angry, but the dance of his touch across her scalp forced business thoughts away. Soon the heavy black locks tumbled past her hips and the residual tension from the comm she'd taken earlier drifted away. What did it matter if her biggest rival had landed a shipload of new slaves? Her shipment was due in less than two cycles.

Her lips curved and self-congratulation flooded her mind. She hadn't succumbed to the temptation to tell Marriot of the imminent arrival of her cargo. Let him discover when her ship docked.

"Let your mind empty, lunaheart."

"Sorry."

Cayle chuckled. "Don't peek. I'm going to guide you to the couch. It's to your right. Perfect. Time to make you comfortable." He paused a beat, no doubt waiting for verbal direction. Yes or no.

"Go ahead, sweet man."

Soon the trousers pooled at her feet and the peaks of her firm breasts tightened, ever sensitive against the cooling lifeforce from the conditioning unit. The sensation arrowed downward to sink into her pussy. She ached for him, yet had learned to wait when Cayle took control. The lovemaking was always spectacular.

"There you go. You were naughty today, going without your underwear."

"I was in a hurry to take a call. You kept me in my gel-bed for longer than usual."

"Because..." He nipped the pad of one finger and the jolt of awareness layered between her thighs, building blocks of the pleasure to come. "You're beautiful and sexy..." He bit the fleshy part between finger and thumb. "...and I can't get enough of you."

"Yes," she whispered and tried to turn into his arms.

"No, lunaheart. You gave me permission to do this my way. You can't take back the reins now."

Firm hands pushed her onto a gel-couch and she settled with a sigh, facedown, the gel cushioning her breasts, her hipbones and the rest of her body with supreme comfort.

"Keep your eyes closed."

The warble of birdsong and the rush of a stream filled her sitting room. She drifted on a cloud of bliss as Cayle dribbled fragrant oil down her spine. The scent of herbs and flowers relaxed her further.

"Where did you get the oil?"

"I went with Hark to do the marketing. She required aid to carry parcels and arrange deliveries."

"You don't need to do manual work any longer. I've told you before."

"I enjoy keeping busy. I did check to see if you had need of me."

He had, she realized, so she bit back her irritation. No need to spoil this decadent treat of alone time. Once her cargo ship arrived she'd become busier with myriad demands on her time. She'd survey the incoming stock, peruse them herself to make sure the captain was correct with his assessment of the captures. She'd need to arrange for their cleaning and grooming and each captive would require a health check.

Cayle straddled her body, his hard thighs riding the outer edges of her hips. The slight pressure set her heart racing, each sense hyperaware as she wondered what he would do next, which method of lovemaking he'd choose. An inventive lover, he was generous and appeared to enjoy the act as much as she.

His hands slid down her spine, feathering then digging into her muscles. A groan slipped free as he massaged and rubbed, the heady floral and herb scent wafting to her as the oil heated on her flesh.

She craved his touch between her legs but bit her tongue to halt the begging words that tumbled unbidden to mind.

He moved down her body, stroked and smoothed his hands over her buttocks. She moaned, and he chuckled.

"Patience, lunaheart. My way."

"Too slow."

"Slow is best." He massaged her thighs, skipping over her weeping sex. Instead, he stroked her calves and her feet until she throbbed with hunger, yet every muscle sang a relaxed song.

How did he do this to her when no other male had ever come close? Every other male in her life she'd used to get ahead, to obtain position and power. Never had she experienced the need to linger, to savor, to possess.

"Turn over, but keep your eyes closed."

She obeyed, resettled with his help. A callused finger circled one breast, drifted between and then higher until he circled her nipple.

Without warning, he tugged.

"Ooh." The sharp jolt frisked her nerve endings.

Warmth surrounded her nipple next. His mouth?

"Don't open your eyes," he warned, the wet heat disappearing with a soft pop.

Yes, it was his mouth, and mercifully, he returned to his taunting and teasing, the faint suckling that drove enjoyable sensations writhing down to her needy pussy.

His fingers played with her other nipple before his mouth switched. She floated, drowning in his attentions, business receding until thoughts of her to-do list for the coming cycle was but a faint memory.

When he lifted his head, she waited with bated breath. A sharp pain at her breast, followed immediately by another, told her he'd placed clamp-pegs on her nipples. She breathed through the wash of pain, allowed the nip and burn to sink its claws into her and emerge at a point shy of pleasure.

"Should I continue, lunaheart?"

"Yes."

He roughly parted her legs, knowing what excited her. Loss of control. The bite of pain. Both things she dished out and never received in return. Except with Cayle. Cayle...

The warm stream of air across her sex made her catch her breath. The rougher caress of his hard fingers as he ran them through her slick flesh. A prickle of sensation converged on her clit, the harbinger of climax, and she caught her breath, ready for the next onslaught.

It didn't come. Instead, he removed his hand but kept her grounded with his touch on her hipbone.

"Cayle."

"Shush, lunaheart."

He moved a fraction then settled between her legs. Some of her frustration eased. He didn't intend to leave her ramped up and edgy.

The next sec a curse leaped from her mouth. "Phrull."

Her eyes flew open to see his concern. "Breathe. Take a deep draft through your nose. Do it now, and the burning will lessen."

"What did you do to me?" She glanced down her body, attempting to see between her legs.

"I've put a smaller clamp-peg on your clit. Breathe the lifeforce. It's a lighter peg with not as much tension as the ones at your breasts. Breathe. The stimulant on the clamp will kick in soon."

Even as he said the words, arousal stirred deep in her womb. It rippled from her breasts as he flicked the clamps. The sensations raced straight to her clit, the burning throb growing, growing, growing.

"Ahhh," she croaked and swallowed at the twirling ribbon of pleasure that frisked but never settled in one spot.

Without removing his gaze, Cayle stripped, baring his muscular body and his erection. Her gaze went to his cock piercing, the glistening drops of seminal fluid on the ruddy crown. She'd ordered him pierced to enhance her pleasure and celebrated the decision. She'd pierce her clit except it was another sign of slave status. No one in her circle had one, or at least admitted to the fact.

As she watched, he opened a bottle and stroked the creamy liquid the length of his shaft. His smoke-gray eyes deepened in color as his gaze collided with hers.

"I want you to leave on the clamp. I'm going to slide onto the gel-couch beside you. Move carefully over me so you don't dislodge the clamp-peg. Take my cock inside you at your own pace."

"What is the cream?"

"A new invention. It will stimulate you inside, the slight nip of the clamp a counterpoint for the pleasure in your channel."

"Have you tested it?" she asked, her tone sharp, jealousy springing to life at the idea of him penetrating another woman.

"I've tested the cream. I used a vibrator to penetrate myself, and I've used it on my hands and my cock. Everything is natural, and I have suffered no ill effects. I can wash it off if you wish."

"No, it's all right."

His nod held approval. "Move slowly. I don't want you to injure yourself."

Ursola did as he requested and clambered onto his body. If she progressed too fast, the sensations stole her lifeforce, and she had to drag in huge breaths to compensate for the nip of pain at her clit. She guided his cock to her pussy and bit by bit took him inside.

His girth seemed larger than normal, the exercise of seating herself more difficult, yet contrarily more thrilling than ever before.

"Feels good, lunaheart." He hissed out a breath. "So damn good. Much better than when I used the cream on my own."

"Yes," she said as she rose and the pressure on her clit eased a fraction. She impaled herself again, the sense of fullness exquisite. "The enhancing cream is amazing."

"It does do excellent things. It makes my cock more sensitive. I can feel the drag of my shaft each time you move. My cock head is more sensitive. Tell me what you experience."

Ursola moved up and down in a dreamy fashion. Her teeth dug into her bottom lip as she focused on the growing swirl of enjoyment. "I feel relaxed, and the pleasure...it's just out of my grasp. If I go faster, maybe I can reach it."

"No lunaheart. Keep at this slower speed. I'd hate you to rip off the clamp due to impatience. I don't want to injure this pretty pussy." He reached between them and ran his finger around the clamp in easy, delicate circles.

The pressure on her engorged sex teetered her to pleasure then pain. She sucked in a hoarse breath. "Don't know if my skin can contain this much delight."

"You can take it. This and more." He sat up, so she perched on his lap, his new position making his cock strike her channel at a different angle. "Move a fraction faster now. Goddess."

Ursola laughed, the tinkling sound taking her by surprise. She sank down and rose, riding his cock at a faster pace. The blissful sensations began to knit together, growing, growing, expanding until she sobbed out her enjoyment. "*Cayle.*"

His gray eyes twinkled with a spark of devilment. One large hand circled a breast, squeezed, clamp-peg and all.

The jagged pain had her crying out, she jerked, her muscles twitching, the resulting flare of ecstasy too much, too big, too huge for her body to absorb. The tipping point. Pleasure and pain danced and mated, swirling in a big ball of satisfaction. A scream ripped from her throat as she convulsed, spasms catapulting along her channel, making her twitch and writhe.

She was dimly aware of Cayle groaning, coming, but her body kept shuddering, and she had to concentrate on regaining her breath. She leaned into his solid weight, smelled the musky man-scent of him. When she was thinking more clearly, she'd play her usual game of trying to decipher his scent. It was musky—yes—but there were elements of spices and maybe flowers.

He ran a hand down her sweaty spine, and she shifted into the embrace. Another spasm radiated from her clit, and she groaned at the spike of gratification. Less intense this time, but still enough to steal her body of lifeforce.

"Easy, lunaheart."

"You sound satisfied." It was difficult to get out those few words, to form them into sounds.

"I enjoy giving you pleasure. I'm going to take off the clamp-pegs," he said. "Don't want to injure you."

Before she could answer him, his hand slid between them to unclip the tiny clamp-peg surrounding her clitoris. A sharp pain sent another coil of pleasure soaring. He lifted her off him and placed her on her back. "Don't move. Take deep breaths."

Something else she liked about him. He read her body, knew how she was feeling, the sensations she was experiencing and how to ramp them up or ease her down. She'd asked him once how he knew, and he'd said it was instinct—something he just knew. But suspicion had lurked in her. Jealousy.

She'd discovered he was everything he'd said. A youth from a poor family, desperate for funds. His mother had signed him up as a slave, taken the cash in return and walked away without looking back. Cayle had started work in her kitchen as a scullery boy. He'd caused no trouble and labored his way up until he'd come to her notice. Now, he could rule the other slaves. She'd give him this power without blinking—if he asked. Instead, he continued to work hard whenever she carried out her duties and social obligations.

She drifted, happy with her thoughts, satisfied and completed. A little sleepy. Her clit burned, but it was a good burn. She was happy, she thought, as she'd never been before.

"Take a breath for me, lunaheart."

Before she could ask questions, something cool and soothing washed over her clit, instantly relieving the remaining heat. She sighed, her muscles relaxed. Her eyes drifted closed.

Cayle released one of the clamp-pegs at her breast. Sensation returned with a fiery kick, and she gasped, tensing to fight the pain. "Cronin's balls," she cursed, jerking from his soothing touch, her eyes wide now with the shock.

"Steady there." Amusement weaved through his words then the ache subsided, batted away by the same cool wash of gel he'd used on her clit. The seductive state of relaxation returned until he removed the last clamp-peg.

This time, she managed to bite back a curse and secs later, it didn't matter since the gel eased the brief agony.

"All right?" he asked.

"Sleepy."

"Why don't you rest? You have nothing urgent to carry out until the soiree this eve."

"I should do some bookwork."

"Why don't I help you later? I can scan the screens or read the necessary data. Whatever you wish."

She blinked at him, fighting her fatigue. "You're too good to me, Cayle. Perhaps I will sleep now."

"I will wake you in time to prepare for this eve."

"Excellent." She caught a weird expression on his face. No, it was her. The orgasm had been so intense, so perfect and now she needed to recharge her body. He was smiling at her—her handsome slave.

Ursola gave up the fight to keep her eyes open. Cayle...sometimes she wondered if her body would expire from the emotions he fostered in her. Happiness. Excitement. Joy.

It was a pity her gorgeous man was a slave.

"One more cycle until recreation time," a purple guard crooned as he pushed food pouches through the feed chute. Several fat red berries and a shiny yellow fruit bounced through secs later. He loaded water containers into another chute and made them accessible.

Royal caught a berry in his paws just before it hit the ground.

"We're on space rations, I see." Jannike fought the craving to scratch her stomach and lost. Her nails raked across her flesh but did nothing to cure her ailment. Luckily, neither of the men noticed since they were more interested in each other. Yet even they fought the true mating, confining their physical contact to skin-to-skin. She clicked her fingers at them. "Pst! I'm gonna eat all the rations. You should hurry if you want to eat."

"Probably stew again." Lynx climbed to his feet with a wide yawn.

Jannike was pleased to see his lower half remained garbed. She told herself to look elsewhere, but her mind disobeyed. Her glance took in a landscape of toned muscles covered with splotches of black. The feline tattoo on his arm had faded completely, and now it seemed as if the black parts wandered his chest. Her gaze moved on to Shiloh, a bulkier man and just as impressive.

"Like what you see?" Shiloh asked in a silky voice.

Jannike forced herself to meet his challenging gaze. "The tattoos have gone from your arms. Your chests are covered with black smears. Turn around."

Lynx turned to present his back.

Secs later, Shiloh followed suit. "Well?"

"Your backs have a few marks but not as many as your chests." Probably because they hadn't had penetrative sex yet, although she didn't share this with them. She tossed them a ration pack each, then concentrated on her own meal.

Lynx cocked his head. "Something is wrong with the engines."

Jannike frowned, listened to the steady drone, and caught the pauses in the revs. "Can't be too serious. The guards aren't reacting."

"They're grunts." Shiloh's tone was dismissive. "They don't know any better."

"Whatever the problem is, it's getting worse," Lynx said.

The ship shuddered, tilting downward without warning. Royal let out a shriek and leaped at Jannike. The missile of calibore pushed her off-balance, and she would have fallen if Shiloh hadn't grabbed her and wrapped her in his arms.

"Phrull," Lynx muttered when the revs became a protesting moan. "I wish I could see what was happening. I hate *this*."

The ship shuddered, screamed, and continued on its downward

trajectory. The entire framework of the vessel juddered again, slowed a fraction.

"We've hit atmosphere. According to the guards we're close to Manx Two. Kelvin," Shiloh shouted above the panicked cries of their fellow captives. "We're crashing. Sit in the corner and brace."

Even as he spoke, he was urging both her and Lynx into the nearest corner. They huddled in a tight group, the men stoic while Royal chittered in alarm, his strong arms wrapped around her neck in a forceful embrace. His small body trembled, and not even the stroke of her hand stilled the shaking.

Panicked shouts came from the guards. Running feet thundered past their cell.

"Hurry! Hurry! We're going down," one screamed.

Jannike didn't bother lifting her head. Instead, she closed her eyes, leaned into the protective embrace of Lynx and Shiloh and enjoyed relief from the constant prickling of her skin.

CHAPTER FIVE

"They've slowed the descent," Shiloh said.

"We're still going down." Lynx's taut muscles indicated tension, indicating that his mind had taken the same path as his. "Phrull, I hate this."

The same sense of helplessness roared through Shiloh's veins. He glanced at the woman. Not a trace of panic. Jannike didn't scream or pray. She didn't cry out or react as most of the Virosian women of his acquaintance would under the same circumstances.

Reluctant admiration filled him. He'd watched her train, even managed to confine his jealousy long enough to let her fight against Lynx. She'd held her own, using skill and cunning to best his friend during some of their bouts.

She hadn't managed to beat him, but he'd found their skirmish satisfying. Challenging even. Grudgingly, he realized he liked her no-nonsense attitude.

"Won't be long now," Lynx said. "Better pray—"

The ship struck the ground. Jannike head-butted him, and Shiloh grunted. Royal shrieked. An explosion sounded, close enough for concern. Screams and howls erupted in the other cells. Cries of agonized pain. The other captives battered his mind with their panic. He tightened his grip on Lynx, on Jannike, but they slid across the floor, whacked into the bars.

Trolleys and feeding implements flew down the outer corridor that ran between the cells. Items crashed against walls with metallic shrieks. Pallets skidded around and hit them.

Shiloh cursed. Lynx groaned. Royal screeched, his fear resounding in the confined area. Jannike attempted to calm him. The ship took off, fell in a sickening drop, punched into the ground again. The floor tilted at a crazy angle.

Jannike pulled away.

"Hold." Shiloh gripped her arm to reinforce the order. "Might bounce again."

It did.

Hard.

Jarring.

Then the synmetal fabric of the big ship groaned.

Shuddered.

Settled to less of a lean.

The screams, the roars, the howls of pain became worse. The cacophony of terror deafened Shiloh.

Instinct made him want to help, yet he could do nothing except look after those who shared his own prison.

Once he was sure the ship had stilled, Shiloh released Lynx and Jannike. He assessed his own body. He groaned and stretched out the leg Lynx had fallen against, pressed his ribs. Blood dribbled down his face, and he swiped at it to clear his vision.

"You all right?" Lynx demanded.

"Fine," Shiloh said and managed to prove it by climbing to his feet. He staggered, balancing precariously because of the uneven floor.

The cries hurt his head, the pain, the fear, the horror of this never-ending nightmare.

"Whoa." Jannike rubbed her temple. "You have a hard head." She wobbled a bit as she attempted to stand. Shiloh gripped her arm to aid her to stand. Royal clung, covering her face in his anxiety.

"It's okay, boy. Let me move you." She shifted his trembling body to another position on her shoulder, pushing closer to Shiloh as she regained her balance.

Shiloh eased out a breath, relaxing even though Lynx was on her other side and still on the floor.

Lynx attempted to rise and collapsed with a pained groan.

"What is it? What's wrong?" Anxiety had Shiloh rushing to his friend's side.

"Shoulder," Lynx gritted out. "Bloody thing has come out of the socket again. Gonna need to shift."

"Not here," Shiloh snapped.

"Ahoy there," a booming voice called above the racket.

Jannike gaped at Kelvin. "How did you get out of your cell?"

"Door buckled with impact. Might be able to force yours. Quick help before guards come."

"The guards are busy," Jannike said to Lynx. "Shift now to speed your healing. Stay at the rear of the cell."

"Phrull, she's right," Shiloh said. "We need everyone at full strength."

Lynx nodded but struggled to remove his tunic.

"Let me." Shiloh maneuvered the fabric up and over Lynx's head. Every wince, every grunt from Lynx felt like a body blow, and not for the first time, Shiloh wished they didn't need to remove their tunics in order to shift. Their trews melted into their bodies, and he had no phrullin idea why their shirts ended up in tatters instead of doing the same thing as their trews and footwear. "Sorry."

Lynx sucked in a harsh breath as he focused. Shiloh watched, aware of the anxiety stirring his gut. Gradually, the transformation took hold. Shiloh released the grip he had on Lynx's tunic and puffed out a relieved breath. Lynx wasn't limping. The shift to feline had helped.

"Where do you think we be?" Kelvin boomed.

"Maybe Manx Two." Shiloh strode forward to check the door. Kelvin was right. The bars of their door were out of alignment.

"If we've crashed somewhere on Manx Two, we're in bigger trouble than before. The deserts are inhospitable and dangerous," Jannike said. "Most people never leave the dome, except to travel off-planet."

"We'll take our chances. You stay here if you want, but Lynx and I are leaving."

"We're coming with you." Jannike stalked to join him. "Let's do this."

Shiloh squinted at the light coming from outside the ship. The crying and screams continued, and animals and beings—those who'd escaped their cells—poured through a rupture in the wall of the ship.

"Wait. I see guard. I get keys or find central control." Kelvin glided away, surprising graceful despite his booming voice and large brown body.

"Yank at the bars on my call," Shiloh ordered. "One, two, now." He put all his force behind the yank and at his side, Jannike did the same.

The bars moved, but not enough.

"I have keys to work individual cells," Kelvin said. "Guard dead. Must have hit head. No central control panel for cells."

"What about the other guards?" Shiloh asked.

"Front of ship took most of the impact," Kelvin replied. "Maybe dead."

"Let's hope so," Jannike said.

Kelvin tried the first key and then the next. On the fifth attempt the key turned.

"Wonder why the locks weren't computerized?" Jannike asked.

"No idea. Don't care." Shiloh wrenched on the door and forced it to open.

"I let out others." Kelvin darted away with the keys in hand.

"Be careful," Jannike called. "Some of them will be dangerous." She started to scoop up the uneaten fruit and nuts plus the ration pouches they hadn't touched.

Shiloh watched her fashion a makeshift bag with approval. "I'll see what else I can scavenge, but we can't take too long. We need to move. Lynx, you feeling better?"

A growl came from the rear of the cell.

"You need to shift and help us carry supplies." A loud roar came from one of the other cells. "Holy phrull. That's a floris dragon," Shiloh said on catching a glimpse of the crimson wings as the dragon flew through the jagged hole in the side of the ship.

"All done," Kelvin said. "Some creatures dead. Others injured. Can't help. Must look after self. Need drink. Liquid before we leave." He hurried to his cell and started to drink, tipping so much liquid down his throat it was a wonder he didn't block his breathing.

"Shoulder better?" Shiloh asked.

"The bone has clicked back in place. I'll survive." Lynx gathered the thin blankets into a pile and used one to fasten a pack in much the same way Jannike had. "Might work as a shelter from the heat. We should use these to cover our heads. It will help keep our bodies cooler."

Shiloh scooped up a basic medical kit and turned to Jannike. Royal clung to her, softly crying. "Let's move out."

She gave him a clipped nod and grabbed pouches of water as she passed the food station of their neighbors. Shiloh snatched up as many as he could and loaded them in another thin blanket.

They picked their way past the debris in the corridor, and Shiloh had to steel himself against stopping to help some of the injured creatures. Couldn't save them. No one could help them now.

A striped tigoth sprang at Jannike but before Shiloh could react, Kelvin had thumped it across the nose with a whiplike arm. The force of the blow deflected the creature and left it stunned.

"Thanks," Jannike said.

Kelvin gave a clipped nod and continued toward the gaping hole in the side of the ship.

"An explosion of some type," Lynx said.

Shiloh nodded. Scorched black edges showed the force of the detonation, the scent of soot, metal, and misery filling the air. The impact had decimated the nearby cells. The inhabitants hadn't stood a chance.

By common consent, they paused to survey the territory beyond the ship. White sand mainly—peppered with gray rocks—stretched in every direction. A breeze stirred the particles. The heat from the solar-star radiated off the sand, making Shiloh squint through the heat waves. Several creatures galloped across the sand while others flew. One nearby crawled, his leg injured. He left a trail of oozing blood behind him on the sand.

"Desert," Jannike said. "We're on Manx Two."

"Which way to the dome?" Shiloh asked. "That's our sole option. Is the planet all sand and dunes?"

"The dome is on the west side of the planet. There's a deserted mining village to the north. These dunes are interspersed with rocky outcrops. There are areas called havens where there is shelter. Sometimes water, but they're not large enough to sustain a village. They're hard to find. Some people believe they're mirages, but my father—never mind. I believe there are havens somewhere within the desert region."

"We need transport," Lynx countered. "If the mining village is deserted, we won't find transport there. We should take our chances at the dome."

"I agree," Shiloh said. "We'll enter and blend then beg, borrow or steal transport."

Kelvin gave a curt nod.

Outnumbered, Jannike gave in and clambered from the ship. She scowled, her jaw set. "Come on, Ry," she muttered.

"Not looking forward to going home?" Shiloh asked, his feline senses hearing her easily. "I thought you said Ry has a mate."

"He's my friend. His mate is my friend. I miss them."

"I understand. I miss my family." He clamped down on his bottom lip to prevent another word.

"I have never missed Manx Two," Jannike said. "If I'm captured, I'll be returned to the widow as an escapee. Believe me, death is a better alternative."

Lynx placed an arm around her shoulders. "We won't let that happen. I promise."

"We'll keep you safe to the best of our ability," Shiloh agreed.

Kelvin dropped to the ground beside them with a thud. Two copper-colored birds with big round eyes perched in his hair. They clung tight with talons and squished together as if they required the security of touch. "Too much talk. This is no social gathering. West is this way. I have excellent sense of direction."

Shiloh broke into a trot. "Like the new decoration," he said to Kelvin.

"I couldn't leave them." Kelvin's green-brown hair rustled like the leaves of a tree while a frown marked his weather-scarred face.

"That's not a criticism." Lynx eyed the birds with interest. "It was good of you to help them."

"It takes a while to become used to Shiloh," Jannike added.

The birds let out a series of low, melodic whistles, and Kelvin replied with a rustling of his hair. "They offered to scout the territory once we are away from the ship."

"You can communicate?" Jannike asked.

"Yes. They speak a little known language."

"Move," Shiloh snapped. "I hear tracker lizards. Jannike is right. We should travel in the opposite direction. They'll assume we'll head to the dome."

"Aye," Kelvin said. "Tracker lizards will follow others going west. I see prints. Lots of creatures escaped before us. Many highly sensitive. They will sense the dome or know of it. Many share information while in cells."

They had? Shiloh hadn't caught the communication between the other cells. Something must have shown in his expression.

Kelvin said, "Tremin have excellent hearing and speak many languages because we are nomadic. Visit many planets."

Nothing wrong with feline ears and he hadn't heard a thing. Of course, he'd been more worried about keeping Lynx away from Jannike and his own urges to grab Lynx and sex him half to death. Shiloh shuddered, blood rushing south to fill his cock. "Enough talk," he growled. "We move in silence. Lynx, you go first, and I'll follow in the rear. Hopefully the winds will sweep away our tracks."

"Won't be able to track all," Kelvin said.

Lynx set a brisk pace—not quite a run but faster than a walk—and headed around the base of the sandy dunes. Overhead the solar-star shone brightly, beading sweat on Shiloh's face, his torso, his arms and legs. Clothing clung and the shifting, unstable sands made balance difficult. Soon, his calves burned.

Lynx walked steadily, and Shiloh kept sniffing the air, cocking his head to discover if the tracker lizards were following their trail. Nothing. The lizards remained behind them, and tension eased from his shoulders. They might have half a chance if no one pursued them straightaway.

The dunes gave way to the rocky outcrops Jannike had

mentioned and footing became easier.

"Damn this place feels like a phrullin' cook fire." Lynx came to a halt.

"Once the solar-star falls lower in the sky, the temperature will plummet," Jannike said. "We haven't gone far, but it would be best if we find shelter. We can travel more easily at blacklight—at least before the temperatures fall into uncomfortable. Shiloh, you and Lynx can shift and guide us through the darkness. Your eyesight is better than mine."

"Sheltering from the worst of this heat makes sense." Kelvin blinked rapidly and stirred his hair.

The round-eyed birds rode the movement and whistled. They seemed to agree with the assessment while Royal remained silent, his furry arms wrapped around Jannike.

"Sometimes the outcrops have caves," Jannike said. "Or failing that we could make a shelter from some of the blankets."

Lynx absently rubbed his shoulder. "I'll watch for something suitable."

Shiloh remained silent, not needing to add to the conversation since the suggestions were sensible. Thank the goddess. The idea of getting landed with a helpless female or a complaining creature would slice their chances of a successful escape.

Now that he was confident recapture wasn't imminent, he allowed his thoughts to drift. His gaze tracked Lynx at the front of their group. His friend favored his shoulder yet kept trudging onward. Pride suffused Shiloh. If he had to shipwreck on a hostile planet, he couldn't have picked better companions.

The message arrived halfway through her official engagement. Ursola frowned at the vibration of the jeweled earlink she'd donned to wear for the gathering. She ignored it to continue her conversation with the ambassador of Nidni. Smiling at a joke, she accepted a goblet of willow sizzle from a slave then excused herself.

Ursola made her way into the fragrant garden and sipped the sparkling purple wine. The lights spread out like a twinkling colored carpet, the building's dark silhouettes standing in soldier-straight rows all the way to the curved wall of the dome. Many other guests had the same idea—lured by the crisp blacklight air, the view and the myriad tubs of rare flowering plants owned by the ambassador of Manx Two. She stalked to the far end and managed to find a private corner.

With a command, she linked to her home. "You called?"

"Lunaheart." Cayle's husky murmur brought a shudder of need to the fore. "There was an urgent call from the captain of the *Asperity*. He wants you to contact him."

"They've landed?" A broad smile curved her lips.

"They've crashed in the desert outside the dome."

The hand holding her wine trembled violently. Splotches of purple splashed onto her black-and-white form-fitting gown. "The desert?"

"Yes."

"I'll call immediately." Ursola gripped her goblet as she fought a scream.

"I'm sorry, Ursola. I know you were looking forward to the *Asperity*'s arrival."

"Not your fault." She clicked off. Every nuance of the turmoil spinning in her gut poured from her in a succinct curse. "Gafinkarse."

She forced herself to suck in a deep breath, let the lifeforce ease out. It couldn't be that bad, not if the captain was calling her from the crash site.

Temper muted at the thought, she put a call through to the ship. "What happened?" she demanded the instant she heard the captain's voice.

"The engine malfunctioned then blew. There was a secondary explosion in the cargo hold. Most of the crew is dead."

"What about the cargo?"

"Some survived, but many have escaped. Piros is out with his tracker lizards now, rounding up the escapees."

"Can you repair the ship?"

"The second officer is working on the problem now, but we require parts. The damage from the explosion is extensive. It would be best to send another ship to transport the cargo to the dome."

"I see." An understatement. She didn't see at all. How could this happen when the *Asperity* had traveled the universe and beyond to collect specimens? Why had her ship foundered in her home territory? "I want to know what caused the explosion and the engine trouble."

"Yes, mistress."

"Make sure you capture every one of my specimens and transport them here. I'll expect regular reports." Ursola clicked off the link and drank the remainder of her willow sizzle. She paced back and forth as she drank, her mind working furiously. The *Asperity* received regular servicing. She made sure of it because efficient working tools made for productivity.

Someone on board the *Asperity* had sabotaged her ship.

A competitor?

A frustrated employee?

Or someone else?

"Gafinkarse." Any number of her acquaintances sought power, fought to steal her achievements.

But she would prevail. Yes. The pressure on her chest eased. She must pretend nothing out of the ordinary had occurred. Business as usual.

Lifting her chin, Ursola stalked back into the mass of party guests, a smile fixed in place.

"Ah, Mistress Verena." The Nidni ambassador held out his hands. "I wondered at your disappearance. I wished to ask you to dance."

His deep brown eyes held good humor and not a trace of sly guilt. She forced her lips to a deeper curve. "I wanted to see our host's rare flowers. They are quite spectacular. Their fragrance 'tis most bewitching, and the lights of the city are very pretty."

"I had a private tour before the guests arrived. Our dance? Would now be suitable?"

Ah! Sexual interest, not a business competitor. This, she could deal with. "I'd love to dance with you." She set her glass aside, accepted the hand he extended and let him guide her through the crowd.

The music became louder. A pleasant enough sound but grating now that she ached to return home and take control of this gafinkarse shamble.

The ambassador swept her into his arms and pulled her against his chest.

Ursola's breath whooshed out when the prod of something hard jabbed her belly. She fought to maintain a level expression. "Ambassador, it's very warm. People are saying experts should lower the dome temperature control to counteract the heatwave. What do you think? Is it this hot on Nidni?"

"Oh yes. Our warm months are hot indeed. We have a beautiful planet. I would love to show you the village of Ytnelpxes and the Ynroh Temple complex. It is a fascinating place." His brown eyes gleamed, as if he told a private joke.

"I haven't heard of Ytnelpxes. You'll have to tell me more." Ursola attempted to wriggle away so the prod of his shaft didn't punctuate her belly with each gliding step.

"Oh my dear. I will."

The music drifted to an end, and Ursola smiled at the ambassador. "I'm afraid we'll have to postpone our discussion until another cycle. I am feeling rather fatigued. I believe I'll leave for home."

"Let me escort you to the skytrain," the ambassador said. "Or did you hire private transport?"

"I used the elite carriages of the skytrain. No need for you to leave the party early. I'm sure others wish to speak with you about the possibility of forming a trade alliance with Nidni."

A senior slave dressed in formal black stepped onto the dais with the band. "Supper is served," he intoned. "Please move into the large reception room."

"Stay for supper," the ambassador murmured. "We can chat for longer."

"I'm afraid my head is aching," Ursola said. "I suffer from headaches and have done since I was young. Once they start, a tablet and sleep is my sole relief." An understatement. A pulse pounded at her temples—the reason being her downed ship. She smiled, infusing it with politeness and regret. "Another time."

"I will escort you home," the ambassador said.

Ursola bit back a sigh. "Thank you. That would be lovely." She wheeled away from the man and made her way to the exit. After stopping to observe the niceties and bid good blacklight to her hosts, Ursola left the party, the ambassador an annoying companion on the short trek to the skystation.

Manx Two citizens—those of low standing—loitered near and inside the public waiting room. She ignored them to code into the elite waiting area.

"Ambassador, I am fine. I intend to contact a slave to meet me at the station."

"I insist."

"Very well." Ursola entered the elite shelter with the ambassador trailing her and twenty secs later, a skytrain pulled into the station, almost silent in its approach. She accepted his arm and entered the car.

"This train is efficient."

"Yes." Ursola smiled. "They're secure too. Even females on their own can travel at any mark of the cycle without the need to fear for their safety."

Thankfully, the journey to her home station was rapid. Ursola sat on a seat with her fingers pressed to her forehead, a ploy to keep the ambassador at bay. She pressed her earlink to signal Cayle, and he answered immediately. "I'm on my way home. Meet me at the skytrain station," she instructed and disconnected.

The train halted at a station and passengers exited. The doors shut.

"I believe we can do business together," the ambassador said. "Your companies are capable of providing Nidni with the turnaround we require for our household goods. However, I will require further discussions to firm the details. Perhaps we can meet over dinner on the next cycle."

Pushy male. He might possess a dashing way but compared to Cayle he came up lacking. "Certainly—if my headache retreats."

The skytrain zapped along the track before slowing for the next station. Her station. Ursola stood once the train came to a standstill.

"This is my stop."

"I'll wait with you until your servant arrives," the ambassador said, his hand giving warm guidance at the small of her back.

They reached the platform and she turned to him. "Thank you, Ambassador, but it's not necessary."

"Call me Lankesh." His hot breath wafted against her cheek.

She blinked and stared up at him.

"Mistress," a familiar voice said from behind them.

The ambassador started, and Ursola caught back a smile.

"My slave."

"Our dinner?" Lankesh asked.

"Comm the house when—"

A flash of light seared her retinas. A crack of sound followed. Lankesh shouted. Another explosive pop reverberated through the station. Hands grabbed her shoulders, tossed her to the stone floor. Cayle's familiar warm body pressed her into the chill of the stone, and Lankesh hit the deck beside them.

People shouted, legs scurrying past their position. When a third shot—and it was blaster fire because the scent of scorched synmetal filled each of her gasping breaths—other people joined them on the floor.

"We need to move," Cayle murmured.

"I've commed law enforcement," Lankesh said. "They'll be here shortly."

A siren sounded, rapidly approaching their vicinity.

Cayle partially moved off her, and she could breathe again. Enough for fury to take flight.

"Let me up."

"Yes, mistress." Cayle shifted aside and aided her to her feet.

"Did you see what happened?" she asked.

Lankesh shrugged, his lazy humor vanquished. "The shots came from that direction." He indicated with his hand. "I do not believe they wished to harm anyone. It was a warning."

Ursola pursed her lips. "Why do you say that?"

"Because the culprit was awaiting us. He or she fired yet didn't hit anyone. I cannot say for sure, but I do not believe they were a poor shot. They aimed where they intended to strike. A warning," he concluded.

"You should go inside the mansion, mistress."

A fourth blaster shot rang out and fragments from the wall struck her face.

Six law enforcement officers arrived. One with extra braid on his uniform looked to her.

"Catch the culprit," she ordered. "I want to display his head in the central city square."

No one fired on her and lived to embellish the tale, and no one threatened her slave's life either.

CHAPTER SIX

S weat poured down Jannike's face as she trudged after Kelvin. Hot. So hot. Each breath seared her nostrils, her lungs, and the bright, bright solar-star caused her to squint. Beneath her tunic, her skin prickled with the heat or maybe it was the mate malady exacerbated by the high temperature. Either way her skin crawled with discomfort.

Her hand slid beneath her tunic, and she surreptitiously scratched her belly as she watched one of the two small birds Kelvin had rescued lift into flight.

Goddess, goddess, *goddess* this itching would drive her to insanity. It directed her mind to the two felines, and she was starting to realize the depths of suffering Ry had gone through for all those rotations.

Shame made her recall her impatience, the way she'd thought his actions were an excuse for sex.

At least her guilt forced her mind from the dryness of her mouth, the tightness of her lips, and the heat on her face.

Royal whimpered and writhed beneath the head shelter she'd fashioned from her blanket covering. "We'll stop soon, boy. Get some water and rest."

One bird returned and screeched, landing on Lynx's shoulder without hesitation. Up ahead, Lynx changed direction, enough for her to glimpse his arse. *A fine one.* The thought jumped into her head, and once there, it took root. She'd had her fair share of males, even experimented with a female once she'd become easy in her own skin.

Sex released battle stress. It relaxed a being, allowed them to recharge. Sex was something for fun, something she did when the urge occurred.

On her schedule.

Sex wasn't necessary, and not sex with a particular male. Two specific males.

She scowled, realized she was still gaping at Lynx's arse and ripped her gaze free.

She would fight this unfortunate attraction.

No way would she leave Ry and her friends. They'd come for her because they valued her presence, her input. They'd come because they were her friends. Ry had promised.

This situation—temporary. Mogens, the ship's seer, would whisk up one of his potions and cure her of this weird malady.

And she'd never feel helpless and out of control again.

Just as she'd promised herself.

A rocky outcrop came into view. Not large. Not perfect, but the elevated position gave them a view of their surroundings. If they used the blankets to screen out the solar-star rays, the spot would suffice.

"Well spotted." Shiloh marched past and slid his hand down Lynx's cheek in an intimate gesture that had Jannike's stomach clenching.

Like a punch at her jaw, jealousy blasted her, spreading through her mind in a blaze of misery.

She didn't want either man, had no right to this level of irritation.

"Jannike?"

Kelvin sounded puzzled, and the sound vibrating past her lips—the growl—cut off abruptly. Royal whimpered and her hand went to his back to stroke and comfort.

Tiny bits of gravel crunched under her boots, the slight incline feeling as big as a mountain to her fatigued thigh muscles. A grunt escaped, and the annoying, irritating prickle started its familiar dance across her stomach. Every urge inside her bade her go to Shiloh and Lynx. She forced her legs in Kelvin's direction.

"Home until blacklight begins to fall." She turned to scan the area behind them and couldn't see a thing out of place.

Satisfied, she studied their immediate surroundings. The rocks piled haphazardly on top of one another, casting small slivers of precious shade. Her belly let out a plaintive rumble, which she ignored. Yet another layer to her wretchedness but something she could use for distraction.

"We'll need to split up to take advantage of the pockets of shade," Shiloh said.

Jannike gave a curt nod. "No prob. I'll set up camp with Kelvin."

"Good." Shiloh strode the few steps to join Lynx. He didn't stop until their bodies touched. The murmur of voices crossed the distance between them, and envy slapped her around again. Wishing for something she'd never have. Gah! Shiloh didn't like her—he tolerated her presence. She ripped her focus off them and forced her mind to the practicalities.

"Any ideas how to secure a blanket to give shade for both of us?" she asked Kelvin.

"Yes."

Jannike frowned, waiting for him to expand, but his eyes merely twinkled with mysterious secrets. "Are you intending to tell me?"

"Show is better."

Kelvin removed the blanket from his back—a larger version than her own. He trudged to an area away from Lynx and Shiloh, one concealed from anyone coming after them.

Jannike opened her mouth to protest because the spot he'd chosen wasn't near the faint patch of cover provided by the rocks.

Kelvin clutched the silver blanket in one hand. A creaking sound began, one that came from him. His face contorted and faded into the coarse brownness of his skin. His loincloth disappeared into his body and his arms and legs expanded, the creaking growing louder. His feet—bare—dug into the sand, writhing and twisting to give him a solid grip on the shifting ground.

A creaky bark of amusement came from Kelvin. "I'm guessing you've never met a tremin before."

Even his voice had changed to whispery—the voice of the forest.

While she gaped at his feet digging into the ground, his arms had lengthened, his hair had acquired spikes and become more leaflike. Now the blanket stretched out, spread by Kelvin's branches and providing a welcome square of shade. One big enough for all of them.

"Rest, Jannike," Kelvin whispered, his voice quieter in this form.

"What about you?"

"This is my resting form. I will have the best rest I've had for cycles. This, I promise."

"Thank you, Kelvin." Jannike dragged her body into the shade, the relief from the constant beat of the solar-star almost instant.

She pulled off her head covering and gently peeled Royal from her shoulder.

The two birds flew into Kelvin's lower branches and settled in the shade. Their round eyes drooped shut.

"See if Royal will rest in my lower branches," Kelvin whispered.

Jannike scooped up the calibore and placed him in the closest branch. Once she saw Royal was happy in this spot, she pulled a large berry from the supplies she'd toted and handed it to the calibore.

Kelvin's eyes closed, and if she hadn't seen them, she wouldn't have known the location of his features. A whispery sigh issued from him. A sense of peace.

Satisfied the birds, Kelvin and Royal were happy, Jannike pulled out a pouch of water. Tempted to gulp the contents, she forced herself to sip and stopped at the count of five. With no idea of when or if they'd discover water in these desert wastelands, conservation made sense.

Jannike set the supplies aside and spread out her blanket. Now that they'd halted to rest, every muscle in her body ached in accord with the prickles of her skin. The weight of her tunic against her flesh irritated her hot, sweaty body.

Take it off. Without another thought, she peeled off the blue tunic and balled it into a pillow. Maybe she should check for their captors before she tried to sleep. Once the idea occurred, it nagged at her, and finally, she crawled to her feet and staggered around to the other side of the rock outcrop.

Shiloh and Lynx had set up here and had discarded their tunics too. Lynx had shifted while Shiloh remained in humanoid form.

"Problem?" His gaze slid over her, and the itchy sensation almost dropped her to her knees.

She clamped her teeth together and forced herself to scan the horizon. "I wondered if anyone was following us, and even though I know you can see from here, once the idea came to mind it wouldn't let go. I had to look."

He nodded and the back of her neck itched—a different irritation to normal—and she guessed he was studying her. She forced herself to sweep the sandy horizon for a second and third time before she moved.

"Nothing. I guess I'll try to sleep now. How is Lynx?"

Shiloh stroked his hand over Lynx's head and the resulting purr had her biting her lip. The nip of pain should deter her from thoughts of joining them. Didn't work.

"Lynx is fine. He's sore, but now that he has the luxury of staying in feline form, he should heal."

She nodded, forced her legs to move away.

"What are you wearing?"

Jannike glanced at her breasts, clad in a red bra—all lace and satin. *Comfortable and practical yet girlie too.* Camryn's words echoed through her mind, bringing a blast of homesickness. At least that was what Camryn had described the feeling as—the desire for the comfort of home and family.

"It is an Earth garment," she said. "My friend, Ry, took his mate back to her home planet for a visit. We spent a twelfth of a rotation on Earth." The memories of their holiday released some of the strain, brought a curve to her lips. "We had a good time. They have this food called chocolate. Kaya—another friend—she purchased much chocolate to take as a memento. She hides it all over our ship and curses when she finds one of us has discovered her cache."

Shiloh had cocked his head, interest turning up the corners of his mouth. The sight was so foreign she gaped for a sec before regaining control.

"I'll leave you to rest," she said.

"Lynx and I intend to take turns at keeping watch."

Jannike nodded. "Call me to take a turn. We all need rest."

"I will."

She turned away, forced her traitorous legs to leave the two felines.

"Jannike?"

She turned, swallowed at the double temptation sprawled out in front of her. "Yes?"

"Sexy Earth garment."

The unexpected words had her gawking until she managed to pull herself together. This time her legs moved on command. Running away. Retreating. At last—her brain had slid into the right program.

Heart beating faster than it should, she dropped onto the blanket beneath Kelvin's impressive tree frame. She balled her tunic into a pillow and attempted to sleep. While exhaustion weighed down her body, her mind gamboled and frolicked with the vigor of a youngster. Lynx and Shiloh. Both felines and —to her mind—mates. So, she didn't understand why the mating bug had struck her too. The insidious longing to cozy up to the two felines—singly or both. It didn't seem to matter to the craving gnawing at her bones. This wasn't her.

She didn't need a man.

She didn't require a mate.

She might use a man.

She might enjoy a man.

But she never, never, *never* experienced the urge to keep one.

Frustration nudged aside the yearning for an instant, the intensity of invisible bugs writhing beneath her skin forcing a groan up her throat.

"Jannike?" The query in Kelvin's whisper had her eyes flicking open.

She pushed to a sitting position and swiped one hand over her hot cheeks. "Bad dream."

"I can listen."

"Thanks, but I'm fine."

"If you're in good health, then why are you shaking like my hair when the winds rise?"

Damn. "Manx Two doesn't hold good memories for me." Not a lie, but not the truth either. She knew it, suspected Kelvin guessed this too, since he didn't strike her as brainless.

Jannike put a stop to the conversation by yawning. "Tired. I think I'll try to go to sleep again."

"You weren't asleep before," Kelvin pointed out.

Yeah, he didn't miss a thing. "I'm gonna try to rest." She turned her back in dismissal and firmly closed her eyes.

She fought the constant crawl of desire, the urge to go to the two felines and beg them to touch her, to surround her with their hard bodies. The needy place between her thighs began to throb in counterpoint with the itch of her skin. Agony to remain still. Torture with each movement. She bit her bottom lip until the metallic taste of blood filled her mouth, fighting her body, fighting the insidious urges. Just fighting.

Finally, she must have fallen asleep. A hand on her shoulder jerked her from slumber, and she bolted upright, lashing out with her fist and smacking Shiloh in the jaw.

"Phrull it, woman," he gritted out, glaring at her and rubbing the spot.

"Sorry." Her gaze darted, jumped, skipped and settled everywhere, anywhere except on Shiloh with his intense green eyes, his sweat-sheened pectoral muscles and his tight black trews that outlined strong, muscular thighs.

The physical outlet had helped. Maybe she should hit him again. Smack. Punch. Jab. Grapple...*okaaay.*

She fought a tremor and failed, the shudder pulling every nerve ending to attention. Saluting. Ready for action...

Jannike struggled to her feet and put some distance between them, just so she could breathe Shiloh-free air. "Is there a problem?"

"The tracker lizards are heading in this direction. Can't see them clearly yet, but Lynx and I can hear their calls. They're on a scent trail."

"Crap." Jannike reached down to grab her tunic and pulled it over her head. She gathered her blanket and resettled the remaining supplies she'd set aside earlier.

"I think we should stay here," Shiloh said.

Jannike frowned at him, batted away the lurch of need in her gut. "Stay here? I don't know about you, but I have no intention of repeating my capture experience. I'm not waiting for the tracker lizards to lead those bastards to us."

Lynx slipped around the corner, slinking in his feline form. He shifted to humanoid with quick efficiency, his trews and boots appearing on legs that had been covered with fur while his chest remained bare. "The tracker lizards aren't following our scent. They're following something else."

"So we sit tight," Shiloh repeated. "If they were going to find our trail, they would have found it by now."

"I agree. The breeze keeps shifting the sand. There is no vegetation out here to help the scent stick. The tracker lizards are following another. Not us. If we move, we run the risk of giving them a trail to trip over," Lynx said.

Made sense. Jannike jerked her chin in recognition of good advice. "Who or what are they chasing?"

"Not sure yet. Shiloh and I need to move around here. We don't want them to spot us. We'll grab our supplies."

Shiloh glided away with Lynx prowling after him.

Great. Just great. Two male chests to ogle and fantasize over, to touch... Another one of those full-body shivers rolled from her head to her toes, leaving her weak-kneed and reeling. Hellfire. She had to keep her mind off Lynx and Shiloh.

"You are attracted to Shiloh," Kelvin said.

"No." She glanced over her shoulder and hoped the felines hadn't overheard.

"Lynx."

"No. All I'm interested in is getting out of this mess alive."

"Thy is kidding thyself."

"No!"

"The men are returning."

Jannike quivered and scanned the horizon from where they stood. She froze. "Is that...hellfire, it is. One of the dragon things is heading our way."

"A floris dragon? Where?" Shiloh demanded.

"To the right." Lynx indicated with his right hand.

"The hunting party will see it." Jannike pointed out the obvious. "The creature's red wings are like a bloody flag."

"The floris aren't fussy about what they eat," Lynx said. "But tracker lizards are difficult to kill. You have to go for their soft bellies."

"How is a dragon's sense of smell?" Jannike asked and edged under the sun shelter. "Their sight?"

"About the same level as a feline." Shiloh crinkled his brow in obvious concern.

"The creature knows we're here," Kelvin said, his whisper flat.

Jannike pushed aside her trepidation. "The question is, did they have more than one specimen on board the ship. Since it's flying toward us and the trackers, maybe it's searching for its mate."

"Soon know." Shiloh's tone indicated he was thinking the worst already. "If the dragon dive-bombs us, we'll know for sure."

"Cheerful Charlie," Jannike said.

"Huh?" Lynx stared at her with his sexy green eyes.

Her stomach did a dragon-style dive-bomb before she pulled a suitable expression together and managed a casual shrug. "Earth expression. Camryn taught us a lot, so we blended better during our visit."

The dragon kept coming. Jannike tracked its progress across the pale sky. Shiloh and Lynx exchanged a glance, one that spoke volumes to Jannike. They were ready to fight for their freedom.

"I'm an experienced warrior," she bit out, pissed at exclusion to their little club. "I'm not going to fall apart. What's the plan?"

"Lynx is going to shift and keep an eye on the advancing tracker lizards. There's no point making a run for it until we ascertain if we're prey. If it's us, I suggest we split up and run faster than a ruby-dotted whippet," Shiloh said.

Jannike packed up the food then placed it by Kelvin. "I take it a ruby-dotted whippet is fast."

"Holds speed records on the planet Playolia," Lynx answered even as the change took him.

"What about you, Kelvin?" Jannike asked. "Are you running with us?"

"No, I'm safer in this form. A floris won't find me an attractive meal. I'll keep Royal and the sienna-eyed markowls safe. Don't worry. The dragon won't bother me. He knows I'll strike out with my whip branches and damage his wings. A wounded floris is a vulnerable one."

"Maintain silence now," Shiloh warned. "Hand signals only."

Jannike nodded and edged from beneath the shelter, her gaze tracking the dragon. It was a beautiful creature, the bright red wings large and eye-catching. Its body, a deeper, less showy red, held streamlined strength. The dragon's giant maw hung open, testing the air for scent. Even from this distance, the sharp white teeth were visible. With rapid wing cycles, the creature sped through the air, cutting the distance separating them.

When the dragon gazed straight at her, Jannike ducked deeper into the shade of their screen. The dragon did know of their presence. She tensed, waited a sec before checking on the creature's progress again. It kept coming, coming, coming until the individual scales protecting its hide were visible from where she stood.

"Get ready to run," Shiloh murmured.

Jannike's muscles tensed. Funny. She'd spent cycles and rotations wishing she were dead, beyond the pain and humiliation. Sure, things had improved once she'd managed to escape, but even then, she hadn't cared if she lived or died as long as she was in control, the one calculating the risk to her person. Now that possible death stared her in the face once again, regrets pressed down on her shoulders.

She'd changed.

Ry, Camryn and the rest of the *Indy* crew were her family, and she wouldn't have a chance to say goodbye.

The dragon let out a bellow. Flames shot from its snout and left scorch marks on the sand and rocks. The dragon angled lower, spiky talons outstretched and fixed its gaze on them. Another spurt of fire shot close enough for Royal to let out a yelp.

"Now," Shiloh said in a terse voice.

Jannike propelled herself down the hill and away from the tracker lizards. Shiloh leaped, twisting his body into feline in a smooth shift.

Every sec she expected those wicked claws to spear her, for dragon fire to torch her skin and roast her until she resembled a burnt potato. Each breath sawed up her throat, sweat blurred her vision.

Flames struck the ground beside her, so close the heat seared her skin, made her stride falter. Off-footed, she didn't see a rock in her path until too late. She fell hard, hands flat to brace her fall. Sand. Dust. Pain.

Death hovered in beast form.

Manx Two truly would be the death of her.

CHAPTER SEVEN

L ynx pulled up, his sides heaving as horror clamped around
his ribs. The floris dragon swooped, its maw wide open to
display wicked teeth. Fire exploded from its mouth—a flare of red
and orange and burnished copper. A snarl vibrated in his throat,
and he changed direction to hurtle toward Jannike.

She'd scrambled to her feet and faced off with the dragon.

Faster, faster, *faster*.

Phrull, he wasn't going to make it.

A scream rang out in the distance. Lynx slowed, head cocking to
hear. The roar rippled through the air again, panicked and full of
terror.

Shiloh?

Fear gripped him by the scruff, and his heart almost beat out of
his chest.

Up ahead, the dragon lifted its gaze from Jannike. His large scarlet wings flapped and his big head tilted.

The third shriek shredded Lynx. So much pain and suffering in the bellow. Shiloh...

Lynx skidded to a halt and whirled to scan the landscape. Not Shiloh. Relief eased from him in a feline hiss.

The dragon tormenting Jannike with its firebreath bellowed in return, the shriek full of fury and anguish. Large wings lifted its red body higher into the air, and he departed with a speed Lynx wouldn't have thought possible, given the size of the beast. Surely they hadn't had this creature on the ship. Containing it... Lynx couldn't begin to think of the difficulties.

A feline bark dragged his attention away from the dragon's departure, and Lynx picked up the speed.

Jannike was down again.

Lynx reached her before Shiloh. He shifted smoothly and crouched beside her prone body. She lay on her stomach, her shoulders trembling, her face hid in her arm. "What is it? Where are you hurt?"

Shiloh skidded to a halt beside him. He shifted. "Her clothes are scorched, but burns are minimal. The bastard was playing with her."

Lynx snorted. "The governess used to smack us over the knuckles with her spoon when we played with our food."

The shudders and tremors increased in Jannike, and Lynx smoothed his hand over her upper arm. He frowned as the quakes froze and suspicion rose. "Was she laughing?"

"Jannike. Jannike!" Lynx turned her over, searched her face then ran his hands over her body to check for broken bones and other less obvious injuries.

"Don't touch," she snapped, the remnants of humor blanking from her expression.

"Where are you hurt?" Shiloh demanded with his usual abruptness.

"Don't fuckin' touch me." Jannike bolted upright and batted at Lynx's hands.

Shiloh sat back on his haunches, his mouth twisted into a sneer. "What's wrong, princess? Afraid of getting feline cooties?"

She scooted away and stood on shaky legs, wavering, her strong features pale. Her blonde hair bore scorch marks on one side, the ends sticking upward in crazy disorder. His mother—the queen—would raise her hands in horror if the same sight greeted her in a looking glass.

Lynx scanned the rest of her body. Dust covered her trews, rips in one knee and another at her calf where a tracker had bitten her on capture. Her tunic carried a mixture of dirt and dust and one sleeve appeared singed. Her hand slipped beneath her tunic to scratch her belly.

In the distance, the whistling shrieks of the tracker lizards had become louder, more frenzied. The floris dragon bellowed, its fury carrying across the desert.

"We need to see what's happening," Jannike said.

"Do you need help?" Shiloh asked.

"No!" She put up her hands in a defensive manner.

Shiloh let out a disgusted snort. "Phrull, lady. What is your problem?" He spun on his heel and strode away.

"Jannike?" Lynx asked.

"Leave me." This time, there was no force in her voice. She sounded...she sounded defeated.

"I won't touch, but I'm not leaving until I know you can get yourself up the hill and back to camp."

"I thought I was dead. The dragon could have had me at any time."

"But he didn't." Lynx wanted to help, to carry her since she moved so gingerly, but he respected her demands and held back.

"No."

"You were laughing."

"Kaya would have slapped me for acting hysterical."

"Kaya?" He gave her space, which seemed to ease her snappish mood. He didn't know a lot about her since he'd spent most of his time with Shiloh while locked in the cell.

"Kaya is one of the crew. My friend."

The climb up the slight incline took Jannike longer than it should. Her gait hitched with a limp, and by the time they reached Kelvin, her breaths came in hoarse pants.

"I'll get the medical supplies. The graze on your knee requires treatment. This heat will bring on infection."

Jannike rounded on him with a glare. "I can do it myself."

"Fine." *Ungrateful female.* Lynx stomped over to join Shiloh. "What is wrong with that woman? She won't let anyone help her and gets hysterical at the idea of anyone touching her."

"Rape," Shiloh said without taking his gaze off the plains below their rocky haven.

"Phrull it. That should have occurred to me."

"It's the only thing that makes sense." Shiloh shifted his weight then scratched his chest. "So we do as she says and keep our distance. You have to admire her tenacity, her determination. She's not the same as other females. You itchy?"

"Yeah. The heat seems to make it worse."

"The black marks are making my skin itch. It—damn. Did you see that?"

Lynx stared at the dragon, part awe, part fear fighting for dominance. The calls of the tracker lizards were deafening, even from this distance. "The dragon is picking them off."

A sword of firebreath slashed and skewered the shrieking creatures even as they ducked and danced, trying to escape the dragon's wrath and talons. A cloud of dust headed at the melee.

"That will be the big bastard who captured us," Shiloh said. "I hope he fries."

"What are we going to do? Push on and pray the dragon doesn't decide to attack again." Lynx rubbed one of the black marks on his abdomen. The relief was momentary, the bugs beneath his skin gathering momentum when he lifted his fingers.

"That's all we can do. No point staying here. The heat isn't as fierce as it was earlier. We should eat and take the opportunity to slip away while they're busy fighting."

Shiloh made sense. "Let's go."

With the heat from the solar-star reducing as blacklight approached, they packed their meager possessions and set off.

The shrieks from the tracker lizards had died away, and the resulting silence lifted the small hairs at the back of his neck. There was little chatter from their party, merely a silent determination.

At least they wouldn't need to worry about the tracker lizards any longer.

Shiloh followed in the rear as he had earlier, his thoughts darting this way and that while every one of his senses scanned for danger.

Progress became quicker now that they didn't need to battle the unrelenting heat. Not long until blacklight fell.

A twitch beneath his skin made him catch his breath. He scraped his nails over the spot in an attempt to alleviate the irritation. It wouldn't help. He knew that, but it didn't stop his vigorous scratching. Maybe touching Lynx...

Once they made camp to wait out the worst of the blacklight, they could rub against each other. He didn't even care about the stink of sweat. He was desperate to gain relief. Perhaps he might persuade Lynx to let him try oral.

The thought didn't raise panic or stamp him with worries of losing their friendship, which told Shiloh how desperate he was for Lynx's touch.

Kelvin walked in his normal stoic manner, tall and sturdy like the trees he resembled. The markowls perched on his broad shoulders.

Jannike marched with a stiff back, a slight hitch in her gait. The calibore clung to her right shoulder. She'd told them she'd been a slave and had used her body to barter her way from the prison. And rape. That fell somewhere into the mix. She seemed to have great faith in her friends. He hoped she was right to place her trust in rescue. They could use a miracle.

Still, she raised his curiosity.

Strong and determined. Dependable as far as he knew. The calibore creature loved her and never left her presence for long. She had a manner about her—an air of command he recognized because he owned the same trait. A bit bossy. His lips twitched.

Not a female that grabbed a male's attention first off. Not unattractive. She bore a subtle sexiness. That red thing she wore beneath her tunic. The way it cupped and lifted her, put her breasts on display. His cock had jolted to life, and he'd wanted to go to her, to run his fingers over her shoulders, press his lips to her collarbone...

He snorted out a breath because, even now, remorse sat heavy on his shoulders. The idea of touching another person in a sexual manner—after that first instant—seemed wrong, as if he was cheating on Lynx.

Luckily, sanity had prevailed.

Still, he wanted to learn more. Ask questions about her friends and the places they'd traveled. He could make the conversation casual, offer a few of their experiences in return. Furtively grab facts to appease his inquisitiveness.

The solar-star fell below the horizon, taking the light and the last of the heat. Shiloh lifted his head, relieved to see pinpricks of light from other solar-stars.

"Can we stop for a drink?" Jannike asked. "I don't know why, but I feel thirstier after eating a meal than before."

Lynx halted at the front of their group.

"I hear some say 'tis best to drink rather than eat when in the desert," Kelvin said.

"You didn't think to say this before," Jannike demanded.

"We don't have many options." Shiloh lifted the makeshift bag off his shoulders and pulled out a water container. "We need to keep up our energy."

Jannike barked out a laugh. "Keep us alive a little longer so we can have a repeat experience of the heat."

"Exactly." Shiloh found himself grinning. She had a subtle sense of humor, one that people might miss if they focused on her scowl.

"What was up with that dragon?" she asked as they lounged against handy rocks. "He intended to eat me."

"He might still eat us," Lynx said. "They're excellent hunters."

"Cheerful Charlie," Shiloh muttered.

Jannike chuckled, the notes hoarse but amusement nonetheless. His heartbeat did a skip. Guilt bounced up and down on his shoulder, this time accompanied by bemusement. He tested the feeling, counted up the clues and came up with a conclusion.

He wanted to stick his cock inside Jannike.

The water smoothed the dust in her mouth, her throat. The hot patches of skin where the dragon had seared her with its fire throbbed and combined with the itches to create a nasty torture. Now, she couldn't rub as hard or she'd break the skin. Experience had taught her infection gained a hand up in hot climes.

She had to stop scratching.

A subtle itch sprang to life on her stomach. She ignored the fluttering prickle.

"Should we start moving again?" she asked.

"Yes," Kelvin said.

Jannike placed a hand on his coarse arm. "You didn't have a drink."

"I drank back at the ship. I don't require water yet."

And if she drank as much water as Kelvin had, she'd pee like a racehorse. Another of Camryn's quaint expressions, and it raised a smile.

She fell into line behind Lynx and forced her achy legs to move at the pace he set. The level of the irritation beneath her skin had subsided when she thought of her friends. Maybe she should focus on the good times and their recent trip to visit Camryn's family on Earth. One of her friends, Amme, had remained on Earth to stay with the man she'd come to love.

Love.

Sex.

And...the fukkin prickles raced back, stronger than before.

All she had to do was think of sex. The trigger apparently.

"Jannike? Jannike! What's wrong?"

Lynx had slowed when the path carving between the rocks they were traversing had widened. Now he walked at her side, his expression quizzical.

"What?"

"You were mumbling." His grin broadened, his teeth a flash of white even in the murky lighting. "I thought I heard you mention sex."

Jannike stumbled over a rock, and Lynx's muscular arm gripped her around the waist before she tumbled headfirst onto the ground.

"I'm okay," she said hastily. "Don't touch me."

"Your scorch marks. Sorry, I forgot." He lifted his hands in surrender and backed up half a step. Royal hissed from his perch on her shoulder. "I was trying to help."

"Thank you." Not that his increased distance made much difference. She'd caught his scent. Yes, he was dirty and sweaty like her, but he also possessed a masculine scent that tugged at the feminine part of her psyche. The tiny prickles increased, leaping around like March hares. Not that she recalled Camryn's explanation at present. She just knew hares jumped. A lot.

"What's the problem?" Shiloh asked.

"It's dark." Jannike reached to soothe her calibore. "I tripped." Even she heard the belligerence in her tone. "Doesn't matter. We should keep traveling because the temperatures will plummet soon."

She caught Lynx studying her and gestured with her head. Thankfully, he didn't voice further questions. He shrugged and moved back to the lead. Jannike concentrated on walking, one foot after the other.

No more sex thoughts. No more sex thoughts. Stupid woman. Why hadn't she realized she was mumbling aloud?

Time blurred, and Jannike kept plodding after Lynx. The darkness hadn't become absolute, just enough to strain her eyes to make out objects in her path. Probably her saving grace. She couldn't ogle Lynx's butt in this light.

A knifelike pain sliced through her belly. Her cry escaped before she could button her lips.

"Jannike needs to rest," Kelvin's voice boomed from behind her. "I will carry Royal if he allows the honor."

The boom took her by surprise, but she was too exhausted to leap in reaction. Inside, her stomach jolted and set off an echo of prickles and itches.

"I can carry you," Shiloh offered.

"No!" Goddess, that would make it worse. She couldn't—wouldn't—touch either of these men. She liked them, admired them, but what was the point? They'd have to go to the dome eventually or die in this sandpit. If the widow heard of her presence or, worse, captured her, she'd die a horrid death.

Mates connected on many levels. It wasn't that she disliked either of these men. Hellfire, she'd only ever wanted one, but now, in her delirium, she craved two. She didn't know what to do with two men. As much as she loved Ry Coppersmith, the man was a handful. She didn't want a boss—not one or two—she wanted a partner.

Her sex clenched at the thought, the prickles stealthily creeping across her breasts. Another soft groan exited before she could halt the sound.

"Jannike." Shiloh scooped her up and their group slogged onward.

"You don't have to carry me."

"Shush. No one thinks you're weak. You're injured, more than you let on to us earlier."

"No, I—"

"Relax, Lynx will choose a campsite, and we'll rest until light."

"We s-should be able to w-walk more during the early whitelight, before it g-gets too hot." The words dragged across the tip of the tongue, digging in heels. She persevered, pushing, pushing, pushing each syllable free until her sentence ended. Finally, exhausted, she closed her eyes. No! She mustn't fall asleep.

"Sleep," Shiloh whispered. "I've got you."

But she didn't want him to get her. He belonged to Lynx. They would be mates, and it was fitting. The two complemented each other—both strong and sure. Longtime friends, they were already partners. Taking a step further to mates wouldn't bring much of a change.

Couldn't get in the middle.

Might cause a fight.

Not the time for romance, for sex, for flirtation of any sort, no matter how much she admired their bodies and minds, craved their attention.

A prickle knifed through her gut and Jannike heard herself whimper.

"See any place suitable?" Shiloh asked.

"A big pile of rocks ahead. Won't be long," Lynx said.

Jannike quivered and turned her face to breathe in more of Shiloh's scent. One whiff and the itching subsided to a low-level hum. Oh goddess. Blissful relief.

Jannike's mind quieted, and she forced herself to take even, steady breaths instead of great gulps. If she could spend longer in his arms or Lynx's arms. Either would do.

She suppressed the immediate urge to sigh.

Not gonna happen.

"Jannike. Jannike, wake up. We're at camp."

The husky rumble was a pleasant way to rouse and much better than the rooster-bird call that Nanu, the *Indy's* pilot and engineer, had rigged to help them rise from their sleep-beds each cycle beginning. Another idea taken from Earth. Life aboard the *Indy* was so different now that Camryn had joined the crew. Improved, she decided.

"Jannike?"

"I'm awake," she said. "You sound much better than the rooster-bird."

"A compliment?" Laughter rippled through his voice, and a different sort of quiver fluttered to her sex.

She tensed, began to struggle.

"Stop wriggling, or I'll drop you on your arse."

She halted, but every particle in her mind wanted to leap from his touch. Her body had other ideas.

After a long, extended sec he eased her down. Their bodies jostled in the process, and sudden knowledge drummed into her brain.

Danger, Jannike Hondros! Danger.

If the spike in Shiloh's pants wasn't attached to his person, then she was an ape's uncle.

Gasping in a girly manner, she yanked from his touch and scrambled backward. In the blacklight his features were indistinguishable, but she heard his huff of impatience.

"It's a hard-on, Jannike. A male gets them. Deal with it."

A splutter of laughter came from Lynx, who stood beside a

gaping Kelvin.

"I get them too," Lynx added, in the manner of one offering advice.

"Keep them away from me. I'm...I'm...not used to that sort of thing." The sec she'd uttered the words, she wanted to yank them back. Kaya would roar with laughter if she'd overheard that particular gem. A tiny snigger bubbled at the back of her mind. *Ridiculous, Jannike.*

"Let me treat your wounds then we'll leave you to rest," Lynx said.

"No!" If anything, her panic escalated while her hormones, in concert with her body, rioted for progress in this touching business. "No, I don't need either of you touching me. You're both tired too. Give me our medical supplies, and I'll take care of my ouchies."

Lynx's brows winged upward. "Ouchies?"

"My translator doesn't know this word," Shiloh said.

"Earth speak," Jannike blurted. "Camryn...I...we...never mind. I will fix the sore spots."

"I will help her before I take root," Kelvin boomed.

"Yes." Another blurt. Could she monkey a nitwit any better? Might be ape—she couldn't recall the order of the animals right now. "Yes, that's fine. You and Shiloh need to rest. Together. Away from us." Jannike buttoned her lips and bowed her head. Goddess! She clenched her hands and slowed her breathing. No, no, no! Lynx stood too close. She needed to remove herself from his airspace before her traitorous body decided to test for spikes in his pants.

"We know when we're not wanted," Shiloh said.

"You'll want privacy." Jannike rushed the words. "To do things."

Lynx cocked his head. "What kind of things?"

"Touching. Sex things. I don't know. I don't know anything. I know nothing. Don't do sex. Don't want it. Go, go." She made frantic shoo motions with her hands, her chest heaving as she struggled to breathe past the knifelike stabs in her stomach.

Shiloh grasped Lynx's hand. "We'll set up camp on the other side of those rocks. Shout if you need us."

Jannike held her breath until the men passed beyond her scent range. When their footsteps receded, and they'd blended with the blacklight, her shoulders sagged.

"Lass. You're in trouble. You need those two males. The lack is affecting your health."

Jannike peered into the blacklight, her heart galloping like a hell-horse after meat. Had they heard? Kelvin had spoken in an undertone. When neither of the felines reappeared, her tension subsided. "No, I don't have a problem, not apart from a few hot spots on my arms where the dragon fire burned through my tunic."

"Lie to yourself, but you're not fooling me." Kelvin shook his head enough to stir his hair. It made a rustling sound, a peaceful brushing and stirring of hair strands.

Jannike sighed. "Maybe you're right. I don't know. Those two are mates, and I mustn't get into the middle. It will cause trouble."

"You don't know that for sure."

"No, but my educated guess tells me to stay away. I'd appreciate your help. I'm so tired I can barely lift my arms. Shouldn't be this tired. Always training to keep up fitness. Ry makes sure we stay fighting fit."

"This cycle has tried us all. Maybe the next will be less eventful."

"Maybe."

Jannike unfastened the laces closing the neckline of her tunic, and grasped the hemline to tug the garment over her head. Grim determination allowed her to complete the chore. She was breathing hard once she dropped her arms to her sides.

"The supplies are in my bag." Kelvin referred to the improvised carrier they'd fashioned from their blankets. "Spread your blanket and sit ye down on a soft spot of sand."

Jannike chose a place at the base of a huge rock, sheltered from the prevailing wind, although it wouldn't do much to stave off the cold. "This will do."

Once she'd settled, Kelvin knelt at her side.

"The right side of my body is worst."

"The heal-gel will take away the heat and promote healing."

A sigh gusted from her when the gel hit her skin, the coolness relieving the burning sensation. Gentle fingers rubbed in the gel. It shouldn't have hurt. Logic told her this, but a screech rippled free. A pained gasp.

Kelvin's hand jerked from her body, and the fiery needles firing her synapses receded.

Footsteps thumped around the corner of the rocks, and Lynx and Shiloh arrived. Their eyes glinted, catching the faint light. When no danger presented, they strode the remaining distance.

"What is it?" Lynx demanded.

"What's wrong?" Shiloh asked.

The two felines stood shoulder to shoulder, prepared to act on her behalf. The feminine part of her sighed and cooed. The warrior part—her brain—tensed until each muscle grew rock hard. She winced when Lynx moved a step closer.

"My touch pained her. Took her by surprise." Kelvin handed over the heal-gel to Lynx. "Maybe ye fingers will be softer on her burns."

"No," Jannike said.

"Ye need this, lass," Kelvin boomed and stood aside.

She screwed her eyes shut, her pulse choppy and loud enough for them to hear with their kitty senses.

"Phrull it, Jannike. We didn't realize it was this bad. You have red patches on your arm and your torso." Lynx fingered one spot.

She winced at the spark of pleasure that shot down her body.

"Give me the gel," Shiloh said. "If we both do this, the job will get done quicker."

No. No. No!

The denial sang through her mind. This won't take long. Not long. Not long.

Wait...red marks on her torso. They weren't there before. The dragon fire had scorched her right arm, and that was all. This meant...this meant the mating urges had entered her system. No wonder she was so jumpy.

She attempted to recall events with Ry and Camryn. Camryn had fought the mating, but Ry had kissed her, fucked her early on, which obviously must make the process different.

Goddess, she had to keep fighting.

"How much longer?" she asked in a low voice.

"A few mins," Lynx said.

"You've been scratching them," Shiloh chided. "Don't. That's the easiest way for infection to take a grip."

Lynx ran his fingers over her biceps. "Jannike, are you listening?"

Good goddess. They were tag-teaming her. "I'm listening." Didn't mean she had to obey or...goddess, their fingers felt so good. The harsh prickles digging into her flesh and crawling beneath her skin twisted together into pleasure. Slowly, the tension released from her muscles.

"There. All done," Shiloh said. "What about your back?"

"My back is fine. No pain at all." She managed not to purr the words. Thank the goddess.

"We'll reapply the gel before we set off again." Lynx rose to his feet. "Sleep well."

"Thanks," she said.

"All you had to do was ask." Shiloh smoothed his fingers over her biceps and skimmed the tender skin of her wrist. His touch left a simmering charge of pleasure, and she closed her eyes to screen her expression in self-defense.

His trews rustled as he stood, but she sensed he scrutinized her before he and Lynx departed.

"Does thy feel better, lass?"

"Yes, Kelvin."

"My touch pained you. Their touch soothed. 'Tis destined."

"No."

"Fight if you must. Yer foolin' yerself, and that's the last I'll say on the matter."

"Promise?"

Kelvin snorted a booming laugh and strolled to another spot. Royal climbed down his body and scampered over to her.

"The *Indy* had better come soon, Royal," she whispered as she stroked his fur. "I don't think I can hold out for much longer."

CHAPTER EIGHT

"What do you think is up with Jannike?" Lynx asked. "I'm not sure I buy your theory about rape. Think back to the start when they first put her in our cell. She didn't react much when she woke with strangers hovering around."

Shiloh stripped off his tunic and spread a blanket on the ground. "Just now, her body was tense, but she wasn't jumpy. She didn't scream, not the same way she did at Kelvin's touch. What do you think it means?"

"No idea." Lynx yawned as he removed his own tunic and boots and started on his trews. "Too tired to worry about it now." He scratched his chest. "Wonder if the heal-gel will work on these black marks. They keep moving, and I feel them shift. It's disconcerting." The weirdest thing he'd experienced in his life.

"I need to touch you," Shiloh said without warning. "Need more than what we've been doing."

Lynx's gut bucked, and it wasn't in fear. "What do you mean?"

"Trust me?"

"Never been in dispute."

Shiloh shifted his weight from foot to foot.

Lynx grinned at the uncharacteristic uncertainty and dropped onto the blanket. He placed his hands beneath his head and smirked up at his friend. "Nervous?"

"Hell yeah. I keep thinking this will wreck our friendship."

"Shiloh, after all the crap we've shared over the rotations, nothing will change our friendship. We've touched, kissed. Think we're way over the line now."

Shiloh stripped off his boots and trews and plonked on the blanket beside him. Lynx grinned again. It was sorta cute for the big guy to hesitate.

He reached out and squeezed Shiloh's knee. "Love you. We're a team. Always have been. Can't imagine my life without you in it."

"But you're a prince, second in line to the crown."

"Doesn't make me special. Doesn't make me rich. Doesn't make me crap superior magic. Still dress the same way as you. Shiloh, when have I ever lorded it over you?"

"I'm scared," Shiloh admitted in a low voice.

"Me too."

They fell silent.

Lynx stared up at the black sky and enjoyed the cool breeze frisking his body. Refreshing after the earlier heat. He replayed Shiloh's words, even understood his doubt. "The parents will freak."

Shiloh snorted a laugh, although they both knew it wasn't funny. "So what's new?"

"This might be the final death knell."

"Maybe, but we have friends. I doubt they'll care. Cimmaron won't for a start," he said speaking of the female Dlog pilot they'd met in a bar several rotations ago.

"Agreed. So why are you dithering?"

"Scared."

Lynx stared at the pinpricks of light that scattered the black sky. "The prickling sensation is getting out of hand again."

"I know. Doesn't mean I like the coercion."

"Agreed. I'll be asking questions if—when we make it home."

"We need to check with the research librarian," Shiloh said. "He keeps the House of the Cat records. There must be information somewhere."

"Fated mates though." Lynx turned on his side and propped himself up on his elbow. "Phrullin amazing when you think about it." He leaned over and pressed his lips to Shiloh's. His lips curled a fraction as he thought how right and familiar this seemed. Not a kiss between friends but one between lovers.

Seemed right. Nothing wrong with love, with loyalty, with friendship when it arrived in the same package.

Shiloh rolled without warning, breaking the sweet contact. His chatoyant eyes glowed with passion and yearning. There was love too. Desire. A hint of his normal challenge, and this settled the last of Lynx's disquiet. Shiloh must have felt the same because he lowered his head and kissed him.

Nothing sweet about this embrace.

Passion spilled out as Shiloh bit at his mouth, encouraged him to open. He tasted, varied the pressure, licked, mated with his mouth until desire roared through Lynx. He gripped Shiloh's shoulders, falling into the smooch with all the passion and honesty he possessed.

Shiloh's hands wandered. He caressed Lynx's chest, his pectoral muscles, and trailed kisses down his throat. A mouth on his earlobe was nothing new, but when Shiloh nibbled, sparks reverberated all the way to his cock.

Lynx gasped, gripped Shiloh's head and did all he could to beg for more without stating the need aloud.

Shiloh laughed, a low intimate sound. "I'm not gonna stop touching you. We can't go all the way, not without gel to make things easier. Never want to hurt you. But with no one watching, we can go further. Trust me?"

"Always," Lynx whispered. "With my life."

Shiloh's smile stole his breath, the hint of wickedness propelling his pulse rate to choppy.

Shiloh nipped his neck, his rough tongue laving away the sting. He sucked hard enough to leave bruises, not that Lynx cared. The bruising would heal, and besides, it felt damn good.

Already, his cock stood to attention, pre-come beading at the tip. The insistent prickles under his skin had subsided, as they always did when he and Shiloh touched.

Shiloh moved lower, paying attention to his nipples. Previous lovers had sucked and bitten him there, and he'd experienced nothing. When his friend licked, every nerve snapped to attention and saluted. The scrape of canines dragged a groan from deep in his chest. His arms went around Shiloh, held the feline to him in case he decided to halt.

"Shiloh," he whispered.

"Feel good?"

"Need more," Lynx admitted.

"More to come," Shiloh promised and dealt his other nipple the same treatment.

Lynx's world became one of sensations, of silken touches, of musky scents, soft lips. Hard lips. Teeth. He loved it all, the cycle's tensions drifting away on a Perian sea of pleasure.

Lynx jumped when Shiloh gripped his cock in his big hand and pumped hard.

"Shiloh," he pleaded. "Please. More."

He expected Shiloh to rise and take him in his arms, that they would writhe and rub together until climax took them both. His next breath caught in his throat. He swallowed as Shiloh straddled his thighs and took his cock into the heat of his mouth.

The warmth, the tight pressure Shiloh managed with his tongue and lips dragged another groan from his throat. Desire. Pleasure. Enjoyment flamed across his skin, hurled him into bliss. His hips bucked, driving his cock deeper into Shiloh's hot mouth.

"Shiloh. Shiloh. Shiloh," he chanted.

Phrull, why hadn't he thought of this before? Suspected that this was what Shiloh had meant? Because he thought of sex in the traditional way. That was why. This was new, unexplored territory. Most people would disapprove. His parents, Shiloh's parents, would act with disgust, but he didn't phrullin care.

Shiloh didn't disgust him and had never repulsed him with his relaxed approach to sex.

Shiloh lifted his head, released his cock with a popping sound.

"Why are you stopping? Don't stop. Please."

"I don't want you to hate me, say I forced you later. Still scared, Lynx." The words came out hoarse and full of passion. His big hand trembled, telling Lynx more than words how much this meant to him.

"I'm all in." Lynx met his friend's gaze and let everything he felt show in his expression. "There's no going back now, and I don't want to."

Shiloh gave a choked sound that held a hint of self-deprecation. "Thank phrull for that."

Before Lynx could formulate a reply, Shiloh swallowed his cock down, taking him fast and deep, driving him into thick pleasure and a sphere of pure sensation. His hips jerked without volition. His hands gripped the blanket at his sides then he gave in to the urge to touch. Difficult though the maneuver was, he managed to sit and slide his fingers through Shiloh's hair.

"Goddess." Another tremor struck and reverberated the length of his body. "Lift your hair away so I can see. Yeah. Phrull, Shiloh. That looks so damn hot. Seeing my cock slide into your mouth."

Shiloh didn't take his mouth off Lynx's cock, but his gaze rose, and what he saw sent Lynx spinning. Pleasure shone in his eyes. He lifted his head, stroking along the underside of Lynx's cock. He tasted the broad head, the roughness of his feline tongue darting spurts of pleasure along Lynx's veins.

Lynx watched avidly, mesmerized by the rugged masculinity of his friend's face and seeing him in a different way. A new way. He caught the flash of tongue, and the corresponding caress forced a groan past his parted lips.

Shiloh's gaze met his again.

"I had no idea." Lynx led with honesty. "Does it get better still?"

Shiloh winked, amusement simmering along with the lust glowing in his feline eyes. With one big hand, he pushed Lynx back to a lying position.

"What are you going to do?"

Shiloh didn't reply. Instead, he started to use his hands and fondled Lynx's balls, rolling them with callused fingers, tugging on them to a point shy of pain. At the same time, he increased his mouth action, taking Lynx deep. So deep Lynx's cock hit solid flesh.

If he'd thought Shiloh was giving his everything before, he'd been mistaken. The rush of pleasure tore through his body, the tight suction of Shiloh's mouth almost more than he could bear. Good. So phrullin good.

Lynx's eyes slid shut. Each breath came in a rough gasp. His hips lifted and he began to use Shiloh's mouth as he'd utilize a woman's pussy. Rapid thrusts that he couldn't control. The pleasure built in thick, juicy layers until he didn't think his body would hold together.

Another suck. A bump against Shiloh's throat. A thrust.

"Shiloh!" His climax roared through him with the rapid propulsion of a spaceship thruster. Shiloh swallowed and continued to swallow, each movement of his throat inducing another series of aftershocks. Lynx came and came, semen pulsing from his cock in rhythmic contractions. Long moments later, he stilled, ceased his thrashing and every muscle collapsed in physical repletion.

Shiloh continued to lick him, gentler now, which Lynx was grateful for because his cock had become tender.

Finally, his limp shaft slid from Shiloh's mouth.

They stared at each other, and Lynx swallowed.

Shiloh narrowed his gaze. "Anything to say?"

"Yeah. Why didn't you tell me it felt this good? Women never use enough force. They treat my cock as if it's going to break off. You...that was perfect."

Shiloh lost his impassive expression, his grin blooming into one of pure beauty. "You weren't ready to listen."

"Maybe," Lynx conceded with a shrug. "Can I do that to you?"

Shiloh's smile slipped a fraction. "You want to?"

"Yes. Besides, I owe you. That was amazing."

Shiloh moved off Lynx's legs and frowned. "You don't have to reciprocate. Don't feel you owe me anything."

Lynx sensed he needed to act fast. If he handled this wrong, Shiloh would back away, and he didn't want that. "I want this more than anything. Giving always brings me just as much pleasure. I want to make you groan. Wanna bet I can do it?"

Shiloh barked out a laugh. "Not touching that wager with a long fishing pole."

Lynx sat up. "Tell me what to do."

"To start with, just do whatever you like a woman to do with you."

"I can do that."

Shiloh lay back on the blanket, and Lynx straddled his thighs.

His friend's cock stood fully erect, the large head swollen with need. "If you feel as if you might choke, use your hands at the base of my shaft to control how much goes in your mouth."

Lynx nodded.

"And tuck your hair behind your ears so I can see what you're doing. I enjoy watching."

"Me too." Lynx listened to his friend's instructions. "If you want me to do anything different, spit it out. Touching you doesn't disgust me, Shiloh. The prickles under my skin have subsided since you touched me."

"In me too."

Lynx grabbed the lace he used to fasten his tunic and used it to tie back his hair. That done, he reached for Shiloh's cock. Not much different from his own. Hard and hot to the touch. He ran his hand up and down the shaft, then used his mouth to follow the same path.

Shiloh hissed, and when Lynx lifted his gaze, he found Shiloh gritting his teeth. Not a shred of horror or distaste filled his expression. This was something different—a combination of lust and expectation. The need to hold back in order to savor a treat.

Remembering Shiloh's advice to do what turned him on, Lynx explored Shiloh's balls with his lips and fingers, just following instinct and letting Shiloh's breaths guide him as to what to do next.

He licked up Shiloh's shaft, breathing in his friend's musky scent. Taste. What did Shiloh taste like at the tip of his cock? Curiosity and an odd sense of hunger propelled him onward. When he took the entire head into his mouth, Shiloh's big body shuddered. His hips lifted into Lynx's mouth, pushing his cock deeper. A musky, salty taste filled his mouth. Not unpleasant or off-putting. He wriggled his tongue back and forth, and the taste intensified. He sucked, lapped, slid his mouth up and down. He coughed when Shiloh went too deep, his eyes watering as he fought his gag reflex. Then he remembered Shiloh's advice to use his hands. He pulled back a fraction, gripped the base of Shiloh's cock and combined tugs and drags with mouth suction.

"Goddess, Lynx. *Lynx.* Whatever you do, please don't stop."

Lynx smiled around Shiloh's shaft. He took him as deep as he could and swallowed. Shiloh jerked, pushing his cock that much deeper. Their gazes met as Lynx lifted his mouth while keeping the tight seal around Shiloh's cock. He upped the pace and soon tasted more beads of liquid.

Whenever Lynx reached this point, his orgasm hovered in the background like an aggravated feline prepared to pounce. With this knowledge in mind, he sucked harder, tried to take Shiloh deeper.

"Lynx. Goddess. Lynx." Shiloh kept repeating his name in a litany, his big body quivering, trembling, shuddering.

Lynx tried to take Shiloh deeper into his mouth and partially succeeded. Shiloh let out a roar, taking Lynx by surprise, then his friend was coming, spurting into his mouth. Lynx tried to swallow, but the sheer amount of fluid shooting down his throat took him by surprise. He pulled back. Semen dribbled from his mouth. Another blast of semen got him in the face. In the chest.

He gaped at Shiloh, watched the amusement transform into a guffaw once Shiloh's orgasm began to trail off.

"Feline, you should see your face," Shiloh spluttered between chortles.

"I didn't expect...goddess..." He swiped at his chest, fighting the urge to grin in return. It was kinda funny.

"Stop."

Lynx's hand froze on his chest. "What?"

"You look hot. I enjoy seeing my mark on you."

Lynx snorted. "I thought it was the wolf boys who marked their territory."

Shiloh cocked his head. "So you admit it. We're partners in the fullest sense now."

Lynx sucked in a breath, waited for trepidation and fear, maybe disgust to trot to the fore. None of that happened. A sense of rightness and belonging assailed him. A sense of wonder. "That's right." His gaze remained steady on his friend.

Shiloh's smile lit up his entire face. Lynx caught his breath, and something in his chest tightened.

Shiloh grasped Lynx's biceps. Without breaking their gaze, he wiped the splatters of semen into Lynx's skin. The laughter transformed, trickling into something darker and needy. Shiloh's lips met his, the contact bringing comfort even as desire sparked through his veins again.

When Shiloh lifted his head they were both breathing hard. "Soon," he promised. "We'll do this properly once we're sure of our safety and have supplies."

"All right." Words that a rotation ago might have terrified him. Now the idea of doing something so intimate together seemed right, and he held not a single regret.

"Let me clean you up," Shiloh whispered, and Lynx blinked at the tenderness coming from his friend. Part of him wanted to tease but he hauled back the impulse. Time and place.

Shiloh wiped away the sticky residue with the corner of his tunic. "We'd better try to grab some rest. We'll need to travel some distance before the worst of the heat."

"The ship owner went to some trouble to collect us and the other specimens. They're gonna want us back. They'll send more tracker lizards after us."

"The specimens that manage to survive this heat," Shiloh said.

"Yeah, that's what I thought, but we have to try to get to the dome. I have no intention of making this easy for them."

"I thought about splitting from the others—"

"No, not a good idea. We're better off together," Lynx said.

"You didn't let me finish. I discarded the idea because it didn't feel right. We're not leaving anyone behind. Together, we're stronger."

"The next couple of cycles aren't gonna be easy. That floris

115

dragon is still out there with its injured mate. And there were other dangerous creatures on the ship."

"Cross your fingers we make it to the dome," Shiloh said. "If we make it that far, finding a means of escape from the city will be as easy as tugging a kitten's tail."

The severe cold woke Jannike. Invisible, chilly fingers pinched her nose, her cheeks, her fingers, her toes. She wrapped the blanket more tightly around her body and covered her face. The reshuffling and rearranging didn't make a bit of difference and succeeded in waking Royal. He grumbled and chattered at her while she tried to get comfortable.

"Can't sleep?" Kelvin asked.

"I'm cold. How long have I been asleep?" It wasn't as black as before, and she could make out Kelvin's expression when she turned toward him. She settled Royal on her shoulder and sat up. Yawning, she rubbed gritty eyes, every muscle in her body screaming for more rest. After stretching her cramped limbs, she clambered to her feet. Maybe if she paced she'd get warm. Where were her boots? Ah!

"You had a few portions of the cycle in slumber," Kelvin said.

Her eyes began to stream, tears flowing as she laced her boots. Not tears, but her eyes attempting to compensate for the dryness. She knuckled the moisture away and blinked several times.

"What's up?" Shiloh asked, appearing from behind the rocks in the same stealthy manner Ry and Camryn used.

"I can't sleep because of the cold." She tried not to gawk at his bare chest. Evidently felines, or this particular feline, didn't feel the cold.

"We've rested long enough. We can move out now and eat the last of our supplies when the heat forces us to stop."

"It's still dark," Jannike said.

Lynx—also bare-chested—appeared beside Shiloh and laughed.

"We can see okay. Same line formation as the previous cycle. I'll pack up our stuff."

Lynx disappeared, and Jannike expected Shiloh to follow his friend but he remained in position, his hands on his hips.

"What?"

"Lynx and I have been talking. We think we should head in the direction of the dome."

"Our captors won't stop looking for us," Kelvin boomed, speaking in his normal voice now that everyone had woken.

"That's what we figured. Our best chance of escape is finding transport at the dome. Go on the offence rather than running."

"Don't you mean steal?" Jannike asked.

"That's what I mean," Shiloh said without inflection. "Do you agree?"

"We don't have an alternative. Long-term survival in the desert is impossible. We have enough food for one last snack and not much more water. The dome it is."

The two markowls tweeted and cooed and made clicking sounds at Kelvin. He clicked and tweeted back and nodded, his branches vibrating with the sharp shift of his head.

"The markowls have good blacklight vision," he said. "They offer to scout ahead. One will fly in front to discover possible danger. The other will check for the floris dragon."

"That would be much appreciated." Lynx appeared to stand at Shiloh's side, fully garbed and carrying their belongings.

Kelvin communicated with the markowls. The birds lifted into the air, their wings extending as they disappeared into the gloom. "They intend to hunt before reporting back."

When Lynx halted by Jannike, she caught a whiff of sex. She gulped, and silently battled the bloom of craving in her achy body. *Stay away. Don't give in.*

She managed to hold her ground, but her knees shook like saplings in a strong breeze. Her gaze shot to her feet. Fight. Fight.

Fight.

"Something wrong, Jannike?" Shiloh asked.

Her gaze flew upward to study him. As usual the man held his true feelings close to his chest. "Not a thing."

With minimal possessions to pack, they were soon on their way. Her belly rumbled, protesting the lack of sustenance. Sheer willpower kept her placing one foot in front of the other and propelling herself along. The coldness receded from her limbs, yet the chill persisted on her cheeks. Her eyes continued to stream tears, and she had to keep brushing them away. She knew she wasn't crying but others might jump to conclusions.

One of the markowls returned and perched on Kelvin's right shoulder. It fluffed its wings before beginning a report.

Jannike focused but heard nothing except indecipherable clicks. She'd recommend to Ry that they update their translator databases with more languages. The inability to understand little known races could place their lives in danger.

"He didn't see the floris dragon," Kelvin said. "He flew over the area where we saw the tracker lizards. The dragon's mate wasn't there either, but there was much lifeforce coloring the sands. Many bones. He saw humanoid people approaching on two-wheel motors."

"Lifeforce?" Jannike asked.

"Blood," Shiloh said. "I'm more concerned about the motor things."

"Motor-skids," Jannike translated. "The rich hold weekend parties in the dunes not far from the dome. They use these vehicles for recreation and have races. The fat tires make travel over the sand easier."

"Anything else?" Shiloh asked.

The markowl chirped.

"The rat-pygmies are tasty." Kelvin chuckled, the humor raspy and hoarse. "He suggests we try some."

"Ugh, no," Jannike said. "During the cold months the creatures infested the slave quarters. They have nasty bites. I still have a scar on my leg where one bit me. Ugly damn creatures." She tripped over a rock obscured by sand and cursed under her breath. No excuse for that one. Pearly light suffused the landscape, and even she could see without difficulty.

Her tongue darted out to lick her lips, the moistening relief temporary. She needed to drink from her dwindling water supply. Jannike ignored the urge just as she avoided acknowledging the never-ending prickle beneath her skin.

The portions of the cycle ticked over, and the chill of the early morn gave way to extreme heat. She arranged her blanket over her head and fashioned it so Royal rode out of the direct light.

"We'll walk to that outcrop." Lynx indicated the skyline.

Jannike focused gritty eyes on the distant rocks. They perched in piles at the top of an incline. Not far. She could make it that far. One step. Two steps.

The second markowl arrowed through the sky before them.

The one perched on Kelvin's shoulder shrieked.

"What is it?" Shiloh demanded.

"Something is chasing the markowl," Kelvin said.

Jannike squinted into the brightness, saw a larger bird. No. "Raptor," she said after taking in the streamline black reptilian shape, the gleaming ebony talons and the black leathery wings. "Must've come off the ship. Distant relation of the dragon. They're not native."

"Bad?" Lynx asked.

"We should run to those rocks. They're powerful enough to take down a humanoid."

"We won't make it. Not in this heat." Shiloh studied the raptor. "Suggestions?"

"Collect rocks to chuck. Their bellies are their tender spot. Keep away from their talons. The tips are poison-coated. Kelvin, what are you doing?"

"Giving you a chance." He did a rapid shift into a tree, his branches bare of leaves this time. When he finished the transformation, his branches reminded Jannike of gnarly roots.

She ripped her gaze away and scooped up fist-sized rocks, piling them at the base of Kelvin's trunk before darting away to gather more.

The markowl arrowed toward them, zigzagging to evade capture.

The raptor's irritated screech echoed across the expanse of sand. Large jaws snapped, talons extended and the markowl faltered.

"Come on." Jannike placed Royal in a fork of Kelvin's branches and dumped her belongings.

To Jannike's relief, the markowl discovered a new spurt of speed. He dived straight for Kelvin's branches.

The sec the raptor came into range, Jannike lobbed a rock. At this point it didn't matter where they struck the creature. Anything for distraction. Missed. She fired another and clipped the raptor's wing.

The markowls squeaked while she, Lynx, and Shiloh lobbed rocks. The raptor screamed and rose out of range. As if wanting to taunt them, it circled above.

Lynx darted out to grab a handful of the fallen rocks. The raptor struck, dive-bombing with breathtaking speed.

"Watch out!" Shiloh roared and hurled a flurry of rocks.

Lynx sprinted for shelter with the raptor snapping his heels. He caught Lynx's tunic, those big talons grasping. Lynx lifted into the air.

"Prince!" Shiloh sprinted at the raptor.

Jannike fired rocks but had to slow for fear of hitting the felines. "Yes!"

The raptor faltered when her rock stuck its chest.

"Shift," Kelvin bellowed. "Shiloh, down." He whipped out a

branch, barely missing Shiloh's head, and struck the raptor on one outstretched wing. It roared and dropped Lynx. Lynx yelped and struggled free of his tunic.

"Shift," Shiloh yelled.

Lynx dropped like a rock, and as Jannike watched, her heart jumped halfway up her throat. The shift took forever. Too slow. He'd hit the ground before he could transform and land on his feet.

The raptor screeched and positioned for another swoop, slower than before. More wary. Still hungry. Still determined. Kelvin's branches whistled through the air, forcing the raptor to change his approach.

Black fur rippled across Lynx's skin, his tunic tangling around his upper torso even as his trews bled into his feline body. He hit the ground, four feet outstretched, claws digging into the sand. Dust billowed around him. A cough erupted. A sneeze.

He was okay.

The raptor came again, this time low and forceful. Still determined to get Lynx. Jannike fired a rock. Score! Right in the face.

At her side, Shiloh hurled rocks while Kelvin whipped the raptor with his branches. The raptor squawked and backed away. His big black wings lifted him to glide on the air currents. As they watched, he drifted away in defeat.

"He's hurting," Shiloh said.

Lynx shifted and strode over to the Shiloh. Wordlessly, he hugged his friend.

Shiloh murmured something, his muscled arms going around Lynx's bare torso. One big hand drifted down to rest on Lynx's trews.

Jannike took a step back, giving the two felines privacy. She ripped her gaze away and attempted to shove aside her flash of envy. Better to concentrate on the weird way the shifters' trews and footwear transformed with them, but their tunics didn't. Once she'd asked Ry why this happened, but he'd shrugged. He had no idea.

"Good work, Kelvin." She reached for her water bottle. The last one. She unscrewed the synmetal cap and forced herself to take a small sip. Her gaze went to the felines again, and she absently took another sip. These two males were good and decent and deserving of the closeness they shared.

As she watched, Lynx kissed Shiloh on the lips. They broke their embrace and sauntered over to her and Kelvin.

"Did the raptor pierce your skin?" Kelvin asked.

"No, he ripped my tunic. My back is burning a little. No scratches though," Lynx said.

"Why did you shout Prince?" Jannike asked.

"Nickname. An old one that doesn't get used much anymore. Guess it slipped out in the heat of the moment." Lynx exchanged a glance with Shiloh and grinned.

The markowl whistled and hooted at Kelvin.

"He suggested we move since the people on the motor-skids are still behind us."

The other markowl hooted.

"That is good news."

"Could do with some," Shiloh said.

"There is a haven not far from the rocky outcrop. We will need to travel farther today, but she thinks it is doable. There is water—a pond. She was going to explore when the raptor spotted her."

"Let's hustle then." Lynx brightened. "I don't know about anyone else but I could do with a bath."

Jannike scooped up her gear and fed Royal the last of the nuts. He took them but didn't start eating. "Water would be good. Royal is much quieter than normal. I don't know if it's the heat or if it's something else."

"Probably the heat." Shiloh caressed Royal, but he didn't

respond. "Try and keep the direct light off him."

Kelvin uprooted himself and transformed to his mobile form while Jannike fashioned a shelter to keep Royal out of the direct heat.

Lynx started walking, and Kelvin ambled behind. Jannike followed Kelvin and the footsteps from behind indicated Shiloh had fallen into formation.

"Please, Ry," she prayed. "Please hurry." For as much as she'd love a bath, she wished her friends would arrive and whisk her away first.

CHAPTER NINE

U rsola stomped into her mansion. The peace, the richness and the luxury normally soothed her and brought satisfaction. Right now, a scream pressed against her chest, fighting for release. Her shoes clattered on the stone floor, echoing in the entranceway.

"Mistress." Cayle bowed with respect. "You are back early from your meeting. Is something wrong?"

"Everything is wrong. Such a simple job. Everything was going so well." She ripped off her solar-star protection since she'd come from the facility she owned outside the dome. The place where she kept her incoming slaves and specimens in quarantine before they went to auction.

Cayle waited, face set in concern, while she stormed around the entranceway.

Her head jerked up when she caught a glimpse of a loitering

slave. "Get out of my sight."

"Of course, mistress." Cayle bowed and backed away.

"Not you." An attempt to tamp down her fury got away from her, the events of the past cycle playing with her mind.

Someone attempting to shoot her.

Her cargo ship crashing.

Specimens scattering across the desert.

Those who remained alive would die in the unrelenting heat.

And now, someone was spiriting away her slaves. Three had gone missing. Three of the most valuable since they were breeding stock.

If she didn't know better, she'd say someone was out to get her, to beat her down until her empire foundered.

Envy—she'd long known others were jealous of her position. And now an anonymous someone was eroding her business and profit margins.

"What would you like me to do, mistress?"

"I have a meeting in my office shortly. Arrange refreshments. Deliver them as soon as my visitor arrives."

"Yes, mistress." Cayle backed away, his palms pressed together in a sign of respect. "All shall be prepared as you favor."

He disappeared, and she cursed under her breath. If she continued to act this way, she'd drive a wedge between them. Cayle was important to her mental wellbeing. The idea of losing what she had now...

Aware her behavior was off, she strode toward her office to ready for her visitor. Calm. She couldn't let anyone see her rattled.

Rumors flew around the dome like winged beasts, and she didn't intend to be the name on everyone's lips.

The company she'd chosen had a perfect record off-planet. Most Manx Two residents wouldn't have heard of this business, let alone used its services.

A tap on the door had her straightening, taking a sharp breath.

Showtime.

"How far is the haven?" Jannike swallowed and swallowed again. No matter how much she worked her throat, she couldn't produce enough spit to quench the thirst of a gnat-fly. And every time she scanned their surroundings, her gaze went straight to Lynx or Shiloh, whichever of the two stood closest. The only good thing about the tingle beneath her skin was that it took her mind off her thirst. "Are we sure this place exists?"

"A markowl has a different perspective of distance," Kelvin boomed.

On her shoulder, Royal whimpered, and she stroked his back in sympathy. "Can anyone spare water for Royal?"

"I'm out," Shiloh said.

Lynx shook his head with regret. "Me too."

"Give Royal to me. I have water," Kelvin boomed.

"Where? You're not carrying anything," Jannike said.

"Royal." Kelvin reached for the calibore. "Trust me."

Jannike shrugged and handed the listless calibore over to the tremin.

Kelvin did a weird partial shift until a tiny twig sprouted from his neck. He guided the twig to Royal's mouth. "Suck on this little one." His big brown fingers coaxed the calibore to move its mouth.

Jannike gawked when Royal began to suck with enthusiasm.

"Slow, little one," Kelvin whispered and recommenced walking. "Ye don't want to make yerself sick."

"We need to know how far the men on motor-skids are behind us," Shiloh rumbled. "I can't see anything, can't hear a phrullin thing out of place, but my back is prickling."

"It's the mating thing." Jannike swiped her forehead. "Haven't you and Lynx done it yet?"

Shiloh glared. "Butt out."

"Don't you want to talk about your love life? Most males gloat." She couldn't seem to shut her mouth. "Tell everyone about their sexual conquests."

"I don't," Shiloh snapped.

"Do too," Lynx called over his shoulder. "You tell me."

"No one else." Shiloh's burst of temper dispersed.

"Aw, that's so sweet." The little imp yabbering in Jannike's ear refused to shut up. Sex. Sex. *Sex.* "I'm right. You haven't done it yet. The black splotches haven't come together to form a feline tattoo."

"Ye tread a dangerous path, lass," Kelvin murmured. Of course, the words emerged close to his usual boom.

"Why is she walking a dangerous path?" Lynx halted to study Jannike.

Shiloh remained silent, his eyes glowing a freaky cat green. His gaze tracked her, his mouth pulled into a knife-thin line.

"Jannike knows about us. She's the one with experience of mating," Lynx said.

Her stomach bucked and her tongue flashed out to moisten her lips. It was like licking a patch of gritty sand. "I'm sorry. The lack of water is playing havoc with my words." Not quite the truth. It hurt to speak, yet the alternative—to think—caused the tingles into her body to morph into sexual territory. The urge to fling off her tunic and offer her breasts...

She shuddered and attempted to swallow. Damn, her throat hurt.

"We be close," Kelvin boomed. "I sense water."

Lynx resumed walking and resigned, Jannike fell into step. Since the morn, her discomfort had morphed from bad to worse. Every step caused her trews to rub against her swollen sex. Part of her was surprised the felines hadn't commented. They'd be within their rights, given the way she'd just poked at their sex life.

Ry...she hadn't understood the torment he'd suffered until Camryn's arrival.

Since talking hurt her throat, she fell silent. She listed all the things she'd try to do in the future, should she escape this sandbox without the widow's notice.

Have sex—no, not a good idea.

First, she'd talk to Mogens, the *Indy*'s seer and medicine man, and ask him to make her one of the potions he'd made to alleviate Ry's suffering.

Chocolate. Hopefully Kaya still had some of the stuff she'd purchased on Earth and would deign to share.

A bath...

Yeah, simple pleasures she'd learned to enjoy, many of which came from Earth and she'd experienced because of Camryn.

She slogged up a sandhill, panting in the heat, her calves burning in tandem with her pulsing sex. Oh, goddess. Her mind had gone to the hot and nasty again. *Yesss!* The little imp inside her hollered, practically beating her chest in encouragement.

"Not far now," Kelvin boomed.

The ground beneath their feet trembled without warning, gradually trailing off into silence so acute her own heartbeat and hoarse breathing became the loudest sounds in her vicinity.

Jannike froze. "What is it? Do you see anything?" No sooner had she uttered the words than the vibration recommenced.

"No talking," Shiloh barked. His eyes had resumed their feline glitter, the pupils slits instead of rounds. A sign of his agitation.

But he was correct. Goddess, this burning heat inside and out had rotted away her commonsense. She scanned the expanse of sand and rocks they'd already traversed. Nothing out of the ordinary snared her attention.

Kelvin rustled his hair, a soft almost sighing sound and the two markowls took flight. The birds soared into the sky, separated and flew in counterpoint circles.

When the vibrations didn't reoccur, Shiloh gestured for Lynx to continue. In the short time they'd stopped, Jannike's legs had seized and a groan slipped past her lips.

Shiloh tapped her on the shoulder, an order for silence, and she cursed under her breath.

A tremor shook the ground beneath their feet, more violent than before. The sand stirred, a sucking hole appearing beside Jannike.

"Run," Shiloh ordered.

An arrow of pain shot up her right leg, making Jannike slow to respond. A pale wormlike head, the size of the two felines combined, thrust upward and roared. The stench almost knocked her over.

She gawked at the antennas, the beady black eyes, its off-white body. For precious secs, she froze then Shiloh grabbed her, propelling her away from the monstrosity just as sharp teeth snapped in an audible click. Jannike ran in the direction Shiloh shunted her. The creature plunged back down the hole he'd made in the sand, traveling underground to where Lynx sprinted along the ridge of the sandhill.

The head came out of the sand, giant antennas switching this way and that, listening for the sounds they made. The creature's black eyes stared straight at Lynx yet didn't seem to see him. Lynx froze and didn't move.

Jannike slogged to the top and from the crest, she sighted the haven, a tiny spot of green in the broad sea of sand.

Shiloh came up behind her and she pointed. He nodded and mimed for her to descend the hill.

Good strategy. The creature seemed to hunt via sound vibrations. She'd draw him away from Lynx and Shiloh would run a different angle to her to confuse the creature. Kelvin didn't have the same speed as them but he moved with stealth.

Taking a deep breath, she pushed herself to speed, taking a

downward path. Ironic, they were always splitting up yet the mating drew them together. A tepid wind blew into her face as she practically flew down the slope. Gritty sand obscured her vision. She stumbled, righted herself by flapping her arms.

Keep your footing.

Don't fall.

The grumbling shift of the sand came from behind. Closer and closer. She sprinted toward the haven and the rocky ground surrounding the oasis of green. Bright light shimmered across the ground. Grains of sand sprayed her face, but she kept propelling her legs onward.

"Keep running," Shiloh hollered.

The reverberation halted abruptly. Jannike forced her legs to keep moving. A tear ran down her face, squeezing from irritated eyes. She sucked for breath, her pants louder than they should be. The rush of tremors started again, still coming for her. Faster, faster, faster.

The sand stirred beneath her feet. She tripped, not seeing a rock in her rising panic. Roll. *Roll!*

Jannike rolled just as the ugly pale head burst from the sand right where she'd stood seconds before.

"Freeze, Jannike!" Lynx shouted.

Goddess, he didn't have to tell her. She didn't think she could move if she tried. Instead, she lay on the sand, fighting to regain her breath, fighting not to moan aloud, fighting not to attract the creature.

The fabled sand worm.

She'd thought them a myth, a tale told to dissuade children from misbehaving. Not a myth. Not a myth. Not a phrullin myth at all.

The creature roared, the stench making her want to dry heave. She fought the urge. The thing could gulp her down in one bite.

"Jannike, we're going to distract it," Shiloh hollered.

The sand worm turned its head, a sticky residue dripping from its fanglike mouth. The pale antennas veered in Shiloh's direction, and Lynx shouted. The antennas revolved.

Kelvin boomed from somewhere behind, and up in the air above her, the two markowls shrieked.

The sand worm reared, its giant maw snapping. A frustrated roar whooshed from the creature, and Jannike swallowed rapidly to battle her need to puke.

Too frightened to move in case she attracted notice, she could do nothing but watch. Shiloh and Lynx shouted in quick succession, their positions taking them both closer to the haven.

Without warning, the sand worm arced through the air and dived into the sand. Jannike watched its progress before pushing sluggishly to her feet. Through stinging eyes, she checked the positions of the others. Kelvin stood behind her, halfway down the hill. Shiloh stood between her and the haven, and Lynx raced across the sand, a short distance separating him from the rocky area surrounding the haven. Goddess, she hoped the sand worm couldn't drill through the rockier ground.

She forced herself to move toward the haven, taking care with her foot placement.

Lynx leaped the last few feet, tucking and rolling back to his feet in an acrobatic stunt that would have made her cheer under normal circumstances.

Once he regained his footing, he kept racing until he hit the green expanse of the haven. The sand worm popped from the sand where the rock soil began. Ah, some of the things she recalled from the old tales were true. Sand worms preferred soft deserts.

The sand worm roared, its large pale body swaying back and forth, antennas vibrating.

"Water!" Lynx shouted. "Last one in is a rotten fodo egg."

Easy for him to say. He stood in a safe zone.

With her gaze on the sand worm, Jannike picked her way across the sand. Shiloh crossed onto the rocky expanse leading to the haven without a problem.

Kelvin continued his steady pace.

Shiloh joined Lynx and hollered. "It's beautiful here. Water to drink. Get your lazy arse here now."

The sandworm reared in the direction of his shout and gave another shriek. Its antenna swiveled and zeroed in on her.

Phrull. She froze, fear curdling her belly. In front of her, Kelvin crossed into the safe zone. The worm sank into the sand, disappearing. The tremor of the ground beneath her feet increased. The worm was heading in her direction.

Indecision tore at her. Did she run or stay immobile?

"Don't move, Jannike," Lynx roared.

His order stayed her in place. Her heart tried to burrow from her chest, and it took every ounce of her control to remain still. The tremors increased until the ground at her feet churned.

She didn't know if Lynx and Shiloh were still shouting at her. Sound had become lost in the rushing approach of the sand worm.

The rapid seesaw of the ground under her feet tossed her off balance. She fell hard, the force of the fall pummeling the air from her lungs. She squeezed her eyes shut, unable to watch death approaching.

"You have a traitor amongst your people," the man said in a crisp voice after listening to Ursola's recitation. His skin was a delicate lilac, and he had the creepy white eyes of the Torgon people, but his heritage came from another race too. His skin was textured, his eye ridges prominent, his bald head gleaming under her office illumination.

Ursola bit back her curse. "That much is apparent, Krarbrock. The question is, what are you going to do to root out the turncoat?"

"We will look at your staff. Those who work in your facilities and your home. We could plant a spy from within our organization."

"Start at my facility. I believe that is where the trouble springs forth."

A knock at the door halted their conversation.

"Come," Ursola ordered with a touch of impatience. It was one thing to suspect a traitor but another to learn the private investigator believed the same. She'd built her empire on fear to halt this sort of treachery. Obviously, she needed to up her game.

Cayle entered her office bearing a tray of the refreshments she'd ordered. Without a word, he set the tray on her desk and poured the pale green fruit juice into tall glasses filled to the brim with crackle ice. The juice began to bubble on contact with the ice. A refreshing drink and her favorite.

She nodded at Cayle, and he retreated without a word.

"Which of your staff are allowed access to this private office?" The investigator's pale violet face remained serene, but his empty white gaze bored into hers. This male was not an idiot. She could see that, and combined with his official success rate, she felt better about this decision. This male would ferret out the traitor.

Then, she'd make a public example of the being who'd attempted to reduce her empire to rubble. Next, she'd gut him with a knife and hang his or her body at the entrance to her facility. A warning to anyone who dared to cross her, to cheat her from the profits she so richly deserved.

This mishmash of incidents would not occur again.

CHAPTER TEN

The ground bubbled and churned like liquid boiling in a cooking pot. Jannike sank into the sand. Her arms thrashed. She struggled. Her panicked resistance made things worse. She sank downward, deeper, deeper, deeper.

Fighting every instinct of self-preservation, she forced herself to still. Her immersion slowed, and she sucked in a hoarse breath. Where was the worm? She turned, trying to see. Sand boiled over her head, filled her mouth. Heat seared her skin along her back. She jerked at the discomfort and tried to shift her body to escape the burning sensation.

Her squirming sent her deeper into the sand.

She spat and attempted to breathe through the particles of grit sticking to the inside of her mouth. No saliva. She spat again and couldn't halt the terror swirling through her mind. A sob escaped. This wasn't the way she wanted to die.

Where was the worm? It was there—somewhere—making the earth rise in waves. Heart galloping, she wriggled and writhed, attempting to move carefully instead of letting her panic reduce her to helpless thrashing. Finally, *finally* her hand grasped solid ground. For secs, she gripped the handhold, then the boiling sand forced her to lose her grasp. She kicked, legs scissoring. The motion popped her closer to the surface and a solid purchase. Her entire head broke free of the sand. She gasped air, choked on the residual sand in her mouth and throat. She sank, the bright light obscured by the dark sands again.

The violent shuddering and bubbling of the sand slowed, and another rapid kick of her legs propelled her above the surface. Air. She sucked in a huge draft of air, coughed.

This time the soft desert didn't suck her under. She kicked again, her fingers scraping across the more solid ground at the far extent of her reach. Her fingers clawed the sand.

She gulped another breath of air, the wheeze of her lungs loud to her ears. The bloody creature was toying with her, just like those worms in the tales she'd heard during her youth. Any second, the sand would seethe, she'd sink down, and the worm would swallow her whole.

Calm now that fate stared her in the face, she waited. She swallowed, the gritty sand aggravating the membranes in her throat.

"Jannike!"

She lifted her head to squint against the bright light. It sounded like Shiloh.

"Stay there," she called back, unconcerned about attracting the worm now. They didn't all need to die.

A tremor rippled through the ground, but it was milder than before. Jannike twisted, trying to see. As her heartbeat and the roaring in her ears subsided, she began to notice her surroundings.

The worm... She crawled inch by inch and attempted to haul her body from the soft sand. For some reason, the vibrations reduced even further. The worm was retreating.

"Take my hand," Lynx said.

"You shouldn't be here. You're mates."

"We're not leaving anyone behind," Shiloh snapped. "Give me your other hand."

His fingers tightened around hers.

"Why did the worm retreat?" she asked, bewildered at its actions. Maybe it was the more compacted ground she'd struck.

"Going after bigger, easier prey." Lynx tightened his grip. "Ready?"

"Ready," Shiloh confirmed.

They yanked her arms, and she popped free from the quick-sucking sand. She lay on the ground, each breath rasping down her throat, tearing at the tender skin of her mouth and gullet. The heat on her back still smarted and now danced down the backs of her legs.

"What bigger prey?" she croaked.

"Let me help you up." Lynx hauled her to her feet, but her knees buckled. She would've toppled if it weren't for him grasping her waist.

"We need to move in case that thing comes back." Shiloh's voice held strain.

A throbbing buzz sounded in her ears. She turned her head toward the sound, frowned at the scream. "Is someone else here?"

"The men on the motor-skids."

Hence Shiloh's urgency to get to the haven.

She forced her knees to hold her body weight. They trembled, but she thought she could walk. Her first step proved otherwise.

Strong arms scooped her up before she hit the ground. "I've got her," Shiloh said. "Move."

Another scream echoed across the sand, carried by the wind. The fear and horror had the hair at the back of her neck standing to attention.

"That thing is feasting on them. The vibration of the motor-skids is drawing the creature."

"It's a sand worm," Jannike whispered hoarsely and that hurt her throat. Everywhere hurt. Her back, her legs, her eyes, her throat. And now that Shiloh held her pressed against his chest, the weird tingles beneath her skin added to her misery.

Lynx glanced in the direction of the screams. "I've never of heard them."

"Thought my mother made up the tales," Jannike croaked.

"Don't talk," Shiloh ordered. "We'll get you water once we get to the haven."

The ever-present vibration increased.

"Move it." Lynx's voice held urgency. "Seems the beast is still hungry."

Jannike's gut bucked, the idea of repeating her experience filling her with horror. "Put me down. I can walk."

"No, you'll slow us down." Shiloh's reply was a vibration against her back. He increased his speed, loping now instead of using careful foot placement.

Jannike squeezed her eyes shut and prayed to the goddess of justice and death. *Please let me live today.*

If the widow was gonna take her life, Jannike wanted to do it face-to-face and fighting. She didn't want to get sucked into the sticky maw of a sand worm.

"Keep going," Shiloh said. "You saw the creature rear from the sand."

Lynx grimaced. "True."

"I can walk."

"It's easier to carry you." Shiloh never slowed. "Besides, I want to get water on those burns."

Jannike frowned. "They're not that bad."

"Your skin is blistered. The backs of your legs too."

"Doesn't feel that bad."

"It should," Shiloh said in his blunt way.

"Just feels hot. Uncomfortable."

Shiloh shrugged. "Maybe the creature has venom of some sort. Anything like that mentioned in the tales you were told?"

"Mostly the stories were to stop us from wandering off and exploring outside the dome. People die all the time. It's why they built the dome. Not everyone starts with water like us or can find a haven." She cracked her eyes open and screwed them shut again. The brightness was almost too much to bear, and her throat protested her long speech. "Need water."

"You'll have it. Almost there."

"How is she?" Kelvin boomed. "I've built a shade shelter for her."

"Water," she mumbled, the tightness of her throat becoming worse.

"The water isn't potable," Kelvin said.

"Phrull." Lynx's shoulders slumped. "What are we gonna do?"

"I can drink and filter it," Kelvin offered. "It will take a cycle."

"She needs water now." Shiloh placed her under the shade. "Let me take off your tunic. I need to see the extent of those burns."

Jannike winced as Shiloh lifted her tunic over her head.

"The water is all right for swimming and bathing," Kelvin said. "I could see nothing disturbing in its depths."

"Nice undergarment." Amusement colored Lynx's voice. "I'll check the pond while you see what you can do with her back." The crunch of gravel marked his departure.

"Once Lynx says the water is safe, I'll carry you down. I think sitting in the water will relieve the heat in your skin."

"It's not bad," she said again. Well, her back was stinging but it was bearable.

Kelvin shunted Royal under the shade and the calibore ambled over to Jannike. He sniffed her leg and sneezed.

"He looks better. Thanks, Kelvin."

"You next." Kelvin whispered to the markowls and the birds lifted off to circle the haven. Kelvin planted himself next to the shade. Thick roots speared into the sandy soil, rooting him in place. His branches spread outward, some swaying low. Amazed by the process, Jannike stared as a thin branch dipped in front of her face.

"Bite into my branch. Slake your thirst."

Jannike lifted her battered, aching body until she was sitting. Lightheadedness struck, and she wobbled, unable to remain upright. Shiloh caught her before she toppled backward. Her heart went into a series of palpitations. Whoa!

"Jannike, are you all right?" Shiloh demanded.

"I can't bite Kelvin."

"You will die if you don't." Kelvin's matter-of-fact summation drove the truth home. Hadn't she decided she wanted to live? "I can replenish my supply and filter the new water intake, make it safe for you all to drink. Bite my branch for her, Shiloh."

Shiloh's glance held uncertainty, but he did as Kelvin instructed. He grasped a thick branch and bit down, his sharp canines making quick work of the task. Kelvin's expression tightened, his only reaction to the tearing of his bark. Shiloh's cheeks sucked in, his dark lashes screening his eyes.

When Shiloh lifted his head, he sighed with distinct satisfaction. "Thank you for sharing your water with us. I am honored at your gift." The formal words of thanks should have sounded silly, but Jannike thought they were perfect. Shiloh was a male of hidden depths.

Shiloh held Kelvin's branch in front of her mouth, and she placed her lips where he'd bitten into Kelvin's flesh. Despite her lingering horror at biting Kelvin, the wash of moisture into her parched mouth had her moaning in pleasure.

"Is that what you sound like when you're having sex?" Lynx

asked from behind them.

"I have plenty of water," Kelvin whispered. "Show him." He arrowed another branch in Lynx's direction. "You will need more moisture too."

Jannike sucked on the wound and swallowed the moisture, so grateful to Kelvin for allowing them to drink from him. The lightheadedness faded as did the dryness of her mouth and throat. Uncertain of how much to take, she lifted her head.

"More," Kelvin insisted. "I will drink to replenish my supply later."

Royal crawled over to her and bit into Kelvin's branch not far from where she drank. He showed no hesitation.

Jannike drank until she'd quenched her thirst. "Will the bite marks heal quickly?"

"No." Kelvin sounded matter-of-fact. "I will ask ye to drink from the same place each time."

Beside her, Lynx and Shiloh finished slaking their thirst.

"Kelvin is right. I sensed no danger at the pond. You should soak in the water." Lynx glanced at Shiloh and winked. "I know I intend to."

"If you two are doing sex things, I'm staying here."

Lynx's grin was broad and toothy. "We can share the pond. It's a spring, and the far end is private. Shiloh and I will head there."

"I want to check on the worm first," Shiloh said. "You help Jannike to the water."

"Ever the bodyguard—" Lynx broke off as if he'd uttered something out of place.

Shiloh shook his head and laughed, his long strides taking him to the edge of the haven.

"What did you mean, bodyguard?" Jannike asked.

"A joke," Lynx said. "Can you walk or do you need me to carry you?"

"I can walk. Do you need anything, Kelvin?"

"No, thank ye," Kelvin whispered. "I intend to sleep."

Jannike noticed the bark bites they'd left oozed a kind of sap. It made her curious, and she wished she knew more about Kelvin and his capture. Kelvin remained in the background, listening rather than participating, yet never hesitating to offer help when it was required.

Jannike followed Lynx to the pond and saw what he meant about privacy. "I'll go over there by those rocks. I can strip off and wash my clothes."

"Your tunic is shredded in the back. Not much holding it together now."

"So, I'll wear my blanket like you do during the worst of the heat." She picked her way over the rocks, and when she reached the water's edge, she plonked her butt on a rock in order to remove her shoes. Now that she'd drunk deep and conquered her thirst, the throb of her back became more apparent. She removed her red bra and stood to take off her trews. The sharp pain in the back of her legs had her eyes watering. Blisters. She peeled off her panties and stepped into the cool water, almost moaning at the instant relief. She waded deeper until water covered her back. Dipping her head under the water, removed a lot of the dust and dirt.

"Jannike, are you decent?" Shiloh called.

"I'm in the water."

"Stay there. I'll bring you some cleansing plant. Kelvin says it's a kind of soap." He appeared around the corner and clambered over the rocks. "I'll leave the plant here on the rock. You just squeeze the sap out the end and lather up."

"Thanks." Jannike watched him leave, her pulse racing a little faster. Close call. She released her tongue from imprisonment between her teeth and waded to shore to retrieve the soap plant. In this short time of relaxation and relative safety, Shiloh and Lynx would consummate their relationship. Once that happened, the mating bonds should click into place, effectively shutting her out.

It was what she wanted.

The way things should happen.

Yet no matter how often she told herself this, the yearning wouldn't leave. It crouched like a black leopard, attentive and watchful, ready to pounce the sec she released her restraint.

Sighing, she dipped her head under the water and washed her hair. The sap that oozed from the spiky green leaf didn't resemble soap. It didn't lather like Earth cleansers or dissolve like the cleansing agent in the sanitizer units on board the *Indy*. It remained thick and viscous like the stuff Camryn called gel.

Laughter echoed across the water, low and intimate. The urge to go to them was so strong she found herself taking two steps from the water before forcing her limbs to stop. Lust swept her in a rogue wave, frisking her breasts, her nipples and her pussy while she struggled in the undertow. A needy moan escaped, squeezing up her throat like a stealth warrior. Her legs trembled, and she returned to the water's edge, plopping down in disgust.

This wasn't going to happen.

She was handling the discomfort. It couldn't get much worse. She pushed herself into deeper water and floated, letting the coolness ease the sting on her back. Swimming reminded her of their visit to Earth, and she wondered how Amme was getting on in her new life with Marcus. She and the rest of the *Indy* crew had spent much of their Christmas visit playing in the pool.

Good times.

More masculine laughter drifted across the water, and a dart of acute pain arrowed to her pussy. She bit her lip as the sharp ache morphed into pleasure. She groaned softly, mindful she wasn't alone. Unbidden, one hand drifted down her belly and slid between her legs. The merest touch of her slit sent spiraling bliss—the like of which she'd never felt before—crawling through her veins.

Maybe this would be enough. She should grab the opportunity

while she had the luxury of privacy. One finger circled her clit, and she sank under the water. She came up spluttering and coughing. Shaking.

"Goddess," she muttered, disgust a hammer pounding on her stupid, thick head. She resumed her floating and kept her hands clamped firmly at her sides.

But now that she'd touched herself, the yearning to do it again, the temptation to do more sucked at her willpower. She walked toward the shore and sat on a rock.

Clothes. She'd wash her clothes. Surely that would drive evil temptation from her mind.

It didn't.

The mundane chore kept her hands busy but let her mind wander. Her traitorous mind galloped straight to sex. *It won't hurt. You won't let us visit the felines. Masturbation will give us some relief.*

"Us," Jannike said in a low voice of loathing. Since when had her body become a committee, voting on a resolution. "I'm the boss, and I am in control."

Not true, a little voice retorted at the back of her mind. The little voice had a face, and it looked a lot like her friend Kaya. The blue hair and pointy ears were a dead giveaway.

What would Kaya do?

Jannike snorted out a sound that was a close cousin to derision.

Kaya would seize the opportunity. The woman loved sex and embraced her sexuality. Or she did now. There was a time when Talor, Ry's brother, had seduced her into trouble. She'd taken half a rotation to bounce back from that disaster.

A sizzle of enjoyment darted from her pussy to her breasts, rebounding to the far corners of her body in a happy leap. While her mind had drifted to the past, she'd dropped her bra into the water and reached between her legs.

Give up. Give up. *Give up, Jannike.*

143

Her personal conscience was persistent.

Gritting her teeth, Jannike picked up her bra and applied some of the plant sap. She scrubbed and rinsed before repeating the actions on her panties and her trews. Her tunic was back at their camp. She'd see if she could repair it later. With her laundry duties completed, she picked a shady spot, inspected it for danger then relaxed into comfort. She'd sleep. That was what she'd do.

But sleep refused to come, her mind focusing on the urgency thrumming through her body, her desperate need for release.

"I give up," she said, her tone screechy yet resigned to the undisputed truth. No rest for the wicked, wicked woman who lusted after two mated felines. "I give up."

Jannike parted her legs, the wash of air a gentle balm against her swollen tissues. Her hand slipped between her thighs, and she dragged her finger down her cleft. Wetness greeted her touch. From the sec her fingers came into contact with her flesh, the prickles beneath her skin settled into humming anticipation. Unable to resist, she grazed her clit with one careful finger. Her breath caught at the spurt of gratification. Harsh yet enjoyable, the pleasure threatened to overwhelm her senses. Still, she repeated the subtle move, a low moan escaping this time. Sex had never been like this before. Intense. Overpowering. Extreme.

See. That's all you needed to do. Give in to the urge, and the problem will back away. Conscience Kaya was a mite smug in Jannike's opinion, yet it seemed this might be the answer to her problem.

With greater confidence and purpose, she stroked her clit. When Conscience Kaya pointed out the emptiness of her womb, she thrust two fingers inside her channel and stroked swollen internal tissues as well as her needy clit.

The climax inside her swelled and swelled then swelled some more until it reached mountainous proportions. Jannike hovered on a precipice, tiny moans squeezing past her tight lips as she stroked, stroked, stroked her flesh. She swallowed and groaned, her eyes squeezed shut while her heart hammered against her ribs loud enough for the felines across the other side of the pond to hear and remark upon.

Yet she didn't stop, couldn't stop.

Tremors racked her body, her skin sizzled as if it couldn't hold her body any longer. And still, the orgasm swelled within her body, straddling a barrier, leaping into pleasure, sometimes diving into pain. Both ways made her groan and twitch. She pressed her thumb harder on her clit, added another finger so three tunneled in and out of her vagina. She was sobbing now, reaching for pleasure, stretching with every particle of her being.

The pleasure whooshed—not quite there, but close. Yes, yes, yes!

One more stroke should do it. Just one more. She licked her lips, wondered if she'd survive the strain on her heart.

Her thumb stroked over her clit and the pleasure leaped upward into freefall.

Yes. Yes. *No!*

The waiting, hovering, impatient orgasm shimmered just out of touch, stood on tiptoes, indecisive and shy, then backed away and went *poof* like one of those magical genies she'd read about in an Earth storybook.

"No," Jannike whispered, harsh disappointment a twisty knot in her throat, knock-knock-knocking for release.

Her breasts were painfully tight and so sensitive to the tiny puffs of air now drifting across the pond that she wanted to scream. She pulled her fingers from her pussy and pressed them to her nipples in an attempt to ease the discomfort. Nothing made any difference. Instead, the scent of sex drifted from her fingers, and an answering dart of demand skimmed through her pussy.

Jannike firmed her jaw and pushed to her feet. On trembling legs she walked into the pond and washed away the evidence of her aborted climax.

It seemed nothing in her world ever came easy.

Same old. Same old.

Shiloh cocked his head, pausing in his bathing routine. "Did you hear someone cry out?"

Beside him, Lynx stilled to listen, attracting Shiloh's attention. Water gleamed on his chest, dripped from his long hair. A scruffy beard covered his jaw, giving him a rugged look his parents wouldn't appreciate. Hellfire, why wrap it up? They'd order Lynx to his chambers and tell him to sort himself out. A wry grin curled across Shiloh's lips. What he'd pay to witness that scene.

"I don't hear anything," Lynx said and turned to face him. "What's so funny?"

"Private joke."

Lynx snorted out a don't-try-and-bullock-crap-me sound, one that shouted busted. One that said he didn't do jokes. Private or otherwise. One that cried he'd tromped far over the employer-employee relationship, so go ahead and confess. Shiloh felt his grin etch deeper into his face.

His lover. Shiloh shook his head, a long lock of his hair flapping over his cheek with a damp slap. He brushed it away with an impatient hand. Lynx, his best friend and the prince he guarded, was his lover.

The idea should panic him, send him running in the opposite direction yet truth waved a placard in his mind. He wouldn't change a damn thing, and in fact, once they found a sheltered, shady spot he intended to go all the way. Hard-out seduction mode. His stomach gave a little skip at the thought, and the damn smile that had no business colonizing his face, dug in its heels and settled in to stay.

"Are you finished with your wash?" Lynx sounded breathless. Shiloh had heard that tone before. It was a let's-get-busy flag, and his friend was waving it in his face.

Shiloh's gut jumped, and he fought the stubborn smile that wreaked havoc with his tough bodyguard status. "I'm done."

"I want to kiss you."

"No one is stopping you."

"Thought I should ask permission."

"You don't ask permission for anything else," Shiloh pointed out.

Lynx's eyes glowed, the pupils narrowing into catlike slits, sharp enough to slice and dice through any bullock shit. "This is different. It's important. Life-changing. I don't want to phrull it up."

Shiloh swallowed—his feelings—the fragile emotions in him expanding with a breath-stealing whoosh. "Do you think I don't worry about the same thing? We've had this discussion. I don't want to have it again. I want this. You. As far as I'm concerned, you belong to me, and I sure as hellfire belong to you. Kiss me whenever you want, wherever you want. I'm not gonna offer a fight."

"You couldn't flatten me anyway," Lynx scoffed, and he advanced, stopping Shiloh's incredulous retort dead on his lips. Shiloh wrapped his arms around Lynx and sank into the beauty of the kiss. It was all lips and gentle passion with none of the urgency that thrummed inside him. Instead of changing the nature of the kiss, he let Lynx lead and found new freedom in this departure from the norm.

Their cocks brushed below the water level, and Lynx pulled away to grin lazily at him.

"Any chance of some good hot sex?"

"Every chance." Shiloh's gut and mind did an uproarious dance and a mental hoorah in celebration. He couldn't think of anything he'd enjoy more right now. "The leaf I gave you to wash with—well, the sap will make a good lube."

"How do you know?"

"Kelvin told me." Shiloh wanted to laugh when Lynx's mouth popped open in an O of astonishment. "He suggested it would be best to consummate this thing between us because he thought it would strengthen us as a unit. He pointed out that, at present, we're still itching our stomachs and backs. If that faded, we would have a better chance of staying alive."

"Kelvin...when did...I see." Lynx snapped his teeth together.

"Yep, the man doesn't say much but sees all." Shiloh lowered his voice. "He's kept us alive. He said he can suck up this water and make it palatable. We'd better check to see if the others need us."

"Stay," Lynx said. "Jannike will let us know if there is a problem. That sand worm is still out there. We need a strategy to leave the haven. I say we relax while we can. Besides, if we're gonna die tomorrow or get captured again, I want to have something good to think about."

Shiloh felt a smile dig in its heels and gave his head a sharp shake. His brother Ellard would *tsk-tsk* under his breath if he saw him. His family's lack of approval hurt and he shouldn't miss them, but he did. Maybe once they got out of this mess they could visit home. "Works for me. I found a spot where we can have privacy."

"Where Kelvin can't see?"

"I know you get noisy." Shiloh wanted to laugh at the indignation on his friend's face. The truth was he was loud too, and he didn't give a flying phrull if anyone heard him. The urgent need for Lynx overrode his inhibitions. He reached for Lynx's hand, shivering at the solid weight, the inherent strength of it, his mind rushing ahead to those strong fingers roaming his body. "This way."

He led Lynx to a grassy area behind a stack of rocks. The area was shady and private with the added advantage of having a view of the surrounding desert.

Lynx threw his body onto the grass and rolled to grin up at him. Shiloh's heart skipped and gamboled like a playful kitten. They were going to do this. It would change everything, yet like Lynx, he didn't feel a scrap of doubt.

"I love you." The words startled him as much as they did Lynx. For a long moment, they stared at each other.

Lynx's expression softened. "I know."

Shiloh's next breath lagged in his lungs, the weight of disappointment holding it hostage. He swallowed to hurry it along, desperate to rid himself of the ball of anxiety.

"Come here." Lynx held out his hand in invitation. "I know actions mean more than words to you. Let me show you how much I love you."

Shiloh's breath eased out in a sigh. He reached for Lynx's hand, and everything slotted into place, his world righting. Lynx's green eyes twinkled at him, a smile—almost shy—curved his friend's lips.

Lynx tugged, yanking him off balance. He landed against a wall of hard muscle, Lynx's arms coming around his shoulders without hesitation. Their mouths met and this time passion exploded along with a wave of lust. Shiloh groaned against Lynx's mouth, the blood draining down his torso to cram into his cock.

Lynx parted their mouths to drag in air. "How does this work?"

"You want me to show you?"

Their gazes met and held before Lynx nodded.

"It will be uncomfortable at first. I'll do my best to make it good, but you're not used to this."

"Don't care." Lynx's growl of certainty eased Shiloh's last reservations. "If full penetration rids us of these cursed itches, I'm on board with this. I want this. You."

Shiloh nodded and reached for the pile of leaves he'd collected before he'd joined Lynx in the pool. He squeezed the sap onto his fingers and noticed they trembled. The last thing he wanted was to phrull up this first time between them. Too important. *No pressure.* He'd start slow. Give Lynx plenty of time to become used to his touch.

Shiloh closed his fingers around Lynx's shaft and teased him with easy strokes. Lynx shuddered, and arousal sank into his face, coloring his cheeks and drawing his feline to the surface. Lynx's other self glittered in his eyes.

Satisfied Lynx was coasting on pleasure, he repositioned his body for better access and allowed the fingers of his other hand to wander. He pressed and stroked, the sap making things so much better. Easier. The stuff was way better than the lube Shiloh favored.

"How are you doing?" He nibbled Lynx's inner thigh while he waited for a reply.

"Feels good." Lynx's voice was thick and full of satisfaction. "Real good."

Shiloh reached for another leaf and squeezed out more sap. He drove his fingers deep past Lynx's puckered entrance, his stroking more aggressive as he stretched and prepared his friend.

Lynx yelped, his eyes growing wide, and Shiloh slowed.

"Problem?"

"No, do that again. There's a spot..."

Shiloh felt the grin riding his lips sink deep into his cheeks. He imagined his expression would hold wickedness. He pushed his fingers deeper, danced them over Lynx's gland, giving him more of the same but not enough to come.

"Shiloh."

Shiloh grinned at the inflection in his name. "I'm going to take you now."

"Should I turn over?"

"No," Shiloh whispered. "I want to watch your face, see your eyes when I come. I want to kiss you."

Lynx's eyebrows rose. "You don't like messy emotion with your sex. You told me you always take your lovers from behind, that it's your favorite position—"

"None of them were you." The simple, unembellished truth.

Shiloh applied sap to his shaft and moved over Lynx. "Remember, it might hurt at first. I'll take it slow." He pushed more of the sap into Lynx and stroked deep before he fitted his cock to Lynx's entrance. He glanced at his friend's face, noticed the tiny pucker of worry between his brows. Shiloh's heart flip-flopped, and he leaned closer to steal a kiss. While their tongues mated, he pushed into Lynx's heat.

Lynx sighed against his mouth, the lingering tension Shiloh had felt receding with the soft sound. The sap made all the difference and left a residual tingling along his shaft. If they survived this adventure alive, he decided he'd grow this plant. Of course, first he'd need to find a place to make a garden.

A home.

He pulled back a fraction and tunneled deeper with his next thrust. Lynx flexed around his cock, the snug, warm feeling making him catch his breath. He trembled, and Lynx puffed out a breath. Shiloh glanced at his face, concerned, but Lynx's smile, his relaxed expression belayed his anxiety.

"It's never been like this before. You okay?"

"This mother bird side of you is cute." Lynx didn't open his eyes, so Shiloh's glare was wasted. "The pain isn't as bad as you indicated. Feels good. Don't be an old lady feline."

Shiloh withdrew and plunged deeper. A laugh escaped at the feline hiss from Lynx.

"More," Lynx demanded, lifting into his next stroke. His canines protruded, and the sexy sight had a growl vibrating in Shiloh's chest before the thought occurred. Goddess, this man—his best friend. The idea of the time they'd wasted getting to this point...

No. He pulled back and plunged balls deep, desire and lust and love a tangled ball in his chest, his gut, his mind.

Shiloh sought Lynx's mouth again, his hips rocking in a steady pace. The heat built in his balls, pushed up and outward until he existed in a world of bliss. Lynx nipped at his bottom lip, urging Shiloh to speed.

Shiloh stroked into Lynx again, and Lynx groaned. He kissed Shiloh's shoulder and reached down to stroke his own cock. Shiloh stopped holding back his pleasure and increased the pace of his thrusts. In. Out. His eyes squeezed tight while he savored the building pressure.

Beneath him, Lynx cried out and sank his teeth into Shiloh's shoulder. The burst of pain released a lever in Shiloh, and his orgasm swelled within him, sweeping from his balls and bursting up his cock in a painful whoosh of pleasure. He felt the swirl of Lynx's tongue over the pressure points of the bite, and a second, less forceful jolt sizzled along his cock. Lynx's channel flexed around his length, and a third dragged a raspy growl from his throat. Without even thinking, he sought Lynx's shoulder, not far from the base of his neck, and bit down. The coppery taste of blood filled his mouth, and he swallowed before grooming the area he'd bitten.

Lynx grunted and clutched Shiloh tighter while he rode out the remnants of pleasure coursing through his body. Shiloh lifted his head to claim a lazy kiss. That...he had never...phrull! Sex with his past lovers—male and female—paled in comparison to loving Lynx.

They lay there, bodies plastered together, savoring the relaxing aftermath. Shiloh pulled out of Lynx and tugged his friend to his feet.

"Come to the pool. Bathing will ease any residual pain."

"I bit you," Lynx said. "I couldn't stop myself. Wait, the wound is still bleeding a little."

"Lick it clean for me."

Lynx moved close. Shiloh's arms went around him, and he held his lover while Lynx licked the wounds on his upper shoulder. The rasp of Lynx's tongue darted pleasure all the way to Shiloh's cock.

He moaned loud enough for Lynx to lift his head.

"That hurt?"

"Feels good." To show Lynx just how pleasurable the act felt, he dipped his head and slid his lips over the bite he'd left on Lynx. His friend quivered in his arms.

"Goddess," Lynx whispered. "It's like a live booster wire straight to my cock."

"An understatement." Shiloh felt as if he might explode, and desire rose headily in him. "Pool. Cleanup first."

"Mr. Bossy," Lynx said, but Shiloh heard the laughter in his friend.

Together, they padded back to the water and began to wash.

"Shiloh?"

"Yeah?"

"I want to take you. I want to feel what you felt."

"I haven't..." Shiloh trailed off. "Yes, I'd like that."

"Wait. You haven't let any man have you?" Lynx asked.

Shiloh felt uncharacteristic heat crawl into his cheeks. He wanted to shift the conversation, or at least avert his gaze, but instead kept stubbornly staring at Lynx. "No."

"But you'll let me."

"I agreed, didn't I?"

"You did." A wicked grin spread across Lynx's face, moving slowly as engine oil in a frigid climate, until it reached from ear to ear. "And I can't wait to breach your virgin arse."

A snort escaped Shiloh, and he managed to contain his mirth to a tight smile. After an extended sec, he gave up the fight. He threw back his head and laughed, the sound echoing over the pool. Emotion clutched his chest in a tight embrace as he grinned at Lynx. Happiness. That was what this bubbling reaction was—contentment. "It's all yours, Lynx. Any time."

"That's what I'd hoped you'd say." Lynx grasped Shiloh's arm. He gave it a tug. "I pick now."

Jannike shifted position, her legs cramping from staying in the same spot for so long. She hadn't meant to watch the two felines, but once she'd spotted them, she couldn't move. One, they would have heard her and suspected she was spying, and two, she couldn't tear her gaze away. Thank the goddess the two men had finished and gone to the pond to bathe.

She yelped under her breath when the blood prickled through her veins and plopped onto her butt. With a whispered curse, she rubbed her calves to restore circulation. This was punishment for acting like a pervy jerk, as Camryn would say. Snooping on lovers.

Assured she'd be able to move without pain, she rose. Shiloh glanced in her direction, and she ducked. Goddess! A spike of adrenaline had her heart bump-bump-bumping against her ribs. Stupid. So phrullin stupid.

This was the last time she let her hormones yank her around. Her hormones had tugged on her ear, whispered she should watch, and she'd behaved like a well-behaved pet. No, she was standing right now. And no, she wasn't jealous. She. Was. Not.

Lecture done, she forced her legs to raise her off the ground. Her gaze darted to the spot where the two men had made love, and she froze. The bastards were at it again.

"Did you hear that?" Lynx asked.

"I saw as well. Jannike is spying on us."

Lynx slanted his gaze in the direction of the sound. "I see her. What do we do? Give her a show?"

"I'm up for that." Shiloh stroked his cock, his slow grin—so unusual it was striking—pushing Lynx's pulse to choppy. "What's wrong? Have you gone shy?"

"I'm wondering where to touch you first."

"Anywhere you like. I'm sparkly clean. You should make the most of that."

Lynx sighed at the reminder. "True that. We're gonna need a dose of luck to escape from the dome. They knew we were here. The sand worm might have killed them all, but they would've contacted someone in charge. They'll come again."

"Doesn't make any difference to our plan. We need to rest." Shiloh's stomach gave a plaintive rumble.

"I'm hungry too." And as if to prove it, Lynx's gut gurgled in sympathy.

"We all are. We can do without food. We can't do without water."

"I'll take our minds off food," Lynx promised.

"You can try." Shiloh's grin flashed, and with a carefree laugh, Lynx pounced.

They went down, and Lynx sought Shiloh's mouth. Kissing his friend was different from kissing a woman, yet he didn't regret a thing. If Jannike was right, and they were mates, it had pushed their friendship to a new level. One he liked.

Lynx gentled the kiss, wanting tenderness instead of urgency. Shiloh's arms came around him, and Lynx shuddered with enjoyment. Firm touches. A slight readjustment of their hips and their cocks aligned.

Lynx groaned at the rush of heat, the push of need in his body. "Tell me what to do. I don't want to hurt you."

Jannike dithered, and to her shame, she couldn't take her eyes off the two felines. The urge to join them hit her so strongly that she found herself taking two steps before her brain lurched into gear. They were beautiful together. A team. A mated pair, and they didn't need her around. The irritating itch kicked to life, sliding stealthily beneath her skin. She raked her nails over the spot, but the itchiness increased.

She didn't understand this attraction. Given her knowledge, she would have presumed she'd be safe since the two felines were mates.

She didn't think they felt the same way toward her, but she had caught them staring a couple of times... Gah! The entire situation was confusing and weird.

The two males were getting into their lovemaking now. They wouldn't notice her retreat, and if they did—too bad.

She stood and stomped up the slight incline to where Kelvin had set up camp. What did she need with a mate, anyway? She ignored the burst of heat within her body, the insidious longing.

The idea was ridiculous.

CHAPTER ELEVEN

"Report," Ursola demanded of her second-in-command, a squat man as wide as he was tall. He had a round face, an earnest, sweet face that hid his inner core of cruelty. His black hair, glossy and long, hung down his back in a complicated plait while his white robes were spotless.

Alain plopped his fat arse on one of the chairs on the other side of her home office desk. His black button eyes held calmness, another façade much like his jolly visage. "Many specimens have been recaptured and are at our facility. Unfortunately, several died, and a few suffered injuries during the crash. My men have located another group on a haven not far from the dome."

"And?"

"They have yet to report on their progress. Once we capture these last specimens, we'll have most of the original cargo."

Not as bad as she feared. "And the ship?"

"I sent out the retrieval team. They're salvaging what they can and effecting repairs. The foreman says they can patch the hole in the side but the propeller engine is in bad shape. They're waiting for new parts to come from Manx One."

"I see." She had other ships. The temporary loss of one was a nuisance but not debilitating. "Keep me informed of progress. I'll need to set another date for the auction. How bad are the injuries among the survivors? Anything that will take the specimens out of an auction?"

"Many were dehydrated, but most injuries are treatable. Nothing that will deter us from making a profit."

"Excellent."

Someone knocked on her door. Ursola started to frown, then decided the interruption was good. Alain liked to linger, and she suspected he had designs on her person. "Come."

The door opened to Cayle, who bobbed his head respectfully. "You have another visitor, mistress."

"Alain, I think we've finished? Keep me informed of progress. My slave will escort you out."

Alain frowned but accepted his dismissal. "I'll be in touch."

Ursola nodded, pleased at the progress he'd reported. The crash was a mere setback, and if anything, the delay allowed curiosity to build. She'd taken care to speak to various buyers, telling them of the cargo and their rare status. The result was daily calls and eagerness from the collectors.

"Ah," she said when Cayle showed in the private investigator. Cayle sent her a private smile that pleased her even though she kept her expression impassive. He shut the door, leaving her alone with the private investigator. "Tell me you have made progress."

"Whoever the culprit is, he or she is cautious." The investigator tugged at his purple tunic to ensure it wouldn't crease when he sat. A frown marred his brow, the network of textured irregular lilac ovals on his skin glinting under her office illumination. "I have followed every lead and have learned nothing useful. I have checked into your staff at the facility and the crew aboard the downed ship—those whom I have been able to contact. There are two ship hands missing. A floris dragon attacked one, and the other disappeared. It is debatable whether she made it back to the dome or not. Events are unclear after the ship crashed."

"Find her," Ursola barked.

"I am searching." The investigator's forked tongue flickered out and back in, tasting the air, testing for currents left by truth and lies. "I wish to interview your house slaves next. I also need to know who has visited you on business or personal matters. My assistant will do a sweep for spy-bots."

"Is that necessary?"

She disliked outsiders peering into her private life. The investigator might learn the truth of Cayle's status. She'd been so careful, and Cayle was discretion itself.

"I demand the utmost loyalty from my household staff. A lesson learned a long time ago." The traitorous bitch. Her husband had paid for his transgressions, and the bitch had spent hundreds of cycles in the dungeon—until she'd managed to escape. If she ever got her hands on the wench again, she'd make her rue the cycle she'd leaped into the master's bed. "My house slaves know the merest infraction will send them back to auction, and they mightn't gain such a lenient owner the second time."

"Even so, I would like to complete my investigation," the male said, unperturbed by the synsteel of her voice.

"Very well." Ursola conceded after a brief duel of gazes. "You may have access to my slaves this afternoon. Make it quick. I do not care to have my routine disrupted." An afternoon of lovemaking tossed away because this pompous man demanded it of her. She pushed the call button on her desktop, and after a short wait, someone tapped on the door. "Come," she called.

The door cracked open and one of the females loitered on the other side. "Yes, mistress?"

"Where is Cayle?"

"He is supervising a delivery of foodstuffs, mistress. He bade me tell you he wanted to check off the items because he thought the trader was cheating you."

"I see. Summon the slaves together. I wish to speak with them in the foyer."

"Now, mistress?"

"Yes, now. Apart from Cayle. He may continue his duties and report to me once he is finished."

"Yes, mistress." The colorless girl bowed and backed away, shutting the door with a soft clack.

"Come," she said to the investigator. "You may interview the slaves one by one in the connecting ante-room."

Jannike watched the felines walk back to the main camp, hand in hand. Their shoulders were relaxed, their smiles easy as they nodded at Kelvin.

A matched pair. There was that envy again. She couldn't keep it tamped down, stuffed at the back of her mind. She wrenched her gaze from their open happiness and worked on keeping her gnawing hunger at bay. Her fingers curled, dug into her palms as she focused on even breaths. In. Out. In. Out. In. Out.

"Would you like to drink?" Kelvin asked.

Royal was already taking a drink.

"If you are willing to grant us that honor." Lynx's come-to-bed voice yanked at Jannike's control. Her gaze lifted, landed, stuck like a prickled burr.

In answer, Kelvin extended one of his branches—the same one they'd drank from earlier.

Kelvin pulled a face when Shiloh bit down, his sole reaction. Still, Jannike suspected that allowing them to drink pained him, making his offer even more generous. Some way, somehow, she would repay his kindness—if they managed to survive this hellhole.

Her gaze went to Lynx, and she found him watching her. He winked, and she battled her blush. If Kaya were here, she'd bust a gut laughing. Her friend would read Jannike's covetousness without difficulty and call her on it. *Think. Talk about something. Anything.* "The bruising has gone from Shiloh's back. Turn around." She stared at Lynx's back—also free of black splotches.

"Have mine gone?"

"Yes." Tattoos had formed on Ry and Camryn after they'd had sex. Even allowing for personal differences, surely something should have happened to show they were mates.

"Your turn," Shiloh said. "Jannike, have you drunk?"

"Not yet. Kelvin was sleeping, and I wanted him to rest while he could."

"Which I thank ye for," Kelvin boomed.

"Could you ask the markowls to reconnoiter the area around the haven? If they are rested and feel up to the task," Shiloh asked. "It would be helpful to know if the sand worm is still around or if anyone else is approaching."

Kelvin whistled and cheeped at the birds, and they took off without hesitation, returning a short time later while Jannike was taking her turn at drinking.

Kelvin chatted with the birds then frowned. "A group of men on motor-skids are coming from the direction of the dome. They didn't see the sand worm but did see the movement of the sand between us and the dome. They think this was the sand worm traveling underground."

"Do we make a run for it or wait?" Lynx mused.

"Wait," Jannike and Shiloh answered at the same time.

"I need to drink and rest to let my body absorb the toxins in the water. Without water, we will not survive the crossing to the dome," Kelvin said. "I would have drank earlier, but I needed rest."

"Let them come to us. They need to get past the sand worm in order to recapture us." Jannike scanned their faces for agreement. "We don't have food, but thanks to Kelvin, we have water. We can rest and wait until the time is right to bolt to the dome."

Shiloh flexed his shoulders and stretched. "The worm will keep the men riding the motor-skids at bay."

"We could shift and sniff out the sand worm," Lynx added his thoughts. "Learn the creature's habits, where it rests, and discover if it is active once the solar-star descends."

Thoughts of escape helped Jannike to focus. Hopefully the *Indy* would appear before the men on the motor-skids attempted to nab them.

"So we're agreed on this plan?" Shiloh asked, his gaze searching their faces.

"Aye." Kelvin answered for them all. "'Tis the sensible plan. I go to drink now."

"Do you require us for anything?" Lynx asked.

"No." Jannike found it surprisingly difficult to utter the word, the tiny voice at the back of her mind waving its arms and practically doing handsprings to grab attention.

"We'll set up camp on the other side of the haven and keep watch for anything interesting," Shiloh said.

Jannike nodded, not trusting herself to speak. Begging words, pleading words, words that would change everything sat at the tip of her tongue, waiting to spill free. She swallowed and was glad when Royal scuttled across the ground and held up his furry arms. She picked him up, cuddling his warm body to her chest. "Kelvin and I will watch this side."

Lynx scratched Royal behind one ear before putting some welcome space between them. "Shout if you need anything."

Jannike nodded again. That wouldn't happen but if her agreement comforted the felines, she'd acquiesce.

The two felines wandered off, their buttocks tight and muscular beneath their trews. Two males in their prime. Such a visual feast. Their soft voices trailed in their wake, husky, private, and full of good humor. Her nipples ached, and she couldn't stop her need to scratch her back.

Stop watching, moron. You're making the situation worse. But she couldn't. A vision of naked bodies. Hers. Theirs. Limbs entwined. Long, thick cocks. Needy flesh. Soft noises. The musky scent of sex. Pleasure. So much pleasure.

Fuck a duck. Fuck a duck. *Fuck a duck!* Not even thinking another one of those intriguing Earth phrases managed to distract her stubborn mind.

She craved sex with the felines, and nothing she did halted her depraved thoughts. With a low groan, she grabbed her blanket and scouted a comfortable spot out of the direct beams of the solar-star. Briefly, she toyed with the idea of getting herself off or at least attempting the feat. No, her experiment last time hadn't ended well. In fact, the elusive orgasm had amplified her frustration.

No.

She'd go to sleep or at least pretend to rest. If her mind wouldn't let her relax, she'd work on a plan for when they reached the dome. The power of positive thinking and all that bull crap.

"Report," Ursola directed Alain. "Tell me your men have captured the last of the escapees."

"The men report there is a sand worm between them and the haven. They tried, but the sand worm killed three of their number."

Ursola ground her teeth together. She might not need these specimens to hold her auction, but she didn't like to lose. She'd collected them once, and she'd have them again. "Send the Renis fighter equipped with experienced guards. We should have done that earlier instead of messing around with the ground crew."

"We were trying to maximize profit. The ships cost more in fuel and labor and reduce our profit margins."

"Yes, yes," Ursola said. "I want these creatures captured. Their escape is setting a bad precedent. Rumors spread, and the last thing I want is for splinter groups to make them into heroes. I can't allow this. I want pictures of the escapees, identification of their species, known characteristics."

Alain coughed, his face puckering on the view screen. "I can't believe I'm saying this, but if they are specimens of lesser value, it might be easier to terminate them."

Ursola considered. "A good point. This is what we'll do. Send a single pilot ship, one equipped with recognition and surveillance tools. Report back once we have their species information, and I'll make the final decision."

"Lynx. Shiloh." Kelvin's whispered boom jerked Lynx from his lover's embrace.

"What? What is it?"

Beside him, Shiloh tensed, battle-ready in the blink of an eye.

"Something is wrong with Jannike," Kelvin said.

Lynx climbed to his feet. "What?"

"She be delirious, muttering in her sleep. I tried to wake. She won't wake." Worry colored Kelvin's voice, taking away some of his usual boom. "Ye should come and see."

Not even bothering to dress, he and Shiloh strode across the haven, Kelvin gliding in their wake. They found her on her blanket. She was dressed in the red garment, the one that covered her breasts, plus her trews. She'd tossed her tunic—what remained of it—on the grass at her head. She mumbled unintelligible sounds. She tossed and turned as if she were trying to get comfortable. Sweat coated her back and chest, making her skin gleam. As Lynx crouched beside her, she began to thrash on her blanket. Her arm snapped out and whacked him across the face.

"Ow," he muttered, ducking the next attempt to knock him out.

Shiloh caught the thrashing arm and pushed it to the ground. "Jannike. Wake up."

"Look at her stomach and chest. It's covered in welts," Lynx said. "Do you think something bit her?"

"She be scratching a lot," Kelvin informed them.

Shiloh frowned as he glanced at the tremin. "Has she said anything?"

"No."

"I think we should get her body heat down. Take her to the pool." Lynx stood decisively.

"Aye," Kelvin said.

Shiloh scooped her up and strode down the incline to the pool. When the water came up to his waist, he dipped her under. She muttered a series of words. Lynx understood one.

Home.

They all wanted to go home, even him. He suspected Shiloh hankered after home too, although he hadn't admitted as much. Even his mother's scolding—her lectures about the proper behavior for a royal prince would be welcome right now.

When Shiloh dunked her under the cool water, Jannike started to struggle. Still not awake, though.

"You hold her," Lynx said. "I'll splash water over her."

"She's lost weight."

"We all have." Lynx scooped up handfuls of water and let them dribble across her chest. Beneath her red garment, her nipples pulled tight. He tried not to notice, but his gaze kept tracking in that direction.

"She's female," Shiloh said, his voice husky.

Lynx's gaze leaped to Shiloh's, and he witnessed an answering heat in his friend. He straightened. "It's wrong to think of sex when she's sick." Shiloh barked out a laugh at his words. Not surprising. Even he'd heard the pompous tone in his words. "I sound like Jarlath."

Shiloh barked out another laugh. "As much as our brothers irritate me at times, I'd give almost anything to have them here bitching at us."

"I was just thinking I'd even be pleased to see my mother."

"Aye, having the queen lecture us would make things seem more normal."

They stared at each other for a sec.

"I think we're punch drunk or food deprived or something."

"Definitely something," Shiloh agreed. "Since the start of this adventure."

Lynx stilled then scooped more water and dribbled liquid over Jannike's forehead. The water ran through Jannike's sweat-plastered hair. "Do you have regrets?"

"Not a one."

"Me neither."

"Good to know," Shiloh whispered and his husky tone sent a pang of longing through Lynx.

Jannike jerked in Shiloh's arms, a shiver racking her body.

Shiloh frowned. "The heat has left her limbs. She's shivering."

"How can she be cold now?"

"Bring her to shore." Kelvin had taken the opportunity to drink more water while they tended to Jannike. He uprooted himself and studied them expectantly. "I suspect she needs warming now."

"We'll dry her off as best we can and wrap her in a blanket,"

Shiloh said.

"No." Kelvin set his hair rustling with a shake of his head. "She be requiring body heat to return to normal. Ye cuddle her. Sleep with her. That should do the trick." Kelvin wandered back to their camp without looking back.

"Why can't he warm her up?" Shiloh asked.

"Shiloh, this isn't about sex. It's a small thing to help Jannike survive."

Jannike jerked within Shiloh's arms, her body convulsing with the strength of her chills.

"Besides, Kelvin is already providing us with water. You've seen his expression when he does so. It pains him, yet he gives without complaint."

Shiloh frowned. "I don't know—the idea of anyone else touching you brings my feline to the surface. He's not angry—more concerned. No, that's not right either. All I know is that you belong to me, and I want to show ownership."

Mindful of Jannike's jerking feet and unpredictable arms, Lynx reached out and squeezed Shiloh's biceps. "I know. My feline is poised at attention. But think about this. I saw you eyeing her breasts. You wanted to touch, to strip away the red cloth. Admit it."

"Yes." A tinge of shame exited with the abrupt answer.

"I felt the same way. And we'll need to strip off her wet clothes if we have any chance of warming her to normal temperature."

Shiloh groaned. "I was trying not to think about that. Makes walking difficult."

Lynx glanced at Shiloh's groin as he exited the water. He laughed and just like that, the residual doubt and angst coming from his feline settled. "We're males. It happens."

"Our camp or Kelvin's?"

"Kelvin's. We might require his help."

Shiloh's brows lifted, a quizzical smile asking a question.

"A chaperone." Lynx gestured at his own groin. "I have no idea what is wrong with us, but I'm having the same problem. You'd think with all the coupling we've done this cycle our organs would want to rest."

"You know what the queen would say?"

"My mother would say nothing." Lynx chortled. "That sort of thing should never be mentioned."

"Lynx, if we survive, I'd like to go home. At least for as long as it takes to become irritated with the folks' attitudes toward our chosen occupations."

"I'm not hiding our relationship, Shiloh." Lynx lengthened his strides to keep pace. He stood clear while his friend settled Jannike on her blanket. "If we survive," he continued, "it's because our friendship is strong, and I won't hide my feelings. I don't care what the king and queen say or our brothers. I'm not retreating to how we were before." Passion rang in his voice. Determination.

"It won't be easy."

Lynx snorted. "When did we ever take the easy way? If the parents hate our relationship so much, we can relocate elsewhere. I find myself wanting a base—somewhere permanent to call home."

"Yes." Shiloh wasn't much for speeches, but his reply held every answer Lynx sought. They were both in agreement, and that made happiness spread inside him.

"Phrull, she won't keep still. I'll hold her while you strip off her clothes," Shiloh said.

Jannike remained unconscious, her limbs shuddering in great convulsions. Her teeth chattered, and tiny chill bumps pebbled her arms and chest.

Lynx grasped the waistband of her black trews and when her hips lifted off the ground in a tremor of cold, he was ready. He peeled the fabric down, blinking when he saw the matching red covering her sex. "Pretty," he murmured in appreciation as he stripped the clingy fabric down her thighs.

"They match," Shiloh said. "I've never seen undergarments of this type."

"She mentioned the planet Earth. Maybe she acquired them there." Lynx removed them during the next series of shivers, trying not to stare at the revealed flesh.

"She was born in a lab," Shiloh said. "See the faint blemish on her upper arm. That looks like an inoculation scar. They gave the fully developed babies vaccinations after a big disease scare."

"Turn her over. I can't see how this garment works." He gave it an experimental tug, then frowned. "Ah. I think I see the fastening." He twisted the back where the pieces met in the middle of her back. "Yes. These parts need to come off her arms. Turn her back over."

Shiloh turned her on her back. "I thought she said her stepfather sold her. If he required the currency, which is what she implied, then why did they order another child from the birth labs? I mean, they must have, since I got the impression Jannike wasn't the youngest."

"I don't know. Unless their circumstances changed for some reason, and they could no longer afford to raise their children. Or maybe the stepfather wanted his own child. That's the logical answer. Ah, there's the slave brand she mentioned. I wish we knew more of this planet," Lynx said. "We should have asked Jannike more questions."

"We've had other problems to solve," Shiloh stated. "You lie there and put your arms around her. Once she's settled, I'll go on her other side."

To his relief, Jannike relaxed as soon as he wrapped his arms around her. Her teeth still chattered, but she cuddled against his chest, the worst of the body spasms trailing off. Shiloh situated himself on her other side and wrapped his burly arm around her waist to draw Lynx closer to him as well.

"My cock feels as if it's gonna burst."

"Likewise," Shiloh said. "I thought Kelvin said if we mated, this damn prickling would disappear. I can feel it now, hovering beneath my skin."

"Same. And it's wrong on so many levels when she's not well. I wish I understood this mating thing."

"At least her shivering has ceased. We've managed that. Try to go to sleep."

"I don't think I can. Talk to me. Any idea what we should do once this is over?" Lynx didn't say *if* they escaped. Confidence made him speak with positivity.

"I like your idea of a home base. We have currency. We could purchase land and build a dwelling."

"Yes." Lynx liked the idea, picturing it in his mind with ease. "Land for us to run and play in feline form. Enough space in our dwelling so we can invite our friends to visit."

"I'd like to see Cimmaron again. I hope she's managed to stay out of the clutches of her captain. That male wanted her bad."

Lynx thought about their friend—a Dlog woman—who'd gone outside the bounds of normal female Dlog behavior. She'd worked and saved and paid her way until she qualified as a pilot. Most Dlog women mated early and settled with a male. "I'd like that. What else?"

"I don't want to give up trade, but I don't want to continue full-time. I'd be happy to do the odd trip. Maybe we could set up as merchants in the city. Hire and train some of the orphan youngsters from the lower city and give them a chance at a future."

Between them, Jannike ceased shivering, gave a soft sigh, and seemed to drop deeper into slumber.

Lynx relaxed, too, and let his mind test Shiloh's vision. "I like the idea of a new future. If we can't find a place to settle on Viros, perhaps we could live on one of the nearby planets."

"Yes. This is a good plan."

"I like it." Lynx spoiled his words with a hearty yawn. "We will discuss this further."

A masculine snore greeted his words, and despite the slumbering female separating their bodies, he smiled. He'd never felt closer to his best friend.

Jannike was having the greatest dream ever.

Sex.

Lust roared through her mind, her heart, her body to settle in her pussy. Warm arms surrounded her and held her with love. Heat seared both her front and her back, and this threw her. Two men?

For a sec her mind faltered at the absurdity of having two lovers, then she realized this was a dream, and why the hell not? This was her dream, and she could do anything she wanted.

She released the tension from her muscles and settled to enjoy the pure fantasy.

One muscular thigh parted her legs, slid against the warmth of her pussy. Sensations tore from the point of contact, and she began to move, rubbing herself against the firm muscles. Pleasure. Blissful pleasure. She pressed harder, faster, desperate to relieve the building ache.

A hand grasped her breast and tugged on her nipple, the sharp jolt of pain driving her over. She toppled in freefall, diving into her orgasm with greedy pleasure.

Her heart beat a fraction faster, and she couldn't halt her cries of enjoyment. Yes. Oh yes.

A masculine chuckle sounded right next to her ear. Her eyes flew open, and another cry escaped.

Lynx. Naked. Shiloh. Naked. And she'd just...

"No. Phrull, no." She scrambled to her feet and realized she wore not a scrap of clothing. Very naked. She crossed her arms and attempted to hide her breasts. Where the hellfire were her clothes? Her gaze darted left and right until she spotted them in a wet heap. A desperate woman couldn't afford choosiness. She bounded over to her clothes, seized her trews, and shoved one foot into a leg. Speed put her off-balance, making her hop before she tripped over a tuff of grass and fell on her arse.

"Let me help." Lynx's lips quivered as if he was trying not to laugh.

"Stay away from me." She backpedaled, using her hands and feet like an Earth crab. Not very dignified since she was still naked. "Look the other way. Who took off my clothes? Why?"

Shiloh lifted his hands in surrender and halted his advance. "We were trying to help. You had an episode. Your temperature rose dangerously, and we had to dunk you in the pool."

"My trews are soaked." Jannike scrambled to her feet, tried not to think about them staring at her naked body, and pulled the wet trews up her legs. When she glanced up, she caught both men ogling her breasts, and she folded her arms over her chest and glared at them.

Lynx bent to pick up something, and when he straightened, he dangled her bra on one finger.

"Give me that," she snapped, incensed to feel heat collecting in her cheeks as she snatched her bra. "Turn around and stop gawking."

"Make me." Shiloh's expression held challenge.

Lynx spluttered, his grin growing to sand worm proportions. He sauntered over to the nearest rock formation and leaned on it, his green eyes dancing with mirth. "Our days have been crappy lately. We take our amusement where we can."

"I was asleep," she said, off-balance and not up to the task of using her fists. "I didn't know what I was doing."

"But you did it well," Shiloh said.

"I can smell you on his leg." Lynx's lips twitched in a macabre dance of humor.

"Shut up," she snapped. "Where are my panties?"

"Panties." Lynx savored the word in his mouth like a ripe piece of fruit. "Panties. Is that what those undergarments are called?"

"Here they are." Shiloh dangled the scrap of red lace between finger and thumb.

"I'm going for a swim to wash my clothes." She stomped toward the pool and stopped abruptly when she heard footsteps from behind. She glanced over her shoulder. "I don't require an escort."

"You were ill. It came on without warning." Shiloh followed her. "We've made it this far, and it would be silly for you to drown because of your sensibilities."

Jannike felt her mouth drop open. "My sensibilities? You big oaf. I'll give you sensibilities." She executed a flawless kick, one that had taken Ry down before and missed. Shiloh grabbed her foot and hauled her into his arms with an ease that prodded her temper.

"Let me go!" Her struggles didn't loosen his grip, but she kept fighting. Goddess, what was wrong with her? She was acting like a panicked virgin. Panting with exhaustion, she ceased fighting yet didn't relax.

"Shiloh, let her go." Lynx's mouth quivered yet again, his eyes dancing right along in echoing humor.

"Are you trying to injure me?" Shiloh asked.

"Yes." She tried to relax, sucked in a big breath. A mistake.

The roar of engines from overhead halted their conversation.

They were here! Excitement and relief suffused Jannike. Ry and the crew had come for her. Finally.

She scanned the sky and puffed out in disappointment. Too small for the *Indy*. The *Indy's* tender was black with silver trim. This craft was a deep blue.

"Friend or foe?" Shiloh asked.

"Not my friends. I don't recognize the ship. No, wait. That ship comes from the dome. The blue-and-gold shield on the side denotes Manx Two."

They all tracked the trajectory of the ship.

"I don't like it. They're not attempting to land," Lynx said.

Shiloh nodded. "They might know about the sand worm. They definitely would if they'd had contact with the men on the motor-skids."

"Too late to hide. They've seen us." Jannike's tone was grim.

The blue ship did another tight circle of the haven before flying off.

"Well." Jannike planted her hands on her hips. "Maybe it's time to rejig our plan."

CHAPTER TWELVE

The communicator beeped, and Ursola stabbed her finger at the receive button. "Yes."

"The pilot captured images of the escapees. Three humanoid. Two males. One female. I'm sending the images through now," Alain said. "We were able to identify the female since her identity was in the slave catalog."

Interest peaked in Ursola. A slave. How interesting. Her fingers manipulated the data Alain sent through. Two males. Both big. Dark hair. Green eyes. Handsome specimens that would bring a good price from collectors. The female's face came on the screen and Ursola caught her breath.

Jannike—a name cemented in her brain.

The slave who'd stolen her husband.

The slave who'd managed to escape her wrath.

The slave who'd thumbed her nose at Ursola.

A slow smile spread across her face, and possibilities spread before her like a decadent treat.

"Send the team of soldiers. I want these specimens taken alive, especially the woman."

"We're not going down without a fight." Determination burned on Shiloh's warrior face. "We make it difficult for them."

"Agreed," Lynx said.

"Running is the best option, but not in this heat." Jannike swiped a hand over her brow. The solar-star meandered, low in the sky, yet already sweat coated her skin. Her stomach punctuated her statement with a rumble.

Lynx rubbed his flat belly. "I don't know. If they had food, I might consider their invitation."

"I saw the ship," Kelvin boomed from behind them. "We are in a trap."

"We're not surrendering without a fight," Lynx stated facts.

Jannike scanned the sky. Empty. Scowling, she studied the flat, endless stretch of sand in front of them. As she watched, the sand worm made a passing sweep, sticking its ugly head above the sand, tentacles twisting. It let out a roar. "The motor-skids are still there."

"They haven't moved off the rocky strip since the sand worm took some of their men," Shiloh said.

"They're gonna capture us again." Lynx verbalized what they were all thinking.

Jannike wanted to dispute his words, but he spoke the truth. While they had water—thanks to Kelvin—and shelter from the worst of the elements, the lack of food would begin to tell.

"What's wrong with your skin?" Shiloh asked.

"Nothing." Jannike glanced at her stomach and saw the cursed black splotches. She swallowed. "I must have bruised when I hit the ground. It's not important." A lie, and one that almost choked her. She cleared her throat. "We need a plan."

"We split up and take our chances," Kelvin said. "They can't chase us all at once. And if we do it under cover of blacklight, we increase our chances."

Jannike kept away from the two men. She ignored the knifelike intensity of the prickles beneath her skin. She wrapped up to stave off the chills and dunked her clammy body in the pool to alleviate the sweats that came more frequently. A cycle passed, and fear morphed into an ugly beast, attempting to derail her from her chosen path.

Shiloh and Lynx might be her destined mates, but she couldn't tell them, couldn't put herself in the position of begging for their attentions, couldn't put them in any more danger than they were already.

Besides, they didn't have time.

Jannike stood and packed up her blanket. She pulled her ripped tunic over her head. It was better than nothing.

"They're coming," Kelvin said.

"It seems they're smarter than we gave them credit for."

Lynx and Shiloh slid out of the blacklight to join them.

"I can't see them yet." Jannike scanned the sky.

"Doesn't matter. Let's move out," Shiloh said.

"A last drink," Kelvin urged.

None of them argued. Jannike winced at Kelvin's hiss when her mouth drew on his branch. Each time seemed more painful for him, yet he never complained.

When they'd finished drinking, Kelvin bowed his head. "May the goddess smile upon ye with favor."

"Good luck." Jannike strode away.

"Wait." Shiloh grabbed her, hauling her into his embrace.

"What—"

He stopped her question with a quick, hard kiss that was over almost as soon as it began. Shiloh handed her to Lynx, who kissed her with a passion that left the prickles beneath her skin singing.

Then the two men faded into the gloom, leaving as silently as they'd arrived.

Jannike took a breath to calm her trepidation, then nodded at Kelvin and forced herself to walk away, not stopping even when she came to the edge of the haven.

She hustled, every sense trained for movement to indicate the presence of the sand worm or the motor-skids.

The drone of the ship's engine became more audible. The pilot circled the haven then headed in her direction. Phrull it all. They must have heat-seeking equipment.

She increased her pace, following the mental path she'd planned after they'd decided splitting up was necessary. Damn if they'd catch her without a fight.

When the ship veered off its circular path, Shiloh halted to study its progress. He and Lynx had decided to walk together until they ascertained the pilot's plan, and they'd talked Kelvin into staying at the haven with the markowls and the calibore.

"Why did you kiss Jannike?" Lynx asked.

"Jealous?"

"That's not an answer."

"I wanted to," Shiloh said, a trifle defensive. "She looked alone and defenseless when Kelvin wished us good fortune. I've been thinking about kissing her ever since we woke with her rubbing against my leg."

"Those aren't bruises on her torso. They've moved since we first saw them. They're the same as the ones we had."

Shiloh nodded. "Sleeping next to her felt right."

"Something to consider. Damn, the ship is going after Jannike." Lynx took half a step before Shiloh grabbed his arm.

"Stick with the plan. Some of us escape and use our resources to save those captured." Shiloh stood his ground when Lynx attempted to free himself.

"You're right. It's just—phrull, I've been thinking about fucking her. It felt disloyal, so I didn't tell you."

"Come on. Let's move and give these phrullin creeps a run for their currency."

Lynx hurried to catch him. "I thought you'd be angry."

Shiloh snorted. "How can I gripe at you when the exact thoughts marched through my mind all of yester-cycle?"

The two felines increased their pace to a ground-eating lope, intent on putting as much distance between them and the haven as possible.

The blacklight fell away, and the heat from the solar-star began to shimmer across the wide expanse of desert.

A second ship appeared on the horizon, and they halted to take stock. The ship was black with silver.

Shiloh scratched his back, watched the blue ship maneuver over Jannike, a silver net come down, hampering her movements and allowing easy capture.

"They've got Jannike," Lynx said.

"Looks like they'll get one of us too. Good luck." Shiloh took off running.

The hum of the ship became louder. Sand blew in his face, his eyes. He kept his legs pumping despite the uneven surface and the threat of the sand worm. Part of him expected a net to descend, just like the one they'd used on Jannike.

Didn't happen.

The ship zipped past him—a tender from a bigger ship. Phrull, he didn't stand a chance. About to change direction and at least give himself a fighting chance, he pulled up when the tender landed.

The door slid open and a large male appeared in the entrance. A smaller feminine figure, squeezed into a gap beside him. Jannike's friends? He sniffed and relaxed at the hint of feline on the air.

Without warning, the ground began to tremble beneath his feet. Phrull! He started to run. "Hurry. Phrull, hurry," he bellowed as he threw himself at tender ramp.

A woman with blue hair elbowed her way past the woman. "Grata, what is that thing?"

"Sand worm," Shiloh gasped. "Take off now."

"He smells like Jannike," the feline woman said.

The feline man and the blue-haired woman reached for him, dragged him up the last of the ramp as the tender lifted off. The sand worm thrust upward, snapping its large jaws and howling at missing its prey.

Before Shiloh could regain his breath, the big male grabbed him by his tunic and thrust his face close. "Where is Jannike? What have you done with her?"

"Other ship." Shiloh had trouble talking. He was trying to catch his breath and breathe around the feline male's chokehold.

The feline woman tapped the male's shoulder. "Ry, let the man breathe. He can't talk with you choking him."

"Bad tidings on the clouds." A new voice and doom invested every syllable.

Shiloh turned his head a fraction and gawked. It was a him—he was sure of that—but black swirled across his features turning them from white—no gray—to a deep black. "I...ah...are you

Jannike's friends?"

The grip at his neck loosened.

"Where is she?" the man demanded.

"They've recaptured her. We split up so some of us would escape."

"We," the feline snapped.

"Ry, this isn't an interrogation." The feline woman offered an apologetic smile and rubbed her rounded belly.

"Damn straight it is," the blue-haired one declared. "Tell us what you know."

The feline woman pushed past the male and shoved him back two steps. "I will extract the necessary information. I'm pregnant and I get to have my own way. You promised."

Shiloh listened in bemusement. The male's jaw tightened but he allowed his female to take the lead. Shiloh wasn't fooled though. This Ry was poised to leap if he sensed a threat. Phrull, they were just as confusing as Jannike. He swallowed and slipped back into the safety of bodyguard mode. Much less puzzling. "You must be Camryn and Ry. Jannike mentioned you."

"And you are?" Camryn prompted.

"Shiloh. I'm from Viros, and they captured us like Jannike. We escaped when the ship crashed in the desert."

"We?" Ry asked in a sharp voice.

"Lynx, my mate, and Kelvin, a tremin. Kelvin remained on the haven with the creatures, and Jannike, Lynx, and I split up, so they couldn't recapture us all."

"Where is this haven?" Camryn asked.

"Captain?" a voice called.

The pilot, Shiloh saw when he glanced in the direction of the voice.

"That creature is after someone. What do you want to do?"

"Lynx." Shiloh stood and brushed past the strangers to peer out the view screen. Lynx sprinted across the sand. As he watched, his

181

friend shifted, his leopard form streaking ahead of the burrowing sand worm. "Please. You have to save him. *Please.*"

"We're gonna save him," Camryn promised.

"Your mate?" Ry asked.

Shiloh met the male's gaze without shame. "Yes."

"We'll fly over the top of him and lift him into the ship. He'll need to shift back to humanoid, otherwise we won't be able to grab him. Tell him to change."

Shiloh gaped at Ry. "How?"

"Can you communicate mind-to-mind?"

"No."

"Fuck," Ry muttered. "Okay. Wait by the ramp. I'll let my pilot know what we're going to do."

Shiloh waited impatiently, his gut writhing. He didn't like relying on strangers.

"You ready?" Ry asked.

Phrull, Shiloh hoped so. They had one shot at this. "Ready."

The ramp whirred open just as the tender sped to a spot in front of Lynx.

"Lynx!" Shiloh roared. "Up here."

Lynx pulled up, limbs skidding in the sand because of his rapid halt.

"Shift," Shiloh hollered. "We'll pull you up. Phrull, the sand worm is still coming."

"Who are the dudes on the bikes?" Camryn asked.

Shiloh guessed she meant the motor-skids. "Hurry," he hollered at Lynx.

Lynx's shift was slower than normal, and he reached for them, his head and arms still covered with black fur. Shiloh gripped his forearm, ignoring the jab of partially transformed claws. At his side, Ry grunted as they took Lynx's weight.

"They've got him. Gain altitude," the blue-haired one ordered the pilot.

The ship shot upward just as the sand worm thrust from the sand.

Adrenaline and fear gave Shiloh extra strength, and Lynx popped through the tender's entrance. Shiloh's arms came around his lover's body, and he buried his face in Lynx's shoulder, breathing through his residual fear. Phrull, that had been close.

"Can't breathe." Lynx struggled in his embrace.

"Sorry." Shiloh gentled his hold but was unable to remove his arms. His brain wouldn't let him as it chanted *mine, mine, mine* in a long, determined litany.

"*Ah-hum!*" A pointed feminine cough came from behind them.

Shiloh lifted his head. The laughter and understanding within Camryn's gaze brought tightness to his throat. His. Lynx belonged to him.

"Jannike," Ry prompted.

"They will take her to the dome." Lynx ran a soothing hand down his back, calming some of Shiloh's lingering fear.

"I thought Jannike said she wore a tracker," Shiloh said.

"She does." Ry grimaced in disgust. "We thought it was faulty. Ours aren't, so hers should work. Something keeps interfering with the signal. Sometimes we can track and at other times, she blinks off our system."

"It's slowed us down." Camryn scowled. "We didn't expect to take a third of a rotation to find you."

"Can we collect our friend from the haven before we go after Jannike?" Lynx asked. "And if it isn't too much trouble, we could do with some food."

"Kaya has chocolate," a young woman said from a seat next to the pilot.

Another feline and unmated, judging by the cat tattoo on her cheek. Pretty, but young.

"Do not," the blue-haired one denied immediately.

"I smell chocolate." Camryn glowered at the female and rubbed her stomach again. "It's been driving me crazy. Damn hormones."

"I have snacks in my bag." The black-and-white man glided toward a doorway. "I'll get them."

"Which way to this haven?" Ry asked, and Shiloh noticed he kept close to his mate, touching her often.

Shiloh met his gaze and nodded in recognition. He felt the same way about Lynx, and it was beginning to look as if Jannike resided in the same region of his heart.

"They won't hurt her," Lynx murmured, although he didn't sound too sure.

"No," Shiloh agreed. "Not if they want to sell her for a profit."

Camryn's brows shot upward. "They're selling her?"

"Yeah, we ended up in the same cell as Jannike. They wanted a breeding pair."

"Nanu, put the accelerator on," Camryn said.

"Is there a clearing large enough to land?" Nanu called, the beads at the end of his braids clacking together as he turned his head.

"A flat area of sand at the edge of the haven." Lynx replied. "The ground is rocky, and the sand worm doesn't like it."

"Show me," Nanu said, with a jerk of his head.

Shiloh climbed to his feet and offered a hand to Lynx. They stood behind the pilot, and Lynx gave directions.

"We're going to Viros," Ry said to Shiloh. "My parents came from there."

"What are their names?"

"Coppersmith."

Shiloh shook his head. "Lynx might know the name, but it's not familiar to me."

"The family left before I was born, I think."

"Lynx and I don't spend much time there. We run a trading and cargo business off planet."

Ry nodded, and Shiloh couldn't tell if the man was pleased or not.

"I see the spot. We're landing," Nanu said.

"It won't take long," Lynx promised. "It's just Kelvin, a calibore and the two markowls."

"Nothing dangerous?" Ry asked in a sharp voice.

"No." Lynx grinned. "We're the dangerous ones."

Camryn gave a grim chuckle. "That's good. Jannike's captors won't know what hit them."

Jannike struggled even as the net closed around her, trapping her arms and legs. Strong hands hauled her aboard the ship and thrust her into a cage. With her movement restricted, she could do nothing except glare at her captors. The six burly soldiers, all dressed in form-fitting black and sporting tattoo script on their faces, stared back in interest.

"Boss woman want you bad," one said finally.

Jannike's gut bucked with foreboding. A reunion she'd rather dodge. She didn't bother replying. Instead, she forced herself to study her surroundings, to search for weaknesses in security. The cage bars consisted of thick synmetal, and with her space limited, she couldn't stretch from her crouch.

The flight back to the dome didn't take long. Frustrating that they'd managed to get so close without getting captured. At least Shiloh and Lynx remained free.

Yes, this was the best outcome.

If she died—no, when because the widow wouldn't go easy on her this time. At least she wouldn't take anyone else down with her.

And there was still an outside chance Ry and the crew would arrive before the widow exerted payback. He'd promised and he never broke his promises. Yeah, all she needed to do was hang on.

The ship landed, and Jannike tensed, ready to take any chance to escape.

But they didn't release her from the cage. Instead, they covered it and wheeled the entire thing off the ship.

"Lift it onto the glide," someone said.

Jannike felt the cage lift. Nearby, someone grunted.

"Cursed thing weighs a ton."

Jannike muffled a grunt. It wasn't her. She'd been on an enforced diet and had lost weight.

Her cage bumped and swayed as workers placed it on a transporter. A whir of sound captured her attention, but she had no idea what it was or which direction she was traveling, the cage cover foiling her attempts to gain information.

"The boss lady wants her in the private high-security cage," a male ordered, his brutish voice making Jannike picture someone huge.

Her chances of escape weren't looking good.

At least it was cooler here. Depending on what they intended to do with her, they might feed her. Her stomach grumbled at the idea of food.

The cage stopped moving, and someone pulled the cover off. Jannike took in her surroundings in one quick sweep. She was inside another cage. Larger. This one had a feeding station and cleansing facilities. Luxuries, but still a prison. Part of one wall propelled her reflection back at her. An observation window.

No escape from this prison.

Her gaze tracked back to her guards. All held weapons, and they pointed in her direction.

"Out." A rail-thin guard, in urgent need of sanitizing, gestured with his weapon.

Jannike stepped from the portable prison, taking her sweet time, watching, assessing her options again, unwilling to accept defeat.

They backed from the cell one by one, taking her temporary cage with them. Finally, the door closed behind them, the locks sliding home.

The guards tromped out, leaving her alone. The scent of the food drifted to her. Hot food. She pulled the bowl out of the container and smelled it. Vegetables in a sauce. Flat bread. Could be drugged.

Her stomach let out a plaintive rumble, and she spooned up a bite. The flavorsome sauce danced across her tongue. A gurgle sounded as she swallowed. A moan. Goddess, that was good. Too bad if it was doctored.

Jannike ate the entire bowl and went back for seconds. This time, she forced herself to eat more slowly.

A robe hung on a hook near the sanitizer unit. Jannike stood and stripped off the remnants of her tunic. Her boots and the grubby linings hit the ground with a dull thud. The rest of her clothing joined the pile, and she stepped into the cleansing tube. Too bad if the guards were watching. She didn't care at this stage.

She completed her cleansing with brisk moves then turned the controls to dry. The cleansing suds disappeared from her skin and secs later, she exited the tube. She reached for the robe and belted it at her waist.

She made quick work of cleansing her clothes and boots and dried them in the tube too. She pulled on her underwear and tattered trews, feeling better now that she was clean and her belly was full.

Now all she needed to do was wait to learn her fate.

Ursola paced around her office then prowled through her home. The servants froze whenever they spotted her and turned to face the walls until she'd passed. Well-trained, she thought. The investigator was crazy to suspect someone from within her home intended to hurt her.

Her slaves knew better.

Her communicator buzzed, and she plucked it from her pocket. "Do you have her?"

"We do," Alain said. "She is at the facility in the high-security wing. What do you wish me to do next?"

"Keep an eye on her, and make sure your men don't relax their guard." Every particle of Ursola wanted to rush to confront the conniving bitch. No, she decided. It would be best to keep the slave off-balance.

Let her fear grow.

Play on her doubts.

"What about the two males who were with her?" Ursola asked.

"The pilot said she was alone."

"I see. Check with our men on the ground. I want them recaptured."

"It will be done. When will you come by to inspect the specimens?"

"The cycle after the morrow," she said decisively. "I have formalities to take care of before I visit the facility. The auction will take place seven cycles from now."

"Very good," Alain said. "I'll make sure everything is organized."

"Excellent." Ursola ended the call and started down the stairs.

"Mistress." Cayle stood in the entranceway.

Ursola smiled before she could stop it—a smile she normally reserved for the bedroom, for moments of privacy.

"*A-hem.*"

"The investigator wishes a moment in your presence." Cayle's gaze flicked back to the investigator standing behind him. "Mistress, my presence is required in the kitchens. I must help make a list and escort the cook to the market."

"Of course." She waved him away, biting back her irritation at the investigator's presence. "Continue your duties."

Cayle nodded and strode away before disappearing through a door to the right of the staircase.

"A trusted employee?" The investigator's arch tone riled her and had a snappish reply tickling the tip of her tongue. She bit the inside of her cheek, struggled for control.

"A slave," she bit out. "Nothing less, nothing more. You have news for me?"

"I've interviewed all of your house staff."

"And?"

"I believe your head slave—the one who was just here—is behind your troubles."

"You have proof?" Something inside Ursola broke, and anger pulsed through her veins, filling the fragmented bits. "Tell me."

The investigator retreated, and Ursola took a petty comfort in the telltale behavior. Her reputation preceded her, and he'd do well to remember she wouldn't hesitate to retaliate should he upset her.

"I don't have proof."

"Then why would you say that?" she snapped.

"It's a gut feeling. Your other slaves are too frightened to do anything other than what they're hired for."

"And him?"

"He's arrogant. He's not like the others."

Ursola frowned. No, he wasn't like the others, which was why she'd started paying attention to him. "He has been in my service for several rotations."

"As I told you. A gut reaction."

"You will investigate further before you make another report," Ursola ordered. "I don't want gut feelings. I want proof. I want you to present the culprit to me so I can deal with them."

Cayle carried the shopping basket for Hark, the cook, and listened to her prattle with half an ear. The slender woman with the ethereal face, who'd been a slave for many rotations, scarcely uttered a word while inside the mansion. The instant she left, her mouth didn't cease flapping. It was the same with the other slaves. Once they left the cloistered environs of Ursola's mansion, their terror faded, and they spoke in full sentences.

Their owner was a monster.

"Where to first?" he asked, shoving Ursola from his mind. Now was not the cycle to allow his hatred to overwhelm good sense, not with the investigator sniffing around. Cool and calm was his motto. Keep victory in sight. The abolition of slavery.

"Meat first then vegetables. We'll visit the baker last." Hark hesitated. "I need to do a large order, but maybe we could enjoy a break with the baker's wife?"

Cayle smiled to ease the anxiousness that had crept into Hark, the tension in her thin shoulders. "I'm sure that can be arranged."

"The mistress expects her meals on time." Thrust back into reality, Hark wrung her wrinkled but capable hands, some of her earlier excitement fading to leave pale cheeks and nerves.

"And we'll make sure she gets it," Cayle soothed, his nostrils flaring. "She will have no cause for irritation."

"Who is that man at the house? He asked me many questions. Why? He implied I left the mansion without permission. None of us leave the mansion without the mistress's permission."

"Don't worry," Cayle said. "I understand the investigator spoke with the off-site employees too. Nothing to get upset about."

They walked in silence now, Cayle focusing on their surroundings. The skytrain whooshed overhead, whisking commuters from one side of the dome to the other. A man—another slave dressed in black-and-gold robes bearing the Starsa crest caught Cayle's eye and gave an imperceptible nod. Good, the next stage of the plan was underway.

Cayle guided Hark past other slaves scurrying to and fro to complete their chores, upper-class men and women, and visitors to Manx Two shopping and enjoying cups of spice dram, a non-alcoholic beverage made from the juice of the dramite cacti.

He noted strangers and had no trouble discerning which were present to attend Ursola's auction. Their confidence, their arrogance, and the way their gazes lingered on slaves on the walkways gave them away. He gritted his teeth and turned his attention back to the slender cook, smart in Ursola's black-and-red uniform for senior slaves. With a gentle hand at the small of her back, he guided her into the butcher's shop.

"You go ahead and choose your meat. Take your time. I'll pass the day with the head butcher."

Hark acquiesced with a bob of her head and hurried away.

Cayle approached a big, strapping man with bulky biceps who looked as if he'd break Hark like a twig—if he cared to undertake the task. "How are you today, sir?" He bowed his head in respect.

"I fare well. Business is good," the butcher replied. "How is your mistress?"

"She is well, thank you. I am glad business is booming. I feared the storms would confine customers to their dwellings."

The butcher cast a surreptitious glance around their vicinity then winked. The tightness in Cayle's shoulders eased. Ah, a successful escape. That was good news, but he wished he could do more.

"We have many visitors, despite the end of the tourist season." A veiled warning of the investigator. "But still—we must tighten our belts until the beginning of the next season."

A swift frown crossed the butcher's face, his dark eyebrows squeezing together, but he gave a curt nod, understanding Cayle's message.

The door to the shop opened, and a couple entered. Strangers. A handsome pair with an air of confidence about them. They'd likely come to attend the auction but today were after one of the butcher's meat pies. Saliva pooled in Cayle's mouth, the urge to spit at them so strong he almost trembled. Goddess, he was losing himself to his need for revenge.

Strangers, they might be, but he shouldn't make assumptions.

The male was big and strong, and his loose gait indicated an easy strength. He wasn't stupid, though, his green gaze slicing and dissecting his surroundings. His hand pressed protectively, possessively against the woman's shoulder. It was easy to see he cared for her and that she returned the emotion. His gaze settled on Cayle's slave arm bracelet.

"Sir." The woman's accent was strange. "We're searching for our friend."

"All the visitors stay at one of the two tourist complexes when they visit Manx Two," the butcher said.

The woman shot a look at the male, and they seemed to communicate without words. "She is here against her will," she admitted in a low voice.

Cayle frowned. This was dangerous—talking to strangers. Ursola had spies everywhere.

"The slave auctions are scheduled to take place in seven cycles," Cayle said.

"We will not be purchasing our friend." Something in the man's voice—the hard note of determination—spoke to Cayle. This man knew of loyalty, and Cayle had no doubt they'd fight for their friend.

Cayle scanned the interior of the butcher's shop and saw they were attracting attention. Worth the risk. He could make plausible excuses. He bent closer and pretended to give directions, gesturing to the left. "The widow keeps her specimens in a facility outside the dome, not far from the private spaceport. All the beings destined for auction are housed there."

"Thank you," the woman murmured. "No one else would speak

with us."

Cayle stepped back and raised his voice. "Don't forget, make sure you take the left turning, get on the glide there and that will take you to the auction house."

"You remind me of someone," the man said. "Have you always lived on Manx Two? Have we met before?"

"I was born here in the birth labs. I have never traveled from Manx Two."

The man shrugged. "Thanks for the directions. My mate would have been disappointed to learn we'd missed the auction."

Cayle took another step back as if to distance himself.

"I hope they have more people to back them up." The butcher gazed after them with narrowed eyes.

"Indeed." Cayle noted Hark had completed her shopping. "Can you deliver cook's order to the mansion, please? We have more errands to complete."

"It shall be done," the butcher promised.

Cayle escorted the cook from the store. He caught a glimpse of the male and female speaking with a pair of big men with similar coloring. A blue-haired woman and a man of a different race joined them. The blue-haired woman froze when she saw him, elbowed the male standing beside her. He glanced at Cayle, frowned and spoke to the first couple. They all turned to stare, and he felt the weight of their gazes until he and Hark turned into Vegetable Alley.

Cayle froze inside, disliking their interest. Too late now. He'd gone with his gut, given them the information they sought. He'd known one cycle his luck would turn. Maybe this was that cycle.

CHAPTER THIRTEEN

Excitement filled Ursola, and she found it impossible to wait a full cycle to view her recaptured female, to gloat in person. With the auction under control, her temper a fraction sweeter, she dressed for her meeting with the slave who'd made her the butt of jokes for rotations before she gained enough power to quell those who considered her misfortune funny.

She dressed in her finest set of embroidered robes, wanting to display her wealth and success. She'd had the female fed and allowed her facilities in which to bathe with an eye to making a profit. Perhaps death would suit better. Something to ponder.

"Mistress." The firm knock on her chamber door ended her primping.

"Come."

"The investigator wishes to speak with you," Cayle said from the doorway.

"I don't have time. Tell him to return later. I will see him prior to meal break."

"Yes, mistress."

Ursola studied his beautiful face. "Shut the door. Come to me."

Cayle followed her orders without hesitation.

"I have need of you." She lifted her skirts to display her legs. "Make me come. I have an important meeting and require relief."

"Yes, mistress." Cayle took her skirts in his big hands, taking the weight and raising the fabric higher to reveal her pussy. While she watched, he took a deep breath, as if he was savoring her scent. The idea pleased her, and some of her tension receded. He crawled beneath her skirts and parted her legs with a gentle hand, allowing the fabric to fall over his head.

If anyone entered the room, they wouldn't note his presence. A finger trailed down her slit, rubbed gently. Ursola sucked in a quick breath at the dart of exquisite pleasure.

Warm lips replaced his finger, the flicker of a tongue. She shivered, knowing she wouldn't last long. His lips slid up and down, and his hands guided her stance wider. The tip of his tongue traced the rim of her clitoris then his lips closed over the tiny organ and sucked.

Her orgasm was quick, her gasp greedy as enjoyment washed over her with the suddenness of a desert sandstorm. He licked her, easing off because experience had taught him of her extra sensitivity after climax.

Perfect.

Just perfect.

Her lips curled in an easy smile of relaxation and peace. A perfect mindset for this meeting with her ex-slave. She'd squash her like the annoying bug she was.

She was still smiling when Alain let her into the cage housing the rebel. As per her orders they'd chained the slave to a central post, and she posed no danger.

Ursola frowned, taking in the woman's obvious strength, her militant air and the jut of a determined chin. She looked familiar...ah, of course. It was the remnants of a youngster left in a female now fully grown.

"I suspect I'm the last person you wish to see."

The woman stared at her through gray eyes. Funny, they were almost the same color as Cayle's eyes. The thought brought a flash of remembered pleasure. There was no comparison between the two slaves. Cayle was reliable and she'd rewarded his loyalty, yet he never took advantage. This one...she'd spit in her face if Ursola stepped too close.

"Too frightened to speak," Ursola mused.

"I'm not scared of you. You're a bully not willing to face me unless I'm chained. Yeah..." She paused as if considering the matter. "That says coward."

No one spoke to her like that. A snigger reminded her of Alain's presence. Ursola drew in a hasty breath, wrinkled her nose at the prison stench—the pungent scent of medic-cleanser and unwashed bodies—and let the lifeforce ease out in a soft whoosh.

The slave was seeking to manipulate, to drive her to anger with insults. That wouldn't happen. She had control and would retain that position.

"I see the years haven't given you a better attitude." Ursola saw pride and determination despite the chains. She'd considered killing her. Slowly. Painfully. But no, her other idea to sell her to a master who reveled in difficult slaves, one who would break her spirit.

That would work. Once she lost her attitude, the master she had in mind would on-sell her to another who didn't wish to spend time training.

Or, she could sell her in the public part of the auction. Ah yes, she mused, smiling at the prospect of an alien owner with different expectations. Options. Once she put her mind to the problem she had many ways to exact revenge.

But first—first she'd give the slave a hint of what might lay in her future. That would strip the arrogance from her smug face.

"Alain," she called.

"Yes, madam?"

"This slave has an attitude. I want it fucked out of her. I give you leave to use her on the condition you do not injure her. I intend to sell her at the auction and don't want her body to bear distressing marks. Do you understand?"

The gleam in his black button eyes, the hint of cruelty he unleashed, said he understood and anticipated carrying out her orders in a creative manner.

"Yes, madam."

"I will inspect the rest of my stock now in order to organize the buyers' catalog." Ursola strode to the cell door, her robes swishing around her bare legs. A pity Cayle wasn't here, she thought, but this sense of satisfaction would last until she returned to her mansion.

Life had its moments of piquancy.

"This way, madam." Alain gestured to the right.

"Bitch," Jannike spat. "I should have killed you while you slept."

Ursola wheeled to face the slave. "You didn't have the stomach for it. That's the difference between us. I learn from mistakes. You didn't because I've snared you in my trap again. Powerless. Think about that, slave."

With that parting shot, Ursola gestured for Alain to show her the way. She pulled out her communicator and enabled the note function. "Link to Tratoy RE possible purchase."

Satisfied, she continued with her day. Killing the slave wouldn't make the upstart suffer nearly enough. This plan was much, much better.

Jannike's heart beat in double-time. Goddess, the widow bitch had given her men permission to rape her. A scream clawed at her throat, but she contained her cry, the lurch of fear attempting to ram from her chest.

History repeating itself, and she was powerless to stop the outcome.

She screwed her eyes shut and attempted to tamp down her escalating panic. A tear ran over her cheek, and to top off her misery, the prickles under her skin fired to life in vicious mockery.

Goddess, Ry and the crew, or Lynx and Shiloh had to come for her. She had to believe they were doing everything they could to mount a rescue.

Don't panic.

It was the worst reaction, yet she couldn't halt the chatter of her teeth, the white-knuckle squeeze of her hands because she knew, deep-down, they wouldn't arrive in time to save her.

The man in charge would take his prize as soon as the widow bitch left.

Fight. We'll come for you.

Ry had made the promise the instant they'd realized the tracker lizards were after them.

Shiloh and Lynx had voiced similar promises, and all three males had meant them.

Despite the nausea dancing in the pit of her stomach, Jannike lifted her head.

She'd survived this before.

She could do it again.

Time ticked away, distinguished by a drip in the sanitizer unit.

Drip. Drip. Drip.

Jannike bit on her bottom lip to stop the tremble.

Drip. Drip. Drip.

Goddess. Too much time to think. Too much time to worry. *Too much time.*

Drip. Drip. Drip.

She examined the chains, the silver synmetal bracelets circling her wrists. Studied the ones at her ankles.

In the distance, male laughter echoed, resounding against the syncrete walls. Footsteps approached. More male laughter.

Jannike swallowed, fought a brief yet hard battle to contain the scream pressing for release.

Shiloh and Lynx would come. They'd promised.

All she needed to do was stay alive.

The male laughter became louder. Excited and full of anticipation.

Drip. Drip. Drip.

A click sounded and the door to her cell sprang open.

She was out of time.

Chapter Fourteen

Mogens greeted them at the gangway of the *Indefatigable*. "I've located Jannike's tracker. It's not far from here in a warehouse facility."

Shiloh and Lynx exchanged a glance.

"That gels with the information the man gave us at the butcher's shop," Camryn said. "Mogens, you'll never believe it, but this guy was a masculine version of Jannike. He had light brown hair instead of blonde but his eyes—his eyes were gray like Jannike's. The shape of his face, his features were the same."

Interest and curiosity shone in Gweneth. "Jannike never mentioned family here."

"Her father—no stepfather—sold her into slavery," Ry said. "She mentioned it not long after we first met but doesn't speak much of the past."

"I've asked." Camryn shrugged. "She changes the subject."

"We need to check out security," Kelvin boomed from the far side of the ship.

Camryn jumped, and even Ry looked startled. Kelvin walked toward them, holding the calibore in his arms. The two markowls perched on top of his head.

Royal let out a plaintive cry and stretched out his arms. Shiloh brushed past and the calibore jumped into his arms.

Kelvin whistled and chirped to the two birds, then nodded.

"The markowls have offered to do a flyover to check out the security outside the warehouse," Kelvin boomed at a slightly lower register.

"You communicate with them?" Camryn asked.

Lynx nodded. "Saved our butts a couple of times."

"As long as they don't risk capture," Shiloh said to Kelvin.

Another series of whistles ensued, and the markowls took off, swooping above the heads of the *Indy* crew, rapid wingbeats taking them outdoors.

"Do you have spare weapons?" Lynx asked.

"I'll get them." Kaya trotted away to undertake the chore.

"Do we wait until the early hours? Or do we go now?"

"Wait for the markowls' report," Lynx suggested. "They'll give us an idea of what to expect."

Shiloh growled. "I want to go now. I don't like her in the hands of those people."

Kelvin peered outside. "The markowls are returning."

The small birds darted through the open gangway door. They burst into a series of chirps and whistles. Kelvin listened closely.

"The outer security is minimal. Two men with weapons. They are circling the perimeter of the building, but the markowls mentioned both men appear in a slumber."

"Let's go," Shiloh said.

The crew looked to their captain.

"My gut is screaming." Ry glanced at each of them. "I don't

think we should wait. In pairs. Camryn, I want you to stay on the ship. I can't function if I'm worried about you."

Camryn scowled. "Understood. I don't like it, though. Take Mogens in case Jannike requires medical attention."

Kaya arrived with weapons. She handed blasters to Shiloh and Lynx. "You might be better off shifting to feline. Better senses. Claws to rip. If they see you, they won't expect intelligence."

"She's right," Camryn said. "You'll have Mogens, Nanu, and Kaya to open doors. The three of you would be better in feline form."

Shiloh considered. "It's not our normal way. We tend to fight with traditional weapons and keep our felines as backup."

"You have backup," Kaya pointed out.

Shiloh returned the weapon. His arm itched, and he scratched it hard enough to leave welts.

"I agree with her," Lynx said.

"Let's move out," Ry ordered.

The heat had faded from the cycle, the solar-star low in the sky but still illuminating the landscape.

Shiloh shifted. He set a fast pace, trotting down the ramp, every sense screaming to get to Jannike. Not that he understood the urges writhing inside him. They were just as irritating as the itch that had returned to his skin. Lynx loped after him and increased his pace until he caught up.

Phrull, Shiloh thought. *Jannike, hang on. We're coming for you. And we're gonna take out those bastards who caught us.*

Wait...what? Shiloh almost tripped over his feet as he turned his head and gaped at Lynx. *What the phrull?*

I heard you and answered, Lynx said.

How? Never mind. Might be handy.

Beside him, Lynx chuffed out a sound that resembled humor. So much stuff their parents never told them. Mates. Who the phrull knew?

The warehouse came into view, and they slowed.

I don't know what's going on, but I need Jannike, Lynx confessed as they scanned their surroundings and searched for danger. *Still need you, but I crave her too.*

Shiloh relaxed at Lynx's confession. He hadn't known how he'd explain his desires, hadn't wanted to scare Lynx or make him think he was returning to his old ways.

A man appeared around the corner of the building. His skin was a pale purple, his garments a darker hue. If the male turned around, Shiloh knew his eyes would be pale and full of nothingness.

What the hell is a Torgon doing here? Lynx asked.

Couldn't get a job elsewhere. No one would hire this idiot. Ready?

Ready.

Shiloh slinked closer with Lynx creeping from a different angle.

Now!

Lynx pounced perfectly in time with him. The Torgon went down with a grunt, not having time to draw his weapon. Shiloh slashed the man's face with his claws. *Snap.* The life seeped from the Torgon, and Shiloh moved, not feeling the slightest remorse for breaking his neck.

They followed the building around and met Kaya and Nanu.

"Is the guard out of action?" she asked.

Shiloh chuffed a positive response and she nodded.

"Small entrance door this way. Ry and Mogens are waiting." Kaya hustled off in the direction she'd come from. Shiloh noticed her constant sweep of the area and how her weapon never lowered.

They're good, he said.

Not surprised after seeing Jannike in action, Lynx replied.

"Ready?" Kaya asked. "We'll split up again and take out any guards we come across."

A noise behind had them all whirling around, weapons trained on the newcomers. Three men. One familiar.

"Hold," Kaya barked. "It's the dude from the market. What are you doing here?"

"I think my sister is in there," the man spat.

Ry shifted, and the man blinked. "Jannike?"

"Yes. Hurry. I don't have much time to do this and get back before Ursola wakes."

"You look like Jannike, but if you're lying and try to hurt her, I'll kill you myself," Ry snapped.

"Hurry," the man urged.

"Ready?" Kaya asked again. At their collective nods, she eased the door open, and their group flowed inside, weapons at the ready.

This way, Shiloh said, catching Jannike's scent. He padded along an aisle. Cages lined both sides, most full of animals and other creatures. Dead eyes watched their progress, creatures that had lost hope. He made a vow he'd free them and stop whoever was in charge of this enterprise. But Jannike first.

A shout sounded from the other end of the building. A cheer, followed by a scream of fury, the clank of chains.

"Jannike," Kaya whispered.

Shiloh increased his speed. Lynx and Ry sped at his side. His gaze took in the horror in one quick glance and temper spread in a red wave of rage.

Slash. Crunch. Slap. He became a frenzy of claws and teeth and cold determination, slashing at screaming men, slapping them down, killing cleanly when they deserved far worse.

Behind him a blaster discharged.

Their enemies didn't have a chance. Taken unawares, only one managed to draw his weapon. The blast shot harmlessly into the air when Nanu swung the butt of his blaster into the fat man's gut.

Shiloh and Lynx went straight for Jannike.

The short, rotund man coughed, held his stomach, and started pleading, "It was just a bit of fun. That's all. We didn't hurt her."

Fury lashed Shiloh, shredding his steely control, and secs later the man lay dead at their feet.

Lynx shifted. Ry scooped up the keys dangling from the dead man's belt, and he unlocked the chains holding Jannike upright.

Ry attempted to take her into his arms, but Shiloh snarled a warning.

Ry froze. "Let me pick her up, damn it. She needs medical help."

Shiloh snarled again, easing his body between Jannike and Ry. He didn't know why, but the idea of another male—anyone apart from Lynx—touching her made his feline panic.

"Captain." Mogens glided closer and yanked on Ry's arm. "Let them care for her, Captain. They're her mates. Remember how you get protective of Camryn?"

Mates. *Yes.*

"Phrull that," the stranger with Jannike's eyes snapped. "Let me see her." Fearlessly, he pushed past Ry and planted himself in front of Shiloh. "Let me see if she's my sister."

"C-Cayle?" Jannike's weak voice pushed past Shiloh's possessiveness. It was the note of wonder, the hint of shock in her croak.

"Here's a robe." Kaya handed over a black garment. "She'll want to be covered."

Shiloh took the robe and gently drew her arms into the sleeves while Lynx held her quivering body upright. Her eyes appeared bloodshot and her cheeks bore the track marks of tears.

"Let me see my sister," the man demanded again.

Lynx took a position on one side, and Shiloh flanked her other, their strength keeping her on her feet. Shiloh felt the tiny quivers of her muscles and had to work to tamp down his wrath.

"They died too easy," he snarled.

"Who is responsible?" Ry demanded.

"Jannike. Goddess, it is you," the man said.

Jannike stared back, her gaze assessing. "You're a slave?"

"It was the only way I had of trying to locate you."

"This is your brother?" Lynx asked.

"Cayle. He's a few rotations older than me," Jannike whispered. A tear trickled down her cheek as she struggled for freedom.

"Goddess, I didn't think I'd ever find you." Cayle ignored Shiloh's snarl and yanked Jannike into his arms.

She didn't fight, which was the reason Shiloh managed to stay the feline protest inside his mind.

Steady, Shiloh, Lynx said. *He's her brother. He's our family now too.*

We're keeping her.

Lynx shot him a look—one that said, are you phrullin crazy? *I'm keeping both of you.*

"Captain, we need to move before someone comes to investigate," Kaya prompted, weapon still at the ready.

"What about the other prisoners?" Mogens asked.

"We let them out and arrange for their transport back to their home planets," Lynx said.

"I can help with that." Cayle turned away from his sister. "My friends and I are part of an underground escape network for slaves. I can arrange transport. It would be best if the captives stayed here at the warehouse and kept out of sight. The auction will take place in a few cycles. I can shift them before then."

"What 'bout your cover, man?" one of the men who'd arrived with Jannike's brother asked. "You're more valuable in place at the mansion."

"They're on to me. Widow has a private investigator, and he's not stupid. He suspects I'm responsible for the widow's problems but can't prove it. Only a matter of time."

"The widow is the biggest seller on Manx Two," Jannike said in a low voice. "We take her out, cut off her business at the knees. Free her slaves. Put the fear of the goddess into the others who trade in slaves."

Lynx stroked Jannike's arm. "She's right."

"Need to strike now," Jannike said.

Cayle spoke to his two friends. "Gather the troops. We'll need five here to help with the captives, reassure them, and arrange passage to their home planets. We'll get them to Manx One and send them home from there. We put our plan into action. All slaves on a go-slow. Those who can leave their place of residence go to the central meeting point. Neil, you take care of passing the word around."

One of the men jogged away.

"Let me clean you up." Mogens edged closer, his attention on Shiloh and Lynx rather than Jannike. "You'll let me?"

Shiloh gave a curt nod, but a growl escaped him. Mogens froze.

"Let him work." Lynx tugged Shiloh away. Even so, they both watched Mogens' every move.

I don't like him touching her, Lynx said.

Shiloh glared at Mogens. *She trusts him.*

Ry and Kaya joined them. "We'll drop by the *Indy* and leave Jannike there. Can you help us or are you going to want to stay with Jannike?"

Jannike's skin burned where Mogens cleaned off the blood. She bit her inner lip and focused on not wincing. She wanted to bathe, to cleanse her body and wash away...well, she wanted to feel clean again.

Her ears pricked. They were going to leave her on the *Indy*. No, no, no. *Hell no.* That wouldn't do. She intended to spit in the widow's face then knife the traitorous bitch in the heart.

"I'm going to the mansion." Jannike was pleased to hear her strength and decisiveness. *More like her normal self.*

"No," Shiloh said. "You've been through enough. Let us take care of this for you."

"This is my right." Unspoken was her need for revenge.

"Revenge doesn't help," Ry said. "It doesn't change the past."

"You killed your brother. Give me the same right." Jannike

winced, the sting from Mogens' touch moving past the point of discomfort. "Enough. That hurts."

Mogens started to argue, but Lynx stayed him and took the cloth from the seer. The stinging sensation faded when Lynx continued the chore.

"I don't think—" Shiloh began.

"You wouldn't wait in a safe place while others took care of your problems," Jannike told them in a low voice. "You're not making Lynx stay on the *Indy*."

"I want to," Shiloh whispered.

"Let me finish this. Please." Jannike caught the slight softening of his face and knew she'd won. Good. Soon she'd knife the widow in her traitorous black heart. She'd never bully or buy or sell another being again.

Ursola woke, confused for a sec about her location. Then she remembered.

Cayle.

She turned her head, expecting to see him beside her on the big gel-bed.

One of the gel-pillows held a faint imprint from his head. He hadn't been gone for long since the pillow hadn't puffed back to its natural shape. He'd probably disappeared to prepare pre-dinner drinks and snacks. Ursola flipped onto her back and smiled up at the gel-bed canopy.

So, this was happiness.

Time passed, and Cayle didn't arrive.

Frowning, she reached for the in-house communicator and rang the kitchen.

"Yes, mistress. Can I help with something?"

"Is Cayle there?"

"Yes, mistress."

A slow smile of expectation curled across her lips. "Tell him to bring my usual evening fare." She disconnected before the slave's confirmation and tossed the communicator on the end of her gel-bed. It toppled to the floor but she didn't bother to pick it up.

She imagined Cayle setting the tray on the side table and padding across to her. She'd tell him to strip and watch as he removed each garment. A tingle sprang to life at her breasts, and she lazily stroked one nipple. The sashay of pleasure twirled down her body and settled in the needy spot between her legs. She moved her hips from left to right in a happy dance.

The door flung open and thumped against the wall stop, taking her by surprise. She jerked upright. Cayle's face held none of its usual tender expression, not a hint of a smile. Instead, he appeared determined, his normal deference absent. This was not the face of a pliable slave, and a sliver of fear inched into her mind. She glanced in the direction of her communicator and saw it was out of reach.

The door opened wider, and several other people marched inside as if they had every right.

All males. Big men. Strangers.

"What do you think you're doing?" she demanded in an icy voice, and she lifted the thin cover in an attempt to cover her breasts. "Get out of my chamber."

Without a word, the men parted, and a woman dressed in black strolled toward her gel-bed. A familiar woman and one she'd last seen chained in her facility.

How? What? If she'd managed to escape, why hadn't Alain contacted her?

"What are you doing here?" Ursola demanded, turning to Cayle in an attempt to regain control of the situation. "Why did you bring these people to my chamber?"

"My sister wanted to meet you." Cayle's gray eyes glittered like the blocks of ice on Manx One—dangerous and merciless—and she kicked herself for not noticing it before. Something inside her cracked, bleeding through her hauteur and confidence, letting in fear. The internal shield that kept her armored—shattered because a man had betrayed her again.

She'd loved him, and he'd deceived her.

Despite the avalanche of emotions, Ursola reverted to normal behavior. She shored up her courage and lifted her chin. "I have nothing to say to this woman. Get out of my chamber."

"You treated slaves like commodities when you were married to Neot Verona. Part of me understood. That was the way you were raised. You changed when your husband died," the female slave ground out.

"You killed Neot."

"We both know you poisoned him and set me up to take the blame."

Ursola stared into those ice-gray eyes and knew Cayle spoke the truth. They were brother and sister. Stupid, she thought. Too self-involved, seeing only what she wanted to see.

"You lie," she said calmly in contradiction of her rioting emotions. Despite trying to keep them at bay, the betrayal beat at her mind like a slave wielding a stout whipping stick.

Ah, her panic button, she thought in relief. If she could slide across the gel-bed and get to that, outside help would come from a trustworthy source. A silent alarm. They'd never notice.

"Let me get a robe. We can talk about this." Ursola glanced at the silent men surrounding the slaves. Her gaze roamed their muscular bodies, and her heart beat a little faster. What a prize they would be. She could force them to wear behavior collars and they'd be under her control. "Perhaps we can come up with a solution." She kept sliding across the gel-bed toward her goal.

"Wouldn't touch you with a long pole," one of them spat, his bright green eyes blazing.

Her breath caught as she saw his pupils narrow to slits. A shifter? Oh, what a stunning slave he would make. Her gaze went to the others, and the thrill of discovery pulsed within her. All three men were of the same race. She let the cover fall from her upper torso, a slice of pique grabbing her in a chokehold when not one of the men reacted to her charms.

"Stop where you are," the female slave ordered.

Confident now of attaining her goal, Ursola ignored the order.

The shot of a blaster rang out. Ursola screamed as fiery pain sliced across her biceps. She slapped her fingers over the spot, but lifeforce dripped through her fingers. "You shot me."

"I warned you," the slave said.

For the first time true fear filled Ursola. Tears filled her eyes, overflowed and ran down her cheeks. Maybe she could gain their sympathy. Worth a try since it was a successful part of her repertoire.

"Crying won't help," the female slave scoffed. "I'm not in a forgiving mood. You gave your men permission to use me."

"You're a slave."

The blaster fired so quickly, Ursola didn't register the pain in her other arm straightaway. The slave's eyes glittered, and Ursola knew she stared death in the face.

"Finish it, sweetheart," one of the men said.

Another male, equally stunning, stepped to the slave's other side. "You're better than her."

"She doesn't deserve a clean kill," the female slave spat.

"I'll pay you." Ursola rapidly calculated the cost of freedom. "You'll be rich with more power than you can imagine."

The largest male started to laugh. "You have no idea who we are. We have plenty of power without taking yours."

"You can use me however you want," Ursola said in a seductive purr.

The female slave laughed, the sound containing not a shred of humor. "My mates. They're not interested in you."

"Now she admits it," one of the males murmured.

Ursola lunged for the panic button, pressing the white circle with a trace of smugness. "You're too late. Help is on the way. They'll capture you, collar you, and I'll take pleasure using you all."

"The panic button doesn't work," Cayle said. "I disarmed it rotations ago. No one is coming to your aid. Finish this, Jannike. The bitch will never repent. She's too self-absorbed."

The blaster fire came secs later. It burned through the center of her chest and stole her breath. Two sets of gray eyes stared at her, not in triumph or passion or excitement but in determination.

She gaped back. How had she miscalculated so much? Used one. Loved the other. The thought haunted her as she gasped her last breath and toppled into death.

Chapter Fifteen

Jannike stared at the widow's body. "I thought I'd feel better."

Cayle moved to her side, pushing Shiloh out of the way. "Take comfort in the fact she can't hurt anyone else."

"Others will take her place. It is the way of this planet."

"No." Cayle's confidence grabbed her attention.

"How are you going to stop a centuries-old tradition?" Jannike demanded.

"Several rotations ago, I helped organize an underground movement to get some of the ill-treated slaves to safety. We've managed to rescue many. With Ursola Verena gone, the auctions won't attract as many buyers. We can get more slaves out, using Ursola's gold and try to put a halt to the remaining auctions."

"We should leave," Ry said.

"Can you take the house slaves with you?" Cayle asked. "Do you have room to take them on your ship? As far as Manx One? I can give them currency and get them help to travel from there."

"How many?" Ry asked.

"Nine," Cayle said. "Two males, seven females."

"It will be crowded, but we can fit that number for a short journey." Ry didn't hesitate.

"I'll get them organized." Cayle strode from the chamber without a backward glance at the widow.

"I get the feeling your brother isn't coming with us," Ry said.

"No." Now that the widow was gone, Jannike felt empty. Exhausted. She wobbled, felt her knees buckle.

Shiloh scooped her up to halt her tumble to the floor.

"Take her back to the *Indy*," Ry said. "Kaya and Nanu are still down below. They can help us with Cayle's people."

"Put me down. I can walk."

"As soon as we get outside and onto the skytrain to the spaceport," Shiloh said.

Jannike knew a compromise when she heard one. The truth was she felt better when either Shiloh or Lynx touched her. Stronger.

The entranceway was full of confused people.

"Silence," Cayle hollered, and the area fell silent. He started to speak, to explain and it was easy to see the hope spring to life on their faces.

Jannike met her brother's gaze and hoped they'd have a chance to talk before the *Indy* left Manx Two.

"I never wanted to return to this planet," she murmured. "And if I hadn't, I wouldn't have found my brother."

"You don't talk about your family," Lynx said.

Jannike made a scoffing sound. "You don't talk about yours either. I know you have a brother, and that's all."

"Which is more than we knew about your family," Lynx shot back.

"We'll have the entire trip to Viros to get to know one another better," Shiloh said.

Lynx and Shiloh shared a glance, and Jannike had no trouble reading their concern. "When we separated at the haven, you told me you'd come for me if I was the one who was captured. You told me to survive." Jannike swallowed, her mind shoving her back into the cell with those men. "You told me you'd come for me. Ry told me he'd come for me. You're honorable men—men I trust. All three of you came for me, got me out of that cell, and allowed me to finish what started rotations ago."

"Jannike," Shiloh murmured.

She swallowed again, finding this harder than she'd ever imagined, yet the words had to be said to help slam the door on her past.

"I know I might have nightmares, times when the past clobbers me over the head, but I hope, I hope you'll both be there. I...I've come to admire you both." As close as she was comfortable in admitting they might have a future together.

"Hope it's a sight more than admiration, sweetheart," Lynx whispered. "Because we want you."

"Maybe a threesome is not the way our people do things, or your race either." Shiloh's voice was a rumble against her neck as he strode out into the street, still carrying her. "But we don't care. We're following our guts."

"Our hearts," Lynx added with a glare at his friend. "We'll be as patient as you need."

"Way to go, Jannike!" a familiar voice called.

"Woot. Woot!" Nanu shouted. "See you back at the *Indy*."

"Your friends are going to tease you," Shiloh said.

Lynx's green eyes twinkled as he winked at her. "Should we punch them?"

"No, they're my friends. I get to tease them back. About the patience thing. That's what I'm trying to tell you. This prickling beneath my skin—it's sending me mad. I need you both."

"But do you want us, sweetheart?" Shiloh asked.

"I...I think so," she whispered. "You're good men. You remind me of Ry, and he's one of my best friends. I've never met anyone like Ry before, and now that I have, I don't... I don't know what to do. You're mates, and I shouldn't want to insert myself into your relationship."

"You fought your inclinations. You're still fighting and putting yourself at risk." Lynx's tone edged to severe.

"There was a good chance I'd die," Jannike said bluntly. "Silly to take you both down with me."

"You could have discussed this with us." Lynx's frown hovered close to accusing. "You know...that talking thing people do?"

"Phrullin' right," Shiloh agreed.

Lynx grinned, and Jannike realized, yet again, that two men would be much harder to manage than one. They intended to maintain their chase, no matter her indecision.

Ry, Nanu, Kaya, and Cayle arrived at the *Indy* with the nine ex-slaves. Each carried a small bag of possessions. Some of the younger ones appeared scared and confused.

"Jannike, can we talk?" Cayle asked.

"Do you want one of us to stay with you?" Lynx asked.

"No, it's fine."

"Can the slave bands be removed without giving them pain?" Mogens asked.

"Yes," Cayle replied. "They're all deactivated and just for show."

By common assent everyone left the bridge, leaving Jannike alone with her brother. They stared at each other.

"I've been searching for you for rotations. As soon as I realized Ralcid had sold you... I'm so sorry. He should have sold me. I was older."

"I was a female, small and puny. I couldn't work on the land. None of that was your fault."

"You're not small and puny now."

Jannike smiled. "No. Our mother?"

"She died of a fever. Ralcid remarried and had other children. They kept me around to work the land until their other children grew older," Cayle said. "Ralcid died in a knife fight at the Garter and Star tavern. I saw this as my chance to find you."

"But you wear a slave band."

"I learned about the widow and how you'd been sentenced for murder. Your escape didn't rate a mention. The best way to learn about you was to enter the widow's household. I asked my stepmother to sell me into slavery. It was good for her since she received currency. I'd learned from my research that Ursola liked strong men and took lovers. I hoped I would attract her."

"You took a risk. Even with your hair that color, you still look a lot like me."

"She didn't recognize me. She fell in love with me," Cayle said with distaste.

"You—"

"Yes, and it made me feel dirty every time I had to touch her. One benefit though—she gave me more freedom than the others. I saw a chance to do good, and along with some of the slaves from other households, we set up an underground movement and took the opportunity to create havoc with the upper classes."

"You're staying." A statement.

"Yes. Not permanently, but long enough to create a better, fairer system for the poor. No one should own another being, it doesn't matter what race they belong to. We are all equal no matter what the color of our skin or our planet of birth."

"You'll come to Viros?"

"Yes. Once things are settled here."

Jannike blinked, her chest tight with emotion—hope and love. Things she hadn't allowed herself to feel when she thought of family. "I can't believe you allowed yourself to get sold into slavery because of me."

"Ralcid had no right selling you. Our mother didn't know," Cayle said. "She was distraught when she learned what he'd done."

"She didn't know?"

"She never forgave him. He told her they couldn't afford the child they'd arranged through the birth lab, and he'd had to sell you to make ends meet. She believed him until she followed him to the tavern one day. He was gambling. He should have sold me. I was older and could take care of myself. I know what the widow's husband did to you, what the widow did." His voice hardened. "Dying wasn't good enough for either of them."

"You didn't have it easy either," Jannike countered. "Neither did any of the other slaves. You—we—can't let past experiences color our future."

Cayle's glance held shrewdness, understanding. "Sometimes it's hard to let go entirely."

Jannike fought the shiver that racked her body.

"Jannike." Shiloh burst onto the bridge, Lynx following close behind. "What's wrong?"

The worry on their faces, the way they scanned the bridge for signs of danger. They were behaving like Ry.

"I'm fine. Cayle and I were talking."

Lynx shot Cayle a hard look, his green eyes distrustful. A growl rumbled from him.

"Stop," Jannike ordered. "Cayle's my brother. He won't hurt me."

"I've been searching for her for rotations," Cayle said to Shiloh. "I'd run out of leads and didn't know what had happened to her after she left Manx Two."

"And now you know she'll be on Viros," Lynx said.

Cayle folded his arms across his chest. "My turn to ask questions. What do you do on Viros? How can I be sure you'll look after my baby sister?"

"We're traders," Lynx said after a quick glance at Shiloh. "We would never hurt Jannike, but she is a warrior, capable of caring for herself. She has friends who will kick our arses if we even thought about mistreating her."

Shiloh met Cayle's gaze with directness. "She is our mate, even though she still fights her body. We're a team, and we'd rather cut off our right arms than hurt her."

Cayle gave a crisp nod. "Where will I find you when I arrive on Viros?"

Shiloh and Lynx exchanged another look.

"We're not sure where we'll be because we haven't discussed our future yet, but I can give you my brother's link code. He'll know where we are should we decide to leave Viros," Shiloh said.

Cayle accepted the code and walked over to her. "I'd better go. We need to prepare for the backlash from the ruling class."

Jannike stood and wrapped her arms around his broad shoulders. She leaned against his chest, drew his scent deep into her lungs. She felt his lips move against her temple and sighed while trying to store memories of her big brother. She'd never thought she'd see him again and had never let herself dare to hope. A visit to Manx Two was dangerous, out of the question.

Despite everything, she couldn't be sorry because she'd gained a brother.

Family.

She smiled as she stepped away from him and took in Shiloh and Lynx.

Yes, she'd gained family and the opportunity for so much more if she faced the risk.

I feel as if I'm bursting out of my skin, Lynx said to Shiloh. *Before, when I thought of touching Jannike, the worst thing that happened was a sense of disloyalty to you.*

The same with me. But we can't rush her. She seems all right, but that phrullin bastard abused her. We have to take this easy, let her call the pace.

Lynx sighed. *At least we have each other. That should take off the edge.*

"I guess you'll be sharing my quarters. I'll show you my cabin and give you a quick tour. You've already seen the bridge." Jannike's rapid steps took her away from them. Lynx exchanged a glance with Shiloh, unsure of their next move. Neither of them knew what to do with this efficient Jannike, who had to be hurting inside.

Jannike will like Cimmaron.

Yeah, they're very alike, Lynx replied.

"Galley. Dining room. If you use the galley, clean up after yourself. Ry likes to keep things tidy. We take turns cooking. Can you cook?"

Lynx spluttered out a laugh while Shiloh plain cackled.

Finally, Shiloh wiped his eyes, and they moved past the square room with its tidy racks of ship ration packs and other pieces of equipment Lynx had never seen before. The dining room held one big oval table, both it and the chairs fixed to the floor in case of turbulence. Colorful pictures covered the walls, many of them depicting Jannike and her friends. It was almost homey, Lynx thought, full of family memories.

"I can cook," Shiloh said. "If we want to eat, we shouldn't rely on Lynx. He can burn a cooking vessel without breaking a sweat. He even manages to muck up ration packs."

"Can't cook or won't?" Jannike asked, her spurt of curiosity bringing satisfaction in Lynx.

"Never learned." There was so much they didn't know about each other. The voyage to Viros would be good, give them a chance to become more intimate and cement their bonds before they faced his parents. Oh, he knew of the outcome already. They'd kick him out of the House of the Cat for good. Jannike was not of the House. And Shiloh...well, Shiloh would be an even bigger source of tension.

Fun times.

And Jarlath, his older brother and heir to the throne—Lynx could imagine his pompous reaction. Ellard, Jarlath's bodyguard and Shiloh's older brother, he might be more accepting. Shiloh's parents—no, he doubted they'd approve.

Yep, anyway he looked at the situation, they were phrulled.

"Recreation room. Training room," Jannike said. "We train most days when we're between destinations. Ry likes us to keep fit and battle-ready. It's saved our butts a time or two."

At his side, Shiloh radiated approval. A selection of weapons, from swords to stun blasters and fighting sticks, sat securely in racks. Much of the equipment in this area was similar to that on their ship. A halo machine to turn the entire room into a fuller training experience. The recreation room, however, was different with more of the strange equipment.

"I don't know what half of the stuff is in here," Shiloh said.

"Much of it comes from Earth." Jannike gestured at a pile of boxes strapped into a wall cage. "Some belongs to Camryn, and some like the games, puzzles, and books we purchased during our visit. We have entertainment discs from Earth. Photos and videos from our visit."

"We haven't visited Earth before. What quadrant is it in?" Shiloh asked.

"It's not in this galaxy. It is far away. We have traveled for many portion rotations and used four different gates to get closer to Viros."

Lynx nodded and studied the pictures and posters decorating the walls. In this room, they were like a snapshot of the different places they'd visited. Colorful and full of family again. He increased the length of his strides to catch Shiloh and Jannike.

"The cabins are down this corridor. We each have one of our own." She hesitated. "There is one spare."

"Do you want us to use it?" Shiloh asked.

"No!" she blurted. "No, you can share mine." She frowned at them. "If you want to."

"We want," Shiloh exchanged a glance with Lynx. "But we're not intending to hurry you either."

"I...thank you," she said in a formal tone. The next instant, she rolled her eyes and laughed. "I like you both—I've told you that—but this...this urge to mate with you feels weird. I don't like the element of coercion. When Ry and Camryn met I thought..." She snorted, a sound of self-derision. "I didn't realize how hard it was to fight the compulsion."

"Why do you fight?" Shiloh asked.

"I...I like my life aboard the *Indy*. I don't want to leave my friends and start a new life. One of our crew—Amme—she fell in love with an Earthman. She stayed on Earth, but at least she knows she will see us again. Ry has promised Camryn we will visit her family in the future."

Lynx jumped in before Shiloh said something he shouldn't. He sensed if Jannike knew of his royal heritage, she'd flee in the opposite direction. "Shiloh and I have spent rotations trading and running freight. We don't spend much time on Viros."

"What does Ry intend to do after visiting Viros?" Shiloh asked.

"We've discussed it but haven't come to a decision," Jannike said. "We're a team," she added. "We all have a financial interest in the *Indy,* and our decisions have equal weight."

"We'll have to pick up our ship from where we left it—if it's still there," Lynx said.

"It better be," Shiloh growled.

"This is my cabin." Jannike pressed a button before the door slid open.

He and Shiloh followed her inside. The cabin was bigger than he'd expected and the gel-bed large enough to fit them all. Photos and travel souvenirs covered one of the walls. Several swords and

blasters sat in a security rack. Storage cupboards filled another wall.
Like the rest of the ship, her cabin was tidy.

"I have my own sanitizer room through there," Jannike said.

"Way better than our ship," Shiloh said.

"I want to cleanse," Jannike said without warning.

"We'll go and see if we can help Ry with anything," Lynx said.

Her expression of relief told him it was the right thing to
do—give her privacy—even though every instinct shouted at him
to stay.

"But—"

Lynx grabbed Shiloh and dragged his friend from the cabin.

"What the phrull?" Shiloh protested.

"If we push her, we'll lose her," Lynx said. "She might have
admitted our mate claim earlier, but she's had time to think. It's
enough that she's allowing us to share her cabin and sleep beside
her. She's not shutting us out totally."

"I don't like it."

"This isn't about you," Lynx snapped. "We should contact
home."

"I don't like that idea either."

Lynx scratched an itchy spot on his back. "On that we agree. One
call. Who do we talk to and what do we tell them?"

"I vote for Ellard. He'll listen before he lectures," Shiloh said.

"Agreed. Don't tell him anything. Just say we're on our way
home."

"Works for me."

Fifteen mins later, with the engines of the *Indy* vibrating
beneath their feet, Shiloh pushed in his brother's comm code.
They'd left Manx Two five mins earlier and already the planet
was a small red circle on the horizon. Lynx watched Shiloh shift
his weight from foot to foot—fidgeting, a sure sign of nerves. He
stepped closer and slipped his arm around Shiloh's waist.

"Shiloh?" Ellard's voice was much clearer than he would've

expected.

"Yeah." Shiloh paused to clear his throat. "We're on our way home."

"Good. That's good." Ellard sounded pleased. "How long?"

"We're coming from Manx Two. Maybe quarter of a rotation."

"Excellent," Ellard said.

The eagerness in his voice surprised Lynx. Shiloh shrugged, and Lynx wished the communicator had visual as well as audio.

"You remember Marcus Cloud?" Ellard asked. "He had a farm out of the city."

"Past the lake."

"That's right. Once you land at the spaceport, call me then tender out to the Cloud farm. Jarlath and I will meet you there."

"The spaceport," Shiloh said. "But—"

A loud crackle sounded.

"Ellard. Ellard? Phrull, he's gone."

The ship jumped beneath their feet, and at the controls, Nanu cursed. "Damn storm. We hit this coming in to Manx Two. Slowed us down. You'd better strap in."

Ry ran onto the bridge and strapped into the last empty seat. "Report."

"The same space storm," Nanu said. "We lost communications. What about the passengers?"

Ry scanned the instrument panel. "Kaya and Mogens are with them. They'll make sure they're safe. Did you manage to get through to Viros?"

"Spoke to my brother," Shiloh said.

"He said something about a spaceport." Lynx's brow furrowed. "We don't have one on Viros."

"We're to meet him at the Cloud farm. He called your brother Jarlath." Shiloh's face telegraphed the puzzlement Lynx experienced.

Nanu tossed his head, and the beads on the ends of his hair

clacked together. "What else would he call him? Does he have a nickname?"

"Yeah," Lynx said. "I've never heard him call my brother Jarlath before."

"Weird," Shiloh agreed. *Ellard is always so proper.*

And why wouldn't we meet at home? Why out at the farm?

He sounded pleased to hear from us.

He did, Lynx said. *Did you plug in the right number?*

Shiloh snorted aloud. *You think that wasn't Ellard. It sounded like him.*

"You're speaking telepathically now," Ry said.

"Sorry," Lynx said. "Didn't mean to be rude."

"Is this common amongst felines?"

"Not that we know of," Lynx said. "We haven't always been able to do this. Not until we arrived on Manx Two."

"What about Jannike?" Ry asked.

"Not so far," Lynx said. "But we haven't... I mean..."

"That's good." Ry's expression belied his words. "She...that bastard..."

"We want her," Shiloh said. "It will be at her pace, but we don't intend to let her back away either."

Ry tapped his fingers on his knee. "A routine will be good for her. And with the two of you around, she won't have time to go into her head too much."

"Any advice?" Lynx asked.

"Don't treat her like a sick person," Ry said.

"Give her a bit of romance." Nanu added his opinion. "Feed her. Make sure she eats."

"Feed her?" Shiloh glanced at Ry to see if Nanu was joking.

"Spend time with her. Learn about each other." Ry grinned. "Woo her."

Lynx frowned. *Phrull, does that mean we can't wander up to her and suggest we get busy in the cabin?*

Shiloh barked out a laugh.

"If you don't want the benefit of my experience..." Ry said.

"Did Ry woo Camryn?" Lynx asked Nanu.

Nanu burst out laughing. "No, every time we turned around, he had her up against the nearest wall with his hands and mouth on her."

"I was wooing her," Ry said.

"If that's what you want to call it." Nanu checked his instruments.

Smirking, Lynx changed the subject. "What can we do to help out while we're on board?" He figured between them, they'd manage to seduce Jannike to their way of thinking sooner rather than later.

"Tell us about Viros," Ry said.

"Sure. It's not a perfect place, but at least none of the people are slaves." Lynx started to tell Ry and Nanu about the class system on Viros, the available opportunities, and how they'd decided to go into trade. He sidestepped several salient points, such as their positions within Virosian society. That could wait until their arrival.

Once the ship was safely through the storm, Shiloh followed Lynx and Ry to the galley.

"You could start on the feeding thing," Ry said, his sly grin bringing a twitch to Shiloh's own lips.

"I don't know." Shiloh winked. "What do you think, Lynx? Do we feed her or shove her up against the nearest wall?"

"Both," Lynx said.

"See, that's what I was thinking."

"I don't want to know. Just promise me you won't hurt her. She's been through enough."

"We know," Shiloh said. "We shared some of the ordeals with her."

Kelvin wandered in, and Royal held up his long arms in a demand for Shiloh to pick him up. He tucked the calibore on his hip and stroked his soft fur.

"How be Jannike?" Kelvin boomed.

The markowls tweeted and chirped from their perch on top of his head.

"She is resting," Lynx said.

"Good. That is good. All of you need to rest."

"You too." Shiloh's gaze went to the wounds at the spots where they'd drunk. They were still evident on Kelvin's arms. "Will you heal?"

"They will scar," Kelvin said. "It matters not. For you and Lynx, Jannike, and the creatures, I would do this again. Tell me, are there forests on your home planet?"

"Yes, outside the city there are farms and forests. The forest is beautiful. Lynx and I used to ride our cambeests there most days. Our brothers too."

"I wish a haven to grow roots and mourn the loss of my mate, my sons. I wish to become one with the land," Kelvin boomed, his expression sad and solemn.

"You wish to die?" Ry asked.

Kelvin's hair rattled when he shook his head. "Life is not the same without my mate. Not die but go into stasis."

Shiloh squeezed Kelvin's shoulder. "I know of several places that might suit. We're to meet our brothers at the Cloud farm. I'll show you then."

"Thank ye," Kelvin boomed.

"We'll be in Jannike's cabin," Lynx said.

"Wait," Mogens said. "I have made a potion for Jannike. It will aid her sleep. And I have a salve. Rub it on any wounds to speed healing."

"Thank you." Shiloh nodded at Ry. "Call us if you require our presence."

SHELLEY MUNRO

With Royal still clinging to him, he and Lynx made their way to Jannike's cabin. Feminine voices came from within, and he hesitated. Lynx showed none of the same hesitation. He hit the door button. The feminine chatter ceased, and Jannike and Camryn watched them with varying reactions. Camryn's expression held intrigue and excitement, while Jannike was plain wary.

Suddenly, Nanu's suggestion of feeding her made sense. It was a caring act, yet not confrontational.

"We brought food and a potion from Mogens," Lynx said. "Some salve too."

For once, Shiloh was pleased with his friend's confidence and swagger. If it were just him, he'd back off, and his gut screamed that they needed to strike a balance between the two approaches.

"Can I pat this handsome fellow?" Camryn asked.

"Royal. He doesn't bite, but he's timid." Shiloh blinked as the calibore sighed in contentment and pushed against Camryn's stroking hand. "Traitor."

The calibore jumped from him to Camryn, and she cried out in delight. "Can I take him with me? I'll bring him straight back if he starts to get upset."

"As long as that's all right with Jannike."

Lynx was sitting on the corner of her gel-bed and plying her with food. Yep, maybe Nanu's idea of feeding her wasn't so stupid.

"Jannike?" Camryn asked.

Jannike ripped her gaze away from Lynx and Camryn chortled.

"Can I take Royal with me?" Camryn repeated her question.

"Sure. He seems to like you."

"I wonder if he'd like some toys. I'm sure I can find something for him to play with—a ball of some sort," Camryn said.

"Maybe you could set him to find Kaya's chocolate stash. I swear she's still got some hidden," Jannike said.

Camryn tapped the side of her nose. "I know where it is. I

tracked down the scent. She tried to camouflage it with perfume, but she can't beat a feline's nose. I might go and have a chat with her, tell her a pregnant woman who is chocolate deprived is a crafty adversary. She might as well give me some." Camryn laughed again and strode from the room with Royal clutched in her arms. A feline on a mission.

"What is chocolate?" Shiloh asked.

"A food?" Lynx queried.

"It's an Earth treat. A sweet. We got hooked on it when we visited Earth at Christmas. Kaya is addicted to the stuff and purchased a large amount before we left."

Lynx frowned. "It's a drug?"

Jannike laughed, and Shiloh found himself smiling at the joyous sound.

"No, it's not a drug though the way Kaya guards her supply you'd think her chocolate more valuable than currency."

"What else did you do on Earth? Tell us while you eat," Lynx said.

"I'm starving," Shiloh said. "We brought enough food for us too. I didn't recognize half of the things on your ration menu. Mogens picked out the things he said you like."

"A sandwich." Jannike gestured at the nearest dish. "That's an Earth food. After our visit we all missed the food. Mogens is good with food and he designed a new menu for us. We were there for a month, which is an Earth word for a portion of their rotation. They celebrate the birth of a god, which is very confusing because many of the people don't believe in his presence. The weather was hot. We swam in a pool and went to the beach. We got a Christmas tree. Wait," Jannike said. "We have photos on a gadget. It will be easier to show you later instead of trying to paint word pictures." She paused to take a bit of her food, which consisted of two squares of light brown stuff and a different type of food squashed in the middle.

"Can I try your food?" Lynx asked.

Jannike held it out to him and he nibbled on the corner, chewing then swallowing.

"My turn." Shiloh was pleased at Jannike's more relaxed state. He directed her hand and the food toward his mouth and bit down.

"My, what sharp teeth you have," she said.

"All the better to nibble you with," Shiloh said.

She froze, her gaze connecting with his, and his heart drummed against the wall of his chest.

Don't scare her, Lynx said.

"Do I scare you?" Shiloh tried very hard to appear nonthreatening. Difficult given his size.

"I know you won't hurt me," she whispered.

Shiloh reached out and brushed a finger over the softness of her cheek. "That's not an answer."

"Eat your meal before it gets cold." Lynx sent him a disapproving glare. *She's not some floozy at the tavern. Jannike isn't a sure thing, and we need her. Do. Not. Scare. Her.*

"Sandwiches don't get cold." Jannike paused and swallowed. "My heart knows neither of you will hurt me, but my mind keeps telling me all men are pigs, that they'll use me, hurt me."

"We won't," Lynx said. "Never on purpose, at least."

"I don't want to eat the rest." She handed the sandwich to Shiloh. "You finish it."

Lynx shifted the tray off the gel-bed. "What do you want to do?"

"I'm so tired. I want to sleep, but every time I close my eyes, I see the jailor and the widow, their gloating faces."

"Mogens said the potion will help you sleep. Why don't you drink that and try to rest. Shiloh and I will sleep with you."

"I don't— I..."

"We're not intending to force you to do anything," Lynx said. "If we feel the urge for sex, we have each other."

Jannike scowled, and Shiloh took heart from that. Next, she raked her nails across her belly, her grimace deepening. "This is your fault."

"Do you think the prickling sensation isn't bothering me or Shiloh? We might not have met in the traditional way, but that doesn't mean our relationship is wrong. Feels right to me. I only have to touch Shiloh, touch you and everything seems right in my world. Hell!" Lynx chuffed out a derisive sound. "I'm even thinking that staying in Viros and having a base would be a good idea. I've never wanted that before."

And you know why. We have to tell her the truth. Shiloh thought Lynx would argue, but he sighed.

"Here, drink this potion thing before Mogens knocks on your cabin and checks. He threatened to, but we said you didn't require his attentions," Lynx said. "You relax and we'll rest beside you."

"I—"

"No sex, but we need to feel close to you. I meant it when I said our skin is jumping too." Lynx yanked his tunic over his head.

Shiloh followed suit then bent to remove his boots and linings. "We can tell you about Viros, then we can have a debate about where we should set up our base."

"We all want a home, to settle in one place," Jannike said. "But we wanted to help Ry find his home planet first. He wanted to learn more about Viros. Maybe we'll end up staying there, or maybe we'll go somewhere else. We decide together."

"We'll go wherever you go," Shiloh said.

"Okay, where to start." Lynx stretched out on Jannike's gel-bed. "Viros has a nearby neighbor—the planet Gramite, which is ruled by the House of Cawdor. There have been periods of war between the House of the Cat and the House of Cawdor. When we left, we were at peace."

"Are the Cawdor shifters too?" Jannike asked, and Shiloh was pleased to feel the tension ease from her body.

"Crow," Lynx said. "They covet our minerals and mines."

Jannike yawned. "Who rules your planet? Do you have a chief?"

"We have a king and the ruling class. The city covers the slope of a hill with the castle at the top. The ruling classes live on the level below the castle. There are many levels to the city."

"Does the king have an heir?" Jannike yawned again and sounded drowsy.

Tell her. She needs to know.

Lynx hesitated, but Shiloh was right. Other women in his life would love his position, but he got the feeling royal blood would count against them with Jannike.

Lynx, tell her.

"The king has two sons. Prince Jarlath and Prince Lynx." Lynx drew a sharp breath, every muscle tensing while he waited for her reaction. "Jannike?"

A tiny whistle escaped from between her parted lips, and Shiloh sniggered.

"She's asleep." Lynx's voice held so much indignation Shiloh laughed harder until tears trickled down his cheeks. "I put her to sleep."

Shiloh wiped his eyes and tried to contain his merriment because Jannike needed her rest. Still, his friend's pique started his shoulders shaking again. "I've been telling you for cycles you don't have as much charm as me. It takes skill to attract both men and women."

"*Grrr*." Lynx bared his teeth. "Come over here and laugh at me."

Shiloh stood and stalked around the bed to Lynx's side. The air grew heavy, and Shiloh's laughter morphed to something more, something bigger, darker.

Lynx's eyes glowed, and his shoulders lost their rigidity. "We might wake Jannike."

"I don't think so. The potion has knocked her out. Besides, if we did wake her, that might not be a bad thing. She can join in any time she wants."

"I want to kill that bastard who hurt her all over again," Lynx snarled.

"Our mate is strong. She survived before and made a life for herself. I think she will do it again, and this time she has us, her friends to help her rather than having to rely on her own resources."

Lynx brushed a strand of blonde hair away from her strong face. "The guard died too fast."

"He did," Shiloh agreed in a hard voice. "So did the widow. Jannike's brother is a good man. He will help those who require aid."

"We should do the same on Viros," Lynx said. "Instead of giving up and letting the broken system continue, we should use our influence to make things better. My father won't change. He runs the House in the same way as his sire and grandsire."

Shiloh gave an irritable shrug, the discussion an old one between them, a solution impossible to find. "My father is the same, and Ellard buys into the tradition. Just because things have been done the same way for hundreds of rotations, it doesn't mean it is right."

"A base on Viros would work. Maybe not in the city, but we could purchase some outlying land, build a trading base and employ some of the locals."

Shiloh rubbed a hand over his jaw and grimaced at the scruff his fingers encountered. His regular use of stop-beard had slowed the regrowth and he couldn't wait to get back to his normal clean-cut appearance. "Set an example for others to follow, you mean."

Lynx nodded, a hint of enthusiasm creeping into his features. "Maybe give some of the street kids a chance of a future."

"And if Ry decides not to stay?"

Unspoken were the words that Jannike would want to leave with her friends.

"That's where my plan comes unstuck."

Shiloh tugged Lynx off the gel-bed and pulled him into an embrace. Lynx leaned into him, seeming to need the comfort as much as Shiloh.

"There is some beautiful land outside the city. Ry and the rest of the crew want to have a home base. We need to sell the idea to them. Camryn is with child. Ry won't want to place his mate in danger."

"I'd never thought about having a child, becoming a parent," Lynx said.

"Our parents are going to disown us."

"I know."

"Ry and his crew have already accepted us."

Lynx flashed a quick grin. "As long as we don't hurt Jannike."

"We have no intention of hurting her." Shiloh strummed his fingers over the mark he'd left on Lynx's neck. Lynx shivered and when Shiloh pressed down a fraction harder, Lynx moaned and pushed closer to align their bodies. He lifted his head, and a thrill shot through Shiloh when he witnessed the desire in his friend. Their lips met, the kiss starting off slow before passion swept them away. The kiss became open-mouthed, tongues dueling and lips nipping until they were both breathless.

Lynx pulled away, gasped in a breath. "I want you."

"We don't have any lube." As always, the practical one.

"I have a mouth, and I want to use it on you."

Shiloh shivered, and without answering, he unfastened his trews and tugged them down his legs.

"I have a new appreciation for your body, your strength, and the solid muscles," Lynx said with a grin. "On the bed."

"What if we wake Jannike?"

"I'll have my mouth full of cock," Lynx said. "You're the one who needs to worry about keeping the noise down."

CHAPTER SIXTEEN

J annike woke to darkness, dread. She froze, her mind dissecting clues. One side of her body felt warm, while the other held a distinct chill. A faint vibration sounded, and with it came a sense of familiarity. That was the *Indy's* engines.

The tension in her muscles faded. She rolled away from the heat and cried out in surprise. Secs later, she hit the floor.

"Ow!"

"What is it?" a masculine voice demanded.

"Lights on," another voice ordered.

Her cabin lights popped on, illuminating two big, naked males. Both were in battle mode, pupils slit, teeth bared, and claws evident.

"What's wrong?" Shiloh surveyed the corners of her cabin before scowling.

"You pushed me off my gel-bed," Jannike said, her tone

aggrieved. "It's a decent-sized gel-bed, meant for more than one person." She rubbed her elbow then her hip.

"Not me." Lynx offered an innocent smile. "Shiloh is big, and he spreads out."

Shiloh circled the end of the bed and extended a hand. It was the first time she'd seen them naked—at least this close. Her gaze slid downward, and she watched his cock lengthen. She peeked at his expression and saw he'd frozen. It wasn't difficult to follow his thought processes.

"I'm not frightened of you. Seeing you this way doesn't disgust me."

"What if I asked you to touch me?" Shiloh asked, his words hoarse, a little raw.

Jannike reached out, her fingertips dancing across his pectoral muscles. The heat coming off him came as a surprise and brought an answering prickle beneath her skin. "You're all muscle and strength." She pressed her fingers down until her palm touched his biceps, and the heat crept from her fingertips and up her arm.

The warmth and a sense of expectation darted to her breasts and dispersed throughout her body. In her peripheral vision, Lynx circled the end of the gel-bed and joined them. He positioned himself at her back, and his flesh was just as hot as Shiloh's.

She swallowed, drew in a deep breath, filling her lungs with their scents. Green and wild and perfect. A memory of the last time—the widow. Her minions. She swallowed again and jumped when Lynx drew her against his chest. In front of her, Shiloh pushed into her space. A tremor weakened her knees, stabbed a sliver of panic into her, and communicated the need for flight.

"I...I...can't," she whispered and closed her eyes, not wanting to see Shiloh's reaction.

"We want to hold you. That's all. This will happen at your pace." Lynx's breath was a teasing waft against her earlobe. "We were talking, and you dropped off to sleep. You missed all the good bits."

Shiloh laughed, the bark of humor traveling through his body and by extension, hers. "You missed Lynx's confession that he is a prince."

Jannike rolled her eyes. "Oh, is that all. He needs to come up with better stories. That's why I fell asleep."

A growl came from Lynx, and he nipped her earlobe. She jumped, but the bite hadn't hurt.

Shiloh chuckled. "See, that's what I told him. He needs new material. Come back to bed. Let us touch you."

"We'll stop whenever you want." Lynx cupped her cheek with one big hand, his eyes serious. "Do you trust us to do that?"

"Yes." An easy truth. After all they'd been through, she trusted them with her life. "Where's Kelvin?"

"He's making himself useful. He and Mogens seem to have hit it off," Shiloh said. "When I went to grab something to eat, they were discussing herbal remedies and telling the future via clouds. Didn't make much sense, but they both seemed happy."

"I've been asleep that long?"

"You slept through our Manx One stop. Our passengers are safely on their way to freedom." Lynx winked at Shiloh. "We managed to keep ourselves amused."

"You had sex," Jannike said. "I thought you looked relaxed."

"We might have."

Shiloh squeezed her shoulder. "You need more rest."

Jannike frowned, not liking the way they were studying each other and her. The idea of sex... It had taken her a while to heal physically and mentally last time, so she was surprised at the urges riding her now.

When she didn't reply, Shiloh scooped her off her feet and carried her to the gel-bed. He set her down with easy strength. Before her mind formulated the order to jump back up, Lynx plopped down, and Shiloh took a position on her other side.

"As much as we like your Earth garments, we'd like you to take them off," Lynx said. "Will you do that?"

"Okay." She turned her back for Lynx to access the closure of her bra.

"Good girl. Just the top half is enough for now." Shiloh peeled the bra down her arms and tossed the lacy blue garment somewhere on her cabin floor. He stared at her breasts, and she sensed Lynx doing the same thing.

Shiloh ran his fingers up and down her biceps. The ever-present prickles beneath her skin followed his fingers like a pet on a leash. On her other side, Lynx mirrored Shiloh's touch, and the tickling sensation darted across her chest to meet in the middle. She gasped as her nipples pulled tight.

"All right, sweetheart?" Shiloh asked.

The endearment flooded her with a sense of well-being and made her insides turn to mush when she caught the worry in his green eyes.

Lynx leaned over. "Can we keep touching you?"

The pure need in his expression drew her more than words. Yes, there was hesitation on her part. Shiloh and Lynx were strong males in their prime and capable of overpowering her. But she could shout for Ry. Camryn had whispered they'd hooked up the security. If the felines did anything to distress her, she was to call aloud. Ry and Kaya would arrive bearing weapons.

Camryn had promised she'd gut both felines if they dared hurt her, and despite her petite frame and her obvious pregnancy, Jannike didn't doubt her friend's fierce vow. All her friends were there for her, and that made a difference.

"I th-think that would be okay." Her words were barely audible. "It stops the worst of the irritation beneath my skin when you touch me."

"We thought we'd rid ourselves of the skin cooties," Shiloh said.

"They disappeared for a time."

"After you had sex with each other," Jannike said.

"After we accepted the claim, I think." Shiloh brushed his fingers over her cheek. "I bit Lynx here."

Shiloh reached over her and touched the spot on Lynx where neck and shoulder met. His finger slid back and forth over the raised scar, and Lynx groaned, his eyes closing to slits.

"Does that feel good?" Curiosity had her reaching to touch the same place on Shiloh. She stroked the ridge of flesh and watched a shudder seize Shiloh's large frame. He shifted his body so his groin pressed against her leg. He rocked, rubbing his erection back and forth on her thigh. Another tremor took him, his fingers dropping away from Lynx's neck.

"Hoy," Lynx said. "This isn't about you."

Shiloh's eyes snapped open, his hips freezing. The tip of his cock remained cozied up to her thigh, and the scent of male musk floated on the air.

"Sorry. I thought...I meant to control myself."

"Don't move," Jannike ordered when Shiloh started to rearrange his body. She recommenced her strumming across the ridged flesh, reveling in the way her touch stripped away his control.

Much different from her time in the prison cell.

Shiloh was willing, and her pleasure fed on his. Different circumstances. Different people. These two men—she'd wanted to keep them out of her life, out of her heart, but they'd gone and sneaked in anyhow. She wanted...needed more. Touch. Taste. Sight. She wanted to hear Shiloh's pleasure and share what Lynx had already experienced.

"Can we touch him together?" she asked, turning to Lynx.

"Of course." Lynx's eyes shone with approval. "We can do whatever you want."

"He should be in the middle of the gel-bed so no one is in danger of falling off."

Lynx stood and walked around to the other side of the bed.

They shuffled over, and Jannike began to touch Shiloh with more confidence. She trailed fingers over his chest, leaned closer to taste him. He quivered and released a lusty groan of pleasure. Lynx let his hands wander, but he touched her too. He'd rub her shoulder, her back then he'd retreat to caress Shiloh.

Jannike tongued Lynx's chest and tasted salt. He smelled of the cleanser she had in her sanitizer room—another feminine indulgence from Earth. The flowery scent should have seemed out of place. Instead, the familiar perfume made him seem more hers.

Lynx's hand strayed closer to a breast, and she lifted her head to stare at him.

"Too much?" he asked.

"I...no. Feels nice." And it did. Pleasure flowed through her, making her want to return the same sense of delight. She licked a path around a masculine nipple, gave Shiloh a hint of teeth.

"Phrull," Shiloh said. "Feels good. So good. Do it again."

Smiling, she applied herself. She stroked and teased and nipped before becoming braver. She moved down Shiloh's body, and Lynx copied her caresses, mirroring her actions.

Shiloh groaned and groaned again when Jannike bit down on a spot a tad below his hip. Lynx lifted his head and winked at her before taking a nip himself.

Fun, she thought. This was fun.

"Shut your eyes, Shiloh," Lynx ordered, his voice huskier than normal.

"Why?"

Lynx winked at her. "Do you trust us?"

"Yes."

"Then shut your eyes." Lynx smiled and reminded her of Ry in a mischievous mood.

Shiloh hesitated then relaxed. "My eyes are shut."

"Good. I want you to guess who is touching you."

A gust of air hissed from Shiloh. "Easy."

"So you think," Lynx said.

These males were smart. Jannike knew what Lynx was doing. He was planting himself firmly in her camp and making what might cause bad memories to flare into a game. Jannike shifted her weight. She leaned over Shiloh and lapped around his belly button. Her hair shifted forward, the ends teasing across his stomach.

Lynx nipped Shiloh's thigh.

"Easy." Shiloh sounded confident. "First was Jannike. I can feel your hair tickling my stomach. Second was Lynx. I felt a hint of your canines."

Jannike pushed off the bed and purposely made a noise at the foot of the gel-bed before tiptoeing back to her spot. She marched her fingers down Shiloh's thigh and back up before fingering his balls. She was still touching him when Lynx started his oral assault. He squeezed one of Shiloh's balls, using faint pressure.

They kept moving, touching, teasing until they both kept their mouths and fingers on Shiloh.

"I don't know," Shiloh said. "You're cheating."

"But cheating is making your cock hard." Lynx dipped his head and kissed one side of Shiloh's cock. A spurt of desire arrowed through Jannike. That looked so hot, and if Shiloh's groans were anything to judge the situation, the sensations felt good on his end.

Jannike hesitated. She wanted to touch Shiloh so much that her hand trembled.

Lynx moved his mouth upward, licking from the root of Shiloh's cock toward the tip. She glanced at Shiloh's face. His eyes remained tightly closed, his bottom lip clamped between white teeth as he fought to contain his pleasure.

Do it. Touch him. He won't harm you, even if this becomes too much for you. Not even if you pull back. He's not going to hurt you.

This absolute truth—the one she knew to the pit of her gut—had her moving to a position opposite Lynx. She settled and shifted closer. Before she could think too hard, she leaned over and applied her mouth to the other side of Shiloh's cock. His taste, his scent washed over her and she closed her eyes too, allowing herself to feel instead of overthink her lingering trepidation.

Yes, she had nothing to fear here. The jailer might have used her at the widow's behest, hurt her when she'd landed a kick in his balls. Not hard enough because it had just made him meaner, but she'd done her best. She stared at nothing, her mind in the horrors of her recent past. The jailer had been a mere tool, the widow's instrument.

If Ursola Verena hadn't been so power-hungry and intent on revenge, Jannike wouldn't have ended up in a prison cell. The thought brought a flash of anger. The widow was spoiling this—a moment that should be one of celebration.

Her eyes popped open, and the first thing she saw was Lynx's green eyes, his expression one of concern.

"Jannike?" Questions shone in his eyes, and she caught the flash of fear he couldn't conceal.

"No. I am not going to let the widow spoil my life, our lives." Because she admitted a secretly held truth then—only to herself, it was true—but still powerful nonetheless. She envied Ry and Camryn. Their closeness. Their unity. Their absolute faith in each other. And now that they had a child on the way, their relationship appeared even stronger.

She secretly aspired to the same but had never thought it would happen.

Now, she held happiness, a future, in the palm of her hand—if only she was brave enough to take a leap of faith and believe in these two strong men. Commit to them.

Jannike studied Lynx's beautiful face and saw his underlying worry. She glanced up at Shiloh's more rugged features. His puckered brow spoke of his anxiety.

Lynx's gaze remained steady. "We'll understand if you want to stop."

"We don't want to pressure you," Shiloh added.

Her throat held a lump that felt as big as her hand. She swallowed once, twice, emotion gripping her until she had trouble breathing. Moisture gathered at her eyes. "Am I dreaming? Am I still on Manx Two?"

Shiloh reached down and pinched her bottom, and Jannike jumped at the thread of pain that wound through her body. She glared at Shiloh and heard Lynx's snicker.

"Don't be stupid. Lynx, you pinch her too, in case she gets some stupid idea you're a mirage."

"A kiss is better," Lynx whispered, his breath warm against her lips. Then he was kissing her, nipping her bottom lip, and using so much expertise all she could think about was rubbing against him. When Lynx pulled back, she was breathing hard.

Yes.

She wanted them.

She didn't intend to let the widow rule her life from the grave.

Jannike leaned over and kissed Lynx on the cheek. "I intend to keep you both."

That said, she resumed her former position and pressed a quick kiss to the tip of Shiloh's cock. During the pause, he'd softened, but she stroked toward the tip and tasted him. He groaned, and Lynx beamed in approval. She repeated the move, a long, slow lap from base to tip. His flavor burst over her taste buds, and she lapped at the bead of liquid that swelled at the crown. Then she felt another pair of lips, another tongue, twirling with hers, fighting to grab a taste.

Lynx's lips moved on the swollen head of Shiloh's cock, ran over her tongue, her lips while his eyes glowed and held another emotion that looked a little like love. Something twisted inside her, but it was a good feeling of something precious unfurling.

Shiloh gasped, his big body jerking and driving his shaft deeper into her mouth. She lapped and sucked before raising her head and letting his cock pop free.

"Let me," Lynx said. "You go and kiss him, drive him crazy."

They could have pressured her for more, but she thought they understood and were happy to give her time. She crawled up Shiloh's body. Her mouth sought the mark on his neck, and he groaned the instant she nibbled on it.

His large hands smoothed her hair as he whispered words of praise in her ear.

"Jannike, sweetheart. You make me feel whole."

His next groan rumbled through his chest.

"You pinched me."

"You can pinch me back. Anytime you like," he said and groaned again when Lynx took his cock deep.

"Maybe later." She stopped him talking by pressing her lips to his. She held him while he trembled in the throes of passion, took pleasure in the grip of his hands at her shoulders, and she felt extra close to him when he gasped against her mouth and came.

As his large frame relaxed, Lynx came up beside them and plastered his body to Shiloh's other side.

"Jannike?"

She smiled and leaned over to silence further questions with a kiss. She tasted Shiloh and Lynx, and the combination was right.

Just perfect.

CHAPTER SEVENTEEN

L ynx woke and realized he felt more relaxed than he had for
cycles. Rotations even. Heat scorched one side of his body,
and disappointment chipped at his good mood. *Jannike.*

"Lights on," he ordered.

He was right. Jannike wasn't here.

"Shiloh." He shook his friend.

"Wanna sleep."

"Shiloh, Jannike isn't here."

Shiloh bolted upright, his gaze darting to all corners of the cabin.
Not a sound came from the sanitizer room. He grabbed his trews
and thrust his legs into them, galvanizing Lynx to action.

"We can't keep her in a cage, Shiloh."

"I know, but I—my feline—gets antsy whenever she's out of
sight."

Exactly how he felt, which was why he'd woken Shiloh. "She's not in any danger here on the *Indy*. She is among friends."

"I— Knowing that doesn't seem to matter," Shiloh gritted out.

Lynx understood since his gut churned. He reached for a tunic. A blue one. Clean. Jannike must've found more clothes. He handed a black tunic to Shiloh. "I need to tell her about my position on Viros."

"Leave it a bit longer. One thing at a time. First, Jannike needs to tell us if she's leaving."

Lynx grunted, pretending he didn't suffer the same urges riding his lover. "Good luck with that. The woman is independent. We might've seen her vulnerability, but she's strong—mentally and physically. We can't order her around."

"Try telling that to my feline." Shiloh flung open the door and strode down the corridor. "This way."

"I know." Lynx allowed his irritation to show. "I know how to follow a scent trail."

Not in the galley. Not on the bridge.

Lynx sensed Shiloh's unease, experiencing the emotion in a weird duplicate, the feelings ping ponging between them becoming more urgent as they failed to find their third.

Camryn looked up from a meal that looked big enough to feed both of them.

"Have you seen Jannike?" Shiloh snapped out the question, making no secret of his irritation.

"And good morning to you too." Camryn's brows rose at Shiloh's growl, and a tiny grin played on her lips. "No, but she'll be training with Ry and Kaya in the rec room. They always train this time of the day—I mean cycle." She clutched at her stomach and gasped.

Lynx screeched to a halt. "What's wrong?"

"The baby—kitten—whatever is kicking."

Lynx had never been around a pregnant female. "It hurts?"

"It's more uncomfortable. You want to feel?" She grabbed his hand and placed it on her swollen belly before Lynx could object.

Shiloh hovered behind him, and Lynx sensed his fascination even as his feline pushed him to find Jannike.

"Whoa!" Lynx said when something gave a definite kick. "Shiloh, you have to feel this. Can Shiloh feel?"

"Of course. Come closer," Camryn said.

She seized Shiloh's hand, his big mitt dwarfing her own, and placed it beside Lynx's.

Lynx watched the wonder come over his friend's face. "We need to have one of these."

Camryn grinned, an impish warning of her intention to tease. "Are you sure about that? You'll have to ask Jannike. And her child would probably arrive with a blaster ready to fire."

"Maybe a crown too," Shiloh said.

"Pardon?"

"Nothing," Lynx said. "Thanks for sharing that with us. We'll go and find Jannike. I thought we weren't saying anything," he said once they were in the corridor.

"Saying what?" Camryn called.

"Nothing," Lynx replied. *Damn, I need to remember this mind-speak thing. You suggested we don't say anything, then you give Camryn a big clue.*

Sorry. Do you think Jannike will want a child?

I don't know.

You'll want to be the father.

What? Lynx stopped abruptly and pushed Shiloh against the wall. *What the phrull?*

Shiloh shrugged and, for once, refused to meet Lynx's gaze. *You're a royal. You need an heir to carry on.*

If Jannike consents to have a child we will both provide seed. We will both be fathers, and I don't give a phrull which one of us the seed came from. A child, any child Jannike bears will be precious, and it will be ours.

But—

No. This is my final word. I will not have this conversation again. Shiloh, listen and comprehend. Lynx gripped Shiloh's chin and gazed deep into his eyes, enforcing his will and his decision. *I don't care what anyone says—my parents or yours or our brothers—I want Jannike, and I want you. Our relationship might be unusual, but we will be a unit. Any child we have will be blessed and loved, and he or she will have three parents.*

"I...your royal blood...this worried me," Shiloh confessed.

"Worry no more. Jarlath will be king. Our mother will pick some vapid woman for him, and they'll have endless offspring to take the weight off my shoulders. I am fully committed to us. It's too late to back out now—not that I'm even considering walking away. I have no idea what the future will bring, but we'll work it out together. All three of us."

"I love you." Shiloh pulled Lynx into a hug, and Lynx's trepidation faded.

"Don't ever shut me out," Lynx ordered. "Talk to me. We've always been a team since we were young. We're even stronger now."

"I love you," Shiloh repeated.

"Good."

They kissed, deep and tender.

"Hey! No mushy stuff in the corridor," a feminine voice called. "Can I look now? Is it safe?"

Lynx pulled away and spotted Kaya, her damp blue hair tied back to reveal pointed ears. Her tunic stuck to her body while her hands covered her eyes. "I was showing this dolt here that I loved him."

Kaya peeked between her fingers, then let her hands fall to her sides. "Time and place."

"Have you seen Jannike?"

"She's sparring with Ry in the rec room."

"Thanks. I— Wait, Shiloh."

"Doesn't look like a man in a listening mood," Kaya said, amusement threading through her words.

"Shiloh!" Lynx increased his strides to a run and grabbed Shiloh's arm just before he burst into the rec room. He hauled Shiloh to a halt, using all his strength. "Wait."

The clash of swords claimed Lynx's attention and his breath eased out in a hiss. Beside him, Shiloh stiffened.

Ry wasn't holding back, thrusting and parrying, the clash of the blades ringing out. Lynx opened his mouth to protest.

"She's holding her own," Shiloh muttered, and Lynx saw he was right. Jannike never faltered or hesitated, her footwork and strikes flawless.

A timer went off, and Ry and Jannike backed away, swords lowering.

Jannike wiped the sweat off her forehead with the corner of her tunic.

Ry waved at them then stilled, his nostrils flaring. "What were you doing touching my mate?"

"We were looking for Jannike and came across Camryn in the galley." Instinct propelled Lynx to speak quickly. The tightening of Ry's mouth reinforced his compulsion. The other feline gathered to spring, claws and sword at the ready. "She grabbed my hand—"

"Both of them touched her?" Jannike asked Ry.

"Yes."

"It was amazing," Lynx said. The wrong thing to say.

A growl came from Jannike.

"She wanted us to feel the baby kick." Shiloh lifted his hands in surrender, gazing at Jannike rather than Ry. "You don't argue with a pregnant lady."

"It *was* amazing," Lynx agreed. "You're a lucky man."

Jannike folded her arms over her chest. "You're lucky too."

"That goes without saying," Lynx said.

"You need to tell us if you're leaving your cabin." Shiloh

advanced on her, a dark scowl on his face.

"This should be fun." Ry stepped back and held out his hand for Jannike's sword.

"And you and you." She jabbed her finger at Shiloh's chest then Lynx's when they started to crowd her. "Don't touch Camryn. I don't like it."

"We have no interest in Camryn," Shiloh said.

Ry growled from behind them.

Lynx offered a conciliatory smile. "She's a very nice feline, but she's not our feline."

"I'm not your feline either," Jannike gritted out.

"Oh, but you are," Shiloh said in a silky tone.

Ry strode for the door. "My cue to leave. Jannike, are you okay with me going?"

"I can handle these two big lugs."

"I don't know what a lug is but it doesn't sound complimentary," Shiloh said.

"A lug is any male who thinks they can boss me around." She glared at him and Shiloh in turn.

Lynx stared, mesmerized by her feisty attitude. She didn't back down. She didn't appear nervous or scared of them. She didn't lose her warrior stance for a sec. Her irritation reminded him of Shiloh when he was in a bad mood. He glanced at Shiloh and rushed into speech in order to head him off. "We were worried."

"What is going to happen to me on the *Indy*?"

Shiloh stalked her, turned her, and shoved her against the wall, crowding her with his bulk. Before Lynx could voice a warning, Jannike lifted her knee and struck him in the balls.

"What did you do that for?" Shiloh wheezed, cupping his groin.

"You were bullying me. I don't like it."

"You liked my kisses last eve," Shiloh countered, and Lynx felt his lips twitch. Not many people stood up to Shiloh. His size scared them off. Not that he bullied people. It was frustration on his part, the need to claim Jannike. Lynx suffered the same urges and had to battle the desire to rush her.

"I want to clean up before I eat." Jannike sidled past them.

"Shiloh and I will get you something to eat."

"No, I want to—"

Lynx grabbed Shiloh's arm and dug in his claws. And they were claws because his feline kept trying to burst forth. "We will meet you in the galley."

Shiloh attempted to pull away. "No, I—"

Lynx dug his claws in deeper to break through Shiloh's determination. "We will meet you in the galley."

He maintained his grip on Shiloh until Jannike disappeared. "Do you want to scare her off? We need to woo her, not treat her like a possession. You're making your promises ring like empty vessels."

Shiloh raked a hand through his hair—a trembling hand. "Phrull, I know you're right. I...just...my feline keeps pushing me to bite her, to mark her in the same way we marked each other. I didn't think the compulsion would be this difficult to control."

Lynx wrapped his arms around Shiloh, and for a long moment, they held each other. "It's not easy for me either. She's safe and among friends. We have to give her space."

"But what about when we reach Viros? We'll be with other males. Single males. I won't be able to hold it together," Shiloh confessed.

"We can't rush her—not after everything she's been through. She shares her bed with us. She doesn't flinch when we touch her. That's a start, and we have to build a solid foundation with that trust."

Shiloh's hot breath blew against Lynx's neck. Resignation. Agreement. "You're right. I know it, but I don't like the delay."

The cycles passed, one bleeding into another and a routine of sorts. They weren't far from Viros now. Jannike marched down a corridor. She nodded at Kelvin and Gweneth, playing with the markowls, as she passed on her way to the bridge. Lynx and Shiloh followed, silent sentinels at her back.

Kaya stood outside the galley with Royal in her arms. She winked on seeing her escort, and Jannike stopped for Royal to hop from Kaya to her. Royal had taken a liking to the *Indy* crew and shared his time with them all. Jannike suspected the treats helped cement his friendship. With Royal perched on her shoulder, she stomped onto the bridge and found Ry giving Camryn a navigation lesson.

"Camryn, are you nearly finished?" Jannike asked.

Camryn cocked a brow at her tone, then spied the two men standing behind Jannike. She grinned. "Ry, can we finish this later? I'm hungry."

Ry jumped to his feet. "Why didn't you tell me? We'll go to the galley now."

"No, stay here. I'll go with Jannike."

"We'll escort them," Shiloh said.

"Yeah, the highwaymen in the corridor are dangerous. They jump out in front of me and cry, 'Stand and deliver'. It's terrifying," Camryn said with a put-on shudder.

"What?" Lynx asked.

"Where?" Shiloh demanded.

Jannike snickered and scratched Royal's tummy. He did a happy dance and stretched to give her better access.

Ry helped his mate stand. "I believe that is Earth humor. I don't understand it half the time."

"I want to speak with Camryn," Jannike said. "In private."

"We will fall back," Lynx promised.

Jannike rolled her eyes at Camryn. "I know how that works."

Camryn stroked Royal on the head and linked her arm with Jannike's. "We are going to visit with Gweneth and Kaya. We will be discussing female things, and there is no reason for any of you boys to stand within hearing range. We will be gone for five mins then we're going to the galley because I am hungry. Is that clear?"

Ry sent Shiloh and Lynx a warning glance, which did nothing to dull their scowls. If anything they were becoming worse, and she never had a sec's peace.

Camryn tugged on her arm, and Jannike followed her down the corridor. They met up with Kelvin again, who pointed them in Kaya's direction. When they knocked on Kaya's cabin door, Camryn growled in distinct feline irritation.

"I can smell chocolate." Camryn hammered on the door. "Kaya, I know you're eating chocolate. You're mean not sharing with a pregnant woman."

"And a woman with male trouble," Jannike added.

"Hey," came a masculine voice. "We're not trouble."

"I see what you mean." Camryn darted a look over her shoulder. "They're like ticks. Let us in, Kaya. Now."

"What's all the noise about?" Gweneth asked, poking her head from an adjoining cabin. Her eyes narrowed. "I smell chocolate."

Kaya's door cracked open enough to reveal half her face, and even Jannike smelled chocolate. "What do you want?"

Camryn muscled past Kaya and Jannike, with Royal on her shoulder, and Gweneth followed in an avalanche of determination.

"No, not you," Camryn ordered when Lynx and Shiloh attempted to seek entrance. "Shoo! Quick, shut the door. Kaya, do you have any Earth music? I feel like listening to country."

"My cabin, my rules." Kaya pushed several controls. "Rock and roll."

"Even better," Camryn said. "Quick, put on the music and give me some chocolate."

"I don't have much left." Kaya shouted over the raucous wail of a male singer singing about not getting satisfaction. "I'm down to my last bar."

"Don't shout. We just needed some sound to play havoc with feline hearing. Did I mention I know how to make chocolate?" Camryn asked. "And other sweets like fudge and coconut ice. If we could find substitutes, we might be able to make our own versions."

"Really?" Kaya cheered, then narrowed her gaze. "You better not be lying. I have knives and blasters and know how to use them."

"Pooh, Ry won't let you hurt me. Now hand over the chocolate, and don't be stingy. Don't let Royal have any in case he's allergic."

"Why are you here?" Kaya asked, her tone sulky. She stalked over to a locker and pulled out the remains of a chocolate bar.

"Dark chocolate." Jannike held out her hand. "My favorite."

Kaya divvied up the chocolate, and they munched in companionable silence.

"Jannike has a problem," Camryn said.

"I knew two men would be too much for you to handle." Kaya settled on her gel-bed. "Give me one. I don't mind which."

"I can handle them, but they won't give me a min of peace. They follow me everywhere and treat me like a piece of breakable glass. I thought it would help if they saw me training, but now they insist on training with me, and they always hold back."

"What about the sex?" Kaya asked. "That must be good, right? Oh, wait. Gweneth, you need to leave. You're too young to hear this stuff."

Gweneth tilted her chin and stayed right where she was. "I'm not leaving. Just because I haven't experienced sex with a man doesn't mean I don't know stuff. Olivia suggested I buy a vibrator before I left Earth, and I've been experimenting."

They all gaped at Gweneth, who had her chin stuck in the air and wasn't even blushing.

"Should she be doing that?" Kaya asked Camryn.

Camryn chuckled. "Go you!"

"Olivia is a bad influence." Kaya's lips twitched in the beginning of a grin. "I wonder how my brother is coping with her staying with him. Knowing Olivia's sense of humor, he's probably tearing out his hair."

"Never mind Olivia," Jannike said. Olivia was their friend Amme's sister-in-law. She'd stowed away on the *Indy* when they left Earth and sent Ry's blood pressure soaring. "We're doing lots of touching, but they're careful with me."

Camryn sobered. "You've been through a lot. I imagine they're thinking long term and want to make certain you're sure of them."

"I'm ready for more sex. It's different—" Jannike broke off and started pacing, unable to remain still. Her hands curled into fists at her sides. "They don't scare me, but their hovering is working my last nerve. They never leave me alone. You manage to escape Ry. At least sometimes."

"Not often," Camryn said. "And not since he learned we're having a child."

Jannike slipped her hand beneath her tunic and scratched her stomach. "I'm tired of this accursed itchiness too. It never stops."

Camryn gestured with a raised hand. "Lift your tunic, and let me see."

Jannike did a twirl, and the three women surveyed the dark patches on her stomach and back.

"Hmm," Camryn said.

Jannike tugged her tunic back into place. "What does that mean?"

"My itching didn't go away until I'd accepted the mating. Tell your men you're ready to go all the way."

Jannike resumed her pacing. "But that won't stop them trying to protect me. I'm used to looking after myself, protecting others. People don't bodyguard me."

"I could do with time to myself," Camryn mused. "A few cycle segments where I don't have Mr. Broody hovering. I know what to do. We'll start a ladies' club. It will be for several segments—maybe an afternoon where we can get together without the men and do whatever we like."

"Good luck with that." Kaya popped a square of chocolate into her mouth.

"Gimme," Camryn said, holding out her hand.

Kaya sighed and broke off squares for them all. She placed the last two squares in her mouth, closed her eyes, and moaned.

Fists hammered on Kaya's cabin door.

"What's wrong?" a male shouted. Jannike thought it was Shiloh.

"Let's go to the galley," Camryn said. "Let them follow if they want. I have a plan to keep the males busy. If we do this right, we can keep them distracted for several cycles, chasing their tails. Take my cue. Gweneth, you remember what a mouse looks like?"

"Yes, but I don't understand."

"Don't worry. This will be fun." Camryn leaned nearer to Gweneth to whisper in her ear. She pulled away, a wide grin in place. "Let's go."

Gweneth opened the door and glared at Shiloh and Lynx. "There is no need to shout."

"We were worried," Lynx said. "What is that horrid wailing?"

Shiloh peered into Kaya's cabin, searching all four corners with a sweep of his gaze. "We thought someone was dying."

Jannike snorted a laugh. "Earth music. Camryn likes it."

They were behaving in the same manner as Ry had when Camryn had joined the *Indy*. Bossy. Demanding. Sexy and even cute, but oh so irritating. Jannike stalked past them, her nose in the air.

As much as she craved their bodies and enjoyed their company, she couldn't spend the rest of her life fighting for personal freedom. She had to make a stand now, show them she meant to stand at their sides and not behind them like a good little woman.

"Jannike, would you like to take a walk with us?" Shiloh asked.

"I—"

Camryn dug her in the ribs with a pointy elbow.

Right. Their plan. "No, thank you."

"Why not?" Shiloh demanded. "Oomph."

Jannike bit back a smirk. Lynx owned a pointy elbow, too. They'd have to compare injuries later.

"Oh, Gweneth." Camryn came to a halt. "Your cabin is nearest. I'm feeling cold. Do you have a wrap I can borrow?"

"Sure. I'll get it. Don't wait. I'll meet you in the galley." Gweneth skipped away and disappeared into her cabin.

"I'm starved." Camryn rubbed her belly.

"But you ate not long ago," Lynx said.

"I need food." Camryn's hostile tone made the two males exchange glances. "Jannike, you can help me."

They entered the galley and found Nanu spooning up some sort of soup.

"Hey, Kaya," he said. "Ry wondered if you could spell him. He wanted to check on Camryn."

"Sure."

A low growl erupted from Camryn.

A scream rippled down the corridor, the sound of running footsteps. "A mouse!" Gweneth screeched. "I saw a m-mouse. It w-was s-sitting in my wrap. It ran over my foot."

Camryn screamed. "God, did it jump in your pocket? I can't stand the things." She darted behind Jannike. "Check her pockets."

"What's wrong?" Ry asked. "Kaya, I've put the ship on auto-control. You'd better take over." He drew Camryn from behind Jannike and tugged his mate into his arms. "You're shaking.

What is it?"

Gweneth let out another shriek so convincing that the hair at the back of Jannike's neck prickled. "There it is. There. There!" She moaned and dropped to the floor.

"I didn't see anything," Lynx said.

"It's a mouse," Camryn shrieked and raced to stand on top of the nearest chair. "I'm not coming down until you get rid of the creature. You're a cat. Do something." She glared at each of the men in turn. "Catch the thing."

Gweneth stirred, let out another shriek, and shuddered. "Good idea." She scrambled on top of another chair, but Jannike beat her to it.

"They carry disease," Jannike said. "And have beady eyes." She made shooing motions with her hands. "Go. Go. Shut the door after you, and don't come back until you've caught the thing."

"Goddess." Gweneth moaned. "It's eaten a hole in my favorite wrap."

"How did it get on the *Indy*?" Ry asked.

"How am I meant to know? It must've sneaked on board with the supplies. They're not stupid. They seek out warm places," Camryn said.

"If I find out you brought a pet mouse on board, Gweneth, so help me, I'll spank you. Smuggling Olivia on board was bad enough." Ry speared a suspicious look at Gweneth.

"Innocent," Gweneth snapped. "I didn't bring it here. Do I look stupid? They have beady eyes."

Jannike bit her bottom lip and tried to look worried and keep her laugh at bay. Gweneth had blossomed since she'd joined the *Indy*. The feline girl made an excellent actress.

Camryn huffed out an impatient breath. "For goodness sake. Stop standing there like big dolts. Do something!"

"It ran down the corridor," Gweneth said, her hands fluttering.

"Shut the door," Jannike directed. "Please, we don't want it in here."

"Come on." Ry's voice held disgust. "We'll shift to feline. It shouldn't take long to hunt it down."

"What's a mouse?" Shiloh asked. "Do they bite?"

The three feline males stalked out, and the door slid shut behind them. Jannike promptly climbed down from her chair and went to help Camryn who wasn't as agile these cycles.

"Have they gone?" Gweneth asked.

"I can't hear them." Camryn straightened her tunic. "Nanu, can you check to see if they're out of sight?"

"What's going on?" he asked. "I didn't see a mouse and was looking in the same direction as Gweneth."

"Neither did we," Camryn said cheerfully. "But if you tell them that, I'll think up a fitting punishment. You will rue the cycle you tattled."

Chapter Eighteen

"It's so peaceful," Camryn said several cycle segments later. "I wonder if they've found anything yet."

Nanu shook his head hard enough for his beads to clack. "You girls fight dirty."

"They deserve it." Jannike didn't have any sympathy for the beleaguered male felines. "How much longer until we get to Viros?"

"Not long. I've located a gate that will get us there much quicker than we originally estimated. All the readings show it's stable. I'll know better once we get through the gate, but I'm thinking about five cycles."

"That would be brilliant," Jannike said. "I'm ready for some downtime without any excitement."

"Can we make some of those brownie things?" Gweneth asked.

"Sure," Camryn said. "I think there is one box of mix left. You can make them. I'll be here if you need help. You'll need to use the powdered egg stuff too."

The scent of chocolate and baking soon filled the galley. Gweneth made them a big pot of tea, another thing from their precious Earth stores.

Jannike sniffed appreciatively. "It reminds me of Christmas. Do you think they celebrate special days on Viros?"

A tap sounded on the other side of the door.

Camryn sighed. "Sounds as if our peace is over for today."

"That mouse has probably produced offspring since it's been on board," Jannike said. "The *Indy* will be full of the creatures."

Another tap sounded, this one holding more impatience.

Camryn prowled over and cracked the door open. "Did you find it?"

"Let us in," Ry snapped. "We've searched everywhere. Didn't hear so much as a squeak. We couldn't find a scent trail either, which is most odd."

"What is that smell?" Lynx asked.

"Brownies," Camryn said. "You'll have to look for the mouse again tomorrow. I won't be able to sleep a wink until it's caught."

Jannike shuddered. "Horrid things."

"I need a drink." Ry's dark hair stood on end as if he'd repeatedly run his hand through it. "Camryn, is there any of that whiskey left?"

"But I can't drink," she said.

"I'll make you a hot chocolate," Gweneth offered. "There's enough for one more. Where are Kelvin and Mogens? They should eat brownies too. You." She poked Shiloh in the chest. "Go and tell them to come for a brownie. And make sure you shut the door after you. I don't want that mouse in here."

A chuckle burst from Jannike, and she slapped her hand over her mouth, her gaze snapping to Lynx. His eyes were twinkling, and she was pretty sure that if Shiloh's mouth hung open any longer, the imaginary mouse might decide to make itself at home. People didn't give him orders. After a low grumble, he departed and returned in short order with Mogens and Kelvin in tow.

The rest of the cycle was more peaceful, and Jannike helped Gweneth make a meal for them all.

They reminisced about their visit to Earth, and Lynx and Shiloh told them more about Viros.

"Who lives in the castle?" Gweneth asked.

"The king and queen. The princes and the staff."

"Do they have balls?" Gweneth asked.

"Yes," Lynx said.

"Have you been to a ball at the castle?" Camryn asked.

"Yes," Shiloh answered. "Is there more of the pie? That was delicious."

"Do you have pies on Viros?" Kaya asked.

Jannike listened to the conversation, content to let the others ask the questions. Instead, she thought about the coming eve. It was time. She wanted to commit to the two felines, but first...

"Ry?" Nanu buzzed through on the internal ship communicator. "There's a ship approaching."

"Be there in a sec," Ry said.

Jannike stood.

Lynx waved Jannike back to her seat. "Stay there. We'll go with Ry."

"You stay," Jannike snapped. "I'm second-in-command, and it's my job. You're guests." And she marched after Ry without waiting for an answer.

"Watch out for the mouse," Gweneth shouted after her.

Jannike grinned and hustled to the bridge.

"Report, Nanu." Ry peered at the instrument panel.

"They're maintaining radio silence. I've commed the ship, but they're ignoring me. We haven't seen any ships since we left Manx One."

Jannike strapped in and studied the instruments. Ry did the same.

"Hail them again. Tell them to identify themselves."

"Can we come onto the bridge?" Lynx asked.

"Strap in," Ry said. "Shields up."

"Already done. I didn't like their silence."

"That looks like a Cawdor ship," Shiloh spoke. "I didn't think we were that close to Viros and Gramite."

"We traveled through a gate earlier this eve," Nanu said. "By my reckoning we're about five cycles from Viros."

"They're getting ready to fire," Jannike warned, her gaze on the instruments. "What the hellfire are those things coming out from the side of their ship?"

Lynx cursed. "That *is* a Cawdor ship. Those are boarding talons. A Cawdor invention."

"Hail the ship," a voice came over their comm. "Power down your weapons. We intend to board."

"Fire, Jannike," Ry said in a calm voice. "A warning shot to show them what they're up against."

Jannike aimed, fired.

Lynx let out a whistle.

"Phrull," Shiloh said. "Good shooting."

"Again," Ry ordered when the Cawdor ship kept advancing. "Nanu, evasive action."

"Aye, Captain," Nanu said.

"Aye, Captain," Jannike said.

The *Indy* tilted without warning. Lynx fell against a control panel, cursed, and Shiloh grabbed him before he damaged something.

"Strap in," Ry barked.

Bright light seared her retinas. Jannike blinked, waited a fraction until she could see again, and fired off two quick shots.

The *Indy* darted forward, nimble with Nanu at the controls, despite her size.

"One more shot, Jannike. Make it good. I want them disabled and unable to follow us."

The ship returned fire before she complied. The *Indy* shuddered.

"Report," Ry ordered.

"Nothing serious." Nanu glanced at his instruments. "The hull is still intact."

"Ready to fire," Jannike said.

"Fire!" Ry ordered.

"Got them." Nanu's voice rang with satisfaction. "Ripped off their talons."

"Good shot," Lynx said.

"Where the phrull did you learn to fly like that?" Shiloh asked.

"We used to run black market goods back when I had a price on my head," Ry said. "We had a lot of practice at evading bounty hunters. Any other ships in the vicinity?"

"Nothing showing on the instruments," Nanu replied calmly.

"I want to check on Camryn. I'll send Kaya to help."

"I'll stay on the bridge for a while," Jannike offered.

"We can," Lynx said. "If we're five cycles from Viros, we'll be able to help Nanu plot a course. I can't believe you managed the journey so fast."

"If you're sure." Ry stood. "Nanu, I'll send Kaya to spell you in two cycle segments. Jannike, I'll be back in three to spell you."

"Aye, Captain," she said.

"Do you have charts?" Shiloh asked.

Nanu brought up a different screen showing a star map. "We do, although I'm not confident they're up to date. I've noticed a few errors."

Did you see the way our mate handled herself? Shiloh asked.

Yes. We've been treating her like a helpless female since we rescued her. She's just as capable as us. Phrull, I think she's a better shot. She didn't panic and held her nerve even when the other ship attacked.

We have to step back and let her be herself, Shiloh said.

Lynx made a scoffing sound.

"Something wrong?" Jannike asked.

"No," Shiloh said. "Private joke."

"This is the most recent chart. Anything look familiar?"

Shiloh studied the star groupings and grinned.

"That's the Rembrandt system," Lynx said. "You're right. Four or five cycles depending upon the conditions of the Stavis storms around the moons Camret and Marcion."

"Nanu is a natural when it comes to locating gates. He's tried to show me, but I don't have the same instincts."

"Yep was even better," Nanu said.

"He was," Jannike agreed. "Yep was Nanu's brother. He died during an attack when we were hunting for a hell-horse to race."

"Hell-horse racing?" Lynx asked.

"We kidnapped Camryn to ride our hell-horse," Jannike explained.

Nanu's beads clacked as he silently laughed. "Our lives aren't boring. We never know what is coming next."

Shiloh glanced at Lynx. "We might be able to comm Ellard again once we get past the moons. We haven't been home for almost a full rotation."

"It's best if you skirt the Stavis storm clouds. It adds another cycle to the journey time, but the storms are unpredictable," Lynx said. "I'd suggest taking a wide trajectory because I've seen bolts of electrical charges zap out and damage ships where the captain hasn't taken a conservative enough path."

Nanu studied the charts, nodded at Lynx's and Shiloh's comments. "This is the course I plotted."

Kaya sashayed onto the bridge. "I saw that damn mouse. Blasted thing ran over my foot. I thought you felines had a good sense of smell."

"It would help if we knew what we were looking for," Shiloh said. "I've never heard of a mouse before."

"I'll draw you a picture." Kaya tucked a blue lock behind one pointed ear. "Ugly little creatures with beady eyes."

If they're so little why are the females getting so upset about them? Shiloh asked. *They could just stomp on them if the creatures attacked.*

I have no idea. When do you think Ry will arrive? Seeing Jannike in action has made me desperate to show my private appreciation.

"Here's Ry." Shiloh stood and tugged unobtrusively at his trews. "Is Jannike finished for this eve?"

Ry clapped Jannike on the back, and Shiloh had to rein in his urge to growl. *Mine.*

Steady. They're friends. Ry has a mate and only feels friendship for Jannike. Lynx's explanation didn't ease the angst twisting Shiloh's gut.

I want to end this.

You don't want Jannike?

Easy to hear the shock in Lynx's voice. *No, I mean we need to finish the mating. Each cycle it's harder to hold back. Even though you and I are mates, I don't feel the same relief I felt after we marked each other. I—we—need to complete the mating with Jannike before I lose control.*

We agreed not to rush her.

I know. I know. But try telling my feline. Even shifting this afternoon and searching for the mouse creature didn't stop the craving for Jannike. My feline tried to take over. Shiloh's thoughts held grimness. *It was difficult shifting to humanoid form.*

"Do you want to go to the rec room?" Jannike asked.

"No," Shiloh barked. Bull crap. That wasn't holding things together.

Lynx moved to his side and slung his arm around Shiloh's waist, which made Shiloh feel worse. Lynx was a prince. It was his job to mind Lynx. Not happening at present. Shiloh sucked in a deep Jannike-tinged breath and forced himself to let it ease out in fractions. His feline rose, fighting him for control.

"I need to return to our cabin," he said, his voice deeper than usual and holding a rumble of feline.

"Is something wrong?" Jannike asked.

"Yes," Ry said. "Go with him. He needs you."

Jannike moved to Shiloh's other side and slipped her arm around his waist, mirroring Lynx's action. The smell of her, bearing a hint of Lynx and his own scent, the warmth coming from her body, pleased him. A purr rumbled free. She pleased his soul.

"What is that noise?" Jannike demanded.

"Shiloh is purring," Ry said. "You've heard me purr."

Jannike wrinkled her nose. "I try not to think about your sex life. My own is frustrating enough."

"What's frustrating about it?" Lynx asked in a silky voice.

Shiloh lost his urge to purr and growled instead. "That's what I want to know."

"You're on your own," Ry said with a smirk that made Shiloh want to apply his fists to wipe it away. "Go. Kaya and I intend to go over Nanu's chart plotting. I want to do it in peace."

Jannike and Lynx led him away. Shiloh heard Kaya enquire about the mouse and Ry's curt reply about sneaky creatures, that they'd get the animal soon.

Lynx opened Jannike's cabin.

Jannike hesitated in the doorway. "I wanted to talk to you both. We could do that now."

Lynx stiffened, and Shiloh felt the same tension slide through his own muscles. He studied her warily. Talking wasn't his favorite thing. Action came easier. "What do you want to talk about?"

He must have sounded guarded because Lynx scowled. *Try to look interested. Don't scare her away with your glare.*

Jannike scanned their faces and started pacing. Phrull, not a good sign.

"What is it, Jannike?" Lynx asked.

"It's you, both of you. You can't follow me around, tell me what to do and how to behave." She whirled and nailed them with a steely stare. "If you don't start letting me have some freedom, let me have my independence, then I'll have to walk away from this relationship. No matter the cost. I can't—" She broke off, shook her head. "I can't let you take over. I can't lose myself after fighting so hard for freedom."

Shiloh's heart slammed his ribs, and his feline rippled beneath his skin.

"Shiloh is the bossy one." Lynx broke the tense silence. "Bossiness is in his nature. He used to be a bodyguard. Please, you have to give us a chance."

"You're just as bad." Jannike's brows rose. "Whose body did he guard?"

"Mine," Lynx said. "I'm a prince."

"You both possess egos the size of a large planet," Jannike snapped. "This isn't a joke. I need you to listen."

"But it's true," Shiloh said. "I still guard his body. It was his fault we got captured in the first place."

"How many times do I have to apologize," Lynx grumbled. "It wasn't my finest moment."

"I wonder what happened to the big dude with the cyberbeest," Jannike mused.

Shiloh wasn't sure where Lynx's and Jannike's thoughts wandered, but he recalled the moment when he knew they wouldn't slide from the neatly set trap, his helplessness at his failure to keep his charge safe. For a fleeting sec, he'd wished he'd been responsible for the staid, conservative Jarlath instead of the rebel Lynx. Now, he thought of all he'd gained. Lynx's love. Jannike.

For once the restless nature that kept him on the go and willing to travel wherever Lynx led felt...satisfied. Happy.

"Jannike." His burst of speech made her start. He stood and went to her, taking one of her hands in his. Her fingers were callused, her hands capable. Her appearance—she was more striking than beautiful, yet he knew there was softness in her heart, her huge heart. She was strong—strong enough to wrap both of them into knots.

How could she not know this?

"I want you so much it hurts. My feline wants you, and I know Lynx feels the same. I can't promise not to be bossy. I'm a feline male. It's in our nature. But I can promise to love and protect you. I can promise to respect you and your capabilities. You're a strong woman, Jannike. You have the strength to knock sense into our stupid male heads if we step out of line. Sweetheart, if you weren't the special person you are, neither of us would be attracted to you. Please give us a chance. The urge to take you, to finalize the mating bonds, is making us more irritable than usual."

"Speak for yourself."

"It's making me grumpy." Shiloh indulged his feline by running his fingers across the softness of Jannike's cheek. Her eyes slid shut, and she inched closer when his hand wandered down her neck and across her shoulder. Even through her tunic, the heat of her skin was evident. A purr vibrated from his throat while his mind cried, *mine.*

"Shiloh is right. We know we're pushing you. We're trying not to, but our felines are—"

"Leading you around by your cocks," Jannike said without opening her eyes.

Shiloh shot a glance at Lynx and met his friend's wicked grin.

"That's my point," Shiloh said. "You're telling us to back off. You're telling us we're bossy. You're standing up for yourself."

Lynx slid his arms around Jannike's waist and tugged her back against his chest, and Shiloh caught her frisson of pleasure. "You see Ry and Camryn every day, the way they interact."

"Ry is bossy," Jannike said.

"But Camryn handles him. My second point." *What else?* he asked Lynx.

You're doing great. I'm impressed.

"Camryn has a secret weapon," Jannike said, and she did open her eyes this time. Her eyes were a dark gray and so, so beautiful.

"What?" Lynx asked.

"It wouldn't be a secret if I told you."

"Could you use the same weapon?" Shiloh asked.

"Already deployed." No mistaking her smugness.

"Then why are you talking about walking away?" Shiloh demanded.

"There are two of you. I worry about losing myself."

Your turn, Shiloh said, not bothering to hide his exasperation and desperation with Lynx.

"We're yours," Lynx said simply. "We can't promise to change, but we can try. We care deeply for you. We admire you."

"We love you," Shiloh gritted out.

Lynx nodded. "That too. Once we arrive on Viros and make some decisions—joint decisions—about what we want to do in the future, I think it will be better. You'll spend time with your friends while you check out Viros. We'll spend time with our families. Here on the ship, it's difficult to find privacy, and that's making the situation worse. Our felines are pushing us to complete the mating."

"Give us a chance, Jannike. Please," Shiloh said.

Jannike listened to everything the two felines said and thought about Camryn and Ry. Ry behaved in the same manner as Shiloh and Lynx, yet she'd never seen him so happy. Camryn listened to Ry, but the petite Earthwoman never backed down if she thought Ry was wrong. Their relationship contained give and take. Compromise. She considered walking away, thought about how she would feel.

Her stomach dipped and dived like the roller coaster they'd ridden during their vacation. Nerves stuttered to life, jumping up and down while her heart began a faster dance.

"I considered walking away, but every time I think of this, I feel ill. So if I can't walk away, the alternative is to turn around and walk toward you. Goddess help me, we haven't known each other for long and part of me is terrified, but yes. Let's do this."

"Are you sure, sweetheart? Are you ready to take us?" Shiloh asked.

For an instant, she was back in that prison cell, chained and helpless. She shoved the thought away, determined not to let the widow sully this moment. "I'm sure."

"It might cure the itching," Lynx said.

Jannike nodded. "A side benefit."

"Enough talk." Shiloh pushed gently away from her and yanked at his clothes. Lynx did the same while she watched.

Of the two, Lynx was the pretty one. Shiloh was more like her, with strong features. His body was big and powerful, yet she'd seen his gentleness too. And when he smiled...

"What?" Shiloh asked and gifted her with one of his special smiles.

"Just feasting my eyes."

Lynx cocked a hip. "Like what you see?"

"The beginnings of a pot belly," Jannike said with a wink at Shiloh. "Ha! Made you look."

Shiloh chuckled aloud.

"Wench." Lynx swept her off her feet. Secs later, the gel-bed was at her back, and Shiloh was tugging off her boots. Soon, she was as naked as them, and the atmosphere took a more solemn tone.

Shiloh slid onto her right side, Lynx her left. They rolled toward her, and her heartbeat tripped before taking off in a jerky dance.

Part apprehension. Part pleasure.

"Your eyes have gone feline," she whispered to Shiloh.

"Mine too, I think," Lynx said. "Do we scare you?"

"No." Jannike kissed one and then the other, at peace with her decision.

Her men took her kisses as a signal. Their hands wandered her breasts, her shoulders, her flat stomach. Fingers tweaked her nipples in twin sensations that bounced beneath her skin and commed pleasure.

Shiloh nipped her earlobe. Lynx laved the base of a breast, his tongue abrasive yet pushing enjoyment through her too. The two men played her body until she gasped and groaned.

"You first," Lynx said.

The two males shared a look, then Shiloh nodded. He moved down her body and parted her legs but didn't rush. Instead, he stroked and kissed her thighs, and strummed his fingers across her pussy, giving her shards of sensation instead of constant pleasure. "Do you like this?"

"Yes."

Lynx kissed her, slow and deep, until she existed in a world of blissful sensation. Her body cried out for more, but still Shiloh waited.

She ripped her mouth from Lynx's. "Please. Please. I need...I need more."

"Shush." Lynx pressed a kiss to the corner of her mouth then turned his head to glance down her body.

She felt rather than saw Shiloh position his cock and lever his body over hers.

"Open those eyes, sweetheart," Lynx whispered. "Know who is loving you."

Jannike forced her eyes open, unaware she'd closed them in the first place. He was right though, she thought as her gaze connected with Shiloh's. His green eyes glowed, the pupils slits rather than rounds. He moved without haste, flexing his hips and taking his time to embed his cock in her flesh.

Lynx kissed her—a lazy kiss that exploded need in every direction. He parted their lips and lifted his head to kiss Shiloh. They kissed differently, she thought, watching them—harder yet the act held sensuality and love.

When their lips parted, Shiloh smiled at her. "My turn for a kiss."

His kiss was forceful and urgent, and his cock thrust deeper while their lips mated.

She'd thought Shiloh would hurry and seize his pleasure. She was wrong. His strokes remained slow and even. Thrust and withdraw. Thrust and withdraw.

"Shiloh," she whispered.

Lynx silenced her with a kiss, his tongue duplicating the pace of Shiloh's measured thrusts. She groaned against his mouth, her climax rolling over her in a liquid swell. Lynx nuzzled her throat, laved back and forth on the fleshy spot where neck and shoulder met. He gave her teeth and bit down.

Pain shot through her, along with the desperate urge to bite in return. A renewed wave of pleasure rolled over her, and when Shiloh lifted his head, she gasped. Lynx lapped at the spot and the craving to bite in return overcame her. Shiloh's neck and shoulder were in the perfect position. She bit down before the thought firmed. Shiloh groaned, and she felt the jerk of his cock within her channel.

She tasted coppery blood, yet it didn't make her want to stop. She cleaned the wound, and Shiloh trembled. A growl slipped from him, feline in its intensity. She glanced up to meet Lynx's smile.

Shiloh pulled free, his confident manner absent. Instead, he appeared shocked and a tad shaky.

"Shiloh?" Lynx had noticed too.

"I'm fine. More than fine." Shiloh settled beside her and

kissed her as Lynx caressed her thighs. Lynx repositioned himself and twirled his tongue around her clit. Jannike groaned against Shiloh's mouth. Then she sighed as she felt Lynx enter her with one seamless thrust.

"He's feeling paradise," Shiloh whispered. "Tight silken pleasure."

Lynx powered into her, the climb to bliss faster this time.

"Me too."

Shiloh laughed. "I want to taste your blood, let our lives entangle and thread together."

Before she could reply, he bit down right on the spot Lynx had bitten her. The pain was keener now. She shuddered as Lynx caught her cry with his mouth. He reached between them to tease her clit, and that was all it took for the pain to transform into more manageable.

"Bite me," Lynx whispered against her lips. Need throbbed in his request, desperation. He pulled back and thrust into her heat again.

Shiloh ran his tongue across the mark he and Lynx had left, the rasp like a prod to her internal organs.

"Shiloh. Lynx." Instinct had her biting. As she bit down, Lynx bucked, shoving his cock deeper inside her.

Shiloh nibbled and sucked at the mark while Lynx kindled her passion higher with a series of quick, hard strokes. She lapped away the coppery blood from the wound, and Lynx's groan reverberated through her cabin. Her inner muscles contracted around his length, each of his thrusts increasing the tempo drumming in her ears.

Shiloh kissed her, and an intense burst of heat filled her, then spilled into a toe-tingling release. She gasped, her head whirling with the force of her climax. Her fingers dug into Lynx's shoulders, and she clung.

Shiloh twisted to kiss Lynx. A raw and guttural moan slipped from Lynx, his breathing as ragged as hers. Jannike squeezed her inner muscles, and Lynx trembled again. The muscles of his arse flexed as he pumped into her. He stilled, fully embedded, his cock jerking as he came.

As his breathing returned to normal, he leaned his full weight on her.

Can't breathe. Even as her discomfort communicated itself and she opened her mouth to speak, Lynx replied.

Sorry.

Get off her before you do some damage, Shiloh ordered.

"What the phrull?" Jannike whispered. "I can hear you, and your mouths aren't working."

I feel whole, Lynx said.

Perfect, Shiloh agreed. *You okay, Jannike?* A tendril of fear flickered through him when she didn't answer immediately.

"I'm feeling excellent. When you bit me—both of you—it felt as if everything snapped into place. Shiloh, turn over."

Shiloh exchanged a puzzled glance with Lynx. "Why?"

"I want to check out your arse. Go on. Turn over for me."

He turned over.

"Wow," Lynx said.

"What?" Shiloh asked, turning back to face them.

"Check out mine," Lynx said and turned his back so they could see the black leopard covering his back.

"The same," Jannike said. "Me?" She twisted so they could both glimpse her back.

"Black splotches," Lynx reported.

"Weird," Shiloh said. "Ry has one too, but this doesn't happen on Viros. My father doesn't have a tattoo."

"Mine neither," Lynx said. "But my parents aren't true mates. Most felines on Viros believe stories of true mates are the stuff of legend."

"Camryn has a tattoo." Jannike reached behind to scratch. "My skin is still itchy."

Shiloh laughed. "You need more practice at this sex thing."

"Yeah," Lynx said.

"I wouldn't boast too much. It might mean you've both had too much sex," Jannike said and grinned. "It might mean you're man-whores."

"Hey." Lynx pinched her bottom. "We might have once spent our leisure time chasing the ladies but no more."

"We want one lady, and that's you," Shiloh confirmed.

Jannike climbed off the gel-bed. "Be back in a sec."

We have to tell her about your status, Shiloh said.

I tried. She didn't seem to believe me.

You didn't say, 'I am Prince Lynx of Viros.' That might have helped.

I've spent half my life trying to forget. It's not as if the position brings any benefits. It doesn't mean anything to me or to you. We're just plain Lynx and Shiloh. Chances are, even if we stay on Viros, we will have our own home, our own business, our own lives. That's what I want.

Me too, Shiloh said. *We'll have to tell her.*

Jannike returned from the sanitizer room. "Tell me what?"

"We were wondering if there is any chance of a child. We didn't—it should be something we discuss first."

"Neither of us thought to ask about preventing offspring," Shiloh said.

"I'm protected." Jannike shrugged. "The morn we arrived at the planet where I was captured, Mogens took one look at the clouds on the horizon and insisted everyone on the ship drink a new potion he'd whipped up to prevent offspring. Apart from Camryn."

"How long does it last?" Lynx asked.

Jannike shrugged then scowled, trying to scratch her back.

"A rotation. Maybe longer, but Mogens wouldn't guarantee the potion for longer than a rotation."

"Come over here," Shiloh said. "I'll scratch your back for you."

Jannike sauntered over to Shiloh, unworried about her nakedness. Lynx smiled, not jealous that he wasn't included in the moment. He received just as much pleasure from watching his two lovers interact with each other.

"I would like children one day. On Manx Two children are made in birth labs. On Camryn's planet, the females carry their young. I think carrying the young before birth would make them more precious." She groaned as Shiloh raked his nails over her back, and Lynx joined them, wrapping his arms around both.

"We can do whatever you want," Shiloh said.

"When we're all ready."

Jannike turned in Lynx's arms so she faced both of them. "That sounds like a good plan."

The next few cycles passed rapidly. Ry wanted a complete inventory of supplies before arrival on Viros. Lynx approved of the sentiment, his respect for the other feline growing each cycle.

"We still have to catch that damn mouse," Ry said.

"I saw it this morn." Camryn waddled closer. "When I was on the way to the galley."

Ry folded his arms across his chest. "Why is there no scent trail?"

Jannike bit back a grin as Camryn calmly shrugged. "Are you saying my eyes are defective?"

Ry strode to the door before trotting back to kiss his mate and pat her swollen belly. "We're going to be down in the hold. Lynx and Shiloh offered to help Kaya and I check the stock."

"I could help," Jannike said.

"I'd prefer you to keep an eye on Camryn to make sure she doesn't overdo things and be there to spell Nanu."

Lynx kissed Jannike and handed her off to Shiloh, who also stole a kiss. They strode after Ry, and the two women stared after their men.

Jannike sighed, and Lynx heard. He grinned and started whistling. A stray thought leaking from Jannike wiped away his grin. He darted a look at Shiloh.

"Did I hear right?"

Shiloh nodded. "I don't know whether to act shocked or impressed."

"What's wrong?" Ry asked.

"We caught a stray thought from Jannike as we left. The mouse is imaginary."

Ry chuckled. "I had my suspicions when we couldn't find a scent trail. I guess Camryn had had enough of my protective hovering."

"Jannike told us we were overprotective as well," Lynx said.

"It's difficult not to with a kitten on the way." Ry dragged a hand through his hair. "I think of all that could go wrong—"

Shiloh turned pale. "We'll go for birth labs when it's our turn."

"No," Ry said. "The journey is amazing. You've felt the kitten kick and stretch. He kicks harder when I talk to him."

"When we were kittens, we were told legends about males who would bring offerings for their females," Lynx said.

"Ah." Ry brightened. "We could use that legend. Why don't we stop by Mogens' cabin and ask his opinion?"

Shiloh grinned. "I like the way you think."

Lynx continued along the corridor, smiling. Shiloh had never been so relaxed. He certainly smiled more. So this was true happiness. Lynx thought he'd been happy before. He knew better now.

CHAPTER NINETEEN

Later that eve, Jannike stomped around the rec room. She dodged the scruffy old chair Camryn had insisted on bringing from Earth and the more modern gel-seating Kaya's brother had helped them purchase to complete her circuit. "Goddess, I wish this itching would stop."

Camryn frowned from the depths of the old chair and stroked her belly. "I wish this kitten would stop kicking. You know the itching stopped for me as soon as Ry and I started having sex."

"She has two males," Kaya said a trifle grumpily.

"And you laughed at my vibrator." Gweneth's tone was full of smugness.

Jannike pressed her back against the nearest wall and shimmied up and down. "It's so itchy. It's driving me crazy."

"So back to the sex," Camryn said. "I presume you're having sex?"

"She's having sex." Kaya scowled. "The walls are thin. I get to hear, and it's affecting my sleep. It's driving *me* crazy. I need my own man."

"I'm available," Nanu said from the far corner.

"*Please.*" Kaya tugged on a hank of blue hair. "It would be like doing it with my brother."

Kelvin and Mogens were chatting in the other corner of the rec room. Royal dangled from one of Kelvin's arms that he'd shifted into tree. A neat trick. Without warning, the markowls started hooting and chirping. Kelvin replied in kind, glanced in their direction, and boomed out a laugh.

"What?" Jannike asked.

"The chatter amuses them. They understand more than you realize."

"Great," Kaya said. "So now they know about my lousy sex life. See, even the birds think my life is a joke."

"They can laugh all they want." Jannike rubbed her back against the wall, giving it more pressure. "But I can't take this scratching for much longer."

"Let me look at your back." Camryn heaved her body out of her chair and padded over to Jannike. She tugged at her tunic and lifted it to reveal Jannike's back. "Ooh. Mogens, come and look. It's covered in black bruise-like marks, but she's rubbing them raw."

Mogens tut-tutted when he saw her back. "Nasty. Does that hurt?"

"You've broken the skin with all your scratching," Nanu observed. "Kaya, sister, it's time to go and relieve Ry and Jannike's men on the bridge."

"Yeah, yeah. Rub it in," Kaya said. "On second thought, I'm glad that back doesn't belong to me. Looks painful. I tell you, Nanu. I need a male. I need to find one on Viros. I couldn't troll when we visited my brother. Earth was a bust."

Nanu laughed and slung his arm around her shoulders. "We

have contacts on Viros now. I'm sure we can get blind dates. We have a few cycles to discuss our needs."

"You mean write a list?" Kaya asked.

"Yeah, then we can help each other find the right one," Nanu said.

The two disappeared, still discussing sex. Jannike shifted her weight and attempted to ignore the itching. It didn't work.

"I don't understand." Streamers of black curled across Mogens' face, turning his features from white to gray. A contrast to his white robes. "Camryn is right. If you're having regular sex, the itchiness should fade. Neither of the men are suffering. Do they have tattoos on their backs?"

"Yes." Jannike stepped away from Mogens' touch and tugged down her tunic. She cursed and gave in to the craving to scratch. "Ooh."

"I don't know. If we could make a stop, I could read the clouds." Another swirl of black darkened his face.

"What's this about reading clouds?" Ry demanded. "What's wrong?"

"Jannike is suffering. I have some salve that might help alleviate some of the itchiness. At least the external symptoms. But I believe the worst of the pain comes from beneath her skin. I've never seen anything like this."

"Jannike." Lynx's tone held chiding.

"Why didn't you say it was that bad?" Shiloh said.

Both Lynx and Shiloh went to her, wrapped their arms around her and the symptoms—the persistent itching—backed off to bearable.

"It was okay, and then it wasn't." Jannike didn't know how to explain the sensation. "I might go to my cabin."

"Stop by my cabin to get some salve first. You've broken the skin, and the last thing you need is an infection. Come with me now."

Jannike nodded and followed Mogens from the rec room. Lynx

and Shiloh fell into step behind.

"Why didn't you say something?" Shiloh persisted.

"Because it was okay until we parted to do our own things," Jannike said.

"You asked us to give you more freedom, but how can we allow this if you're in pain?" Shiloh's exasperation came through loud and clear.

"Why do you think I didn't mention it? I knew you'd behave like a grumpy bear. I still want time alone or with my friends," Jannike gritted out.

"There must be some reason for Jannike's mating remaining uncompleted." Mogens' robes rustled as he walked in front of them. His skin had returned to a normal cheery white. He opened his cabin door and gestured them inside. "It won't take me long to get the salve." Mogens disappeared behind his floor-to-ceiling shelving. Each shelf was crammed with containers and vials of all shapes and colors. Dried plants hung from a rack above their heads, perfuming the air with a green floral scent.

"He has a lot of stuff," Lynx said. An understatement since every available surface held mystery ingredients.

"Ah, yes," Mogens muttered from the other side of the shelving. "This salve is perfect." The rustle of his robes indicated his return, and he beamed as he handed over a glass container. "This salve has healing properties. It will leach the heat from your flesh and help alleviate some of your symptoms. This salve also makes an excellent lube. It's cooling and moisturizing to allow less friction." His beam widened to toothy. "I speak from experience since I have tested it myself."

"Everyone on this ship is sex-mad." Jannike had to work hard to contain the heat in her face. When all three males laughed, she threw up her hands and strode from Mogens' cabin.

"Thanks for the salve," Lynx said. "I'm sure Jannike will thank you herself once she gets over her snit."

Jannike froze on the spot then backtracked, the heat increasing in her face rather than fading. "Lynx is right. I have no manners. Thank you, Mogens. It's much appreciated. My hearing is much better. Is that normal?"

"Don't ask us," Shiloh said. "Because we don't know either. Mating doesn't occur on Viros, as far as we know. There are legends, but no one we know has mated in the same manner."

"Shiloh's right. Sorry, sweetheart, but we're just as confused as you."

"Camryn's senses improved until she turned feline," Mogens said.

"Phrull, I hadn't even thought that far. Will I turn into a feline?"

Lynx and Shiloh shared an astonished glance.

"Is that possible?" Lynx asked.

Mogens frowned. "I don't know. Your body seems to be fighting the changes."

"Imagine running together through the forest," Lynx said.

"Magical," Shiloh breathed, and he looked like Gweneth had on receiving her Christmas presents.

"My back is painful enough. Thanks for the salve, Mogens." And with a curt nod, Jannike strode away. Stupid males. All they thought about was themselves. They weren't going through this aggravation. No, they had, she recalled. It had been worse for them when she'd first been captured.

"Wait, Jannike," Lynx called.

She slowed her steps, guilt smothering her temper.

Lynx and Shiloh flanked her, and the three continued to Jannike's cabin.

"I'm going to sanitize," she said.

"Want some help to wash your back," Shiloh asked.

"No. When Lynx helped me this morn, the cleansing suds went everywhere. You're even bigger than him."

"Good try," she heard from Lynx as she entered the sanitizer room.

"Spoilsport. At least we have a big sanitizer room on Viros."

A male laugh sounded, a teasing, almost sultry one. Her men were starting without her. She'd better make this quick.

Around ten mins later, she stalked into the main room and found Shiloh and Lynx naked and entwined on her gel-bed.

"We have an idea," Lynx said.

"One that might help push you past the itchiness," Shiloh added.

"Spill." She scooped up the container of salve. "Can one of you put this on my back please?"

Lynx accepted the container and opened it. The scent of herbs and flowers wafted into the air.

"Smells like lavender, an Earth herb," Jannike said. "Much better than some of Mogens' other concoctions."

Shiloh issued a soft curse. "Phrull, Jannike. Your back is a mess."

Lynx smoothed salve over achy spots, and Shiloh started applying it too.

She groaned and arched her back. "Oh, that's good. You said you had an idea?"

"We haven't tried double penetration," Shiloh said. "We've made love in lots of different combinations but not together."

"And now we have salve to help," Lynx added. "What do you say?"

"I'll do anything if it means I'll get rid of the bugs beneath my skin."

"Something for us alone," Shiloh said.

"Yes," Jannike said. "We're not inviting anyone else to join in if that's what you're thinking."

Shiloh reached around to tweak her nipple, and it was hard enough to startle a squeak from her. "Any other male comes near you, and they're in for a fight."

"Yes, sir," Jannike said. "Likewise, any female or male sniffing around you will get a bloody nose."

"So we're going to do this?" Lynx asked. "When you two are finished, of course."

"Yes. Yes. *Yes.* I'm desperate enough to try anything." She waved a hand. "Organize. Please."

What are we going to do with her?

"Love her," Shiloh whispered.

The two felines crawled closer until their bodies and limbs surrounded her. Jannike's blood pumped a fraction faster, and to her amazement, she could hear both her body's response and those of Shiloh and Lynx—their heartbeats increasing in concert.

Arousal was a fast simmer as usual. The sec they started touching, caressing, stroking, her nipples pebbled, and the craving began to swell in her pussy.

A hard male cock prodded her hip. Another grazed her stomach, leaving a damp trail. Their musky scent heightened, and it fed the urgency gathering within her mind and body.

Shiloh placed tiny kisses, tantalizingly brief, down her neck, then headed unerringly for the mark high up on her shoulder. A low moan built at the back of her throat, and she gave voice to it the sec his lips grazed the raised scar.

"Let her lie flat on the gel-bed," Lynx said. "I want to taste her."

"Goddess, yes. Let me move so he can lick me," Jannike pleaded, trying to wriggle free of Shiloh.

Shiloh's big hands cupped her buttocks momentarily as he helped to rearrange her body. She parted her legs and beckoned to Lynx. "I'm ready."

Desire kicked at the twinkle in his eyes and increased when his pupils contracted to feline slits.

"You think you're ready." His voice emerged thick and low, distorted by his protruding canines. He made a dark sound as he lowered his head and licked along her slit. A long, luscious taste that rasped across her tender flesh. Deep in her womb, she felt a tightening sensation, a readiness as if her body waited for something extra special.

Her breath caught, and her hips jerked with Lynx's next taste. He stopped frustratingly short of her clit, the puff of air against the swelling nub not enough. Not nearly enough.

Shiloh fondled one breast, teasing her nipple while he dragged his tongue back and forth across her mark. Raw need blazed in her, pushing close to desperation.

"Please. I want more. Please fill me."

"Soon, sweetheart," Shiloh whispered. "We don't want to injure you." He kissed her slowly. "You're very special to us."

The coil of energy in her lower body pulsed, insistent. Needy. "I'm hurting now."

"No, you're not," Shiloh murmured. "What you're feeling is velvet tension. That's the good kind of pain."

She gave a soft sigh then a complaining moan when Lynx lifted his head.

"Shift over and give me space." Lynx's cock jutted upward, the head a ruddy and swollen red. "Climb on top of me. Take me inside you. Make it slow, easy. Tease us both while Shiloh gets ready, but don't come. If you climax, we'll spank you."

Jannike frowned. "I don't want to be spanked."

"Then do as we tell you," Shiloh's breath was warm against her ear as he aided her into position. "Tell me how it feels as you take Lynx's cock."

Jannike's mind went blank.

"Jannike?" Lynx asked. "Tell me."

She grasped Lynx's cock, explored his length with her hand, and was fascinated when his shaft pulsed and thickened. Her gaze went to his, taking in the fine delineation of muscles in his torso, his pure sexiness and strength. She glanced over her shoulder to sneak a glance at Shiloh—his bulging pectorals and flat stomach, his ridged abs and his beautiful cock.

"When did I get so lucky?" she asked.

"We're the lucky ones," Shiloh answered for them both. "Go. Move your arse, so I can get you ready." He cleared his throat, his gaze full of love and caring. "I want this more than anything."

"I want this too," Jannike said. "I've fought for the longest time."

"Maybe that's why the mating hasn't taken," Shiloh said.

"Maybe." Jannike guided Lynx's cock to her entrance and bit her lip as she sank downward. He stretched her and glided deeper, creating exquisite friction along her sensitized walls. Fire and chills warred in her body. Every instinct told her to move, but she resisted.

"Phrull, that feels good," Lynx said. "You'd better hurry, Shiloh."

"Someone is impatient," Shiloh teased.

At another time she might appreciate Shiloh's good humor since he was the most serious of the pair. Right now, she wanted to end this sensual torture. She swiveled her hips to increase the friction, and a growl escaped.

"We'll make a feline out of you yet." Lynx layered laughter into his words.

Shiloh trailed his fingers across her back, and the caress sent tendrils of pleasure to tug deep in her belly. Another sound erupted from her, one she'd never made before. Shiloh gave a delighted laugh and stroked her again. The sound repeated.

"You're purring," Lynx said.

"We'll make her purr louder," Shiloh promised. "Lean against Lynx's chest. Do some kissing, but that's all. No touching marks. Not yet."

"He's bossy." Lynx's breath puffed against her lips.

"Newsflash, so are you." Jannike kissed him to take her mind off what Shiloh was doing.

"What's a newsflash?" Lynx asked.

"An Earth term. We catch them from Camryn."

"We're going to have to visit this Earth one day," Shiloh said. "It sounds like fun."

"We'll go for Christmas," Jannike said and groaned as Shiloh rubbed salve over her hole. It was cold. Not unpleasant though, and it did ease the penetration of Shiloh's finger.

"Relax. Breathe," Shiloh said.

"It's not bad," Lynx said. "You've seen Shiloh do it with me. He knows what he's doing."

The muscles of her inner thighs quivered as the sensation of fullness increased. Lynx nuzzled her neck, his lips skimming her mark, and she fought a whimper. His abrasive tongue flicked across the hollow of her throat while Shiloh stroked and worked his fingers into her. A heavy fog of desire descended, pushing her to a place of pleasure where the only important things were her felines. So giving. Every cycle, they showed their love. They'd even told her they loved her, yet she hadn't returned the sentiment. She didn't know why.

Shiloh withdrew his fingers, and the loss of contact left emptiness. Yes, Lynx still held her and kissed her, but without Shiloh, she didn't feel whole.

"Shiloh." A verbal protest.

"Just slicking up, sweetheart." His hand on her buttock pushed back her distress, and another one of those purrs whispered through her cabin.

"I'm going to dream about your sexy purrs," Lynx whispered.

Shiloh draped himself over her back. "I'm going to dream about being inside you, about stroking into you and feeling Lynx's closeness. I'm going to dream about us coming together."

His husky voice, the inherent promise, had her quivering. She felt the pressure as Shiloh gradually worked into her, the coolness of the salve. She twisted and squirmed between the two masculine bodies, desperate for movement.

"Patience, sweetheart." Lynx stilled her complaint with a kiss.

Finally, finally Shiloh was fully seated, and he stilled. Her channel pulsed around Lynx's hardness, the vibration setting off other pleasurable reactions. A soft, needy cry fell from her lips.

"Ready, Shiloh?" Lynx asked.

"Feel as if I might explode," Shiloh said.

"Yes," Jannike said.

They set up a rhythm of invading and retreating, so she always filled with one cock. Unable to move—not more than a squirm—she writhed, buffeted between their bodies.

Lynx kissed her with an easy stroke of his tongue while the pleasure in her body grew. The pulse at her throat beat a ragged tattoo, the orgasmic buzz stretching and expanding until she worried her body wouldn't handle the experience.

Lynx faltered in his strokes, cursed. "Can't hold on."

"Thank phrull," Shiloh muttered, and Lynx laughed. "When you're ready."

Lynx's mouth fastened on her mark. He sucked as he drove into her body.

"Yes," she cried out, Lynx's mouth the detonation she craved. Pleasure burst to full, fiery life. Her vaginal walls clamped down, sensation pulsating from both cocks. The twists of bliss went on and on, dragging whimpers from her each time one of the men moved. She was vaguely aware of the wash of seed inside her, the wetness, but the overriding perception was one of enjoyment and satisfaction.

Of rightness.

Shiloh eased from her body and lifted her from Lynx's softening cock.

"Let's get you cleaned up," he crooned.

"Tired."

"I know, sweetheart. You'll feel better after a wash," Lynx said. "We all will."

Shiloh cleaned her up and held her drooping body while the cleansing and drying tube did its work.

Then they were lying down together, masculine arms wrapping her in comfort.

"Love you," she said sleepily, and that was the last thing she recalled.

That was amazing, Lynx said.

Shush, you might wake Jannike.

I don't think so. She's exhausted.

It was the best, Shiloh said. *The best I can ever remember. There was something about the three of us being together in that way. It felt right, as if we connected like a key in a lock.*

She loves us. She said so.

It was never in any doubt, Shiloh said.

Fatigue weighted Lynx's eyes, yet his mind kept busy. He heard the rumble from Shiloh, indicating his friend had fallen asleep, but Lynx's noisy mind wouldn't let him rest.

They still had to tell Jannike about his true position on Viros. Yes, they'd had chances to confess. Multiple times. He kept changing the subject or offering a joke instead of a confession because he feared change. He was happy now, but as soon as they landed on Viros, the prince's mantle would drape over his shoulders. His mother would make sure of it. She'd start her infernal matchmaking again until he put his foot down and told her about his mates.

Then she'd freak out even more.

He could practically hear her shocked lectures. He'd mated with not one commoner but two, one of them a male.

Lynx snorted. Fun times to come.

His mind wandered to Ellard's request for them to journey to the Cloud farm once they landed. At least that put off meeting his parents for a bit longer. The cycle after the morrow, they'd land on

Viros.

A pained moan snapped him from his troubled thoughts.

Jannike.

A nightmare dream?

He eased back, giving her space and caught a glimpse of her back. Phrull, Mogens had been right. In a state of awe, he watched the black splotches reshape and join until they formed a black cat with gray eyes.

"What is it?" Shiloh asked, his voice full of sleep.

"Jannike's dreaming."

Shiloh rolled off the gel-bed and turned to face Lynx. A curse escaped. "She's not dreaming, she's bloody shifting."

"In her sleep?" Despite his disbelief, Lynx saw Shiloh was right. Her bones twisted and snapped and reshaped while black fur grew across her body. The air shimmered around her as the shift completed.

"She's beautiful." Shiloh scarcely breathed in his bemusement.

"At least mother can't complain she's not feline," Lynx said.

"I'm sure the queen will find other things to trouble her."

"She will. I can't believe she shifted in her sleep."

"What are we going to do? Wake her?"

Lynx studied the graceful lines of her powerful body. "She's exhausted. Why don't we let her sleep? Unless she shifts again, she can't go anywhere. She can't open the door."

"Good point. Let's leave her sleeping. We're bound to wake if she does and can help talk her through a shift."

He and Shiloh resettled on either side of the black feline. Their gazes met and both grinned.

Life was so sweet.

A light tap on the door woke Shiloh. He climbed off the gel-bed, pulled on his trews then rubbed his eyes as he went to answer the door. He blinked at Ry.

"It's too early for a smirk like that," Shiloh said.

Ry leaned closer. "Not if you've talked Mogens into making you a mouse. Since you and Lynx have spent so much time searching for the mythical creature I thought you might like to witness the commotion. You need to hurry, though."

Movement behind him had Shiloh turning. Jannike blinked at him with her beautiful gray eyes. She leaped off the gel-bed and barreled straight for him, those eyes full of panic and confusion.

"What the grata?" Ry had opened the door and was now gaping at his second-in-command.

"Jannike," Lynx called. To no avail.

She mowed Ry down and shot through the door in clear distress. Lynx shifted and tore after her.

"Hurry. She'll be confused. She shifted in her sleep." Shiloh ran after them, considered shifting, and decided one of them needed to be able to speak with her unless...

Jannike. Jannike, slow down. It's okay.

"What's all the noise about?" Kaya demanded, her blue hair in disarray after her slumber.

"Jannike has shifted to feline, and she's panicked," Ry said.

"Oh!" Kaya said. "Entertainment. I need to see this."

Shiloh sprinted down the corridor after his mates. Ry ran behind him.

"Are we under attack?" Gweneth wanted to know.

Shiloh heard Kaya's voice but didn't slow.

Royal's shriek sounded in the rec room. A shout from Mogens, followed by Kelvin's boom.

Jannike!

She's here, Lynx replied. *Don't scare her. Ease into the room.*

"She's in here," Shiloh said.

They entered the rec room, both scanning the inhabitants and their surroundings.

Mogens, Kelvin, and the creatures stood in their usual corner.

Lynx sat against the wall, and Jannike cowered in the corner, her sides shaking in distress.

"Didn't you discuss the possibilities with her?" Ry demanded in a low voice.

"Of course we did. As far as we knew them. None of this process is familiar," Shiloh said, not bothering to hide his irritation. "She was tired and we decided to let her sleep. She wouldn't be loose on the ship in full panic if you had stood your ground."

Camryn waddled into the room, and Kaya and Gweneth jogged in secs later.

"What's happening?" Kaya demanded. She scanned the room and lifted a gadget to her face. Her grin was visible beneath the silver of the device.

Camryn continued to her chair.

"Crap," Ry muttered. "Camryn, wait—"

Camryn's terrified scream cut off his words. "A rat!" she managed, backing away from her chair.

Something moved on the chair, and Camryn's second scream almost deafened Shiloh. A flash of black streaked across the room. *Jannike.* She was running straight at Camryn.

"Jannike!" Shiloh shouted.

Camryn turned her body, her mouth opening when she saw the black cat springing at her.

"No!" Ry croaked in horror.

Shiloh, Ry, and Lynx rushed forward, but Jannike didn't attack Camryn. She leaped onto the chair, grabbed something black in her mouth, and shook it furiously. She jumped off the chair and growled, a hair-raising sound of fury. She shook the black thing again.

Ry grabbed a trembling Camryn and pulled her out of the way and into his arms.

"What's going on? Who is— Jannike?" Camryn connected the clues at speed.

"Jannike? Sweetheart?" Shiloh approached her carefully.

Lynx showed no such trepidation. He prowled up to her in feline form and rubbed against her.

Jannike. Good job. It's dead now. You can let it go, Lynx said.

Hurt, Camryn.

No, Camryn is safe. See. Ry is protecting her.

Jannike spat something back from her mouth. It hit the floor and jerked. She seized it again.

Gweneth clapped her hands together. "Oh, good. You've caught the mouse."

"Here's a bag," Mogens said. "Drop it in here, and I'll dispose of it." Swirls of black raced over his face and his arms. "Captain." The single word held disapproval.

Jannike dropped the thing into the bag then backed away. Her legs became tangled, and she tripped, ending up with her nose on the floor and her butt in the air.

Lynx gave a bark of humor and trotted to her side. Shiloh fought a grin. When he'd first shifted at age twelve, the extra set of legs had given him trouble, especially if he thought about them too hard.

She growled, the threads of panic in the sound alerting Shiloh to potential problems. "Everyone out. Gweneth, can you grab a robe from Jannike's cabin?"

"I'll get one of mine," Gweneth said and trotted away.

"What was that thing?" Camryn asked. "I'll have to fumigate my chair."

"That was an imaginary mouse," Ry said.

"A mouse? That wasn't a...wait." She smacked her mate hard in the middle of his chest. "You knew! This was a trick."

"You had us running around the ship for cycles looking for the creature," Ry said.

"You scared me half to death."

"An unforeseen event. I didn't think it would scare you. Are you all right?"

"Out," Shiloh said. "Let us speak with Jannike in private."

"Let me help," Camryn said.

Mogens and Kelvin ambled past. Royal clung to the branch Kelvin had made for him while the markowls hooted to each other. Kelvin's mouth twitched, but he didn't comment.

"No, leave Jannike with her mates. Kaya, stop waving that camera around. Out," Ry said.

"I got it all," Kaya crowed. "Took a movie. Nanu is gonna bust his gut laughing."

Jannike growled.

"*Oops,*" Kaya said. "Gotta run."

"Call if you need me," Ry said then he grinned. "I used to be the sole feline. Now, there are six of us, if you count Gweneth."

The door to the rec room closed behind Ry.

Lynx shifted. "He counts us among his crew."

"Yeah. It feels good," Shiloh said.

"It does." He turned to Jannike, who was trying to coordinate her legs. She plopped onto her butt, and a growl of frustration emerged. A cranky one. "Jannike, listen to me."

Her ears flattened, and she growled again. Her tail swished.

"Stop that," Lynx ordered. "We're trying to help. Picture your humanoid self in your mind. Have you done that?"

Another grumpy growl.

"Concentrate," Shiloh said. "Picture yourself. Your face. Your body. Your two legs."

She growled again.

"Look," Shiloh snapped. "Do you want to eat your meal with us, or do you want Kaya to film you drinking a bowl of liquid?"

Tough love, Lynx said in approval.

Easy for you two. You've been doing this for rotations.

And she's back, Lynx said.

"Let Jannike concentrate. What do you want? A seat at a table or a saucer on the floor?"

A shimmer formed around Jannike's feline body, and the tension seeped from Shiloh. It was going to be all right. Occasionally, newly changed felines panicked and couldn't shift back. Some remained that way for cycles, sometimes rotations. But this wasn't going to happen to their mate. Her body transformed, bones cracking, reshaping. The black hair on her body receded. Jannike groaned then stood on two unsteady legs.

Lynx wrapped his arms around her trembling body. "Good job."

A tap sounded on the door, then it opened.

Gweneth poked her head into the room. "Here's a robe. Oh, good," she said and stepped inside. "You're back. That was so cool." She handed over the robe. "Everyone else is breaking their fast. Should I save some for you?"

"Please," Lynx said.

"I need to go and bite Kaya," Jannike said.

Shiloh held up the robe for her. "Would you like to dress first?"

"How was it?" Lynx asked.

"Terrifying. Exhilarating. Deafening. So much extra sensory input."

"You shifted while you were sleeping," Shiloh said. "We didn't expect Ry to let you out before we could talk you through the shift back."

"You saved Camryn." Lynx's mouth twitched at the memory.

Jannike shuddered. "What was that thing? It tasted disgusting."

"That was a mouse," Shiloh said.

"But there was no mouse. It—" Jannike scanned their faces. "Oh. Maybe I'll bite Ry, too."

CHAPTER TWENTY

They spent the last cycle before arriving on Viros cleaning, stocktaking, and packing belongings since they intended to stay planetside.

"We should have told Jannike by now," Shiloh said.

"I know." Guilt slapped Lynx around the ears. She wouldn't take their news well. He knew it, which was part of the reason he'd shoved the topic to the rear of his mind. Running away. *Again*. The acknowledgment didn't stop the roiling in his gut.

"Told me what," Jannike asked from behind them. "Did you contact your brother?"

"Yes." Shiloh controlled his start, but just. He glared when Lynx grinned. "I passed on the directions Ellard gave me for the new spaceport. I still can't believe it."

Lynx shook his head, wondering who had convinced his father and the council to build a spaceport. They needed a medal. "We live at the castle—when we're here on Viros."

Jannike scowled. "The castle?"

"We're about to land," Ry interrupted over the internal communicator. "I want everyone strapped in, especially you, Jannike."

"Huh!" Jannike threw up her hands and wheeled away.

"What does he mean?" Shiloh asked, halting her retreat.

"Jannike keeps injuring her head because she's not strapped in," Kaya said. "I have the camera this time. I'll be ready to film."

Jannike let out a distinctly feline snarl. Kaya shrieked—with humor and an impish smirk—and took off at a run. Jannike raced after her, a feline on the hunt.

"I guess we tell her once we land," Lynx said.

The landing went smoothly, and with the *Indefatigable* secured, they prepared to board the tender, which Nanu had relocated to a neighboring landing pad.

Two men dressed in navy blue tunics and matching trews marched in their direction. "Who is the captain? We have paperwork to complete."

Lynx froze at the familiar voice. He recognized the man but couldn't recall his name. "The captain is coming."

"Your maj— Ah, Lynx," the man said hurriedly, and Lynx recalled bloodying the feline's nose as a youngster for insisting on using his title instead of his name. "D-did you arrive on this ship?"

"Yes." *Hellfire.* He needed to speak with Jannike.

"We'll do the paperwork later," Shiloh said.

"Yes, yes. Of course." The second man almost stuttering in his haste.

The pair backed away, stopped, and bowed from the waist before departing at a trot.

"What was that all about?" Jannike asked.

Lynx shook his head. That had been weird. The subjects didn't usually bow to him. "I've no idea."

"What did they want?" Ry arrived at the tender with two large bags.

"They had paperwork but said we could sort it out later," Jannike said.

"Is everyone ready?" Ry asked.

Camryn trotted over, carrying a smaller bag. "Are you sure your family doesn't mind all of us descending on them?"

Shiloh shrugged. "Ellard said there is plenty of room for ten of us plus the creatures."

"Let's go." Ry scanned the vicinity. "I'm eager to see some of Viros. You say the spaceport is new?"

"Yes," Lynx said. "I didn't think there were plans to build one."

The tender door closed, and they all took seats. Nanu had them in the air in secs.

"I can see the castle." Gweneth had her face pressed to a porthole.

"Lynx and Shiloh live at the castle," Jannike said.

Everyone turned to stare.

Lynx swallowed, feeling both trepidation and guilt. They should have told Jannike earlier of their positions. "We—"

"*Ooh*," Gweneth squeaked. "Look at the trees. Kelvin, look at the trees. It's so pretty here. I can't wait to explore."

"You will not go exploring on your own," Ry ordered. "You will take at least one of the crew with you, and you will inform me of your intentions. Is that clear?"

Gweneth folded her hands demurely in her lap. "Yes, Ry."

Ry blasted her with his fierce expression. "I'm not joking."

"Yes, Ry."

Camryn giggled, and Lynx found himself smiling too.

"The female portion of my crew is a bad influence on her." Ry's tone came close to a growl.

"Yes, Ry," Camryn said.

"Yes, Ry," Kaya said.

"Yes, Ry," Jannike said.

"The next person who speaks will get my boot applied to their backside."

"Phrull." Shiloh spoke into the weighty silence. "I'm so tempted."

"We've arrived," Nanu called. "Where should I land?"

Lynx unfastened his safety harness and strode over to Nanu. A silent Shiloh joined him.

"There's Ellard," Shiloh said. "Nanu. He's pointing over there. Phrull, he's smiling."

"Where's his arm?" Lynx asked, as Nanu maneuvered the tender into position and landed. "Goddess, is that Jarlath?"

"He looks like you," Jannike commented as she pushed between them. "Not as handsome, of course."

Lynx exchanged a puzzled glance with Shiloh. Both Ellard and Jarlath were wearing unadorned tunics. Dressed as they were, they could pass as commoners.

"What's wrong?" Jannike planted her hands on her hips. "Why are the pair of you looking so shocked?"

"We're considered the rebels in our families. Our brothers don't welcome us with smiles." Lynx didn't understand this reception. "We receive lots of lectures."

The tender landed, and Nanu powered down the engine. Gweneth danced up to them, her pretty face alive with excitement and interest. "Is the big feline with one arm your brother, Shiloh?"

"Yes."

"Can we disembark, Ry?" Gweneth asked. "Can we?"

"Yeah, Ry." Camryn's eyes twinkled. "Can we go now?"

Ry threw up his hands. "I'm the captain. You should respect me, not treat me with irreverence. Lower the ramp, Nanu."

"I'll bring the presents." Gweneth sashayed away.

"She is going to give me gray hair," Ry told no one in particular.

"Let's go." Lynx felt unaccountably nervous. "Jannike, with us."

"But don't you want to meet your brothers in private?"

"You're our mate." Shiloh slipped an arm around her waist and propelled her down the ramp.

Jarlath grinned. *At him?* His brother looked younger, happy without the normal stick up his arse. Lynx blinked. Definitely a grin. As Lynx gaped, Jarlath shared a mischievous glance with Ellard. An instant later, they bowed.

"Why is everyone bowing at you?" Jannike demanded.

"I've no idea." Lynx sucked in a quick breath. "Jarlath. Ellard. This is Jannike, our mate."

"Your mate?" Ellard stared at Shiloh. "Both of you are mated to Jannike?"

"Yes." Lynx swallowed, the truth more radical now that he had to tell his brother. What would he think? "Shiloh and I are mates too. We are three."

"A triad." Jarlath chuckled, then he beamed. *Beamed at them*, Lynx saw in shock. Jarlath seized Jannike in an embrace. Secs later, he handed her off to Ellard. He embraced Lynx in a fierce hug. "I'm so glad you're home, little brother. So glad. We have much to discuss."

Did you hear Jarlath?

Yes, Shiloh said. *Are we in an alternative reality?*

Why shouldn't your brothers be happy for us? Jannike asked in confusion.

"They're mind-speaking again," Kaya said.

Ry inclined his head in greeting. "Ryman Coppersmith. This is my mate, Camryn. My crew." He went through introductions.

The markowls took off, rising into the air with excited squawks. Royal let out a screech and scampered off Kelvin. He raced to Jannike and jumped into her arms.

A woman appeared, accompanied by three youths. She possessed pale green skin, brown hair and her golden eyes glowed with welcome.

Jarlath held out a hand, his smile one of pride as he slid her against his side. "Meet my mate, Keira."

Keira curtsied to Lynx. "Your majesty. Boys, bow to the king."

The three boys executed perfect bows. Two bore the coloring of Red Mumbers, while the third had a similar coloring to Jarlath. Beyond that, Lynx didn't recognize them.

"Why is everyone bowing at Lynx?" Kaya asked.

Jarlath chuckled and crinkles appeared at the corner of his eyes. "It's a mark of respect for the king."

Lynx gaped at Jarlath—the brother who seemed like a stranger. Jarlath had a mate. A mate who wasn't a feline. He finally recognized the scent, and his hand tightened on Shiloh's shoulder. She smelled like a Cawdor. Wait. "Father is dead? Why didn't someone contact me?"

"Father isn't dead," Jarlath said. "But he's not well and passed his power to me. Mother disapproves of Keira, so I agreed to abdicate. Congratulations, Lynx. You're it."

"No." Lynx's gaze darted from his brother to his brother's mate to Ellard. All three faces held the same expression. Certainty. "No."

Kaya started laughing. "Does that make Jannike the queen?"

"No," Jannike said in distinct horror. "I'm not staying here. I don't like this planet. I'm just visiting."

"Yes," Jarlath said with a twinkle in his green eyes.

A twinkle, for phrull sake. Lynx clamped his mouth shut and groped for understanding. He frowned and then brightened. "I'm mated to both Jannike and Shiloh. I love them, but neither have royal status, so I can't be king. Mother will make sure of that."

Jarlath shared a glance with Ellard before he turned back to Lynx. "Things have changed around here. Given the situation, the council might agree to amend the constitution. I believe there is a clause about exceptional circumstances that might work for this situation."

"What exceptional circumstances?" Lynx demanded.

Jarlath sobered. "The House of Cawdor attacked us with magic. They struck us from within, using magic and a triad to help power the attack. I believe the council and our parents might see the benefit of having a triad at the head of the House of the Cat. Ellard and I will approach the council later this cycle, but since I'm king until I officially hand over power, I can award Shiloh a title to give him higher status."

"Make him a duke, like in the books we read on Earth," Gweneth piped up.

"A king, a queen, and a duke." Jarlath beamed, and once again, Lynx found himself full of incredulity. Jarlath placed a hand on Shiloh's shoulder. "I give you the title of..."

Ellard whispered in Jarlath's ear.

"Perfect." He tapped Shiloh on one shoulder and then the other. "Duke of Westbury. That's a newly zoned district on the other side of the mining area. I've been wondering what to do with it."

"No," Shiloh said in evident horror. "Hellfire, no. I can't be a duke."

"King Lynx, Queen Jannike, Duke Shiloh," Keira said. "Please come into the house. We've prepared a meal. You'll want to discuss the coronation with Jarlath and Ellard."

"This is a joke," Lynx said.

Jarlath placed a hand on Lynx's shoulder. "No joke. The House needs you. I've tried to do my best, but the House of the Cat requires your leadership skills, your foresight, and your ideas to make us less vulnerable."

"Jannike's right. We're not staying," Lynx said.

"We're leaving tomorrow. Got to collect our ship," Shiloh said.

"Running away again, brother?" Jarlath interrupted, and he grinned as if he was enjoying himself. Lynx was beginning to hate that grin. "You've always done that. It's time to stop running and put your ideas into practice."

Was that what they did? Run away? Lynx glanced at Shiloh, who stood poised to retreat at his sign. They *did* leave home, instead of fighting for their beliefs. "Who built the spaceport?"

"Ellard and I ordered it," Jarlath said. "We've made other improvements but it's not enough. We were vulnerable to the Cawdor before. Their trio of rulers almost destroyed our city. The three of you mated is a sign, which will resonate with the people. You'll see. They'll rejoice in your mating. We needed to change, to make advances to ensure our House becomes strong."

Lynx opened his mouth, shut it, opened it again. "Who are you, and what have you done with my brother?"

A laugh burst from Jarlath. "Keira has everything prepared. Come inside. We'll talk. I'm so glad you're home."

"We'll leave and give you a chance to talk," Ry said.

"No, there's plenty of room in the garden," Keira said. "Please, it's good to have guests. I've been looking forward to meeting you since you contacted Ellard. Please stay." She reached out a hand to Camryn. "Hilda, my cook, makes excellent pies."

"I'm not going anywhere," Kaya said. "I might miss something important. *Ooh*, does that mean we can visit the castle since you're the queen, Jannike? Please say yes. I can slide down the banisters. I've wanted to try that since Camryn read that Earth story to us." She curtsied. "We're going to have so much fun."

"No." Jannike turned to Lynx and grabbed two handfuls of tunic. She shook him. "Why didn't you tell me this could happen?" She shook him again. "You should have told me you were a prince."

"I did," he said.

"I thought you were joking," she shouted.

"I..." Lynx trailed off and raked a hand through his hair.

"He's still the same feline," Shiloh said.

"You're his bodyguard, aren't you?" Jannike asked. "You told me and I... I thought I could carry on being me, spending time with my friends. I want things to stay the same. I don't know anything about being a queen."

Jannike squeezed her hands to fists. A mistake. The prick of her claws against her palms almost forced a yelp from her. Almost, but she managed to internalize her surprise. She glared at Lynx then at Shiloh. *I can't be a queen.*

"Don't worry. There are no 'queen' rules," Jarlath said. "You can write the book for queen rules. All I ask is you listen and consider the idea. Ellard and I are willing to help with whatever you need. We've made changes, but more are needed to drag the House of the Cat into the future, to make things better for all the people who live on Viros."

"Jarlath," Keira said, with a smile of apology at Lynx. "We don't have to discuss this on the doorstep. Give them a chance to think. Meantime, we have pies."

Their friends wandered toward the house, chatting easily with Lynx's and Shiloh's family members.

"Hey, this is getting heavy." Gweneth stomped up to Ellard. "You. Carry this basket for me. It's a gift for our host and hostess." She thrust it at Ellard, and he grasped it with his one hand in self-defense. She smiled sweetly. "Thank you so much. Please take it inside for me."

"Gweneth," Jannike snapped. "You can't order Shiloh's brother around."

"Why not?" Gweneth studied him as he walked away, then turned back to them. "Do you think it would be all right to pinch his bottom?"

Shiloh made a spluttering sound that might have been a laugh.

"Why?" Lynx asked.

"I like him. He has pretty eyes and a nice smile. Sexy. I wonder what happened to his arm. I'll go and ask him." Gweneth skipped off to catch up with Shiloh's brother. "What happened to your arm?"

"The Cawdor attacked, and one of their soldiers shot me." Ellard's reply carried back. "They couldn't save my arm."

"I'm sorry to hear that," she said. "Here, let me get the door for you."

"Phrull, I can't believe the Cawdor attacked," Lynx said.

"I don't know whether to feel sorry for Ellard or glad." Shiloh shook his head. "Did you see her expression? Her eyes shifted."

"Never mind Gweneth and her intentions, whatever they are," Jannike said. "What are we going to do?"

"Investigate." Lynx could feel Jannike's rising panic, yet this proposition aroused his curiosity. This was an opportunity—one he'd never thought to receive. "We'll talk to Jarlath and Ellard. Learn everything we can. Then we'll go into the city. If the council votes against a change to the constitution, it won't matter anyway."

"I don't want to be a queen. It's not in my job description," Jannike said.

Lynx glanced at Shiloh. "We collect information and make a joint decision once we learn more."

"I vote no," Jannike said. "Let's go and have pie."

They entered the house and came face-to-face with a woman with bright pink hair that seemed to writhe up and down. Her pink eyes seethed with curiosity as she bobbed a curtsey. "I'm pleased to meet the new king and queen. And a duke! You'd better hurry or they'll eat your share of the pies—royalty or not."

Jannike elbowed her way past Shiloh and pushed Lynx out of the way. "They'd better save me pie." She followed the noise. Lynx trailed her through pretty yet functional rooms that smelled of flowers. She burst outside through a set of double doors. Lynx strode in pursuit and sensed Shiloh behind him. They found their friends grouped around a table and others lounging on comfortable outdoor gel-chairs. Jarlath, Keira, and Ellard, plus the three boys—Lynx couldn't recall their names—stood and sat with the *Indy* crew.

"Ah, Queen Jannike," Kaya said.

Jannike narrowed her eyes. "Does the castle have a dungeon?"

Lynx decided he'd better intervene before things became nasty. "We're going into the city to check things out. Anyone want to come?"

Jarlath nodded approval. "Ellard and I can give you a tour of the city and show you some of the changes. We need to call a council meeting anyhow."

"Can I come?" Gweneth asked and fluttered her eyelashes at Ellard.

"Keira is going to show me around her farm," Camryn said. "She has creatures called malpacks."

"We keep our cambeests in the stables here too," Jarlath said.

"Kelvin and I are going for a walk." Mogens looked to Jannike. "We'll take Royal with us. He'll enjoy playing in the trees."

"What's a cambeest?" Camryn asked.

Lynx tuned out after Jarlath started describing his cambeest, Black, his shaggy coat, and big feet.

I can't get over the changes in Jarlath, he said.

And Ellard, Shiloh said. *They both look relaxed instead of formal. And Ellard is still with Jarlath, despite losing an arm. If I know my father, he'd have tried to have Ellard replaced.*

We haven't argued yet.

They haven't lectured us about our responsibilities and reputations, Shiloh said. *And Jarlath's mate is from Cawdor. I remember her. Recall the rumors when she was married to Marcus Cloud.*

Ry and Camryn like them, Jannike added to their conversation. *Everyone seems happy.*

Apart from Jannike. Lynx's gut bucked at the thought of losing her. Jarlath was right. He and Shiloh had always run away from their responsibilities. He got the feeling that fleeing wasn't an option this time. She might be stubborn enough to leave if they decided to stay, despite the mating bonds.

Later that cycle, they relaxed in the garden again. The city had been much like others they'd visited. Good points and bad, Jannike thought as she leaned back in her chair and enjoyed the breeze on her face. The scent of flowers and herbs filled her lungs, and somewhere, an insect buzzed as it flitted from flower to flower. Camryn, Kaya, and Gweneth sat on adjoining chairs. They each had a drink and Keira had organized snacks for them. Jannike wasn't sure what the white things were, but the saltiness contrasted nicely with the tartness of her pink drink.

"Tell me about the castle," Camryn said.

"It's beautiful inside. Full of treasures from other planets," Jannike recalled. "I was frightened to touch anything."

"It's much bigger and grander than my father's mansion," Gweneth said, referring to her previous home on the planet Ornum.

"Could you live there?" Camryn asked. "Did you meet Lynx's parents?"

"They're away, taking a vacation on a resort planet." Jannike scowled. "Not that it matters because I'm not staying. No one can make me. I don't care what the stupid council decides."

"Why don't you want to stay?" Camryn sipped from her drink, her eyes slicing and dicing until Jannike wanted to squirm.

"What's wrong with how things were, how things are now? We have a good life. Why do we have to change?"

Silence fell as she stopped talking, and the urge to squirm intensified. Something—no, it was her feline—rolled under her skin in reaction to her turmoil.

"Good God." Camryn cocked her head. "You don't like change. Why haven't I realized this before? If we ever have a vote, you're the one who votes for the status quo." The slicing and dicing continued, Camryn relentless in her search for answers. "You like to maintain control. I always thought that was a good thing, but maybe not. Of all of the crew, you were the one who was slowest to warm to me when I joined the *Indy*."

Jannike broke and reached for another mystery snack. Pretty close to a wriggle if she analyzed her movement closely. "I don't know what you're talking about."

But she did. She liked to know the plan when it came to her own life because all semblance of control had been ripped from her when her stepfather sold her into slavery. So what if she liked routine and knowing what each day would bring. Control over her own actions and her own life made her happy. Change brought uncertainty and jerked her from the routines that made her feel safe.

"I want change. I want Ellard," Gweneth blurted. "I've been thinking about it ever since we arrived."

"But he's older than you," Camryn said in surprise.

Jannike stopped mid-reach for another snack. Ellard was plain too, until he smiled. Shiloh had inherited the best looks in the Tetsu family. And she hated to think it, but one arm would have its limitations.

"Looking at him makes my heart beat faster, and I felt, feel the urge to touch him whenever we're in the same room." Gweneth's cheeks colored at their obvious curiosity and unspoken questions. "My insides feel like stretching, and I think it's my feline. I've never felt anything like it before."

"Wait until you get to the shift," Jannike said. "It hurts."

Camryn picked up her drink and took a sip. "Shifting gets easier with practice. Jannike, I think you're wrong. When we first heard those tracker lizards you didn't hesitate to deviate from our plan. You ran straight into the face of danger without a hint of uncertainty."

"When Camryn went missing on Ornum, you were the one who went looking for her because Ry was out cold," Kaya said.

"But that's different."

"Why? Why is it different?" Camryn asked. "When you and

Shiloh and Lynx were in danger, and you split up so they couldn't capture you all again, you didn't dither about making hard choices. Why is this so different?"

"That was friendship. You and Ry are my friends. Shiloh and Lynx had become my friends. They were mates." There hadn't been any other option, so she'd chosen the lesser evil. The choice that let some of them remain free. "Stop. Please. I don't want to remember."

"Jannike." Camryn's voice gentled. "Don't you see? This is something that would be good for you. If you end up as queen, you would make a fine one. Fair and compassionate. You're fearless and calm under stress. You have such a big heart."

"No." Jannike bounded to her feet, sending the small table and the platter of remaining snacks flying. "I'm a slave from a poor family. I don't possess the right qualities. People will laugh. Rumors will start. The House of the Cat will become a joke because of me." She spun around, intent on fleeing to the privacy of her assigned chamber.

"Jannike." Lynx stood in the doorway, blocking her escape, Shiloh at his side.

To her mortification, Jarlath and Ellard had heard her outburst too.

"Excuse me." She tried to make herself small enough to squeeze past her mates.

"Jannike." Shiloh spoke this time as he moved to block her exit. He reached for her hand, his warmth a balm to her bruised soul. "We'll go for a walk to talk in private."

"Take the flymo," Keira said. "It's a nice eve. I'll get Hilda to pack a basket for you, and you can take your meal in the clearing by the pool."

"I know the one you mean," Lynx said. "A good idea."

Jannike found herself packed onto the flymo—a chubby gray utility vehicle that appeared to be used for shifting cargo and people around the city—and in short order, she was disembarking in a clearing surrounded by trees on three sides and a pool on the other.

"Pretty." It was all she could force past the lump in her throat.

"Want to go for a run?" Lynx asked.

"Yes." It beat an uncomfortable talk. Some of the tension faded from her shoulders. She started to strip. "I picture my feline in my mind, and the shift begins." At Lynx's nod, she took off the last of her clothes and stood naked in the clearing with her eyes closed. Her skin prickled both inside and out, heating uncomfortably until she had to bite down on her bottom lip to stem a cry. She felt a bursting, a rush of pleasure that morphed into pain.

She cried out, but it was too late. The shift was on her. Horrid popping sounds filled her ears. A sharp prickle opened her eyes, and she saw long, vicious claws digging into what was left of her humanoid thigh. Scents burst upon her. Trees. Grass. Water. A hint of some sort of animal.

Jannike dropped down onto her newly grown legs. A black tail flicked across her nose. A feline grunt filled her ears as the two males flanked her, and sudden joy bubbled up, the stress of her cycle pushed to the far recesses of her mind.

They ran and jumped and played until Jannike's sides heaved, and thirst drove her to the pond to take a drink. Lynx and Shiloh shifted and waited while she focused on effecting the change.

"I'm starving," Shiloh said. "Let's eat."

The meal was delicious, although she had no idea of the identity of most of the foods. She lay back on the blanket Hilda had given them and stared up at the trees and the dappled patterns created by the beam of the solar-star.

"You're not that scared child any longer, Jannike," Lynx said.

Jannike bolted upright and reached for her tunic. She pulled it over her head, feeling better for the protection of the fabric. "Maybe not." Damn Camryn for slicing open her scars, exposing her inner wounds for Lynx and Shiloh to see. "I don't want to listen." She scrambled to her feet and reached for her trews. More protection.

Shiloh snagged her hand. "Don't run. It's what Lynx and I have done for all these years. The problems don't go away. You just pretend they're gone. We heard what Camryn said. All of it."

"Camryn was right. Out of all the women we've met over the years, no one is better qualified to rule as queen of the House of the Cats. You're a feline with two incredibly strong and clever mates."

"Don't forget handsome," Shiloh said. "We're both extremely good looking."

Jannike tugged her hand free. "This isn't a joke."

"No," Lynx said. "You're brave and intelligent. You have a good heart because you know what it's like to be treated like bull crap. You fight for your beliefs. You would champion the people—all the people who live in the city, whether feline or not. You have trusted friends to help you. All you need to do is ask."

"This isn't a natural fit for me either," Shiloh said. "The locals know us as young, spoilt felines who were always causing trouble. Although my family has always guarded the king and his family, we don't come from wealth. Not like Lynx." Shiloh paused as if ordering his thoughts. "My point is we can all learn together. You saw the people in the city, those in the castle. Jarlath said they'll accept us as rulers if we present a confident, united front. That's if the council votes for the changes. Jarlath believes they will. He spoke to most of them earlier."

"It's not going to be easy," Lynx said, taking over. "We're not pretending that. My mother can be a real bitch. I hear Keira has felt the lash of her insults, but the people who live in the city—they're the ones who need our help. You could show them how effective a good queen can be."

Jannike sank back onto the blanket. "What if I make a mess of this? I have no idea what a queen does. I own one dress."

"One more than I own," Lynx said.

She cuffed him on the shoulder. "This isn't funny."

"What Lynx is trying to say is we think we should stay here for at least half a rotation. It will allow us all to relax and grow into the position. If you don't want to stay after that, we'll devise another plan to suit all of us." Shiloh tugged on her hand again until she leaned against his chest. "We can set the rules. That's what we're saying."

"If this vote thing goes through, would we have to live in the castle?"

"Yes, but there's no reason why your friends can't stay there too. There is plenty of room. Kaya can slide down the banisters as much as she likes. Gweneth would have a chance to woo Ellard." Lynx winked. "We can give everyone a job and pay them. All we're asking is to give this a chance. None of us should consider fleeing until half a rotation passes. What do you say?"

"Make up the queen rules," Shiloh whispered in her ear. "This sort of opportunity doesn't come along for people like us. What the phrull does it matter if you came from a poor family or that I don't have aristocratic breeding? We caught Lynx without possessing wealth or prestige. He loves us for who we are, not for where we came from."

The words resonated with Jannike and made her realize she was still letting the widow win in a warped kind of way. She sucked in a deep breath and let it ease out nice and slow, then she turned in Shiloh's arms in order to see her felines. "I love you both very much. This will be difficult, but if the council votes to change the constitution, I'll try for at least half a rotation." She pulled a face. "Though I'm telling you now. I won't do tea parties or play nice with upper-class ladies, not those who gawked at us today. I'll need a project, and I'd like it if you could find jobs for our friends—if they want to stay."

"Deal," Lynx said, his eyes glowing a feline green as he bent closer to kiss her. "You'd better start the timepiece because Jarlath is convinced the vote will pass."

"I'd like the same deal, King Lynx," Shiloh said. "No tea parties with prissy ladies. I had to suffer through enough of those as a kitten."

"Deal, but Duke, if you call me king again, we'll have a fistfight."

Shiloh growled, an affronted sound that made Jannike smile. She had no idea what the future held—not a true idea—but suddenly the unknown didn't scare her in the same way. She had two sexy mates. She had friends. She had a purpose.

"Instead of a fight, why don't you employ your energies in other directions?" she asked, removing the clothes she'd hastily donned earlier. Jannike strolled toward her felines, putting a sway into her step. Their attention zeroed in on her as she sank onto the blanket beside them. "We should celebrate our social elevation in private. I've heard that sex is a good remedy for stress, an excellent way to celebrate."

"She is exquisite," Shiloh said.

"You won't get an argument from me." Lynx pressed a kiss to Jannike's back.

The solar-star continued to shine through the trees, casting dappled shadows on the ground and their entangled limbs as they kissed and caressed and made love.

The perfect way to seal their private deal of love and togetherness.

The perfect way to step into the future.

Just perfect.

Thank you for reading **Seized & Seduced**. Did you notice the way Gweneth was eyeing Ellard? She has fallen for the somber, one-armed man and is about to make his life extremely difficult.

Check out **Hunted & Seduced**
(https://shelleymunro.com/books/hunted-seduced/)

to learn how Ellard deals with this new turmoil that's about to punch him in the chest.

About Shelley

USA Today bestselling author Shelley Munro lives in Auckland, the City of Sails, with her husband and a cheeky Jack Russell/mystery breed dog.

Typical New Zealanders, Shelley and her husband left home for their big OE soon after they married (translation of New Zealand speak - big overseas experience). A twelve-month-long adventure lengthened to six years of roaming the world. Enduring memories include being almost sat on by a mountain gorilla in Rwanda, lazing on white sandy beaches in India, whale watching in Alaska, searching for leprechauns in Ireland, and dealing with ghosts in an English pub.

While travel is still a big attraction, these days Shelley is most likely found in front of her computer following another love - that of writing stories of contemporary and paranormal romance and adventure. Other interests include watching rugby (strictly for research purposes), cycling, playing croquet and the ukelele, and curling up with an enjoyable book.